A TIME TO TELL LIES

A TIME TO TELL LIES

Alan Kennedy

LASSERRADE

ISBN 978-0-9932023-2-2

First published in the United Kingdom in 2016 by Lasserrade Press

For Elizabeth

"I have done that," says my memory.
"I could not have done that," says my pride.
Finally my memory yields.

Friedrich Nietzsche
Beyond Good and Evil

PROLOGUE

Friday October 16 1942
Saint Aunix, Gers

That night there had been half a moon in a clear sky, an autumn moon catching the puddles on curfewed cobblestones. It had rained all afternoon then stopped as night fell. It was often like that: it came from being near the sea, that's what they said.

There was a strip of light from the Pharmacie leaking round the blind. He'd get it in the neck for that if they saw it, stupid old fool. Not that you got many about on a Friday night. The place is deserted, all of them stuck inside, drinking floc, wireless blaring away, minding their own.

Why did she think he'd do it? It was always Thierry that got to do things, anything stupid - him or one of the crowd. *Why me?* There must have been something about him: soft or something.

It had been Wednesday - two days ago. They were in the Café Flore, just messing about, bitching about the new coffee, not that it was coffee. Thierry saying he wouldn't pay, not for that muck. A real row starting, when who should come in but the Englishwoman. They called her that, although not to her face, you wouldn't risk that, her so sure you took her for French. Nobody did. It was that way she had of tilting her head up. And that stupid smile. A smile for everybody, and that's one smile too many. People don't smile in Saint Aunix, funny she'd not noticed. And that hat: how come she didn't know only tarts wore hats like that? But more it's the other things - the way she's always that bit too familiar, wanting you to like her. The way

1

she leans over the table letting Thierry give her a peck, letting him see down her front. Too familiar, that's her trouble. Too familiar that Wednesday as well, squeezing in, jockeying the others along the bench, letting you feel the warmth of her, Thierry pushing, nuzzling you into perfumed fur and soft flesh.

There's nothing to do in the Café Flore. Just a place to sit until Joël in the bar across the square takes the shutters down and leans them against the door. You'd think he'd shift them, but he never does. After the shutters you wait till the covers come off the billiards table, then the whole crowd shoves off. That morning, trying to get past, shaking coins out onto the table, struggling against her knees, feeling his coat snagging. Until he saw. Not snagging - a hand, very small, milky white, holding the coat under the table. A single tug, nothing more.

She waited till they'd gone, the glass door smashing closed, Thierry gawping back inside, grinning. You could tell what they were thinking. *Why him?* That's what they were thinking. He'd asked himself the same.

"Don't bother about them. Look here."

A nice voice. Really proper French, like the School Mistress. A little book in her hands. A book of poems.

"I'm going to write something inside. You can say your girl gave it you. What's your name?"

"Rémy."

"What's your girl called?"

"How'd you know there is one? Fabienne, if you want to know."

"Nice name. I'll put *For Rémy from F* – you don't want anything sloppy. Now, you can do something for me," shaking her hair back, glancing to the door. But they'd gone, already halfway across the square, Thierry bent over, cupping his hands round his crutch, pretending to gag.

"Number eight. There's a brass plaque on the door. Knock just the once – d'you understand? Like this. Just one tap. Somebody will answer. Give him the book."

"You can do that yourself – it's just over there."

That was when she'd smiled. Little wrinkles round dark blue eyes. She'd forgotten that as well: girls round here don't have blue eyes.

"No, I can't do that, Rémy. It has to be Friday. I won't be here. That's why I'm asking you. Nine o'clock, remember. That's not late. Wait for the church clock, that would be best. Just one knock. He'll hear."

"What about the curfew? The Germans. Curfew's half past eight - I'll get myself done for that."

"Nine o'clock's not late, not really. Tell them you're going home. But nobody's going to ask. Everybody knows you – they won't make a fuss. You're a good boy. And there's this."

A banknote folded in two, a picture on the front, a woman with a squint perched up like a statue. Hell - a thousand! He'd never seen a note that big.

"I don't want that much. It's too much."

"No, you take it. Buy yourself something nice. Or your girl. You take it. Just do this for me."

One

There were seven of them – five men, two women. A truck picked them up at Strathcarron in a blizzard, the stiff tarpaulin cover whipping open, feeble light inside cutting yellow across tumbling swirls of snow. At Achnasheen they stopped to take on the last of the women then, as the snowfall eased, turned West to Kinlochewe, creeping along a narrow glen, impossible ice walls rearing into a night sky. At the far end of the valley, huge frozen stars hung low over the brooding hump of Liathach, all the time Alex thinking how odd it seemed to find the blackout in Torridon. Alright, there was a war on, but who the hell would want to bomb this place? Even finding it would be a miracle.

The driver nearly missed his turn, jolting them against each other on the slatted wooden seats. The sound of the engine changed, echoing back from rows of little stone houses. Alex pushed the cover aside. They had passed through gates, grinding up a gravelled incline, engine screaming. A rectangle of light reached out across the snow: a man framed against lamplight at an open door, rhododendrons banked high on either side closing over him.

At the top, the truck drove straight into a kind of barn, wooden doors flung back. They stumbled out one by one into the smell of cattle. As Alex jumped down, stiff with cold, he collided with the woman who had got on at Achnasheen, grabbing her arm with a gloved hand to steady himself.

"Sorry. Where the hell are we? Do you have the faintest idea? Only don't say Scotland – I worked that bit out."

4

"That's the best I could do, I'm afraid. I'd say a good long way from anywhere else. Will that do?"

She had a nice voice: deep, just the faintest hint of something foreign. Nothing unusual there, the whole lot of them were a little odd in the language department, all walking with a slight limp you might say, accent-wise. The little imperfections that had got them here in the first place, had got them through the training. The knowledge they were that bit special keeping them sane, more or less. This was the third training camp, his last, but he'd not seen her before.

"Were you at Ringway? Funny, I didn't see you?"

She shook her head. "Parachutes? No, did that ages ago. I'm here for a course. The bloke who gives it wouldn't come South. Hell of a way."

She turned to look at the distant house set against the steep slope of the hill: high mullioned windows, stone balconies, pepperpot turrets decked out with aerials. "Although I must say it's a pretty place."

"Only the best for us. SOE - Stately 'Omes of England and all that. Except it's not - England, I mean." It was an old joke, she didn't smile back. "They do us proud, don't you think? Reminds you of nice young women in drawing rooms debating whether the milk goes in first or second."

"And you would know what, exactly, about nice young women?"

So that was how it had begun, the two of them watching the rest of the group, a little knot of weary people crunching through packed snow, dragging kitbags. Nearing the top of the drive a sudden splash of light sparkled out from an open door across the ice - wavering candles on polished mahogany, the glint of silver.

The two left behind stood together in an empty shed puddled with cowpats, neither making the first move. That was how it began. It's a mistake to fall behind, you get that drummed into you – it's a golden rule, it really is. But not this once. Falling behind paired them for whatever time they had left.

Her name was Justine Perry. She had grinned telling him, saying he could call her Just for short if he really wanted because she always tried to be. She had lived in France most of her life, getting out after the fall of Poland. Came home, she said, to do her bit. Married, he thought. At least, she wore a ring because she had displayed it in that first session when they'd gone through the usual *personal effects* rigmarole. Pulling it off with a jerk, ostentatiously dropping it into the cardboard box, putting up with the Instructor's predictable coarse joke. They smiled on cue. Best to smile, because you could see at once this one was a vindictive bastard. So they all smiled, even Justine.

He found a place next to her that evening at the dining table. The house must have been grand in its heyday: an Edwardian folly thrown up at titanic expense by a Glasgow brewer in search of a peerage. Glass fronted cases lining the walls of a deserted gun room bore witness to long-forgotten shooting parties, even Royalty, so they said. Before the Great War had put shooting to other uses, leaving the brewer with both his sons dead at Ypres.

Faint patches on the figured wallpaper showed where pictures had once been: fake ancestors, somebody on a horse perhaps, more likely some animal about to die. They should have left that one up, Special Operations Executive having its own brand of humour.

They were sitting at a massive table, borrowed regimental silver winking in candlelight. High above, cherubs blew kisses to muscular painted nudes inside three enormous plaster cartouches. Beyond the point where dusters could reach, cobwebs waved in the rising heat. Huge mirrors in gilded ormolu frames set off each end of the room, the glass speckled with age.

Someone had screwed a wooden plaque into the polished mahogany of the figured double door, declaring *Mess Room*, the tiny act of vandalism reminding those few who might doubt it that war changes the rules. The place was already blue with cigarette smoke.

"Really married?"

At first he thought she was going to snub him. Cold blue eyes, rather large for her face, insolently fixing his. Then she smiled, glancing down at her hand, accepting a cigarette.

"Looks like it."

So he had had to settle for ambiguity even at the start. Still accept it three nights later, lying hard against her in a bed big enough for Victoria herself, army sheets smelling of carbolic soap. Even then she had not elaborated, beyond saying she was here for specialised training. She had done all that boy scout stuff long ago. She was trained – made her sound like a performing seal, didn't it? Although this particular seal had a few last tricks to learn. Otherwise she was going to keep out of the cold. She already had missions under her belt - *aye, and still alive, the noo*, mimicking the Highland accent of the Instructor.

Perhaps it was the nonchalant cruelty of that wiry little chap that drew them together. A gymnasium had been improvised in a dusty ballroom, but he had declared it useless, fit only for faggots. What the hell was the army coming to if you trained *indoors*? He managed to make the word sound blasphemous.

Training was conducted in a pitiless landscape, snow banked so deep that walking was impossible, air so cold breathing was eked out to spare the pain. Their days were spent cracking ice to drag themselves through water tasting of blood. Fumbling the silencer onto the Standard Model B, fingers bloated by frost, then screwing it in again, this time blindfold. Then firing the damned thing.

You'll never win a goldfish that way Captain Vere, sir. It's not a rifle. Don't look. Dip. Up. Point. Squeeze. Go for the body, man, always the body. Two shots, sir. Rat Tat. Better sir, much better. Except he's shot you by now. You're dead and he's half way to Paris. Get a move on for Christ's sake.

Their days were so coloured with violence there was no time to remember he had once thought it might have been different, might have been about something else. Knife work in the second week confirmed otherwise. A stubby little thing, the standard issue knife, barely longer than your fist. Double edged, what's more, the better to work both ways.

You're slitting throats Captain Vere, not stabbing anybody. Stabbing's for girls, begging your pardons ladies. Stab him and he'll take too long to die. Take you with him more than likely. No. Like this. Over the top. Pull. Head back. Slit.

The snow was so severe one day they crowded into the Mess briefly to consider traitors, a blessed relief to be indoors.

Now the manual says you have a choice. You pay him off, you warn him off or you kill him. I beg to take issue with the manual on this. Kill him. Search him if there's time. But kill him first.

Then codes: a tweed back all they saw of a supercilious man scribbling on a blackboard. *The Playfair Code is for boy Scouts. Broken like this. Now watch carefully please - scratch – and this – scratch. You see?* Not that they did. *Poem codes. Double transposition. Chose your poem. No Captain Vere, I'm afraid* Rule Britannia *is taken. The code's as good as the poem, so write your own. If they break it – and they will – you might as well send* en clair. *We're working on one-time keys. Printed on silk. Alas, not ready yet. Questions?*

Spared this, Justine lay on her bed listening to the sporadic crackle of live fire across the hills, watching snow nestle quietly into the corners of windowpanes, thinking of *A Christmas Carol*. Perhaps remembering what Mr Dickens had in store for her, curled up on granny's sofa a lifetime ago, when Christmas seemed to mean something.

She would smile at Alex and his day in the field, him telling her he could barely remember Christmas and he wasn't going to start now, not when the whole caboodle was about to go up. Not when you need a bath, she'd say, and call him a maudlin bugger, letting him burrow into the heat of her, letting him find a way to forget they didn't have all that long.

Six weeks, the little man said, seeming proud of the number, of its precision, strutting about in the uniform of an army major. Not that he *was* a Major in anybody's army: that fooled nobody. It's what you learn first in this enterprise - people are never what they claim. Then you remember that applies to you as well. That's when you understand all you have is pantomime to hang on to.

That first evening, seated in lines on hard chairs, wondering who this man really was, a rickety blackboard out of place in a forlorn room someone once had called a library, leather spines untouched for fifty years releasing a foxy smell into the air, Alex had shivered. The little Major on his dais, catching the movement like a dog scenting prey, fixed him with soft eyes: a doctor bearing bad news.

"It's Captain Vere, isn't it? An average, of course. Unpleasant, but true. Operational lifetime - six weeks. But look, we're here to change all that."

A quiet laconic style that somehow managed to suck the truth out of his words. Best not to believe a word this chap says – he'd be better off selling cars.

"We're getting better though. Quite a lot, lately. Thanks to what you pick up here. What McIntyre's putting you through is going to be worth your life, believe me."

Getting into his stride, the room wondering how many times he had said all this before. How many dozens of previous faces, dead now, their six weeks being up? They said he'd been driven across from Inverness. In a huge staff car, its grey anonymity shouting Secret Intelligence Service. Flown up that morning. Surely not just for a pep talk? Ian somebody or other: Major Ian somebody, SIS. If he really was a Major.

"If you're going to survive – and it's our job to see you do – you must believe in the system. We designed it to save your life ..." The theatrical pause for effect spoiled rather by a Sergeant's choosing that particular moment to bustle in with the stack of little cardboard boxes. He had to relieve the guard at the gatehouse. Could they be handed out now, sir?

Two pills in each box: Benzedrine, wrapped in a paper spill printed *as required*. Use it right and you might keep awake for thirty hours. Or not … it wasn't a guarantee. And the other? The 'L' tablet in its little rubber shell. Well, bite that and you were fifteen seconds from eternity. Expected, of course, but all the same leaving them peering into their tiny pillboxes, thinking complicated thoughts, the flying Major quite forgotten.

Alex would always remember Justine at that moment, catching his stricken face, winking, twirling the little tablet between her fingers like something she might pop into her mouth any minute, finally poking it into the pocket of her blouse. Keeping the sweetie for later, her expression said. He couldn't even look in his box - he'd get round to that eventually. That was the difference between the two of them.

The Major, having lost his audience, was busy switching to another page of his script. He seemed almost too young to be in long trousers, although when he got going you could see why they had given him this job, nodding to the Sergeant, stepping just the right inch back, suitably solemn, gracefully ceding the floor, *of course*. *Carry on Sergeant, carry on*, voice adopting the slightly parsonical register reserved for these odd bits of awkwardness.

"Perhaps a good time to say when to … er … *bite* is not a solely personal decision." He let the pause stretch out an uncomfortable beat too long, "Please accept that if there is no choice, there is no choice. That's the logic of the enterprise we're all committed to. Obviously, if captured - whatever your rank - you will not be in uniform."

He let his glance flick over the heads of the women, coming to land on Justine, "Ladies too … although in your case the uniforms of the First Aid Nursing Yeomanry. We have to trust to the FANY to give you the necessary protection of a uniform …"

He seemed not at all discomforted by the embarrassed silence that followed, until Justine burst out laughing, calling out, "That name! It's a joke. Anyway, we're hardly Yeomen, are we? Hasn't anybody noticed? So we're to go to war with *Fanny* tied round our necks. I ask you! Women of pleasure – *filles de joie* - was that the idea?"

It was a long time before he replied, turning aside to stare at the bleak landscape outside, waiting for the laughter to subside, the scrape of chairs to fall silent. "You work without uniforms. Obviously. But that's not to deny your right to one – man or woman – and the enemy should respect that right. They probably will not. If you are taken, you will in all probability be considered a spy. You will be coerced – tortured - activities outlawed under the laws of war. And you will succumb. That's why taking your own life is not solely a personal decision. A whole circuit may stand at risk."

The last day was a Sunday. Albeit the Sabbath, it seemed appropriate to squeeze Assassination in before breakfast: *Written orders in all circumstances.* Someone had pinned up a Notice in the hall, *Morning Service 1100 hours, Torridon Kirk. All welcome.* Alex and Justine walked through the snow in blinding sunlight to the tiny church, to hear the Reverend McClure rail against the Pope. It was hard to say what they had expected: perhaps that god, having an interest in the ways of Special Operations, had, after due consideration, suspended a commandment or two. Perhaps that God, reflecting on the distinction between lawful killing and the other sort might appreciate how their cause sanctified their deeds. But on that Sunday, God had other things on his hands. He had the perfidious ways of Catholics to reckon with – apparently a consuming preoccupation. At which Justine kneeled on the dusty boards to pray, the papist gesture drawing loud tuts from the old ladies sitting behind.

"How did the old fool know I wasn't one?" Walking back, clutching his arm, already thinking of bed.
"You mean Catholic?" thinking of the little pill. "Are you?"
"Could be … he wasn't to know. He was taking a risk with the six weeks brigade: *You're trained to kill, lassie – Aye, remember that.* I could have strangled him. I'm inclined to go back right now and do it."
Back at the house they traded black jokes about the Pope. About the time they had left. About brief lives. Traded jokes all through that

last afternoon, drinking gin in bed, curtains open to the darkening sky, the window glass figured over with crystalline ferns. White feathers she said: they looked like white feathers. And he flying into a sudden temper asking what the hell she meant by that, she saying nothing, nothing at all, they just made her think of home. And which home would that be? Shouting for the hundredth time, importunate, thinking of *personal effects*, thinking of the ring. She flaring back, it's none of your business, pestering him into one last hopeless coupling, screaming drunken improvisations on the letter L into his ears as her breath grew heavy.

And that was the end of Justine. He thought never to see her again.

Two

He had thought never to see her again. After all, six weeks doesn't give much time for casual encounters. Yet, incredibly, here she was, pressing against him, squeezing a greeting on his arm through the stiff flying suit, the two of them restlessly perched on a wooden bench in a draughty hanger at Tempsford, the place reeking of paint and aviation fuel. Dressed for the drop, a full moon staring down through the hanger doors, frost outside turning the asphalt silver.

Only an hour before, Alex had been sitting alone in the harsh light of a single light bulb in a shabby little room, staring at a blackboard not properly cleaned. What teacher did with the class before - you couldn't help asking, could you? Someone had written *Dame souris trotte* in rather an illiterate scrawl. Presumably a Playfair key - no accents, which was useful. Verlaine - a poem called *False Impression*. Who said SOE lacked a sense of humour?

The Major glanced at the board, frowning, "There'll be two of you jumping," fretfully checking his watch, "your courier's been held up. On the way, I gather. You take off in an hour. The Whitley's on the other runway. There's a decent moon but I'll get somebody to lead the way. Your wireless operator's flying on ahead. A woman: name Simone. This is her first mission, so go easy."

"It's my first as well."

"Sorry, I didn't know. Simone will be with the reception committee sorting out the drop markers for you. She's joining the local circuit. Called *Colombine* – god knows where they get these names."

"The poems of Verlaine, apparently."

"Right. The reception will allocate someone to look after you. The exact date we get you back depends on settling Simone in – she's to let you know. You'll probably be coming back through Northolt, not that it matters. Now … here's the money."

Two chunky parcels pulled from a drawer, green oilskin, bound with tape. "I can't say how important this delivery is. If we're to keep the French playing for us they need liquid funds. They're taking the risks, of course, but I wish it wasn't this way … a bit sordid, things coming down to cash."

Alex found the package suddenly plonked into his hands. "A hundred thousand French Francs. Take good care of it. And see you get a receipt. God, makes me sound like a bank manager, doesn't it?" Glancing across to the door, suddenly shifty, "And this …" A parcel, much the same, only this one bound with a white tape, printed *RM* for its whole length.

"Our Intelligence people sent this. Baker Street. Apparently it's German currency. Reichmarks. We make them. De La Rue, I think."

"You mean they're forged?"

"Let's say *printed*, shall we?"

He was busy stripping off the white tape, tossing it into a wastepaper basket. "Look, just see your courier delivers the goods. They're expected. We have to keep a regular service. No need to tell you it's important – this is one of those *or else* operations, I'm afraid. Alright?"

Alex nodded, holding his parcels, feeling foolish, feeling locked out of something, as if he'd missed some essential piece of information, wishing the man would finish a sentence for once in his life.

After the briefing he stood in the empty hangar smoking a last cigarette, watching a dull black Lysander burst into deafening life. The Torridon Major followed him through another door with a little mouse of a woman in tow, clutching a leather case to her breast. Woollen mittens briefly shook his hand, a tiny face framed in curls: a schoolgirl out too late, a schoolgirl fallen in with the wrong set. So this was the WT Operator. God help them all – she should have been at home swotting for her exams, planning for Oxford tea parties and Rupert Brooke. This bewildered little mouse should have been at school, not messing about with wireless sets in the middle of the night. He wished her luck, fearful eyes, bright blue, catching his own and looking away. They seemed only a touch away from tears.

As he watched the Lysander disappear, a car bounced over the tarmac, skidding to a halt. A woman jumped out, fishing her kit off the back seat, slamming the door. Justine, striding towards him before he had time to be surprised, wrapping her arms round him, beaming.

"They said it was you. I couldn't believe my luck. Now say you're glad to see me. Like the proverbial bad penny, that's me. Briefing done? I got mine driving down. We're delivering loot, I gather. And I'm to carry it. Lucky me. Hand it over, I'll have to stow it. A bit of a miracle I made it, there's one of those random raids. South of London. The docks I think. Briefing alright otherwise?"

"I suppose so. I don't like that chap."

"Who? The gallant Major? He's alright – a bit stiff, but alright when you get to know him."

"That what you propose doing?"

"I may get around to it. What number is this for you? It's my fourth. This one's special, though - I'm going back home. I used to live not far from the drop zone."

"Four! God – how did you manage that? This is number one for me. My first drop. Rather explains the quivering frame, so don't laugh. But seriously, you've done all that?"

"I'm a bit of fraud, really. I've been across twice in one of those," waving towards the faint rumble in the sky. "A Lysander. Remember that training session, how they said they can carry three? Well, all I can say is, not unless you're a dwarf. It's as cramped as hell with two – you end up really good friends after an hour. But two of my so-called missions amounted to exactly three minutes in a damp field, somewhere called Fauquembergues, not far from Paris. Both times the reception committee was no-show. You get used to that – unreliable buggers the French. These pilots don't hang around, either. I think they resent ferrying the likes of us when they could be giving it to Jerry. Mine didn't even taxi down the other end for a run at it – simply took off. Back home for supper. That was it."

"What was the other mission?"

But she didn't reply, turning to watch a faint finger of torchlight sparkling on the grass, bobbing towards them. Justine pulled at him as he started forward.

"No, let him find us. I'm not stumbling about in the dark just because our precious Major wants to keep his shoes dry - John Lobb shoes, by the way. The Major wears bespoke shoes, isn't that odd? London though, not Paris. I notice things like that. Still, it makes you wonder doesn't it?"

But it wasn't the Major. A voice, a little out of breath, came out of the dark, a bulky form looming up close, "If you'll follow me, Miss. Keep close. You too, sir. It's not far."

Across the field the cough of an engine made the three of them veer towards lights high up in the cockpit of the Whitley. Figures standing, bending over something. Two engines now, rumbling over the frosty grass towards them, a man leaning out of the long frame of the fuselage, pushing a ladder down.

Problems started almost as soon as they had taken off. An earnest Flight Lieutenant came staggering back from the cockpit, to bawl into Alex's ear, "Weather closing in. Looks like we'll lose the moon." The noise made speech impossible. Alex pointed up to the jump lights showing red – it was a question.

"Can't say, old boy. We've a good way to go yet. Skip's going to soldier on. Says sit tight."

Justine leaned over, pulling Alex in, her lips touching his cheek, "Don't tell me. Another bloody no show."

They looked across to the tiny porthole of a window as the plane banked to starboard, a huge moon illuminating endless prairies of rumpled cloud, the sky beyond jet black, limitless. Justine cushioned her pack against the grey ribbed metalwork, smiling to herself. She seemed almost content.

He had been dreaming. Incredible to sleep in this hell, but terror had seduced him into a kind of desperate anaesthesia, nestling on Justine's breast. Standing at his bedroom window looking down. Stiff with terror. Bedtime. Behind him darkness thick and black. The street below bright as day. Always someone standing looking up. The doctor again come to call. No reason at all for terror. He was calling for Mother to come and see. She would be cross: he ought not to be out of bed, not without slippers, not in this wind, not with Justine jerking him awake into a solid mass of noise, Flight's face looming down, misted with sweat, fumbling for his strap.

They had opened the jump hole, the Whitley tipping nose-down, taking your stomach with it, Flight hooking Justine's strap, tugging it, shaking his head as she struggled up, pushing her back against the cabin wall, pointing at the jump light. Red, pulsing like a heart.

A seated upright posture, ladies - the standard joke - Nº 1 Parachute Training School, Ringway, the Instructor a fearsome Mancunian, rearing up seven feet high. *Back straight like this* – giraffe neck, a comic line - *or your stupid head will hit the jump hole. No Captain Vere, I didn't design the damned thing. Just try to arrive with your head attached. Can you do that one and all?*

The jump light still red, the Whitley banking, engines resenting the turn, clips rattling, fumes turning your stomach. Flight glanced along the fuselage to the open door of the cockpit, pulling Justine's shoulder, her body juddering with the plane. The jump light still red. Banking harder now, Flight bracing himself against her, swaying at the rim of the jump hole.

"He's making a go-around. Can't see a bloody thing. Cloud."

The engine settled to a dull drumming beat, straight and level. Straight and level in the wrong direction. A pass right over the drop zone could easily put them half a mile adrift. With a go-around you could make that five. Or ten. They were coming round, hydraulics to the flaps stuttering, screaming. Where the hell were they? Tipping to port, cloud caught the edge of the drop hole, pouring ice cold fog into the cabin space. Coming round … coming round, the final bank steeper, too steep, the floor bucking under their feet. Level now … straight and level, Flight tugging clips on the rail, mouthing, "On my go." The jump light still red.

It was green, suddenly green. And Justine gone. Dropping into nothing: upright posture, back straight. His turn: the shoulder tap almost a shove, a shadow running huge and dark above him, air hard in his mouth, stinging like sleet, hurting his nose. One thought tumbling with him: the Whitley had been too fast, far too fast. Something like frozen steam was tearing his nose. Tumbling faster, a ferocious wind ripping at his legs. Too fast, too fast, too fast. Surely it was all wrong? Candles … don't they call them candles, dropping like this?

Something monstrous punched between his shoulders, jerking his head back with the strength of it, sweet silk, vast as the sky, billowing out over him. A rush of new thoughts: how low? Justine? The dark of trees below … there shouldn't be trees … trees suddenly gone, jerked out of sight … tipping back … the swell of a hill canting across his view, grass between the trees, a rushing black advance of solid nothing. *Legs together ladies – you know it makes sense. Legs together.* Thump. Roll. Thump. Legs dragging through wet grass, bouncing your breath out, boots gouging clods of clay, a mountain of silk heaving above, dragging you in its wake over wet grass. Everywhere, the sweet smell of wet grass.

Justine was standing on the rise of the hill, already bracing against the wind, hauling in. Alex hit the box release, webbing pulling past his shoulders. Justine was looking down at him, the rumble of the departing Whitley filling the distant valley.

They followed a path across the field and jumped a ditch. A road sign proclaimed *Aste-sur-Torre* in red and white. Beyond that, two lines of sleeping houses, shuttered and silent. Barely a village.

The moon had gone again. Alex unfolded the map, risking the torch, squinting close to the paper, Justine nudging him aside, running her finger along the black streak of the main road.

"It's alright, I know Aste. I know where we are – I lived not far from here." She stabbed a finger on the map. "The drop zone's here. Your Simone woman will be waiting."

"God, it's a hike. Why the hell does nothing ever go right? Will she wait?"

"It's not just her – there's a reception committee. They'll wait. They have to: we've got their money. About five miles I reckon, but easy walking on the road. And we're not late, just a bit adrift."

Burying their flying gear they realised how inadequately dressed they were. Alex went to drape his coat over her shoulders, but she shook him away, "No time for that. I'll warm up walking. I've got all that cash weighing me down, remember? But first I'm going over there ... and don't ask why."

She vaulted the low wall, slithering down a steep bank into the dark bulk of the wood. A dog started up, surprisingly close, setting off a chorus of answering howls. There must be a house somewhere in the trees. A single yellow square of light appeared suspended in the dark, sending him scuttling for the ditch.

But the other light was already on him. He had not seen the car running silently down between the houses, twin headlights sweeping shadows of massive platanes across the road. Alex stood helpless and blinded in light as bright as day.

The car came to rest alongside, a huge engine panting fumes into the night air. A face in the rear seat peered out: a mouse of a face set under girlish yellow curls, fearful bright eyes catching his own, twitching away. A single gloved hand pressed against the glass, little woollen mittens, sky blue, the kind a child would wear sent into the snow to play. No recognition – her anonymous expression filled with the resignation of defeat.

A door on the other side opened then slammed shut, slow footsteps clicking on the metalled road into the headlights, a figure blotting out the light.

"Your colleague? You were three. The other woman? Where is she?" He was no more than a black silhouette against the headlamps, tall, angular, no hat, light catching the frayed ends of a woollen jumper unravelling at the neck, the kind of thing farm workers wore. But you'd take your oath this chap knew nothing of farms. The voice settled it: English with just enough of a controlled German accent. A cultivated voice, expensively acquired on English playing fields, mildly put out by the frailty of the forces assembled against it, a slightly peevish tone, as if somehow it had deserved better.

"She is with you? Please. It would spare us all a cold night."

They must have been waiting for the Lysander to land, dressed for the part, waiting for Simone. Without that go-around he would have dropped into the same trap, Justine as well. Thinking of her watching, Alex tried desperately not to glance into the woods, peering blindly forward. Best not speak at all. Once you start to speak it's hard to stop.

You must hold out for forty-eight hours, the Highland accent gentle for once, singling Alex out. *Captain Vere, sir – you understand me?* Alex nodding like a keen schoolboy, Justine not even looking up, fiddling with her cardboard box, rattling the tablets inside.

Forty-eight hours to hold out, to give the circuit a chance to repair, time for those who could to escape. Forty-eight hours for Justine to slip the net. This man would not be scouring woods tonight.

Standing alongside the car Alex felt something in his stomach move and clenched against the worst. They always said your bowels would give you away. But then, they said a lot of things. *Forty-eight hours*. They started now, those forty-eight. He never imagined his first mission this way. Stillborn. At least he could give Justine something.

Three

A flag was all that marked it as the Gendarmerie. Grander than its neighbours only by virtue of a flight of stone steps and a double door. The hall inside reeked of sweat and gitanes, cheap disinfectant not quite masking some other smell, vaguely disquieting, like children's vomit. They kept Alex in the car while Simone was bundled inside, the driver returning to haul her WT set off the back seat. By the time it was his turn to be prodded up the steps she had gone. He was steered into a room off the hall and allowed to sink down on a wooden bench. An old man in Municipal Police uniform glanced up then went on typing.

Alex saw his German for the first time. Surely not more than twenty-five, pale oval face, fair hair, thin lips. *People with thin lips are cruel* – didn't Mother always say that? Although this one didn't look cruel. Tired perhaps, pulling a grubby pullover over his head, wool muffling his voice, emerging to catch his breath, smiling.

"I suppose I speak to you in English?" There was a kind of weary superiority in the voice.

"You are English, aren't you? And now you are going to deny it. This ..." holding out the papers Alex had helplessly handed over by the side of the car, "this says you are French. Born ... let me see ... born in Toulouse. A pretty place, Toulouse. La Cité Rose, is it not?" He threw them back onto the desk.

"Have you ever been there? Look, this is a stupid game. Do you really want to play it?" enjoying himself, sprawling into a chair, showing off in front of the old man who had stopped typing to watch.

"You know, most of you Britishers pretend to be Dutch. Did you know that? You pretend to be Dutch and we have to hurt you – just to discover you are not. Not Dutch. Or in your case, not French."

He waited, letting the silence spin out, the old man settling back in his chair to listen to the strange language. Faintly from down the corridor muffled voices reached them, perhaps a woman – too far to tell.

The German stood up.

"It's late. I have got better things to do than round up sheep. In the morning my superiors will need to know who you are, who sent you, why you are here, and where your missing colleague might be. You will have an uncomfortable night to think about it."

He came across to Alex, resting a hand on his shoulder, embarrassed. He seemed very young,

"Look, I speak frankly. I am a soldier. You - you are a soldier? Pretend you can't understand, if you like, but I ask where is your uniform? Where is your identity token – your disk? You know perfectly well why I ask. Is this your idea of war? Giant Albion – isn't that what your poet called you? Parachuting women to do your fighting. Is that what the Giant has come to? Hoodlums and criminals firing pistols from ditches."

He perched himself on the edge of the desk, leaning forward, soft face excited. Unused to conquest, this one - having caught his fish, wondering what to do with it. Hard to believe he was long out of school.

"Listen. If you are helpful, it is possible you could become ... how can I put this? Something other than a cheap bandit. A French criminal perhaps? It might be arranged. You have the night to think about it."

The squeal from down the corridor took Alex by surprise, a primal sound setting his heart racing. The old policeman stopped typing. For a moment it seemed that everything stopped. The second scream was louder, as if someone unused to screaming had decided to rehearse. The scream of someone who, in all her life, had never found reason to scream. A door somewhere crashed open, the sound billowing down the corridor, running feet halting, the scuffle oddly demeaning, someone intoning, *No, no, no,* over and over again, a tiny voice insane with fear.

The typewriter began again. Alex stared at the floor. *You're meant to hear this. You're meant to hear this.* Torridon said this would happen, said there were things you were meant to hear. They had even rehearsed it, roping Justine into the pretence, her screams that morning bringing complaints from the kitchens.

This is something you are meant to hear. Although no pretence could prepare you for schoolgirl's screams. She didn't know how to scream, this little girl, not properly. The German was patting his pocket, looking for his cigarette case. He seemed embarrassed at these unpractised moans - sounds that tore your heart out.

Something heavy shuddered on the wooden floor, making the old policeman glance up, the silence broken by the scrape of a match. The policeman yanked sheets of paper out of the typewriter, watching the German light a cigarette. He shook one of his own from a crumpled blue packet.

The German was back in his chair, shuffling through papers, tossing them one by one onto the desk. He kept the passport till last.

"It is a remarkably bad forgery, you know. You English usually do better. Here, I will show you something. It will amuse you."

He drew a folder on the desk towards him, taking out a single sheet of paper, dangling it in front of Alex. "No? Very well, I will read it to you. ETA 0130 STOP HOME DELIVERY SIMONE STOP DROP GERALD AND MARIE STOP ETA 0210 WCP STOP ARCHER STOP END. You see it is in English. Well, a sort of English. Ah, perhaps you Dutchmen don't understand English. WCP - that would be Weather Conditions Permitting, would it not? And it appears they did permit because you are here. Frankly it was a surprise. We had been told of heavy cloud. Shall I call you Gerald? Tomorrow you will tell me who you really are and where we can find this woman Marie. I will discover her real name myself."

He turned away, the single word, 'Jorg!' barked at the top of his voice bringing the clump of hurried feet to the door, polished boots clicking a salute. A whispered exchange ended in a stream of muttered oaths, Alex risking a glance saw this shiny Untersturmführer was SS. Nobody said there were German troops here - just the Vichy police to deal with, London said. London was certain of it: somebody should have told the Germans.

His arms were being pulled hard behind his back, wrenching his shoulders.

"My regrets. The handcuffs remain. I am told the discomfort becomes less. It is too much trouble looking for wherever you have hidden your little tablet. We shall discover tomorrow. You English, always flirting with suicide. There was a boy at my school … no, I will tell you that story when we meet tomorrow. There will be time." He nodded to the soldier and turned away.

There was an odd faecal smell in the passageway. Through the open door Alex could see the chair Simone had been tied to. It had fallen with her. She lay splayed across a tangle of split wood, her blouse torn open, the pink brassiere, something a girl would wear, curiously innocent. Her head had lolled back at an impossible angle, the mouth crusted round with something white. This child had been sick before it died. Her eyes followed him as he stumbled past. They seemed fearful even in death.

The window in the room where they left him was barred but you would hardly call the place a cell. It must once have been someone's living room, scuffed linoleum worn through at a spot near the empty fireplace. An ancient horsehair mattress had been thrown on the floor. Apart from a bucket by the door there was nothing else. Alex crouched down and let himself fall awkwardly back onto his tethered arms.

Captives must fight the temptation to create a rescue myth. Odd he should think of that particular lecture now. They had dragooned a tame psychologist in to talk about fear, all of them faking attention, thinking how best to spin it out - anything for a few more hours out of the snow. The man spoke of myths of rescue, of their corroding effect, of the dangers of hope. Nonsense, of course. Alex had no thoughts of rescue. Hope had ended with that car sliding silently between the houses. Life had ended then. *Your six weeks are up, Captain Vere.* There was a peculiar kind of peace in that realisation.

Forty-eight hours to survive. He would focus on that. How many gone already? Four? Five? They had not taken his watch, but he had no way of looking at it. No way either of extracting the tiny lump from his coat lapel. Women sometimes put the L-pill in a broach – something to pin to your heart. High enough to get at, of course, if you were so minded. Poor Simone had been so minded.

There was a terrible racket in the night, shadows passing across the slit of light under the door, footsteps heavy on bare boards, the rattle of buckets. There were two of them, muttering to each other. Not police, though. They sounded aggrieved. Eventually, an outer door slammed and the place fell quiet. It must be six hours gone. But these were the easy hours. The German would come back - the one with thin lips.

Alex had been desperate for the bucket for ages, discomfort inexorably progressing to pain. Legs writhing in ludicrous efforts to stand, he somehow rolled off the lumpy mattress, inching himself upright against the wall, tottering across the room dragging urgently, hopelessly, at the back of his trousers. There was no point: a thick warm stream was already running down his legs into his shoes, piddling a thick black snake across the floor. A blissful, shameless, shameful relief.

Humiliation by the removal of clothing or denial of personal hygiene. Torridon had had words for this as well. Hardly a consolation, if you think about it, more a perverse validation of the process. Yes, they said, you will feel humiliated. And he did.

A church bell had started up, not telling the time, just clanging slowly a long way off. That bit of Verlaine about the mice came back to him - hadn't he composed that in prison? *Dormez, les bons prisonniers.* He thought he would never sleep on that stained mattress but sleep can be born of misery easily enough.

He awoke dreaming of Simone's terrified face, oddly indistinct with its halo of curly hair, the bang of a distant door jerking him back to terror.

Still early, a little winter sunlight red on the houses opposite, shutters propped open a crack for the air, the occupants surely still asleep. What did they make of all these stumbling people dragged up their neighbour's steps? What did these sturdy French burghers think of all those goings-on? Did they even wonder? Probably not. You got used to things in France now, even screams.

A cockerel behind the house started to crow, got into its stride, and couldn't stop.

Someone was making coffee, a wireless punching out snappy bits of morning news, louder as a door opened, feet thumping past his door, his heart thumping in step. *Get on with it. Get on with it.* Forty-eight hours was two days. Get through today and that would be one gone: he would be into the second. And what then? They were going to kill him, but you can still ask how. When you are this close to death, *how* is all that matters. What thin lips that German had – you notice things like that.

With thoughts of death off the leash Alex lingered over them, wondering why fear refused to come, why it had stayed so stubbornly aloof. What was the matter with him? All he felt was an odd numbness about the heart. Perhaps there is a point beyond which fear cannot grow? And Justine? She was free. Of the three of them, one caught, one dead, one still free. Would he betray her? Could they bring him to that?

He stood at the window, looking out across the vacant street, wet trousers draped cold against his legs. She was free. At least they had secured that much. And he was going to die. All he had left to discover was how.

He would be having his breakfast, that German with the thin lips. He had asked for a name. Surely any name would do? Why should the German care what Alex called himself? What would be lost in telling? Nothing at all. What was the point of torturing him for that? Perhaps he did not need a point. Perhaps torture would be satisfaction enough. If so, nothing in god's world could help him – nothing at all. *You will succumb.* Oh, there was truth in that. If only they would not hurt him, he would succumb alright. Hurt him how?

A million secret thoughts invaded him, fear as he'd never known it curling over him, doubling him up, pressing him crouched into the corner, fettered arms shaking, crying *No, no, no* into the pointless air, his little tablet wedged out of reach. Dear God, he would bite it now. Oblivion was more desirable than anything he had ever known: even than Justine.

Her name is Justine Perry. Her name is Justine Perry. She's a spy. We're both spies. Get on with it. Open the bloody door. Get it over. Only please God, don't hurt me too much. Please, not that.

The wireless clicked off. Real voices now, one lighter than the rest. That German with the oval face must be back. He seemed dreadfully young, this man with thin lips. Was he here already? New voices talking, the old policeman with his smoker's cough, clearing his lungs, somebody laughing as the door opened, feet thudding along the corridor, taking their time, a key in the lock.

He wouldn't get up. Crouching, knees pulled up, face buried in the stink of his trousers, they could leave him here, a little foetal lump, not worth the taking. The old policeman pulled at his collar, dragging him to the open door, casually prodding him to walk ahead, trousers flapping wet against his shins. At the door he leaned past Alex pushing it open.

A tall man in the uniform of an officer of the Gendarmerie was standing by the door spitting out French words in barely supressed fury. Justine, a heavy purple overcoat incongruously draped over bare shoulders, stood listening with the air of someone patiently waiting for a storm to blow itself out. She had rested one hand on his sleeve in a curious proprietorial gesture, tugging it slightly as Alex came in.

The man prised her hand off, turning away, staring out of the window. They stood together, their backs to Alex, in urgent whispered conversation, voices barely audible. Finally, the man erupted with a snort of laughter and swung round to stare at Alex, the old policeman scuttling back against the door, standing erect.

For a split second Justine's glance flashed danger and Alex knew – although god knows how – she was begging him not to speak. On tiptoes, lips inches from the tall man's ear, she murmured something that drew another reluctant smile.

Alex could only guess who he was, this tall man with his crisp uniform, elegant fingers unconsciously paddling Justine's bare arm. Clearly somebody - undeclared authority reason enough for the old policeman to stand nervously eyeing his cigarette burning itself out.

There must have been an order given, no more than a nod, Alex wincing with relief as he saw the handcuffs for the first time, surprisingly small, tossed onto the desk. He watched as a bundle of papers was pressed into Justine's hands.

She was already tugging his arm, pushing him ahead through the door. In the corridor, the double entrance doors stood wide open, the street beyond bathed in cold sunlight. The same cockerel was crowing.

As they came out, two women on the pavement looked up then went on talking. Alex stopped, consumed with a sense of anti-climax, Justine murmuring, "For Christ's sake, what now?"

At the foot of the steps she suddenly pulled the overcoat from her shoulders, "Damn, I'll have to give him this back ..."

But the man had followed them, standing looking down, one hand outstretched for his coat, a faint smile of concession on his face.

29

He looked at Alex, his English faultless, "You are fortunate in your friends, Monsieur the Frenchman. I will give you some advice. Keep your passport as a souvenir. Take it home with you to London. Explain to your superiors that France is not a playground for the English, do you understand? I will not apologise for your discomfort - you brought it on yourself. Go home."

Slipping his arms into the coat, looking at Justine, his expression was impossible to read, "Go home both of you. You do no good here." Turning back inside, he called over his shoulder, "Perhaps you will be good enough to explain, Madame."

At the corner of the street a battered lorry waited, a young man pulling at a starting handle, trying to get the engine to catch. The two women stopped talking as it exploded into life, watching them squeeze three abreast onto the dusty leather seat. At the crossroads they veered onto a narrow clay track, an impossible gradient, the engine screaming in first gear, climbing to a ridge high against the dawn sky beyond.

The driver barely stopped at the summit, circling a patch of open ground, nodding for them to jump. They stood listening as the sound retreated back into the valley below, Justine smiling at last.

"God, that *Madame* was a right old slap in the face."

Four

"Captain Vere sir, Captain Vere," Mother shaking him. No, somebody else shaking him. Wide awake now in his chair by the bed. He'd been dreaming. The same fetid smell everywhere.

It was too hot in here – you never get used to that.

"You've a visitor, sir. And why are you sitting out like that without your cover? You'll catch your death." She means well, this one. It would offend her to say he'd already caught it – but she wouldn't understand anyway. How she does rattle on.

"You don't get all that many visitors. Out of hours as well, but this one's got a chit. Top Brass I'd say, this chap, you can tell, little rose in his buttonhole an' all. I can ask Alfred to pop along and give you a shave if you like. He's busy this morning with the new lot, but just for you. Shall I do that? He'll wait, your visitor ... ever so keen to see you. Important looking. I've to give you his card. Now ... what about that shave? Spruce you up a bit."

This nurse was called Cecily. He'd always thought of her as his, she seemed to spend so long tending to him. Before Alex worked out where he was – and that took a long time – Cecily had been his only way of staying sane. Although that had been part of the problem – he couldn't be sure anymore that he *was* sane: not exactly.

She used to live at Epsom with an invalid mother before they moved here. Away from the bombs, she said, although that was a joke because the bombs followed them. She had a boy friend, Arthur, although that couldn't go very far - *you know what I mean* - because he'd been called up. Likely to go to Egypt or some such, so he said.

Alex liked listening to Cecily talking about moving here because eventually he found out where *here* was. Southampton. A hospital, although god alone knew why he was in a hospital in Southampton.

When he'd woken up he thought at first he must have been injured because there was a war on. Some battle or other. Shot perhaps? You get shot at in wars: he knew all about the war. But he didn't seem to be injured, certainly not shot.

He spent one whole morning indulgently working his way up from his toes to his eyelids, inch by inch and everything seemed to work. True there was a moment's panic remembering people with no legs think they are there all the same. But no, his legs had not been cut off. He could touch them. If the sheets hadn't been so tight across his chest, he could have looked at them. He had only the headache to concern him: an endless dull pain, making it hard to think.

He knew it was a hospital because Cecily was a nurse. Netley Hospital, she called it, *and a right old dump*. That made him smile: talking about how the nurses had only cold water to wash in, *and wasn't that a crime? And the lavvies … well, you wouldn't want to know about them.*

That first night she'd spent befuddled hours with him, pushing him back into bed when he'd tried to get free of the sheets, when he'd asked where Justine was, when he'd tried to go home. Not that he knew where home was. That was when he decided she was nice, trotting off every few minutes in her starched white cap to attend to some other bed, always coming back.

That was the other thing - the place was full of beds, hundreds of them, row upon row. You're in Netley she said, as if he'd understand, although he didn't. *Block D, but don't you go making anything of that. Lots of the new ones come in here first. No call to go making anything of that.*

But he wasn't making anything of it. He just wanted the headache to go away and was too tired to ask. All he could remember was something about mice and it didn't seem reasonable to trouble her with that.

Of course, he did understand eventually. Block D was where they put the mad ones. Although Dr Hoffmann had explained he was no longer mad, which was to imply that he had been. Dr Hoffmann did not elaborate. Simply pronounced in her matter-of-fact way that he appeared to be suffering from a psychological reaction to some extreme event. And the fractured skull – there was that as well, of course. Severe trauma was the term she used, explaining she was a psychiatrist and it was her job to uncover it.

It would be hard to think of anything more pointless. Alex was surprised to realise he knew about psychoanalysis: a weird Viennese cult best practised in church - or synagogue, if you wanted to be precise. As scientifically legitimate as phrenology and about as much use. Talking about uncovering when there was nothing covered in the first place - patently the good doctor Hoffmann was happy to waste her time. Alex was hiding nothing. After all, he had nothing to hide.

Since there was nothing to recollect, their encounters seemed entirely futile: him sitting in front of her, staring into space, trying to be polite, she leaning back looking at him, a little like his mother, a kindly serious expression on her face, breaking the silence now and then to ask if there was anything he wanted to say.

They filled the time with games. She would say a word and he would reply with what it reminded him of. It seemed he knew all about that as well, had read the books. She would write down his answers and often the following day they would talk about them, an activity that slowly became not completely uninteresting.

Alex grew to look forward to these daily sessions with Dr Hoffmann. Gradually, they took on a different character, the two of them slipping into a kind of complicity, as if they shared some unspoken common purpose.

Imperceptibly, he came to believe there were three people present: obviously, Dr Hoffmann and himself, but also someone else. Not entirely nice this other chap, shifty, devious, wriggling, cleverly shying away when things closed in on him, when things got too close.

It was one Saturday morning that the two of them finally pinned him down. It was a kind of trick. There were never sessions at the weekend and Alex had protested when the escort arrived, but Dr Hoffmann had come in specially that Saturday. Perhaps she had hoped to take this other person by surprise: it was her way of cornering this absent presence. The trick worked.

For the first time, he let them into a little part of his secret. Of a sudden, he remembered Justine, dear familiar Justine, shouldering open the battered door of the safe house, a derelict stone hut overgrown with brambles, his memory charged with the smell of the animals that had invaded the place.

It belonged to Claude Barte, she said, the man who ran the local circuit. He had olives up here years ago but it got to be too much trouble. They were to stay until dark. Turning to him then, looking tired, but somehow triumphant, her question quite casual. *That WT, Simone, wasn't it? Where have they got her, do you know?* And he did know, this wily secretive chap, although the words wouldn't come, apart from I'm going to be sick, Justine grabbing his arm, shouting, no way, you can't be sick here. And you should take those trousers off, clean yourself up. They smell like you've pissed yourself.

Dr Hoffmann was smiling at Alex like Mother smiled long ago when he'd been particularly good, when he'd come home with a gold star. So he smiled back, a little crooked, but it seemed churlish not to. Both of them quietly smiling because they'd tricked it out of him. Pleased the two of them were getting somewhere, Dr Hoffmann leaning back in her comfortable chair, waiting for more. Now he'd started they both knew there would be more. And true enough the other chap remembered. Saying she's dead if you must know. Simone's dead. Swallowed that bloody pill thing. Remembered Justine saying hell, we could have got her out.

He could not remember how the session ended. There seemed to be a gap. Sometimes Dr Hoffmann would give him an injection, something to make him sleep, an odd sort of dreamless sleep with a sweet chemical taste all of its own.

It was Sunday before he woke to the familiar headache, that same taste in his mouth. The ward was always quiet on Sunday. Those allowed to, had gone to the chapel, a red-brick barracks of a place incongruously topped off with a florid green dome. Not Alex. He was in no need of prayer that day.

He would lie on his back, remembering Justine.

"Are you going to tell me how ..."

"How I turned up with the rescue party, you mean? You poor Guffin. You looked a mournful sight I must say."

She was rummaging inside a khaki rucksack left on the table. "God bless him, Claude's left us a bottle of wine. Shall I open it? We can drink it outside. It stinks in here." Turning to him, suddenly serious," I saw that car before you did – that's all there is to it. I cut and ran. Scarpered. Ran like hell. Until I realised I was making too much noise and nobody was coming after me. By the time I'd crept back, you were being bundled into the car by your German friend. Then you drove off, the lot of you."

They sat on damp grass under a plantation of umbrella pines. In the valley below, mist still wrapped itself round tiny stone houses. Endless ripples of wooded hills stretched to the horizon, steel-grey in faint sunlight. She let her hand rest on his arm, holding him there. Although he surely had nowhere else to go.

It was an age before she spoke.

"I told you I used to live here. In the village. You won't like this. Hear me out. That man. The one all dressed up who made the little speech – slapped me in the face with Madame. He had a little house the other side of that wood. He used to call it our love nest. Something he'd read in a book, silly chap. I don't think I was the first girl he'd had there."

As she felt him free his hand she sprang up, "Don't you look at me like that! Don't you dare! What the hell gives you the right to look at me like that? Alright, I slept with him. Why not? Stop gawping Alex. It was years ago. I was very young. It was flattering if you want to know. He said he loved me. He even gave me a ring. You've seen it. Mind you, he'd already given one to his wife ... that was a disappointment. Hotel decoration he called it. Alright, I know it sounds cheap ..."

"You don't have to tell me any of this. I've no right to hear it."

"You mean you don't want to hear — I'm not sure I think well of you for that. Listen. I joined SOE in thirty-nine. What was the chance of me ending up in this place? Seriously. Quite a coincidence, wouldn't you say?"

"You said you lived here. They must have known that."

"Oh, they knew alright. Why send women on missions at all? Why do you think they do that? No, don't look away. Don't tell me the thought never crossed your mind. Why send me? I guess there's a Pascal Renault lying in wait for all of us. What else do you think I was supposed to do? Can you seriously ask? And that stupid expression on your face. What's that supposed to mean? That I'm yours now? How do you think I feel about it, gold ring and all? I'll tell you how I feel — angry."

Alex had walked to the edge of the clearing, smoke rising from a chimney far below bringing a faint smell of woodsmoke. A cock was still crowing.

Justine's voice drew him back.

"Once you'd been arrested Pascal was our only hope."

"But who the devil is he?"

"Who? He's a Colonel in the Gendarmerie. He used to be a big fish in the Deuxième Bureau. Now he's in something called the Office for Anti-National Affairs. Counterespionage. Gathering information on German infiltration of the Vichy setup. He knows your SS chum is spying on him. The hunter hunted — he was the target. Pascal loathes him. He told me once his job was to stop them infiltrating our networks. I never dared ask who our was. My first real mission was here — after the two trips to Paris and back. When I was settling in, the gossip among the girls in the village was all about Pascal. You're best to say yes when he asks, they said. I turned up to get my papers stamped and he couldn't believe his eyes. Went on and on *about the old days. About how it had been a real coup de foudre, there was nobody else, never could be. Very French – as if I cared who else he'd been bedding."*

She reached out, taking his hand in her own, searching for his eyes. "But I said yes, Alex. You may as well know, so there's no misunderstanding.

After that first time I realised he must have meant some of the things he said. A week after I'd landed I was lying low. The telephone went. I knew the voice - it was Pascal – but all it said was clear out *and put the receiver down. The apartment was raided later that morning. That wasn't the only time. I owe him my life several times over."*

"I owe you my life."

"Perhaps you do, but don't go calling it a trade, don't you dare. It was with Pascal. I was buying security and I knew what I was buying it with. There's a name for that, if you want to use it."

"You think you were sent here because they knew you had been ... close? It sounds cynical enough."

"Not really. They don't care about the particulars. It's what women are for – that's what they think. I doubt anybody knows about Renault. For one thing, he doesn't like the English. Says Englishmen make him feel inferior – and they have humiliated France. It's just that he really hates your German. It's something personal."

"And you told him about me? He had no reason to let me walk away. Every reason to keep me, in fact."

"That was what he was going to do, believe me. He asked why the hell he should. Said he was damned if he would help my lovers – the French do make that plural sound so prurient. That's what he was screaming about when they brought you in. But I convinced him."

"I can't see how."

"Can't you? I'm afraid I told him there was no way you would hold out when that SS officer got back. Wimpish – that was you, I said. Given what he thinks about the English, he appreciated the irony. I told him they'd prise my name out of you, no trouble. No, Alex, don't get on your high horse. I happen to be right. You don't know that German. He has a reputation. He gets pleasure out of hurting people. Pascal realised they were bound to get

me and he would be next in line. He knew it wasn't going to take much to prise his name out of me. I told him he couldn't expect me to hold out long. They'd get his name as soon as they arrested me. God, he was furious. Went into one of those comic Gallic frenzies. Called me a little blackmailer, a bitch, a whore, and a good few other words he hadn't used in a while. But I'll give him this, he knows when he's cornered. You know, I've just realised he knew if he was arrested his wife would get to hear of his English mistress. I think that worried him as much as anything ... men really are ridiculous."

"But that German will turn up this morning. He must be there already. It's us that's cornered."

"No. Both of them are at a conference all morning. Pascal arranged it. About clandestine operations, would you believe it? He issued a warrant to have you transferred to the special security prison in Limoges – with immediate effect. He has the authority to do that. It's all in the Station log book. They'll get back to the Gendarmerie this afternoon to discover their bird has flown."

"But they'll check with Limoges. They're bound to."

"Of course. You won't have arrived. And Pascal will deny signing anything. Warrants like that get forged all the time. The desk Sergeant should have followed procedure and telephoned ahead for an escort. The poor bastard will get it in the neck. But he'll keep his mouth shut."

It was not until the following day that Dr Hoffmann heard this story, breaking her habitual silence to wonder aloud whether there might not still be something. Something more to fish for.

"That dream. I've been looking at my notes. You describe a dream you had on a flight. You say it was light, although it was night-time? That interests me. I am reminded of your description of the headlights of that car when you were arrested. In which case ..."

"No, it was before I was arrested. I've had that dream since I was a child. A nightmare really, because it's always filled with feelings of dread."

"And you are always at a window in the dream?"

"Yes, in my bedroom. Looking down. And this woman's on the other side of the street. Look, do I need to talk about this?"

"I suppose not. You say the figure is a doctor? I did wonder about that. I am a doctor."

"When I was a child our doctor was a German woman."

"Hoffmann is a German name."

"She came to the house sometimes when we were sick ... she is just standing there, looking up at me."

"Looking at you?"

"It seems so. But I know this: the fear ... dread really ... was to do with the light."

"And perhaps the fact she was German? You could say you were in the dark. Would you say that?"

Alex let out a sigh of exasperation, "Look, if I was in the dark about something, I would know. Right? Why should I go to the trouble of dreaming, just to tell myself? It doesn't make sense. It isn't as if I was Joseph bringing news to the Pharaohs. D'you think we could stop? My headache's worse."

"But it means something to you – this light, this dark. Do you think it means nothing? Yes, I'm sorry, we should stop. If we had time ..."

But they did not have time. Three days later Dr Hoffmann signed his discharge papers, mumbling about unresolved childhood trauma. But there was a war on and she had other cases. Alex could be returned to the world, if not completely whole, whole enough.

He was looking at the slip of embossed card Cecily had left on the bed - *Neville Archer, MC, Lieutenant Colonel* - when the man himself appeared in the ward, working his way from bed to bed, checking names. Alex half rose in his chair then sank back, clutching his blanket.

A stumpy barrel-chested old buffer from another age was eyeing him from the other side of the bed, breathing heavily as if the stairs had defeated him. Older than Alex expected, he seemed a relic of quite another war. This bloke properly needed a horse to sit on and a sabre.

Tiny black eyes peered out of a wide florid face with the astonished expression of a stunned ox, huge moustaches, their flaring days not quite over, jutting out like tufts of cotton wool making his square head look unnaturally big.

He was uncomfortably dressed in tweed civvies, a rosebud in his lapel. He extended a hand across the bed then, realising it was too far to reach, awkwardly withdrew it, sitting down heavily on the other side, looking for somewhere to put a pair of yellow kid gloves, finally placing them on the bed.

"Captain Vere? That's what it says, but always best to check. You don't know me. Name's Archer. Baker Street. I don't think our paths have crossed."

He started a condescending laugh then thought better of it, withdrawing it like the handshake.

Archer. Alex was sure he had heard the name somewhere. It wouldn't come. "No sir, I don't think we've met. I'm pleased to see someone from the unit. A few more days and I'll ..."

The glittering eyes were darting warily round the ward. "Not the best place to talk, here. About your last mission. I've read the report. It seems you were damnably unlucky. Damnably,"

He lapsed into silence. He had found something on the ceiling and was staring at it disapprovingly, shuffling a little to get straight. The wooden chair seemed too small for him.

"And you ended up in this place?" It was a question, but Alex was lost for a reply. "I've not come to hear your story. Time enough for that."

"I don't think it could be much of a story, sir. I've suffered some memory loss. Still piecing things together. It was the immediacy of everything, I think. Barely time to bury the chutes and we're picked up." He managed an awkward laugh. "Still, better luck next time. Don't they say that, sir?"

"We can't send you back, Vere."

You could tell he rather enjoyed blurting things out. He had composed his face, trying to look serious, but you could see there was almost a smile behind it all. Perhaps he didn't even realise it himself – this ancient relic actually enjoyed bearing bad news. Perhaps it was the last bit of power left to him.

"You do know that? It's impossible."

"Because I've been taken? I know the rule, sir. It just seems arbitrary in this case. Given the circumstances."

The unfortunate secret smile escaped. Archer turning it into a half-hearted kind of laugh, no more than a little catch in his throat, trickling away to nothing.

"Can't change the rules just for you, you know." He leaned forward, tapping his nose in a strange conspiratorial gesture. "You don't realise what a rare bird you are, Captain Vere. Once an agent's taken they never come back. You appreciate that? Never come back. And here you are. You're the first."

"Meaning you can't trust me, sir? Is that what you mean?" Alex realised he was blushing. This old fool actually believed it. What made it worse, his protests would only confirm it.

Archer glanced round the deserted ward, picking up his gloves. "Don't be too hard on yourself. And don't be too hard on us. Let's just say we have to proceed on that basis. That's logical isn't it? Doesn't sound so bad put that way, does it? Who's to know whether somebody's been turned? Or what it means, come to think of it. The world's not black and white is it? You'll know more about that than me."

"But Mrs Perry's report. She must have explained ..."

"It's true we have a report. But ..."

"... I was only held overnight. A short night at that."

"There'll be time to go into this when we get you back to London. Tomorrow, isn't it? The point is you've been seen. Your papers have been seen ... "

"He said the passport was a bad forgery, by the way."

"Who did?"

"The German who arrested me. SS. A young chap but quite senior I think."

"They always say that – throws you off your stride. Your passport is perfectly sound. More so than the rest of the papers if it comes to that. People at Duke Street made it – even the ink's French. There's a point you're missing, Captain Vere - they've had it in their hands. You're *known*. I'm sorry to bear bad news, but you won't be going back. It can't be a surprise to you."

"I was thinking perhaps an exception, given the whole operation was a disaster: an utter shambles."

"You're bound to see it that way, but you don't get to see the whole picture. Overall, even taking your ..." he stopped, struggling to find the right word. The slightly supercilious smile seemed painted on his face. "... your *escapade* into account, overall, we were not dissatisfied. All in all, in terms of objectives, it went well. Hellish unfortunate for you, of course, but for the rest ... on the whole, a success. Yes, a success."

Five

At first, pleasure in being free of the smells and discomfort of Netley was enough and Archer's summons seemed suitably remote. But gradually Alex understood his discharge had been in a sense provisional: he had been left incomplete.

Each morning, he awoke to welcome the dull pain in his head like an old friend, lying for a few painful minutes sorting among scraps of remembered detail, checking what memories sleep had delivered back to him. The immediate past remained a once-familiar place, endlessly taunting him: he lived with his life on the tip of his tongue.

Archer's unit turned out to be unprepossessing: a warren of dusty rooms over the Post Office in Bedford Square. A wooden plaque, newly-stencilled TPSU in white paint, army-style, had been screwed to the wall at the foot of a flight of tiled stairs.

Archer, in dress uniform, was standing at the banister rail, peering down beyond Alex into the gloom of the stairwell as if he expected someone else.

"Take the tube?"

"No sir, I walked. It's not that far for me. Dr Hoffmann says I need the exercise. To tell the truth I don't like being cooped up in the tube."

"Do I know this Dr Hoffmann?"

"Somebody at Netley, sir. Helped put some of the bits together. My bits, that is."

"Never met him. Go through," pointing to the door immediately behind him, "I'll be with you in a minute. We're only just getting settled in here. All a bit primitive, but it serves, it serves. You'll find a chair. The last lot left us that. They didn't leave much else. Park yourself, I won't be long. There's just the two of us so far."

When he bustled back he plonked a pile of brown manila folders onto a battered desk and stood leafing through the one on top, rustling pages, pursing his lips as though he was about to start whistling. Alex had stood up. He might as well have not been there.

Archer tossed the file down, slumping behind the desk.

"Right. You think you know why you're here. But you're wrong."

Alex recognised the familiar piece of yellow card clipped to the front of his Personnel file. He had last seen it at that final briefing in the little room with the Torridon Major. Before the drop. It seemed a lifetime ago.

"I've your file here, Vere. And it's not my intention to add to it. That surprise you?"

Alex found himself looking into the same glittering intense eyes he'd seen at Netley: the painfully puzzled stare of the slightly barmy, somebody always a step behind life, never quite getting the point.

But he was a Colonel, for heaven's sake – how had he wangled that? It must have been the MC - the reward for being brave. Or suicidally impetuous – sometimes that came to the same thing. Either way, this old boy's few mad seconds in the field had lifted him into command. It must have been in his sabre days. It seemed unfair.

"Never been very interested in files. Mostly lies. Here's a question – it says you speak French. How's that?"

"My mother worked in France after the war. In Paris. I picked it up at school there."

"And your father?"

"No father, sir. He was killed in 1918. I don't really remember him. It was a trench booby trap. His platoon walked into it. The war was over by then. They were just unlucky."

"It's no use going into all that now. We've work to do. We had WT confirmation you were captured, by the way. Although by the time the signal was decoded, you weren't, if you see what I mean."

The sudden stare was unnerving, "Mrs Perry's account of how that trick was pulled off is ... what's the word? ... *vague*."

He raised a hand, "No, I'm not interested in your version until we can debrief the two of you. She's still in France."

He closed the folder and went on staring sightlessly through Alex, obviously miles away. "We can't send you back, you know that. The MO says you're not fit yet anyway. You know the rule. Once they've clapped eyes on you you're out of the game. The question is what are we going to do with you?"

"I don't think I'm much use for anything ..."

"Now that's defeatist talk. I don't like that, never have. Gets you nowhere," tapping the folder with the nail of his forefinger, "no, you'll be some use alright. That's what I want to talk about. It says here *Psychologist, Authority on Memory*. That right? Psychologist – that's some sort of medic?"

"Not exactly, sir. And, please, I'm not an authority on anything. I'd barely started my doctoral work. I was a year into it when I joined up."

"Alright, you were going to be a medic, let's not split hairs. It's the same thing. Honestly Vere, this mock modesty is girl's stuff. Drop it, we don't have time. It says authority here in black and white, that's good enough for me."

"I don't know who wrote that, sir. Was it Professor Burt? He hardly knows me. He probably thought he was doing me a favour, you know, putting me in a good light. We've only met a couple of times. He's not my supervisor."

"Who wrote it is not your business. And you shouldn't be fishing. You should know better. What's in here is secret. Stays that way. Look, I need three things." He raised a huge blotched fist, clumsily extending one finger. "First, somebody who can keep his mouth shut. And we know you can do that."

The laugh, when it appeared, was a kind of bark, a sudden mirthless explosion, "Come to think of it, you seem an authority on that as well. Right? Right? You can keep your mouth shut, alright –

we've not heard a peep about what you were doing after that miraculous escape."

"Dr Hoffmann says it may come back, but there's no knowing when, not with a blow to the head."

He managed another finger.

"Second. Somebody who understands the setup - how we work, what you can do, what you can't, and so on. We trained you, so you fit that bill. Trained you at some expense, I may add, so you meet that bill in spades."

A stubby final finger joined the others, making three, bound together with his other hand. "Third. Somebody who knows what makes people tick. And I don't want damned Intelligence people crawling over the operation ... they're the last thing I want. Do you understand?"

There was a peculiar defiant expression about his face, daring Alex to deny something. "I want somebody with a bit of imagination. Months, I've been looking, and then you turn up. A godsend. My own trick-cyclist. Isn't that the term?

"Well, that's a psychiatrist. I'm not a medic."

"Oh, for god's sake don't start quibbling again. Look here, I want somebody who knows what's true, what's a lie ... that sort of thing. You're an authority on that. I may have prisoners for you to see."

It was impossible to see where all this was going.

"*Prisoners*?"

"That's right. Mind you, not your regular POWs," looking up at Alex, an odd ingratiating smile under the white fuzz, "think you can manage that?"

"Manage what, exactly, sir?"

"Sort out the truth, of course. Understand?"

"You mean interrogation? That's not really my ..."

"You're not listening. Not interrogation. We've people for that. I want you to listen. Think you can do that?" A sudden panic flared his face, "God - should have asked. That comes of you raising objections ... lost my thread. You've signed, of course?"

"The Official Secrets Act? Yes. Before I ..."

"No need to say when. Now ..." He waved Alex back into his chair, leaning towards him across the desk.

"What I'm going to say stays in this room. Stays in your head. Understood? Nobody hears about it – that clear? Not your dear old Mum, not your girl, not your dog. Perfectly clear?"

"Perfectly clear, sir. And I don't have a dog."

"I'll make the jokes, alright? What do you know about Special Operations in Germany?"

"You mean the SOE German desk?"

"No I don't mean the bloody German desk. I mean Special Operations in Germany."

"But there aren't any, are there? I know something was tried in thirty-nine or forty. In Aachen wasn't it? I heard it was a complete flop. It must be completely impossible - that's what we were told at Torridon."

"Those chaps don't know everything. Good on theory, but life's not theory is it? Humour me."

He went across and closed the door, dragging his chair round the desk, sitting too close, eyes flicking to the closed door.

"What if I'm going to tell you there is organised resistance in Germany?" his voice a kind of rasping whisper, "on German soil. Now, what can we offer them by way of support?"

"You mean if there was any? Supply drops, I suppose, that sort of stuff. But to tell the truth, if there was organised resistance on any scale, it wouldn't last half an hour. We'd be wasting resources. To say nothing of the risks of low level drops over enemy lines. We're not talking about occupied territory, are we? From what I understand, the regime is pretty well supported."

"Oh, absolutely," nodding a little too vigorously, the smile broadening, "we supported it ourselves until quite recently. I've seen some of the memos, joint action with the Abwehr against the commies. Not all that many moons ago either. Lots of red faces now among our Intelligence brethren down the road ... damned embarrassing ..."

"I'm sorry, perhaps I don't understand."

"Don't understand what?"

"About this organised resistance. Or are we talking about Austria? I suppose that's possible."

"No, I'm talking about the glorious Fatherland. Here's a question for you. What if I say I have the evidence? What if I show you documents, files, WT traffic, the lot. Would you believe me then?"

"We've really got this, sir? It seems incredible. No ... I'm sorry ... I'd still say it was more likely some kind of Jerry disinformation."

An oddly demonic grin appeared, "Good thought, Vere, excellent. What if I could do better?"

"You're telling me there really is organised resistance inside Germany. Do you mean civilian or military? Sorry ... can I ask questions?"

"Of course, my dear chap. Which would you prefer?"

"No, thinking about it, it must be military. Military personnel. That might make sense. How long have we known? Can I ask who knows about this?"

"Ah, another excellent question. I knew you were my man. And the answer is, nobody." He leaned back, satisfied, enjoying the silence. "But you would believe me if I showed you evidence?"

"Of course, sir ... I didn't intend to imply ... what I mean is it's not that I'm questioning ... I'm just not sure exactly where I come in. If it's signals evaluation, that sort of thing, I assume SIS is on top of it."

Archer was shaking his head, tipping back, blowing through the white of his moustaches, "To repeat myself, Captain Vere, our brothers in Secret Intelligence know nothing at all of this. And they will go on knowing nothing at all. This secret is ours, d'you understand? I specifically pressed you on this point and you agreed. You keep your mouth shut – that's an order."

He carried his chair back to the desk, dropping into it, his expression a kind of weary benevolence.

"Here's the point. Thought I'd never get to the point, didn't you? But I come to things my own way … always have done. You're the trick cyclist, the memory man. Given I have enough copperbottom information about this organised resistance, would it persuade you? Yes or no."

"Yes, sir."

"Well, that's what you're going to do, my boy. You're going to deliver me that information. You're going to copperbottom it."

He leaned forward, tapping his nose, rather spoiling the ancient conspiratorial gesture by changing hands in mid flow, "Check that door will you?"

Alex opened the door and looked down the dusty corridor, "Nobody aboard, sir."

"Come back in and keep your voice down. Now … what I'm going to tell you stays between these walls, understood? Might give you an idea. I'm talking about the last war, you understand? Fighting Turks … greasy devils. This chap leaves his kit in the desert. Looks for all the world like he's come up against it and fled the scene. Now … what's inside his kit? Can you guess?"

"Sounds like Colonel Meinertzhagen, sir. False battle plans left for the enemy to discover – is that the idea? I think they call it The Haversack Ruse."

Archer's fixed stare was so unnerving, Alex found himself blushing. "Ah, you've heard something about it? But you don't know everything. He left his binoculars behind as well." He managed a triumphant snort, "Didn't know that, did you, eh? Not about the binoculars?"

Alex thought it best to shake his head.

"They clinched it … that's my opinion. Crucial. Looked like he'd scooted in a hurry, you see. You don't go dropping your glasses like that. Clever."

He suddenly stood up, waiting until Alex had come to attention.

"Just an idea. Something to think about. Now ... you'd better get on, Captain."

So that was it. He was to exchange his one failed night of active service life for nothing much - see the war out accommodating to the dismal routine of a disinformation bureau. It seemed demeaning. Puzzling, what's more, given Archer's obsessive concern with secrecy. Disinformation and deceit were the stock in trade of SOE: it was why they existed. What was the point of trying to keep this ramshackle little enterprise a secret from the people best placed to do the job? It seemed inexplicable.

Two days later, the third and final member of Archer's miniature army arrived. John Cabot was a disappointment: short, bespectacled, running to fat, smooth face slightly puffy, large vacant eyes. Archer boasted he had recruited him in Oxford, adding proudly he could speak German like a native.

"Depends on the native, old man." Cabot had strolled into the room bearing a cup of coffee, looking for somewhere to place it on the desk in front of Alex.

"Drink this. It may be a while before you taste its like. I got one of the servants in the Buttery to fill my thermos flask."

He settled himself into the chair by the window, already at ease. "Are we to be the sum of everything here? *We are but few* ... I forget how the rest of it goes - that the idea? I volunteered, you know, but that doesn't mean I know what I'm supposed to do."

"It's mad, I know, but I'm sworn to secrecy. I'm sorry – our leader's hot on secrecy. He'll spell it all out for you. I warn you, it's not very exciting. But written German's going to be an enormous help. Mine's pretty hopeless."

Feeling slightly ashamed, Alex tried to compose his face, "And you really volunteered to join this unit?"

"Well ... not quite. I was called up, of course. Army. They booted me out in week one. Here ... my secret shame," Cabot held out a pair of spectacles, pebble lenses set in heavy tortoiseshell frames.

He stared vacantly at Alex, blinking nervously. "The buggers wouldn't have me. I thought for a while I might wangle a job breaking enemy codes. That sounded fun. In fact our Bursar got me an interview. You know, I think he's a kind of spymaster. I was sent to some God-forsaken place next to Bletchley railway station. Trouble is, arithmetic's not my strong suit. So here I am – blind as a bat, one more willing recruit to the service of the TPSU. What's that stand for, by the way? Nobody seems to know."

"I haven't a clue. I suppose Archer will tell us. He's not here today."

"A chap in my college knows a bit about our Colonel. I pumped him. You know he's Hungarian? So his name can't really be Archer. Odd choice, given the Arrow Party is a Hungarian version of the Nazis. He comes from Eger. I've been there. Lovely cathedral. Apparently, his parents were very well to do. *Stinking rich* was the phrase used. The how and why of these great riches are a secret. I'm afraid that's Oxford code for Jewish. People in my college are like that - it's all they live for. Archer was shipped off to school in England. Never went back."

"He doesn't look Jewish. Wait till you meet him - I think all this is going to be a bit of a let-down for an Oxford Fellow."

"Steady on, nothing so grand. Junior Fellow, old boy. Even that may come to nothing. I'm working on a collected edition of Gotthold Lessing. Heard of him?" Alex shook his head. "No, few have. My contract here says *German Language Specialist*. I must bend my mind and accommodate to the new century. What do you do?"

"Archer insists I'm his Psychologist. But for heaven's sake don't go making a song and dance about it. You probably know more about Freud than me."

Colonel Archer arranged a surreal opening ceremony on Monday of the second week. By that time, telephones had been installed and there were sufficient desks and chairs to go round. He produced a bottle of Highland Park malt whisky, three assorted glasses and a plate of sandwiches bribed out of the charwoman.

That same afternoon, as a mark of good intent, and only slightly the worse for wear, Alex and Cabot began work on a list of imaginary dissident German officers.

Archer vetoed the suggestion that they simply obtain the current German staff lists from Records, forbidding any kind of direct approach to SOE in Baker Street. Cabot suggested they invent the necessary personnel, drawing on French and German newspapers for inspiration.

At that time the Paris newspapers were carrying reports of the recall of a German military attaché. There was even a blurred photograph. Alex drafted the first TPSU letter, addressed to Kommodore Ralf Spier at the Paris Embassy:

This comes to you from someone who shares your patriotic ambitions to warn you that others have become aware of your activities on our behalf and the Wehrmacht cell we are both concerned with. You will be aware of the appropriate action to take.

Cabot translated it, typing it himself on blank French stationery, adding a masterstroke of his own: *The meeting you had arranged for the 10th must be postponed.*

They hesitated over the question of a signature. It presented an opportunity to deploy one from their growing list of imaginary officers, but equally it would not take long to discover the person concerned did not exist. A compromise was found in the signature: *A brother officer.*

The letter was carried through one morning and laid with some ceremony on the polished surface of Archer's empty desk before his arrival. He was enormously proud of his first-born. He could only read restaurant German, but spent much of the day admiring the document.

Ignoring SOE channels, he sought out a contact in Boodle's, arranging for passage to a double agent in Lisbon. It was to be delivered, *strictly sealed*, to the unsuspecting Kommadore. The day Archer had confirmation the letter had been despatched he returned to the TPSU office in triumph.

"That Portuguese creep will open it, nothing's more certain. We'll just have to see how the information spreads. It's a first step, gentlemen. From small acorns, you understand. In six months we'll have our resistance cells functioning all over Germany. And we'll be pulling their strings."

His optimism was unwarranted. This first small step involving the unsuspecting naval attaché remained the only acorn actually planted.

Archer proposed an extension of the idea, using drops from low level flights depositing briefcases containing the personal papers of selected members of the High Command. Mixed with genuine documents were to be forged papers referring to resistance cells in Berlin, Hamburg and Munich. The plan was stillborn, stalling in the face of SIS opposition.

It was at this point Alex realised how little operational authority the TPSU actually possessed. In particular, access to flights involved a sclerotic clearance procedure, permission invariably denied.

At one particularly ill-tempered meeting an anonymous person, vaguely described as *Technical*, asked who was going to guarantee that objects thrown from a plane (and the question arose *by whom?*) would not be caught in the slipstream, with consequential damage? It was bad enough having to repair planes shot up by the *Luftwaffe* – were we now expected to repair self-inflicted damage? Archer had stormed out in a rage, slamming the door, the expression, *bloody civilians* floating up to them from the stairwell. He did not return for several days.

For Cabot at least, the fact he had time on his hands seemed not entirely disagreeable. He took to bringing notes to work from his Oxford days, working on the poems of Gotthold Lessing.

Watching him endlessly tinkering with translations, it was difficult to escape the conclusion that the TPSU would have little impact on the future conduct of the war. For Alex, at least, a conclusion tinged with the suspicion that the outcome had been intended. Even the unit's name, when eventually discovered, seemed demeaning. Rummaging in a drawer one day, Cabot pulled out a delivery notice for rubber date stamps (18s 6d) directed to *Third Party Supply Unit*.

Archer himself appeared to be waiting for some unspecified event to happen, unconcerned by the lack of concrete action. On occasion, he even spent a desultory afternoon with the two of them, working on the chain of command in the resistance movement, allocating duties, juggling the relative status of fictional German officers.

The telephone call came late one afternoon. They had spent much of that day discussing fish. Before leaving for his club, Archer had asked Cabot to concoct a rumour that two hundred man-eating sharks had been introduced into the English Channel. The rumour was to be spread within the *Luftwaffe*. Exactly how, was left as a matter to be decided.

With Archer gone, Cabot sat in silence, doodling on a piece of paper.

"I know bugger all about sharks. It's not really what I joined up for. Would they survive in cold water, do you think? I thought they were tropical?"

"John, it's not going to matter much, is it? It's not as if they're actually going to exist. It's a mad idea. Who'd believe it? They'd attack our fliers as well. And where would you get two hundred sharks? He seems to have forgotten there's a war on."

Alex was consumed by a sense of frustrated anti-climax. Accepting the Torridon version of war was always slightly tainted -

falling a little short of honourable - at least it was to have been fought on enemy soil. And he had come to believe the end truly did justify the means. But this? Stuck in a dusty room, unwashed teacups buried in piles of paper, old newspapers curling brown in sunlight. All the pointless detritus of a pointless office. He had hoped for something more.

Cabot was prodding his arm. "I'm walking across to the Museum. I'll see whether I can find you a shark that dines only on German flesh."

The telephone rang so rarely Alex was startled. He scraped it across the desk leaving a wake of crumpled paper and lifted the receiver.

"*Captain Vere?*"

"Yes."

"*Please hold.*"

Whoever it was disappeared with an abrupt click, leaving nothing more than a faint hum.

A second click.

"*Connecting you.*"

"Is that you Alex? I only have a second."

"Justine! Is it really you? You've made my day. I was feeling a bit maudlin: this damned headache. Where are you? It's not late, we could ..."

"Yes Guffin, let's take all that as read, I'm in a hurry. Just wanted to pass on a friendly hello. How are things treating you? Getting enough to eat?"

"Eat? Yes, I'm fine. Look, I can get away, can we ..."

"Not right now, my dear. So long as you're getting your grub. Just wanted to say all's well. God bless."

The purr of the dialling tone left him feeling strangely bereft.

Six

The next day Alex was late for a meeting. He'd never been late before, but there's no accounting for a bomb. In this case, a thousand pounds of high explosive, a direct hit on the church at the corner of the street. He stopped for a second to look at the smoking hole, thinking how quickly you come to accept things, to adapt. A few years back the newspapers would have been full of this.

Of course, that had been a time when churches didn't explode. A time before German bombs thumped and crumped their indiscriminate way across London, night after night after night. Until you gave up flinching and became inured to the wantonness, even finding a kind of exhilaration in it. If you get the scale right, destruction has a certain majesty about it. You creep up from your burrow to smell the daylight, almost welcoming that sick lurch about the heart at the sight of what had gone. In the end you crave it, thinking of all those lost things. Paper mostly - how easily paper burns.

The bombs stopped as abruptly as they started, German wrath turning to find other targets. It was that had made Alex pause, because the blackened chunks of St Michael and All Angels distributed across the street that morning were out of the ordinary.

Unintentional, people had mumbled.

Everyone knew the story now: released by mistake on the way back from bombing Canterbury. Although what Canterbury had done to deserve a bomb was for God to know. Surely, there was nothing there but a cathedral? The thought was not consoling. It was our fault apparently. Some angry German thumbing through his Baedecker to find an English place pretty enough to bomb in revenge for Lübeck. Alex could only think that war deserved something more than revenge.

It was a lovely morning for December, cold, with a bracing wind chafing your face. A bright low sun glanced off a leather-bound booklet impaled on the railings - pristine blue, embossed *Order of Service*. A pity - prayer had come into its own recently.

He picked his way through the rubble, remembering Justine kneeling on the floor in that church at Torridon. Justine still alive: against all the odds, still alive. For weeks he had not allowed his mind to venture to that dark place, choosing to keep her alive. And the miracle was true - six weeks were not enough for Justine.

At the corner, firemen wearily hauled at flattened canvas hoses sprawled over the pavement. A bitter smell of woodsmoke in the air reminded him of something not altogether disagreeable but the memory eluded him.

He followed the chalked sign past the silent queue at the temporary bus stop. It would have been comforting to see their wind-chilled faces as defiant, but they seemed merely resigned.

As he reached Bedford Square, a splash of reflected sunlight cast him instantly into his domestic prison in Saint Aunix. That memory, at least, was safe: Justine pushing him into fresh air, liberation filling his lungs, he would never forget that. But there was a gap, nonetheless, a soft patch where nothing held, where he could not go. How strange to know with absolute certainly that you didn't know something.

He stood immobile, the sun in his eyes, the forgotten something so close it was like a pain; far away, a muffled squeal of brakes, someone shouting.

Bloody Fool! You want to kill yourself?

An unfamiliar army Sergeant stood at the top of the steps. He straightened up, stifling a grin. "You'll be Captain Vere? You're the last. Almost caught me there, sir. Me watching you dodge the traffic like that. Wouldn't do, me saluting you in civvies, like. Go along up, sir. They're all there."

"You mean I'm late. No need to be polite."

"Let's say just in time, sir. Quite a crowd today – that's why I'm here. Security. I suppose you heard about the bomb, sir?"

"Security for a bomb? But it was half a mile away. Security for what?"

"Really couldn't say, sir. Top of the stairs and on your right. Oh, sorry, you know the way, of course you do."

As he took the stairs two at a time he could already hear the drone of Archer's voice. He tapped and came in, resting for a second, back against the door, a little out of breath. The place was thick with smoke. The bewhiskered head behind its defensive wall of files paused just long enough to nod. Cabot looked up from his doodles, pursing his lips into a tiny moue, flicking a warning glance across the room.

So this morning it wasn't to be just the three of them. A thin-faced chap in smart Air Force blue had positioned himself at the other end of the table, poised to take over should Archer ever stop. Nobody ever sat there. As Alex dropped into his chair, a crisp blue sleeve was pushed aside, the glint of a steel watch.

There was somebody else.

Set a little apart, standing with his back to the window, the Torridon Major, smiling agreeably, lowering his head in mock-solemn greeting.

Archer caught the gesture, managing a vague irritated wave, "So you two know each other?"

"We met at Tempsford, sir."

"But you don't know Connor here." He let Alex bob up, waiting while they shook hands.

"I knew you'd be held up. Heard about the bomb, you see. A stray apparently. But we've not started. I was just filling in a few bits of background."

Connor's cadaverous liver-spotted face reared up, as if to say he'd come for more than background. He seemed about to speak then thought better of it, slumping back, letting Archer keep the floor.

"Wing Commander Connor's here because we need his take on things," craning round awkwardly over his shoulder to look at the Major, "I don't know how long you two can stay ...?"

If it was a question, the Major, staring down into the street below, didn't bother to reply.

There was a watery glint in Archer's eyes. Alex wondered, not for the first time, how on earth the old boy had engineered this job. Peering out over his barricade, puffy cheeks veined purple with too many late nights at Boodles, sagging eyelids little pools of tears, he was completely out of his depth. Emotionally labile, that was his problem. Perhaps his age, but in Archer's case he must have always been that way - always the tearful schoolboy.

Connor had opened a gold cigarette case to light a cigarette, the scrape of his match breaking the silence like a rebuke. Archer threw a resentful stare into space, pulling down a file, opening it, lost for words.

"Right ... right. We're all here so we'll start. I'll skim through this – quicker that way. To put you in the picture, Alex, we're talking about an operation that took place a bit over a month ago. The morning of Tuesday the tenth of November, to be precise. At Saint Aunix. That's Columbine territory. A pickup for an agent called Perry. Mrs Perry."

Cabot looked up, puzzled by the sudden tension in the room.

Alex was conscious of Archer's glittering eyes fixing his own, staring him down.

"The two of you were dropped earlier last year, weren't you Alex? To join the Columbine circuit." He turned to Connor, "That's the drop that went wrong. Captain Vere and Mrs Perry got themselves into a bit of trouble. But we've got him back, at least." The smile was not friendly. "Bit of a miracle, that. But there you are. Anything new to add, Alex?"

"I wish I could, sir. The fact is, I can't remember anything much after I was arrested," looking desperately at Connor," they tried to get what happened out of me at Netley - at the hospital. No go, I'm afraid."

Connor went on looking at his cigarette end, picking off a loose strand, barely listening.

"It's alright Alex," Archer left the smile where it was, "we're not here to talk about that. Now, where was I? Perry was one of the first to join SOE. With us from the start. Effective, disciplined, no black marks." He prodded the file, "*Fearless*, it says here. Sounds like a disadvantage to me, but who am I to say? Connor's people were to pick her up from Saint Aunix in the morning …"

He was furiously underlining something on the paper in front of him. "A point here, Connor. Probably nothing at all. Your Report has ETD – hard to keep up with all these acronyms. I assume that's estimated time of departure. It's down as eleven twenty. But that's the same as the ETA."

Connor looked at him, smiling. Rather a pleasant smile. In better times you could see him as good company.

"You can take it they don't wait around, Colonel."

"Thought it would be that. Now … the complication. There was another passenger to be picked up. An artist. Name Lucile Beyrou. It's an assumed name, she's English actually - got herself stranded after war broke out. Known to the frogs I assume, but live and let live, they didn't trouble her."

He nodded to Connor, "Alright so far?"

Connor went on looking vacantly into space.

"Right, I'll go on. When the Germans moved South last November somebody – no, Cabot, don't ask – *somebody* decided the propaganda value of this artist person was too valuable to be left to the glorious Reich. Worried they'd put her on show in Paris, I suppose. No worse than all these commie writers fleeing in a funk, I'd have thought, but not for me to say. In a nutshell, it was decided to get her out. We've got her safely tucked away somewhere up North haven't we, John?"

"I gather she's in Dundee, sir."

Archer pushed the Report back into its file. "The War Office ordered us to give Perry's place in the car to this artist woman. It was left to the local people to find Perry some other transport to get her to the field. High handed, but there you are. Now, here's the point. The car they used for Perry was carrying thirty pounds of TNT."

Connor threw his pencil down, grinding his cigarette into the ashtray, "Bloody maquis. And they call it *resistance*. If I'd known it was going to be within fifty yards of one of my planes ... Saints preserve us from amateurs."

"But you didn't know, Connor. Neither did we." Archer raised a hand, glaring at Alex, "Neither did Mrs Perry I imagine. Uncomfortable sort of thing to be travelling with. Of course, the damned thing went off. There wasn't much time to check, but it looked as if a grenade had been rigged up as the detonator, that and the usual alarm clock thing."

He ran his finger along a line of text, "Says here, *Yellow body fragments in the debris, almost certainly MK II TNT grenade*. You can see where this is leading, can't you Alex? Are you with us, Alex? Are you alright?"

Archer's stare was oppressive, false concern welling up into wet eyes, moustaches raised a little, a sadistic little twitch of his lips.

Alex felt sick. The answer was no, he wasn't alright - not alright at all. The bastard had orchestrated this whole recital simply to watch him as he discovered Justine was dead. All this talk about debris was for his benefit. Perhaps the old fool thought his grotesque trick would trigger some lost memory. It would have triggered something - if Alex hadn't spoken to her yesterday he would have been out of the room by now, heaving his guts up in the corridor.

But she was not dead. That must be why she telephoned.

Images of Justine were sliding over each other in what was left of his memory, coloured with a sense of incredible relief. She was alive – somewhere, she was alive. That was all that mattered. And as the thought slipped back into the dark pool, a tiny focus of pain in his head flared like the sharp pierce of a needle. He felt hopelessly vulnerable, aware all the time of the Major's silent scrutiny.

Cabot was trying to retrieve Connor's pencil.

"We're not dealing with a regular army, are we, sir? They're just rural guerrillas. Not exactly your disciplined force. Chaps on the run from the call-up or forced labour in Poland, or Magna Germania, as they insist on calling it." A thought struck him, "How did they get hold of TNT?"

Archer shuffled through the papers, "Yes, there's something about that in here. A quarry in the area with what you might call obliging security." He gave Alex a final vicious knowing look.

"While they were boarding the passengers, somebody shifted the TNT from one car to the other. This was a daytime pickup, you understand, best not to hang around. The car had barely left the field when it exploded. The chaps left behind did what they could but it was hopeless. Just got themselves burned in the process. Hands too damaged to drive. They abandoned their own car, set fire to it, and made off on foot. Terrible affair."

He closed the file, looking at Connor, "I think that's a good place for me to stop, Wing Commander - the point at which your plane took off. Can you take it from there?"

Connor was already making a fuss of reaching down into his briefcase. A little piece of theatre - dragging out a single slim file, posing it unopened in front of him, squaring it off with two hands. He let the silence run on.

"I'll give you our angle if you like. Not that we had much to do with it. Mind you, if there's SOE politics in this, we're out of it, understand? We were just the transport, is that clear? We'd ferried your agent Perry before. We got the news about the extra passenger the day before – that would have been the Monday. Not entirely welcome news, people don't always understand you can't just add weight like that. But nothing to make a song and dance about. Anyway, the instruction was from the War Office."

He looked up at the Major and for the briefest of seconds they exchanged glances. "Of course, we know why now – Jerry was about to move South in force. So we had two passengers – your agent Perry and this artist, Mrs Beyrou - I'm afraid none of us know anything about her. Still don't, for that matter."

Alex was glaring at Archer. The fact Justine had survived seemed of no interest to him at all. Anger left him blinking stupidly. That single abortive solitary venture was to be his all - they would see to that. And here was one more bloody shambles to be picked over in a stuffy office in a back street in Bloomsbury.

He could feel Connor looking at him, Eton and Cranwell exuding world-weary disdain, always knowing that little bit more than you.

He was Air Intelligence, that much was obvious. And his chum the Major, standing with his back to the window, tagging along? What was he? Secret Intelligence Service, or worse.

Watching the ancient relic at the head of the table, staring forlornly from one face to another, Alex felt a surge of pity. Archer thought he was in charge. He hadn't even the wit to see this secretive duo was playing him like a fish.

"Actually sir, not 'Mrs'. She's not married to anybody." Having blurted it out, Alex fell back into his seat feeling stupid, realising too late he'd got even that wrong. They were talking about this artist - he'd been thinking of Justine.

Connor's cool look rested on him a condescending beat too long, "Ah. Right you are then. So not *Mrs*," making to open his file, changing his mind, leaving his hand resting on it, looking up to the ceiling, reciting from memory.

"We'd used that Saint Aunix strip before. Neat little place, tucked away. You can risk it in daylight. This was to be the last for a while. The passengers were back at Northolt at seventeen hundred hours."

The smile to Alex was complicit, almost friendly, "We entrained Mrs ... I beg your pardon ... your other passenger later that evening. You won't want more on this artist, Colonel? She's not really germane."

Not waiting for a reply he spread a sheaf of papers across the table. "Here's the tricky part – and I'm going to stick to the script if you don't mind. Your agent Perry was to go by car from Northolt to Randoph Square for debriefing. Now, everybody accepts debriefing is not our pigeon, but we took the view *eventually* that somebody had to get her back and since nobody turned up for her, it seemed that fell to us. Rightly or wrongly."

He had saved a cold stare for Archer, "Wrongly, as it turned out. But there you are. One of our drivers took her."

He had stopped. That was all they were going to get. Stuffing things back into his case, a little gesture of irritation as they snagged.

Alex glanced across to see Cabot roll his eyes.

Archer had taken a fountain pen out of his inside pocket, screwing the top on and off - something to play with.

"Connor, my dear chap, we're not here to squabble about who lost her. The fact is she's lost. Of course, if our men *had* collected her it might have been different. But they didn't, and we won't go into why. Water under the bridge. As I say, that's not why we're here."

This was too much for Connor. He scraped his chair back, "They didn't pick her up because they bloody well didn't turn up, that's why. You know that perfectly well. Two hours your Perry kept at it, belly-aching her life was in danger, she had to get back to London. We're an operational airfield, not a nursery. There was the hell of a flap on - a raid on the cards. This Perry woman kept saying she had to get to London urgently. So we took her. There was a spare seat in the milk run car." He saw Cabot frowning and added, "The daily briefing papers – that's what we call it. Arrives with the milk."

"Can I check something with you, Connor?"

They had forgotten the Major. He had shifted to lean against the bit of wall next to the window. Connor shrugged, throwing Archer an insolent request for permission to speak, "Check away. If I know the answer. I probably don't. This has nothing to do with me."

"I just wondered whether an SOE car ever did arrive. Do you know Colonel Archer?"

But it was Connor who answered. "The answer's no, Major. I asked. It never did. Right. I'll finish the story. Coming into London, Perry asked our driver to pull over outside Tufnell Park underground – the Tube station. Said she was nipping across to get some cigarettes. There's a kiosk there. That was the last we saw of her."

Cabot looked up, murmuring, "Clever choice."

"Why'd you say that?"

"No escalator. Just lifts down. Anybody following would have to wait for a lift to come back up."

"Why the hell would anybody follow her? We thought she was getting some fags. After five minutes the driver went across to see what was up. She'd gone, of course."

Archer turned to Cabot, "That's the Northern line, isn't it? Well, John, what do you think? Do we set the bloodhounds onto this trollop Perry? It's over a month she's gone. We can't have that, you know. We've got to lay hands on her."

He tapped the file in front of him with the end of his pen, smirking, "Here's a thing – did you know she's called Justine – seems appropriate."

Connor looked blank.

"The lady Mr de Sade had his way with. Never read it? I asked for her file – our Justine, that is - all the operational stuff. I must say, there's enough to suggest we may have a problem. Let's say well informed. She was pretty central to the Columbine operation – responsible for liaison with the frogs."

He broke off, scooting the file across the table to Cabot, "John's done some research on the setup down there. Tell us what's afoot, John. It's your turn."

Cabot, his face shiny with a mist of moisture, pulled the back of one hand nervously across his top lip, scrabbling at a spiral-bound notebook with the other.

"I'll go back a bit, sir, if that's alright? For the benefit of the Wing Commander. And the Major. The Saint Aunix cell was set up in late forty, the leader a chap called Claude Barte. An accountant, incidentally. Not your typical left-wing rebel, inclined the other way, in fact. It was Barte who drummed up the extra car for Mrs Perry." He glanced awkwardly at Alex, "So we have to assume the bomb idea was his. I can check the WT record if you like, sir"

Archer shook his head, "We don't need that. Hurry on a bit. The point is he got the message and he did the necessary." He looked at Connor, "We've had an operator down there for a while. Very reliable. She was part of your drop, wasn't she, Alex? Name of Simone. Go on, Cabot."

No longer listening, Alex was back in the draughty hanger at Tempsford, watching the Major coming out of the side door, a little mouse of woman walking ahead. Simone: the curly-haired child with the woollen mittens. Simone: smashed up among bits of broken chair in the Gendarmerie, a sickly smell of cyanide everywhere. She was dead. You can't have your neck like that and be alive.

He found he was staring into the Major's eyes. Not friendly at all, that expression. The room was too hot. Too many sweating men suddenly tense with something.

"You with us, Alex?" Cabot had stuttered to a halt as Archer shouted down the table, "You seem miles away."

"This WT operator. Simone."

"What about her?"

"She was arrested the same time as me. In fact, she ..."

"That's nonsense, Alex. You're talking nonsense. And you're holding us up. Look, it's damned hot in here. You're getting muddled. My fault, I put things badly. She wasn't dropped with you. I meant she went on ahead."

He craned round to the Major, "That right?"

"She flew down in a Lysander that night. Ahead of the drop. She had her set with her."

"That clear things up, Alex? On you go, John."

"As I said, Barte arranged the extra car. The driver was a chap called Scaffe. Declared unfit for active service. He had a terrible limp. Club foot. The Jerries didn't want him. He transferred the bomb from his car to the other one. That meant he survived, of course - lived to tell the tale. Although it seems that wasn't intended."

As Connor leaned forward to speak, Archer had his smile ready, flapping a hand at Cabot, "A minute John. Yes, Wing Commander, we tried to see what he had to say. But before you get too excited, we'll get nothing out of this man Scaffe. He's dead. Shot two days later. Trying to run away from an armed patrol. Not that he could run, of course. It was in a cake shop. He'd slipped inside hoping to use the back door. Apparently he'd used that way out often. So you could say there's something of interest here - because the door was locked."

"Poor bugger."

"Alright John, spare us, we know there's a war on."

"You could question that in his case, sir. He was just a kid. I doubt he'd even handled a gun."

Connor was still leaning forward, looking at Cabot, the first real spark of interest he'd shown all morning, "Anything about why the door was locked?"

Archer conjured up the slightly unpleasant nervous smile he had reserved for Connor, "Quite so: the pertinent question, Wing Commander. We shall have to discover. Go on Cabot, if you would."

"Not much more to say, sir. They must all have been very nervous on account of the daylight run. You can see the point – somebody was bound to hear the take-off even if they missed the landing. The car with the bomb exited in short order, leaving the others to follow. It exploded just past the gate."

Archer cleared his throat, fishing a sheet of paper out of the file in front of him, holding by one corner, letting it hang down, looking like a man whose moment had arrived.

"This is the last wireless contact we had from Barte. It's been complete silence since. Concerns a young chap arrested for curfew violation. Nothing too much out of the ordinary. He'd been hanging around the local knocking shop. Sixteen – I ask you? Should have been in bed with a book. He had the misfortune to bump into a hard-bitten *SS-Rottenführer*, a squaddie. Hauled the kid off to the local police. They slapped him about a bit. Probably told him to run home and get his mother to sew his trousers up. But here's the point. On the way out, there's a door open. Barte reports this boy saw Mrs Perry in a side room sitting at a desk dictating something. Very much at home."

"When you say, *slapped him about a bit*?" There was a look of distaste on Connor's face. "What do you mean exactly?"

"You can only go by what these chaps say – they exaggerate. He'd be in trouble out after curfew. That would be for the French police, although the fact a German was involved could have made things worse. Apparently, the local station used to be a butcher's shop. Things still there, I suppose ... mincers ... that sort of thing."

Connor was not going to let go.

"So he could be making this story up. He would have been scared witless. Anyway, an agent hobnobbing with the local police – isn't that what they're supposed to do?"

"Except Perry doesn't work that way. She operates through the local maquis. Cultivated them – kept them close, if you like. That bunch don't go in for subtleties. If they thought she was chatting to the wrong people she was not going to last long."

Archer stopped, holding on to the silence, enjoying himself. "My conclusion, gentlemen, is that the car carrying Mrs Perry was never meant to arrive - it was meant to explode en route. The trip must have been faster than they expected."

Connor, head down, was making a pencil note on the corner of a file, "Then why transfer the thing to the other car?"

"I thought about that, of course I did." He managed a smug little grin. "You'd have to give the driver a reason for carrying it. They probably told him he was making a delivery. They never imagined him actually delivering anything. He was going to be dead, along with Mrs Perry. The damned thing went off ten minutes too late. My conclusion is Perry was the intended victim. The wrong people escaped."

"You mean the wrong people were killed, don't you?" For a second Alex could not place the voice. The Major had come up directly behind Archer, unaccountably angry.

Archer shrugged, pushing a bundle of papers into his folder, his tone mutinous, "I suppose you could to put it that way ... all the same ..."

"Actually her driver didn't escape, sir," Cabot folding his book closed, trying to keep the peace. "If you think that locked door was no accident, Scaffe didn't escape. There's really only Mrs Perry to account for."

Connor scraped his chair back, "Then you'd better find her, hadn't you?"

Seven

The Major was the first to leave. He stood silently in the doorway sheltering his shoes from a sudden shower until a grey staff car mounted the pavement, the driver struggling out with a vast umbrella. At the car door he distributed a perfunctory salute to the group left huddled on the stone steps.

Connor, bare-headed, let Alex wave down a taxi. They watched him disappear into the wintry gloom.

Archer stood for a second then took Alex's arm steering him back inside. "Got a minute? I'd like a word. Didn't get a chance before the meeting."

"If it's about sharks, sir, Cabot's on to that. He's gone back to work on it in the Museum. He's getting somewhere – I'd better leave him to say."

"Sharks?" He seemed lost. "Oh, yes, sharks. No, it's not that. Leave all that to John. Something else. We'll go into Records if that's alright."

Records had been Archer's idea. It wasn't even a room, just the end of a corridor blocked off by a new door with an impressive security lock. The tiny space had been lined with filing cabinets, now awaiting something to put into them. It was airless and stifling hot. There was nowhere to hang a coat. Alex draped his over the top of a cabinet, shaking his head as Archer held out his cigarette case.

"Quite right. Shouldn't smoke in here." He lit a cigarette, elaborately perching a solitary spent match on top of a cabinet.

"Look, I want a straight answer. What do you know about this Perry business?"

"Apart from the operation we were involved in, I don't know anything, sir. She got me out, of course. I owe her that. It's quite a debt."

"You weren't in her debt at Torridon." He was smirking. "Got to know her well enough there, I gather."

It wasn't worth a reply. Alex felt himself reddening. Of course: the Training Report from Torridon. Some sweaty clerk blessed with a prurient imagination hearing tittle tattle from the maids who turned the beds down. He was damned if he was going to answer.

Archer was standing so close you could hear the breath wheezing in his barrel chest. "What you get up to is your business, Vere. I'm broad minded. But this chap Connor is Air Intelligence, hence no fool. And the other one, the one who barged in. You weren't there - he doesn't seem to think it necessary to introduce himself. Just swept in with Connor. He's SIS alright. They're the bastards vetoing our every project. They want us closed down. He smells something about this Perry business, mark my words. I've been asking myself why he turned up at all. Why come knocking at my door? I'm asking why, Vere, because I think you may be the reason."

"You're talking about that explosion at the airfield, sir? Until this morning I knew nothing about it."

"Oh, I accept you *say* you know nothing. But that's the trouble, isn't it? And you know nothing about Perry's whereabouts either, I suppose? I notice you haven't said that."

Close to, there was something unsettling about Archer's eyes. Perhaps no more than the vanity of an old man in need of glasses but you could believe someone else behind them, someone else inside that huge whiskery head, peering out at you.

"I can certainly say it, sir, if you like. I don't know where she is. I haven't the faintest idea. But at least I knew she was not dead." No sooner had the words escaped than he regretted them. Never respond if someone goads you – it's a golden rule. As satisfaction mounted in Archer's face Alex could have hit him.

"Yes, I noticed that. You could ask how you came by that information. The way the story came out, it wasn't obvious she had survived, not obvious at all. Most people would have assumed she'd …"

"I'm aware of that, sir. It wasn't particularly kind."

"What the hell's *kind* got to do with it? You'll say I'm harping on about that remarkable operation of yours, but think about it. No sooner were the two of you dropped – you and Mrs Perry - but you get yourself arrested. Somehow they missed her - let's say they walked on by. Then by some miracle she plucks you from the jaws of death. I don't think miracle overstates it. And you can't remember much after that. Now we learn there's every likelihood the locals - her own people – are out to kill her. And she's upped and vanished. Are you surprised people are taking an interest? Where the hell's she got to? Look here Vere, I explained when I took you on I didn't want Intelligence crawling over our patch. I've got my reasons. And you've saddled me with exactly that."

He was standing so close that Alex could see tiny beads of sweat in the white fuzz of his moustache, a slight tremor working at the edge of his mouth, readying itself for something.

"Just stop playing the innocent. You took a telephone call yesterday afternoon. Came through the Baker Street switchboard. Want to say anything about it? Want to tell me who called?"

"Evidently since somebody was listening, you'll know as much as me."

"Careful with your tone, Captain. I don't need to tell you we've just spent an hour talking about this woman. All that time you knew she had made a telephone call yesterday. She asked for you. And you didn't think to mention it? Thought nobody would be interested?"

"I apologise, sir. I took the view it was a personal matter. If you've seen a transcript, you will know that's the truth. It was a very brief conversation. You know she said nothing about an explosion. I think Mrs Perry wanted me to know she was safe and well. I don't need to explain why. But she didn't say where she was or where she was going. You know that."

"So I do. And no need to apologise to me. Just be aware if one or another of those two think you're playing games, they'll be back to roast you. That's your damned lookout - up to a point. *But I do not want them back here*, do you understand me?"

He was speaking in a ridiculous whispered shout, flecks of supressed fury spurting from his lips, Alex standing immobile.

Archer broke away, lighting another cigarette, turning aside to cough, prodding Alex in the chest, his oversized head nodding to the rhythm. Incredibly, there was a sly smile on his lips.

"Pull that door to, will you. This hole is virtually the only place I'm a hundred percent sure isn't *bugged* – that's the word isn't it? Ears everywhere." The stubby finger went on prodding. "I'm asking you to do something for me. Think you can do that?"

"Of course, sir."

"An end to secrets?"

"No secrets, sir"

"You won't know Abbott Court?" Alex shook his head. "It's a reception centre. Belongs to SOE, although I doubt you'll see that on the rent book. Collect a chit from my office before you go. It says you're our Psychologist – alright? They're wary there, so watch what you say. And for god's sake don't start quibbling if anyone asks. They've got somebody there who might be exactly what I've been waiting for. A German. I want you to go and have a look at him. Let me know. Just me, you understand."

"Let you know what, sir?"

"He'll have a story to tell. They all do. He'll be telling lies, of course but it won't be all lies. That's where you come in. I want to know which bits to believe. They say you're the expert on lying. When I've had your opinion I might go and see him myself, find the best way to make him one of ours."

"You mean turn him, sir. With respect, I don't think that's a job for a psychologist."

"Who then? His mother? - if he's got one. His priest? I need to know what makes him tick. That's your job."

"I only saw interrogation from the other side, sir. That's what we were trained for – how to take it, not how to give it. Wouldn't someone from SIS …?"

"How many times do I have to say it, Vere? No - you'll have to do the best you can. I want an opinion. That's all."

When he eventually found the place, it was to discover that Abbott Court had suffered the same fate as St Michael. The houses along the rest of the street, Edwardian villas that had seen better days, stood intact, a dreary subdivided warren of bedsitters. Abbott Court was a bomb site, the building cut off well below the waist, stone stumps black with smoke, its driveway blocked off with a high corrugated fence, newly erected, painted army green. A tiny door cut into the metal opened onto a gravelled courtyard and a large wooden hut.

Alex rang the bell and waited. It was getting dark, a frost setting in, his breath hanging in clouds of white mist. An army Sergeant snatched the chit from his hand and retreated inside, slamming the door, heavy boots clumping away on bare wooden boards. It was several minutes before lighter footsteps returned. An unsmiling WAAF led him along a narrow corridor running the length of the hut. The place was filled with a sharp antiseptic smell, the lights almost too bright.

She tapped on a door, pushed at it, and scuttled away. A man in a short white lab coat was getting up from behind a desk, the chit still in his hand.

"This Colonel Archer. I'm afraid we didn't know him. Your outfit's new to me. Sorry to keep you. We had to check. Security is tight here. Your Colonel says he wants you to see our latest acquisition." He grinned as he saw Alex trying to read the name plate on the open door - a varnished panel with MO/2 stencilled on it.

"I'm afraid no names here. You can call me MO, that's what everybody does, although I'm not much of a medic. Not really the other thing either - more Gentleman than Officer, if you know what I mean. Hence the civvies." He was laughing, "Sorry to be mysterious. I'm showing off. It's what comes of being shut up in this place all hours god sends. The truth is I inherited the room and I've no idea what oblique two stands for – all I know is there isn't an oblique one. Colonel Archer says you're his psychologist. Sounds impressive."

"He insists on putting it that way. I'm doing my doctorate – or I was before the call up. With Professor Campbell."

"You mean Campbell the Ganser man? I've met him. I've always thought the Ganser syndrome was just a fancy name for malingering, but I suppose I'm wrong."

"Professor Campbell has been working with prisoners of war. The Ganser syndrome's quite common in prisoners. I was going to work on it in the context of interrogation ... but I'd barely got started."

"Sane people feigning madness. That what you think our latest's doing?"

"It's a possibility."

"Well you've come to the right place if you're looking for liars. What's special about this prisoner? We've not had him long. How did you know about him? No, sorry, I shouldn't ask ..."

"I'm afraid I don't know, you're better asking Colonel Archer. But not long, I think. I only got the order today. Colonel Archer wants me to report back on this chap."

"I would have thought it was pretty obvious people will lie to get out of prison. Or lie not to get there in the first place. That's why I never believe a word they say."

"It's the *sort* of lie that's interesting - particularly with patients who might be pretending to be mad. It's not so easy to distinguish pretence from the real thing. My idea was that approximate answers might be the clue ... then I got called up."

"Approximate answers?"

"Ganser called it *vorbeireden* – talking past the subject. You ask a patient how many fingers he has, and he says eighteen. Alright, it's a lie, it's nonsense, but it's only *approximately* wrong. It's a number, after all – it isn't as if he'd said *fish* or *custard*. There's the question - if you are pretending to be mad, which way do you jump? Do you have to be mad to make a really convincing madman?"

"That or a professional psychologist, I suppose." Suddenly embarrassed, laughing awkwardly, "Oops. Sorry – just my little joke. Look, your journey might be in vain, Captain. This chap's not pretending to be mad. Pretending lots else, but not that. Mind you, he's certainly lying, but then, that's true of all of them. He's as cocky as hell. Here's what we know about him. By the way, I wouldn't call him a patient if I were you – he's starting to get touchy, quoting his Geneva rights, you know. We've been using amylobarbitone on him … to get a bit more than name and number. No, don't look like that - it's nothing to what they're using on our chaps. And we've got all the right consents, I assure you, given this chap's status."

"No, I wasn't doubting that … of course not. It's just that I wonder about drugs, that's all. Professor Campbell says truth and drugs don't mix."

The MO turned away, irritated.

"Professor Campbell can afford his views … scruples are a luxury for us. Tell him there's war on next time you see him."

He went back to his desk, scrabbling for a file. "The background on this chap. The French Military Security Service delivered him. He's been turning Jews in to the local SD. It's not his business and the French resent it. I don't think the Gestapo appreciate his efforts either. It has all got a bit delicate – on both sides if you know what I mean. I suppose you have to know when to look the other way. The Germans weren't that interested in Vichy Jews until recently – so it's only recently they've realised the French enthusiasm for the business. It took them by surprise."

"The Business? You mean rounding up Jews?"

"If you want to put it that way. There was already zero trust between the Germans and these Vichy people. With some cause I may add - plenty of the French old guard still dream of the next uprising. Anyway, our prisoner got above himself and denounced the girlfriend of his local Gestapo chief, a man called Kloss. She's Jewish, although she hadn't registered. You realise that's a hellishly dangerous accusation. So the good Captain Kessler simply vanished - to general satisfaction, I gather. Spirited away on a dark night. The French arranged for it to look like he's gone AWOL. A bit hard on him, but no fear of reprisals that way. They squeezed him onto one of our flights coming back from near Poitiers. That was a few days back. Squeezed is the word, I gather - you wouldn't want to know the details. He didn't travel in comfort. Arrived as slightly damaged goods, but we straightened him out. I'm not surprised he thinks he's in a hospital. But he's talking alright. One tall tale after another."

"It sounds interesting. If I can just see him …"

"Archer's SOE isn't he? Sorry, shouldn't ask, but that's what Records came back with. I'll just say this - if you are one of that lot, you do need to hear what this man's saying. I don't think interesting quite cuts it - *startling* is more the word. Whether any of it is true is another matter … but I suppose that's where you come in …"

Alex followed him down the corridor into a room without windows, shiny linoleum freshly swabbed. This little room filled with the smell of ether and disinfectant was not somewhere you would ask to be.

The Sergeant who had answered the door was standing next to a kind of operating table, glossy steel-framed lamps pulled down low, unlit.

A man in the crumpled dress uniform of a German officer was slumped in a wooden chair in the middle of the room, arms handcuffed from behind. He raised his head as they came in, sweat dripping from his chin, eyes dark with supressed fear. Alex looked away, remembering Aste.

"What you are doing is … incorrect."

A dry croak of a voice, a crust of white round his lips, the German's breath was pungent even from across the room. There was a sickly smell like pear drops in the room. An educated voice, the English correct, although the accent hard to discern - not completely German. Perhaps he'd spent too long speaking French.

"I am an Officer in the Wehrmacht ... Hauptmann ... you say Captain ... Hauptmann Kessler. My name is Kessler. I offer my name and rank. You have my identity disk. Why have I been brought here? Is this a hospital? Why am I in a hospital? I am a prisoner of war."

"There are some problems with that, old boy." The MO had dragged two chairs across from the wall and slumped down on one, waving Alex into the other.

"You see, your colleagues - your colleagues in the French Service think you're a spy. That's the Bureau for Anti-National Affairs. You understand the term *Anti-National*? That would be their nation, not yours. They tell us you're a spy. That's why you're here. So no, you're not a prisoner of war unless we decide you are. In fact, you're not anything. You don't even exist until we find out what you were up to."

As Kessler leaned forward the sergeant stepped across and put a hand on his shoulder, almost affectionately, "You go easy mate, no point getting agitated."

The MO saw Kessler look at the hypodermic lying in the metal kidney bowl on the table. He leaned over to Alex, "Two and half percent. Sodium amytal. A good response. Alright Sergeant, no need to stand over him. Take the cuffs off would you, let him get comfortable. Hauptmann Kessler isn't going anywhere."

They watched the German wincing to ease his arms, rubbing his wrists, wiping the sweat from his face. Alex felt a sudden irrational surge of pity: we have you, and I know exactly how you feel. You feel death would be better than this.

He settled for the ritual packet of cigarettes, leaving them on the desk, Kessler shaking his head, eyeing them cautiously. For a brief second their eyes met. How young he was. Not so long ago Herr

Kessler had been sitting in a lecture room, perhaps taking notes on Schiller – *When we love we are as Gods! We are dead matter when we hate.*

The MO suddenly got up, walking to the other side of the room spitting out brusque German as he went, "Our requirement, Captain Kessler, is you tell to this Officer what you told to me earlier. All details. If you refuse, we shall inject you and pose our questions again. Your complete cooperation will avoid that consideration."

The German strained forward, looking at Alex, replying in his own language, "I cooperate. I already explained."

"We wish you to speak English, if you can." The MO raised an eyebrow to Alex.

Kessler relaxed for an instant, the smile for Alex condescending, almost insolent.

"You are right. Denying me the liar's armoury: I would have made the same decision."

He continued in English, speaking quickly. "What I told you was this. The Officer leading your group – his name is Archer, his rank Colonel. I can describe him for you, if you wish," looking directly at Alex, "you are not he. I have already explained to this … what should I say? Is it *doctor*? I explained we have a chart of SOE, Section F. It is complete. That is your section, is it not?"

He was trying to take control of things. Alex raised a hand, slowing him down, "You say *we*. Who exactly do you mean by *we*?"

Kessler's frown suggested the question had revealed some unexpected level of ignorance, the frown of someone realising his advantage was greater than he had imagined. A tiny shake of the head wearily acknowledged he must be patient.

"The *Sicherheitsdienst*. Counter-intelligence Centre. Avenue Foch," the same lazy superior glance about the room, "in Paris … you would know that. Colonel Archer is head of your Work Group. It is called TSPU. We do not know what the letters mean."

He looked warily towards the MO.

"You are going to ask for names again. I repeat, it was not my business to know names." He turned back to Alex, "But I believe you are Captain Vere. It is a guess, but you cannot be Herr Cabot because he wears the spectacles. You are the Captain Vere arrested at Saint Aunix last November."

The blow had been calculated. Alex saw the look of satisfaction as Kessler registered the shock in his face.

"If you're so well informed, Hauptmann Kessler, perhaps you can give us some names that are not in the Telephone Directory."

It was a brave effort, the best he could manage, difficult to master the shake in his voice. Kessler's impassive face confirmed the damage had been done.

"There are so many names ..." He paused, head cocking up at the thump of passing boots in the corridor, shaking the floor. A distant door slammed. "English names are hard. *Patrick*? Is that a name? I recall a Patrick. He confessed to being a spy. He was shot. And a woman - you send women on such missions - no German would do that. We call them *Schmetterlinge*, you know. Fluttering into a net. We have them all. I remember one name: Simone. A French name, so I suppose I should say *papillon*. We stood in the field laughing while that one looked for her wireless transmitter. On her knees ... how you say it? ... on her hand and knee. We had collected it for her. She told us her name was Simone. She was persuaded to tell us her real name. Margaret. It is almost a German name. We had her. We have had all of them for months."

He was in his stride now, rattling on like some garrulous stranger in a railway carriage with a captive audience, "Since March is it? Perhaps earlier. It took time to get her transmitter to work. Ours are better. Your agents were cooperative. Even signal checks – your, how you say it? ... your error bluffs. And these poem codes. A poor choice I must say, but we accommodated. We own your circuit, as you call it. For months you have been talking to us. Your orders come to us. And we obey them ... in a certain sense. Your arms drops come to us. Your food drops come to us. Your money ..."

He had stopped, cunning eyes furtively assessing the effect of his story. A long way off, traffic sounds spilled in to fill the long silence:

a whisper from a sane world somewhere else. Alex remembered something, turning to the German, addressing him in his own language.

"What circuit? This one you say you own. A name would be convincing."

"Someone – I forget who – told us the name."

"But you have unfortunately forgotten."

"No, I have not forgotten. The name is Columbine."

They stood outside in the cool of the corridor, the MO grinning at Alex. "See what I mean? Cocky bugger, isn't he? You're right of course, most of that stuff is in Records. We've got their Staff Lists so what's to stop them having ours? You can't stop leaks. He's lying alright, here and there, I can see that. All the same, bits ring true. All that about drops."

"We don't make food drops any more. At least, I don't think so. I'll have to check. And money is never dropped … never … obviously," remembering that little room at Tempsford, waxed packages piled on the table, a single bulb swinging yellow overhead, everywhere the sharp smell of aviation fuel. *A bit sordid, things coming down to cash.* There had been an odd expression on the Major's face. Distaste? No, something else: the two of them complicit in something. Justine as well … Justine grinning, stuffing loot into her rucksack.

Alex realised the MO was waiting for him to go on, "No, money always goes by courier. Pretty well always, I think."

"What's this *bluff* stuff about? I was watching you. He seemed to score a hit there."

"Yes. He won't have got that from *Records*. I'm not sure I should say too much about it. There's a security check in the code protocol. We're still using poem codes – with double transposition it's just about adequate, because the traffic is always time critical. I imagine their code breakers have bigger fish to fry. Our WT people used to use Playfair code, can you believe it? You get sent out with a code a child can break - you could get angry about something like that. The security check is a deliberate coding error agreed with London. It lets us know you're captured – letters transposed, words of a given length … that sort of thing. It's not going to save anybody, but it does give you a last roll of the dice. Jerry spots it, of course …" Alex pointed to the hypodermic, "and uses that stuff if you're lucky … or torture …"

"We know Jerry has started using Cardiazol. We've not gone that far. Not yet. You can control the convulsions, more or less. But the patients end up frightened stiff. Hellish stuff."

"You're trained to hold out as long as you can, but they get it out of you in the end. That's where the bluff comes in. When they fire up and start transmitting with the bluff error, London knows the position because there's a second security check and it will be missing."

"This chap's saying they've got both. He said *bluffs*."

"I know, but he may be fishing. I'm not sure. It wasn't a point I wanted to pursue. His story does sound bad, but it's pretty well all circumstantial. He's actually told us nothing that confirms any sort of penetration - apart from the security check and that may be a lucky guess. In fact, if I'd been briefed to give that impression, it's exactly how I would have played it. Can I ask who gave you this German?"

"The Free French people. The usual story. Violating the sacred soil of France. They're always ranting on about that, I suppose because they gave up the sacred soil a bit too easily. They saw a way of getting rid of this one and took it."

"So he might well be a plant?"

"Oh, almost certainly, my dear chap. We invariably work on that basis. Actually, in this case, I don't even trust the frogs not to be in on the act. You can get a bit incoherent with the amylobarbitone, but Kessler has already let slip a hint along those lines."

He gave a curious jerk of the head, pulling Alex away from the door, drawing closer, "You can't expect the French to love us, can you? Not with chaps like your Colonel fighting the last war. It's bad enough losing your fleet, but when it's your allies that sink it ... I can see the way they feel. I'm going to assume this Hauptmann Kessler was intended to fall into our hands. He says he worked for Military Intelligence, the *Sicherheitsdienst*. I don't know if you read the stuff I see - that's a monstrous sinister crowd. If he's a plant, we have to assume he was sent to sell the story that they have turned the Columbine circuit. It's frightening how confident they are – we're expected to believe the whole rigmarole on his say-so."

"But he must know if this turns out to be just another disinformation stunt he's had it. He can count his life in days. That would make our Fritz in there a very brave man."

"That's the point - he doesn't strike you as brave. Cocky, yes, but not brave. Not suicidal anyway. He knows we'll check."

"Well he's won a round whether we believe it or not. And here was Colonel Archer hoping to persuade him to our cause."

"Turn him, you mean? A double agent?"

"That was the idea. But I think we'll have to add one to the tally. Let's say triple."

Eight

When Alex got back, the only sign of Archer was an ashtray full of stubs on top of a cabinet in *Records*. Yellow light spilled out from the room at the end of the corridor.

Cabot was peering myopically at a large-scale map draped over his desk, humming to himself. He called out as Alex tapped his door.

"*Oceans of the Earth* – pretty isn't it? Got it on loan – chap at the British Museum. The things we're asked to do. But I've made a bit of progress. One snag, though - the Channel's far too cold. I did warn you. Why are you looking at me like that?"

"Sorry. I was lost for a minute. You're on about sharks?"

"What else? Come round here, I'll show you. Archer's not going to like it. He has a choice - sharks that might survive but wouldn't dream of biting anybody, or the reverse. The bloodthirsty sort are all tropical. A damned tricky question to pose, I can tell you. People kept asking why I wanted to know. What was I supposed to say? I bluffed it out as best I could. They said *Prionace glauca* might answer. The Blue Shark. Not really aggressive but it doesn't mind the cold. It turns up at what they called maritime disasters. It's all a bit grisly, but that should satisfy him."

"I'm sorry John – I think Archer will be giving sharks a rest for a while. Tell me, what do you know about Abbott Court?"

By the time Alex had finished, it was late. Street sounds from beyond the blackout had long since ebbed away, London lapsing into dark. A distant random explosion from far across the river, flexed the windowpanes, bringing a fleeting change of air to the tiny office.

Cabot sat thoughtfully running his finger along the contours of the map.

"I can't work out how this Kessler chap knew about you being arrested. I don't want to be rude, Alex, but you're not that famous."

"I'm not famous, but I suppose that escape was. He got the story from the people at Saint Aunix I suppose."

"You realise he could fill in some missing bits for you – things you've forgotten. Did you ask him?"

"Of course not. You can't believe a word he says. These Abbott Court people have got themselves an expert at making a story out of nothing at all."

"Professional opinion?"

"If you like - yes. Take the way he threw Archer's name at me. Impressive, until you think about it. Archer's signature was on that WT message the Gestapo man was waving about. This chap got it from him."

"But your name? And mine? Where'd he get those? I know they intercept WT traffic but you can't get names that way," shuffling awkwardly in his chair, "you're ignoring the other possibility ..."

"Look, they weren't my orders the SS chap was waving about, if that's what you're implying. Or Justine's, come to that. They must have got them off Simone at the Gendarmerie. It's a dreadful sin to fly with operational orders in your pack. I suppose she was green enough – just a kid. The German that arrested me read bits out. It was authentic alright – the who, where, when of the whole operation. God, what a mess. You don't take your orders with you – you'd have to be mad. Alright, an unfortunate turn of phrase."

"Calm down Alex, I'm hinting nothing. I can't help looking this way."

"I'm not mad. I'm as sane as you. All I've lost is my memory. I can't remember what happened after Justine got me out. The people at Netley hospital are sure I got myself a knock to the head - I've still got a terrible headache most of the time. It doesn't change the fact Jerry was waiting for Simone. I was taken back with her."

"Archer did rather stamp on that story this morning. Said you were muddled." Cabot started to roll up the map, "To tell the truth Alex, you did sound a little bit muddled."

"There's no muddle. We overshot the drop site and got picked up on the road half an hour afterwards. Well, I was picked up ..."

"And Mrs Perry?"

"She got away. She was lucky."

Cabot looked down, frowning. He went on rolling the map.

"I know it sounds fishy, John. She was just lucky – it does happen."

"Why did Kessler say Simone was crawling about looking for her set? If she flew down in a Lysander it would have been in her pack. He tripped up there."

"Kessler wasn't part of the reception committee. It's something else he got from the people at Saint Aunix. He assumed she'd been dropped with us."

"She was arrested?"

"I watched them drag her into the Gendarmerie. She looked like a frightened schoolgirl."

"And this chap Kessler's saying they got her working for them that same night. You can see why Archer's doubtful – even if they scared the living daylights out of her ..."

"Listen to me. You're not listening. She's not working for anybody. She's dead. I saw her after she'd swallowed her L tablet. You don't forget something like that."

Unconsciously inured to sounds of war, they were suddenly aware of complete silence outside. One of the periods of calm that punctuate larger raids had fallen on the city. Far away, a fire engine bell came funnelling in waves along deserted streets towards them.

"She can't be dead, Alex. Archer says she's sending. You heard him."

"Whoever's using the set, it's not her. She's dead."

Cabot sat aimlessly polishing his spectacles, staring sightlessly at Alex, the bell tearing past in the street outside. The room fell quiet.

"If you say so, old man."

"God, don't you go indulging me. She's dead, I tell you. And what if Kessler's right about all those agents? What if they've ended up on the Avenue Foch or in Frenses prison. Have you any idea what goes on in those places? What if we've been talking to the Germans for months?"

Cabot lit a cigarette, drawing hard, shaking his head.

"I'm sorry Alex. You've the field experience, I grant you that. But honestly, I don't buy it, my dear chap. A couple of years ago you only had to telephone Baker Street, ask nicely, and you would get whatever you wanted. Security was a joke. It's not all that much better now."

"How would you know? Is that what Archer says?"

"I'm Archer's shark expert, remember? He doesn't talk to me – barks, but doesn't talk. No, security is what keeps my College high table entertained. That and the doings of our Colonel Archer – they talk of little else."

"What about him?"

"Our little Hungarian was packed off to some dire English prep school and then to Rugby. An ancient don claims to have taught him. Eton wouldn't have him. The religion thing – you know. He turned himself into a proper little English gent. That's why his accent's so good. Mind you, I always find it a bit too perfect, if you know what I mean, as if he was still taking lessons. He picked up his MC in the retreat from Mons. Royal Warwickshires. Apparently led a platoon in a completely hopeless charge against a machine gun nest and found himself the only man standing when their gun jammed. Killed four and managed to blow himself up with his own grenade. Invalided out for best part of a year. It's hard to believe, but he actually went back. Wounded again at Arras."

"If he's Hungarian, he was fighting on the wrong side."

"I wouldn't mention that if you value your scalp. He's ended up more English than us. His family was wiped out by the end of the war. Every last stick gone. War's personal for him. A word to the wise, by the way. Keep off Hungary – he doesn't appreciate it."

He leaned back, exhaling smoke, grinning sheepishly, "Tutorial over. About your Kessler chap. You know who he reminds me of? It's us. He's here to sow disinformation. If you get too close to people like that you become blind to the obvious. You know that better than anybody."

"And the obvious is?"

"Come on! A whole circuit penetrated? I'm sure somebody hopes we believe it, but it's schoolboy stuff, Alex. History doesn't teach you much, but it certainly teaches you that the real world's too messy for secrets to hold. Think about it - every one of those agents has ways of signalling they've been captured. And it only takes one to get through. All of them operating under German orders? Do you seriously think we'd not know?"

"You weren't at Abbott Court."

"That's what I mean – you get sucked in. It's like one of Archer's schemes - Archer and his bloody man-eating sharks."

He pushed the map across the desk, failing to catch it as it fell, chasing like a plump puppy across the floor to catch it as it rolled itself up. He sat looking up at Alex, rubbing one knee, mild ingenuous face shiny with sweat.

"If you want my opinion, Kessler got his information about Columbine from loose talk. And the occasional leak. Sorry Alex, leaks do happen ... I'm sorry, old man ..."

"Why don't you spit it out? Feel free. Archer's already ahead of you, there's no need to hint. You think they got something out of me, don't you? When I was arrested. You think that's what I conveniently can't remember. Do you imagine I don't ask myself the same question?"

"Alex, Alex, I'm not hinting anything ..."

"How many times do I have to say it? You hand paperwork in after the briefing at Tempsford. Justine watched me do it. I watched her do it. Everything went into the personal possessions box ..." Alex checked, suddenly leaning forward, tapping Cabot on the head.

"Christ - I've just realised - all that stuff must be logged. Why don't we ask? Go on. Just lift the telephone. That Air Intelligence chap. What's his name? Connor. Why don't you ask him?"

"No need to shout. You really want to bring him down on our head? You're forgetting something. If there's a leak, I'm in the spotlight as much as you."

"If you're a spy, John, England really should tremble. Without your specs I don't think you could find your way home. No, to state the obvious, a leak from this pathetic little crew would have to be me. Me or Justine Perry, I suppose."

"Archer? You could point the finger at him," he was grinning.

Alex smiled back, "I'll let you do that bit of pointing, old boy."

Cabot struggled to his feet, looking at his watch, "D'you know what time it is? I don't think the haughty Connor would appreciate being dragged from his bed to attend our summons. It's Mrs Perry he wants. You can't deny it's awkward, her vanishing like that. No, Alex, no need to get on your high horse."

"Justine's no more a spy than I am. I owe her my life."

"I'm not sure I follow the logic there, old man. There's that business with the explosion. If she was the target, you have to ask why. *Why?*"

Alex sat silently rehearsing Justine's telephone call, a kind of weary depression seeping into his mind. What could he say? *Her lover was a Colonel working for French Intelligence.* What would Cabot make of that? What if Justine had joined the ranks of those judged too great a risk to leave alive?

The drone of a solitary engine far away brought a desultory bark of ack-ack. A single breathless thud from across the park rattled the fire-irons in the grate.

He would never see her again. It was almost a surprise to discover the bitter truth of this would end his life.

"You won't tell, will you John? Archer warned me off mentioning Abbott Court."

Cabot ran his hand across his throat, "Hope to die, old boy. Your secrets are safe with me. Not that I get much intercourse with the great man."

"Seriously ... there's something else. Archer found out I took a telephone call from Justine Perry."

"God almighty, Alex! You're a deep one. Still waters and all that. Why on earth didn't you mention it at the meeting?"

"Honestly, I don't know. Connor, I think. He got on my nerves. He knew anyway – I'm sure of it. It was all a sick game. The toffy-nosed bastard didn't care whether Justine was alive or dead. They just wanted to see how I took the news. You could just as well ask why Archer didn't mention it. She didn't say anything. Just that she was alright. And now I've got to tell him we'll never turn this chap Kessler."

Cabot had wandered over to the window pulling the blind open a crack, peering into the street below. "I'm going home. That name Kessler put me in mind of something. You don't think I could talk to him, do you? Would Archer let me, d'you think?"

Alex walked home, blind apart from his tiny torch, conscious of the plodding echo behind. Whoever was tailing actually wanted to be heard or at least didn't care. As the thin penetrating rain unique to London started up, filming his face, he could only think *poor bugger*. Archer must have commandeered one of the SOE resident walkers. If he thought Alex was going to lead the way to Justine at half past two in the morning, it was one more proof the man was mad.

He hurried on, the feeble glimmer of torchlight bobbing ahead on the paving stones. Beyond the narrow circle of light, invisible masses of stone exhaled a faint warmth. The snort of a tug on the river was the only indication the road was opening out, the plodding echoes behind quickening pace.

At the corner, Alex was tempted to stop, let the chap catch up, tell him he hadn't the faintest idea where she was, tell him to go home, have a smoke, go to bed. Tell him, if he didn't know already, that he was employed by a lunatic. All he wanted was to get home and find something to eat – since he had started this job he was hungry all the time.

The thought struck so abruptly he instinctively stretched out a hand, finding the wet bevelled metal of a lamp post. How many times Archer must have combed through that grubby transcript of Justine's telephone call. Wasted effort, old man, because she knows her job, because she had worked out people like you years ago. He was smiling into the rain like an idiot. Archer could have read it for ever and still not understood. She had told Alex exactly nothing and told him exactly what he needed to know - because she had worked him out as well. All she had had to do was wait for the penny to drop.

He stood smiling into the dark, remembering how she called him *Guffin*. She had got into the habit and he treasured it, whatever it meant. Sometimes he would fall asleep remembering the husky fall of her voice: you take what comforts you can in a grim world. But, *my dear* - those listening ears in Baker Street were not to know she had never called him that. Not once. Not ever. They could not have known the lurch of his heart at the sweetness of it. A little boy home from school for the holidays, Mother pinching his ribs, *I'm sure you're not getting enough to eat*. Mother would always say that. And as the penny dropped, he realised Justine knew her job. She was something he would never be.

It had been two days before her last mission, just off the King's Cross sleeper, legs a little stiff, Justine looking for a telephone box that worked. Alex awake long since, waiting. Pushing the blinds aside to see into the street below, early sunshine falling yellow on his hand.

He remembered her voice soft in his ear, *It's me Guffin. Ready for breakfast? You little boys never get enough to eat. The usual place.*

An all-night café behind the station. Filled with weary ARP men delaying going home until the wife was up from the shelter, red-faced firemen smelling of smoke, a few women no better than they should be. Even if the food was awful – and it was – Alex thought it the most human place in London. He could have hugged the fat woman behind the tea urn, could have hugged Justine peering dubiously at her plate, the woman shouting *fried, missus … all I can say is it's fried*. There was a dash of whisky in the tea. They had sat on opposite sides of the metal table, holding hands.

She would be waiting for him. Early. Sleeper time. She had told him as much and, miraculously, had allowed him to deny knowing for days.

As Alex reached the front door the footsteps behind had already stopped, the walker huddling into his habitual doorway. A match flared, the scent of fresh tobacco blowing past. He had a long night, poor bugger.

Nine

She was there. In the usual place, head bowed, idly pushing scraps of greasy food round her plate. She did not even seem surprised when he sat down opposite, fearful eyes dark from lack of sleep, warily checking the door.

Two women at a table turned long enough to size Alex up then resumed their conversation. Alex glanced at the clock over the counter and shrugged an apology.

"Hello Guffin. You're a welcome sight. I knew you'd be slow coming." Her hands were cold as she pulled him forward, "A day or two, I reckoned," leaning up, for a second her cheek touching his, almost a kiss. "Here's one hell of a mess. I'm scared. Never been frightened before ... should have known it would strike one fine day. Silly isn't it? There's me jumping out of aeroplanes, hardly a flutter. I didn't have a clue what it was all about. Do you know, Alex? Do you really?"

"All I know is thank god you made that telephone call. If you hadn't I would have probably killed somebody. Or myself. He had every intention of saying you were dead."

"Who did?"

"Archer. Vindictive bastard. They listened to your call, of course."

The first hint of a smile, "They were bound to. That's why I had to telephone. I knew that explosion story would get out. I knew you'd be fretting. I've been running like a rabbit ever since. I'm surprised nobody twigged where I'd got to."

"You can include me."

"Apart from the smell, those deep level stations are quite comfortable. Even camp beds if you get there early. I've spent a good few nights in one or another on the Northern Line. The only problem's eating. Not the weather for living on scraps, I can tell you. When I realised nobody was looking, I took the night train to Dundee ... it's alright, I'm not mad. I wanted to find that woman on the flight back from Saint Aunix."

"No, I don't think that's mad. I had the same idea. It would make a sort of sense. Artists, hobnobbing with the Boche - that sort of thing. It's bound to cause resentment. Her name's Beyrou. Archer said she was famous, but I can't find anybody who's ever heard of her. Not even Cabot."

"How do you know all this? No ... tell me later. When I finally tracked her down, she seemed a miserable soul. Looked half starved, but then who doesn't? It was hellish hard to get a word out of her. All she would say was the people who helped her to escape had been killed. They were in that car. I think she felt responsible."

"There was a meeting this morning about you going AWOL: the hell of a flap on. This artist came up – that's where I heard the name."

"I don't think she had anything to do with it, Alex. It was a wasted journey. But a meeting about me – that's stupid. Did they think I'd just sit still waiting to be bumped off? Your six weeks are up, Mrs Perry, please go quietly. That the idea?"

"Archer brought the meeting down on himself. He's as stupid as they come. He convinced himself I knew where you were. He set one of his old SOE minions to dog my every step and paid the price for his obsession. Crowds of Intelligence people fell on us - lured out of the woodwork."

She leaned forward, tugging at his arm, "God, you weren't followed here? You fool."

"Don't panic - credit me with some sense. I took my morning tail by surprise. He was half asleep. I don't think his heart's in the job. He didn't even see me until I was jumping onto a bus. Just stood watching me go. I think he was laughing. There'll be hell to pay when the news gets back to Colonel Archer. I'm not his favourite son right now."

"Alex, can you sit quiet and don't ask questions. Please. It'll be quicker that way. I want to tell you what happened at Saint Aunix that morning. After we got you to the big house."

"What big house? I don't remember anything about a house. I can't very well sit quiet if I don't know what you're on about."

"What d'you mean, *can't remember*?

"It's a long story. Something happened after you left me. Did you leave me? I can't remember. I remember the little hut and you going down the track, walking away. After that, nothing."

"You were in a bad way. Reaction, I suppose. That and wine on an empty stomach. We'll talk about you when I've finished, alright?"

Alex was barely listening, remembering the scent of woodsmoke drifting up through a canopy of green leaves, birds just starting, a low sun warm on his face, Justine smiling, shaking the hair out of her eyes as she tilted the bottle towards his glass. Barely listening. Remembering one morning in his life when he had been happy.

"When the lorry came back we got you inside. You remember?" Alex frowned. "You did seem in a daze, but you were alright. I hung around for a bit, tidying the place up, listening for enemy feet. Then I walked back to the village to hand over the money."

"I remember the money. At Tempsford. Loot, you called it."

"I knew Claude would have worked out something had gone wrong with the drop. The fallback rendezvous was the church. It was a Sunday morning but that didn't matter because the place is locked up. You're not allowed to go there anymore – some edict about mass gatherings. Claude was already there - most unusual for him. And not alone. I'd never seen the other bloke before. I just assumed Claude had brought a new recruit along to show him the ropes. A tough looking character, the strong silent type. We exchanged nods and I handed over the loot. The usual litany of complaints while he counted it – it's not enough, why can't we bring smaller notes, and so on ..."

"The German stuff as well?"

"What German stuff?"

"Reichmarks. The Major said one of the packages was German currency."

"I'll lose the thread if you keep interrupting. I didn't see any German stuff. Claude always makes you wait while he counts the notes, but he was making a mess of it, fumbling. I must have been really slow that morning - that business at the Gendarmerie had taken it out of me. And I'd had no sleep at all. Listening to Claude grousing I realised his heart wasn't in it. He just wanted to get it over as quick as possible. He was like a bad actor - incredibly nervous, voice trembling, hands shaking, sweating like a pig. It's stuffy in that church but it was quite cold. Usually he's the perfect little accountant - chop chop, even a receipt. He kept looking across to the side door. Obviously, I smelled a rat. I'd got myself into some sort of trap. On a hunch, I asked this other chap if he'd been with us long. Nice and friendly. He just mumbled *not long*, and walked off, lighting up. He'd had to risk saying something and must have hoped I wouldn't pick the German accent. He had his back turned for a second and Claude gave me this really desperate look. It was the cigarette that clinched it. The locals may be a tough bunch of atheistic commies, but they wouldn't dream of lighting up in the church."

"He was alone? Just the one?"

"In the church, yes. But I couldn't know who was outside waiting. I decided to bluff it out, I'd got nothing to lose anyway. Said I was in a hurry, shook his hand, gave Claude his usual little peck and trotted off. Not too fast, either. I'm no actor and I think he was suspicious, but he let me go."

"No reception committee outside?"

"Nothing at all."

At first Alex thought she had finished. She had not released his hand, rising in her seat to look through the greasy window.

"No, it's alright. Somebody loitering across the street. It's nobody. I've got so I'm seeing ghosts. Where was I?"

"Nobody waiting outside."

"That's what I said. The place was deserted. Obviously Claude has been picked up. They'd sent this German chap to see what went on. Clever if you think about it. He was a witness. You know how they do love due process. Poor old Claude's going to end up against a wall and all they think about is their bit of legal paperwork to put him there."

"They just let you walk away?"

"I know how it sounds," she had dropped his hand, "I think they knew they could pick me up any time. I can't explain it. I can only say what happened. Alex, don't look like that - it's the truth. That's exactly what happened. I was hooked - they were just letting out a bit of the line. God, and they wonder why people hate them."

A man in khaki uniform standing at the counter looked up. Alex shrugged. The shrug of a man with a hysterical woman on his hands. The wife, perhaps - determined to get something off her chest. The shrug of common cause. We all know who we hate, after all. The soldier looked away.

"Perhaps he thought I was armed. I was, of course, but it wasn't that. I was the mouse and the cat wasn't biting right then. I didn't rate my chances. All I could think was one more catastrophe of a mission. But I'd got you safe, at least. One of us was going to get back. Perhaps one out of three was enough. You think that way, it's a consolation."

"So you went back to that Renault chap. Is that what you did?"

"That look on your face, Alex. Honestly, it's the nicest thing I've seen in weeks. No, I couldn't do that. I'd be signing the poor man's death warrant. I'm not that selfish. I hid behind the wall until I heard them coming out. I remember thinking that's the last time I'll see old Claude. Him and the money lost, and me as well from the look of things. I had thirty hours to get through before the flight out. All I could think of was going back to the church and locking myself in - the old tricks are the best, I suppose. I spent the next twenty-four hours behind some baskets in a sort of vestry, smelling of mothballs.

Look, you'd better eat. Go and get something, they won't come to the table."

Alex shook his head, "I'm not hungry. This headache makes me feel sick. We can't stay much longer, we're getting looks."

"I've finished. You know the rest anyway. Next day I was out of the church miles too early for the pickup. It was still dark and perishing cold. The car was at the crossroads. Not the usual one, which made me panic a bit, but I knew the driver. He hangs about in the square all day - a young chap with a gammy leg, drives like a madman. When we got to the field it was deserted."

He was back in Archer's stifling office, fighting rising nausea. Watching the old fool stumbling over the words. *Yellow body fragments in the debris, almost certainly MK II TNT grenade.*

"About five minutes later this other car arrived. Delivering that artist woman, the one in Dundee. She was scared stiff, bewildered. Kept looking at me as if I was going to tell her what to do. They don't turn the plane at Saint Aunix, there's room to run straight on. The damned thing barely stopped long enough to get us on board. Took off straight down the field and circled back quite low. I saw the cars on the field below. Then there was one hell of an explosion. We flew through a huge plume of black smoke, flames spurting up. That was when I knew why nobody had bothered to arrest me."

She was leaning forward across the table, two hands gripping, pulling him closer. He had never seen tears welling into those dark eyes.

"God, Alex, I'm crying, would you believe it? I'm in a hell of a state. I can't manage much longer like this. It must have been our own people." She pulled away, pressing the back of her hand against her mouth. "Claude organised the cars. Why would he do something like that?"

He could barely hear her. She let her head drop forward, hair covering her face, "What's the point? A bunch of homicidal thugs with a grudge against the English." She looked up, her cheeks wet,

"Remember what Pascal said? Pascal Renault. *Go home bloody English* – something like that."

He waited while she fumbled for a handkerchief, watching her crumple it into a ball. He dared not find her eyes.

"Justine, listen to me. The locals think you're playing both sides, holding out on them ..."

"Don't be stupid."

"Alright, they're wrong, but that's what they think."

"Why the hell should they? No, you're wrong. You've not tried to live there. If they wanted rid of me they could do it any time. God, why am I saying *them*? They're us: I'm one of them. There's no need for bombs, don't you see? I'm completely dependent on them. It only takes a word and I'm dead."

"Unless they wanted it to look like an accident ..."

"Who the hell's *they*?"

"How should I know? The usual incompetant maquisards blowing themselves up. The point is, that way, no reprisals."

She sat idly pushing the tip of a knife round an empty plate. It was a long time before she looked up. "What are you saying, Alex?" her voice setting his heart drumming. "Why would there be reprisals for killing me?"

Shutting up soon, Miss. Can I take your plates?

Alex pushed his chair back, scooping things off the table, carrying then across to the woman wiping the counter. When he got back to the table, Justine was standing. She threaded her arm through his.

"And there was me thinking you were my rock," somehow a brave little smile didn't suit her. "I usually go back into the station when this place shuts. Every day bar Sunday. They have the fire lit in the waiting room. It's safe enough there for a couple of hours."

On the way out he found her hand, praying she would yank it away. Praying she would shout, *for Christ's sake, what now*?

She clung on like a child.

The Waiting Room at King's Cross was packed with noisy sailors togged out in blue and white. With the arrival of two civilians the hubbub fell, only to rise again, the amorphous cacophony of children on a school trip. Most were little more than schoolboys, the old hands sitting apart in gloomy silence, crumpled uniforms not quite clean, a surreptitious silver flask doing the rounds.

Alex found a place on a draughty bench far from the fire.

"I'll tell you what came out of the meeting this morning. Not much really. One thing though: your runner boy was arrested. Picked up on the Friday night."

"Who told you that?"

"*Who?* Why d'you ask? I don't remember."

"René? I think that was his name. Poor little René."

"What could they have got out of him? What could he tell them about you?"

"Nothing. Really nothing. He was carrying a message, but he didn't know what it was. I suppose he guessed it was something a bit fishy because I paid him. Claude had asked for my code book. Poems. The sort of thing any schoolkid might have in his pocket. *Poems by Verlaine.* You know - *Il pleut sur les toits.* I put his girl's name in it. He hadn't the foggiest idea what it meant. Why are you asking me?"

"It's not the poems. You knew he'd been arrested, didn't you?"

She had seen the trap spring too late, letting her eyes fall, an imperceptible nod, whispering, "Yes," rushing on, "is this you quizzing me? Are you saying I should feel bad using a kid? Of course I feel bad. Does that satisfy you? Don't play naïve Alex. What is it your lot call it? A proxy risk. Isn't that the phrase? But I ask you? Out after curfew? Half the kids in the town do it. It's not a hanging offence."

She shook a cigarette out of his packet, striking the match, drawing in hard, letting a tiny haze of smoke escape.

"Look, if you're going to say I should have been creeping around the place myself ..."

"Don't keep saying *your lot*. If you think I'm still an agent, I'm not. I'm nothing. I've been declared dead in the water. My effort's over. I harboured thoughts once I'd be fighting in a war, doing my bit. Maybe dying the best way I could for something … something I believed in. I've ended up as a kind of second-grade clerk, working for a deranged Hungarian with peculiar obsessions. He's close to deciding I'm a traitor, by the way. He's sure they got things out of me when I was arrested."

"That's ridiculous."

Alex reached for her hand, abandoning the gesture as she leaned back, "At the meeting this morning he produced a message from your man Barte. Apparently, the last one he sent."

"And?"

"Well … according to him … and before you jump on me, I repeat it's his account, you were seen that Friday night. After the curfew."

"*Seen* – what's that mean?"

"Barte's version has you chatting to the local Gestapo chief. His story is the local maquis didn't appreciate the company you were keeping."

"The night that kid made his delivery? That Friday I was in Toulouse."

Alex leaned back, deflated, "Well, there you are. If that's right …"

"What do you mean *if*? There's no bloody if about it. And tell me: what exactly did this message say I was doing there?"

"I'm not sure … it was vague on that point."

"There's a surprise! Listen. On that Friday there was a functioning circuit in Saint Aunix, including Claude. The next Monday there was nobody. Even Claude was being led about on a lead. Well there was me, I suppose, but plainly that wasn't intended. I'm not a traitor, Alex, I'm a mistake. If the idiots had known how to set a timer I wouldn't be here talking to you. I'd be a few scraps of flesh in a field."

"We've got a German prisoner from Saint Aunix at an interrogation centre. The frogs let us have him. He was spying on them and got a bit too close. He's talking."

"Talking about me? And you believe him? You know better than anybody he'll say anything to save his skin."

"No, he's not talking about you, but he does seem to know a lot about Columbine. I didn't want to believe him but what he said confirms what you're saying."

"No point being coy is there? Isn't it obvious we've got a spy of our own? And no, I don't think it's you. I saw you at Saint Aunix. You were in a mess, but I don't think anybody had laid a hand on you. And don't look at me – I skipped off because I was frightened, not because I was guilty. Every single operation has failed. Don't you think it strange they always seemed to know in advance?"

"Who seemed to know? French or German?"

"Both probably. Pascal Renault knows something, I'm sure. It's your setup that's leaking. It's your lot need interrogating, not me."

"Justine, you're tired. This isn't some John Buchan story. There's only the three of us in the TPSU: Archer, Cabot and me. SOE pay us, but our boss spends his life ordering us to tell them nothing. To make sure we comply, he's ensured we have nothing to tell. We don't even have anybody to do the typing, just a WAAF every other afternoon. We don't plan missions, we don't select operatives, we don't order flights - in fact, SIS won't let us get near one. You think intelligence people are ... what's the word? *Intelligent.* But they're not. They spend most of their time creeping round politicians hoping for a pat on the head. TPSU hasn't a clue. What are you saying? We haven't got anything to leak."

"What about your Colonel? You don't trust him."

"Only because he's pretty well gaga. I sometimes wonder whether he can find the way to his club. He's a nasty bit of work, but if he's a master spy, god save the Union."

"He's had you followed."

"Oh, he's done that alright. He doesn't trust me – of course he doesn't. He doesn't trust Cabot either. But only because we're cleverer than him. Believe me, that's not at all difficult. He's suspicious of us, but he's too stupid to know why. Most of the time he needs somebody to tell him what day it is. *Why?* What would be the point? Why in god's name would we send people and equipment to a godforsaken dead end like Saint Aunix simply for the local Gestapo to pick them up? It doesn't make sense."

Ten

Evening was closing in when Alex made the decision to find a hotel. Walking aimlessly through pelting rain, he had stifled Justine's protests, pointing to the vast terracotta palace sprawled along one side of Russell Square.

The one hotel in London that had inexplicably escaped the interest of the War Office had not completely escaped the interest of the *Luftwaffe*. Another unintentional bomb had left the entrance cluttered with broken glass and fire buckets. Improvised duckboards lay across the stone steps, a poster with a picture of Winston Churchill improbably declaring the place open.

Alex paid in advance, the man at the desk insolently eyeing Justine, his smirk evaporating as Alex pushed their identity cards towards him.

"Oh, so you're Services?" There was something disturbing in Justine's eyes: something that made him look down, writing their numbers in his book.

"I'll still need a ration card."

"We're not eating."

"All the same ..."

Justine gave him hers and walked away, not bothering to reply to the question about luggage.

It was a long traipse along interminable dusty corridors, but the room turned out to be surprisingly clean, albeit smelling faintly of cordite.

Justine peered down into the Square below.

"I think I've been here before. Years ago. I was a little girl. I remember how pretty it looked when the lights came on in the square..."

She jerked the blackout curtain closed, turning towards him, "You were right, it beats sleeping in the underground. Reminds me of that gothic place at Torridon. But we're taking a risk."

"What risk? You're not on the run from anybody. Not in England anyway. Neither am I for that matter. We can go where the hell we like. I'm damned if I'm going into hiding."

Justine's sudden smile turned his heart over. "Don't look so *defiant*, Alex. It doesn't suit. And it's not convincing. You know you shouldn't be with me. Even if I'm not fleeing your lot – sorry, I mean *them* - you should hand me in. I'd hand myself in if I wasn't so scared. Two goes at killing me in as many days. I know they say it goes with the job, but it makes you wary when your own side starts on it. I'm sorry you're dragged into the mess ..." She checked, "I was going to say my mess, but that's not true. It's nothing to do with me - things have been going wrong for ages. Speaking of mess, I wonder whether there's hot water through there?"

"I doubt it. More to the point, do you think that ration book of yours runs to real food?"

She grinned at him, relaxing a little, "I haven't done much shopping recently, if that's what you're asking. There's a telephone in the corridor. See if it works. See whether they can make us some sandwiches. I'm going to inspect the bathroom."

The corridor outside was lined with dark polished wood, windowless like the interior of some transatlantic liner, the telephone on a spindly gilt table with matching chair. There was something absurd about the pretention of this little tableau, intended to preserve the dignity of the rich and important going about their communications. A single lugubrious electric lamp hung over it all.

Alex lifted the receiver, read the little card, and dialled the desk.

"Is it possible to make us some sandwiches? Anything ... oh, no, not anything ... not tinned fish. If you can? Room 208."

"Captain Vere, sir. I was just going to come and ask ..." A long pause. "About your Identity Card, sir."

There was something strange about the voice – curious how you always know when someone else is listening. This chap was rarely obsequious, you could tell that, but the insolence had evaporated.

"What about the card?"

"I didn't take the number down, sir."

Suddenly alert, heart pounding, "I'm sure you did. Alright, I'll come down."

"Don't you bother doing that, sir. I'll come up and see to it. With the sandwiches. We've got cheese, sir. Will that do? Anything to drink? There's only beer."

"Beer's alright. The number - I saw you write it down."

"No, it's not here, sir. There's no mistake. That must have been the other card."

When Alex got back to the room, Justine was lying on the bed, eyes closed.

"You were right. Cold water. It runs brown. As bad as the underground. Still, the bed's soft. Any luck with the food?"

"Cheese. I hope that'll do. That chap on the desk is up to something. I don't know what. Says he wants to check my ID again."

"You don't think ...?"

"No. Not really. It's just that he sounded a bit queer. We're alright here. At least you can get a bit of sleep. Then tomorrow ... look, Justine, the best thing is you just turn up at the TPSU, my unit. I'll take you in. We'll brazen it out."

"Like hell I do. I'm not going near the place. My mind's made up. I'm going to write and tell them I'm un-volunteering. I can do that. I just have to tell them."

"They'll still have to debrief you. I don't mean SIS. I get the impression Archer wants to handle it. I know why. He wants to

106

know about Aste – the bits I can't tell him. He's desperate to keep the SIS people out of it. He thinks he's got the advantage because it was Air Force Intelligence lost you."

"They hadn't captured me, for heaven's sake. I just got off. Quite a neat trick really."

"Archer's bound to pump you about me. He's not that interested in Columbine, he just wants to know what went on after you got me away."

"Alex, I thought you understood. I've done eight missions. Eight missions is impossible. Couriers last longer than WT people, I know that - but my six weeks were over long ago. I've changed from being a walking miracle to a walking embarrassment. By rights, I should be dead by now. The fact I'm not is going to kill me. The locals don't go in for finesse. Simone's arrested ..."

"Simone's dead. I told you. Swallowed her pill."

"Yes, I remember now. Poor kid. And Claude's probably in Paris already. Dead, if he's lucky, poor devil. That means there's nothing secure left of Columbine."

Standing close to him now, eyes blazing into his. "So why am I alive? That's what they're asking. Even you have doubts, don't you? Tiny little ones. You think perhaps she's up to something – nothing too serious, but *something*. I saw it in your face when I told you about Pascal. And in that café when you started quizzing me. Even you, Alex."

"I was trying to connect things. I can't see how you can even say that. If we start suspecting each other ... no, I'd trust you with my life. In fact I have trusted you. I'd be lined up with Claude Barte if it wasn't for you. I could ask the same question. Do you think I'm responsible? There, you looked away. You can't answer, can you? Because it's possible. Ask yourself what could have been prised out of me at Saint Aunix? Names. Contacts. That's what Archer believes. How the hell do you think that makes me feel?"

She went on staring, silently waiting. She knew. She saw it in his face. Knew there was more to say. Knew he would never speak the words. And as the recollection of his sordid cell flooded his mind, Alex felt his face hot with the shame of it. Remembering *her name is Justine Perry,* he looked away.

He would recall that betrayal for the rest of his life, endlessly consoling himself that it is deeds that condemn, not intentions. Confronted in reality by that thin-lipped monster, perhaps he would have kept silent. Torture is mostly in the anticipation after all. Confession is spawned by fear, not pain - he knew that well enough. He had read the books. The men in the Avenue Foch had read the books. He felt Justine's cool gaze on his face.

The sudden drone of an aircraft saved them, huge engines rattling the windowpanes, something monstrous, low in the sky, just beyond the blackout. Dangerously low. Alex dashed across pushing heavy curtains aside, opening the tall window, stepping out onto the tiny balcony, cold air whipping his face.

A rumble of heavy vehicles rose up from the blackness, bells echoing between the chasms of distant buildings, a coarse stench of hot metal in the air. Justine's voice from inside the room was muffled by the thick cloth.

"I'm not going anywhere tomorrow. I've finished with it. All of it."

Alex looked down into the Square below, feeling his stomach turn. It was not so very far. Nothing, compared to the drop at Ringway. It would be quick, a fall like that.

This war – his war, Cabot's war, Justine's war – was surely lost. England's war, one catastrophe after another, all lost. Even London, falling brick by blackened brick into ruin, London above all had lost. German troops everywhere else would soon enough be here. What then? How could a few faked letters, a few faked officers, mend that? How could any sane man think that would do any good? He was fighting a war with paperclips. Only a fool would think that rumours planted in embassies were going to win a war.

It wasn't that the struggle was so unequal. When it had started he had shared the suicidal pride in certain defeat. No, it was the humiliating futility of his own part in it - fighting bullets with lies, like some seedy crook in a back room. How many German fliers were going to turn back, repelled by thoughts of Cabot's sharks?

"Alex, that's the food at the door. Somebody's knocking."

As he pushed the curtain back, stepping into the light of the room Justine was opening the door.

Archer stood there, looking at her. Wearing his walking out uniform, a little swagger stick under his arm, immensely pleased with himself, a wide smile under the moustache.

"Mrs Perry isn't it? I think we did meet some time ago," pulling off one glove, hand outstretched, Justine shaking it like an automaton, her face frozen. "At Baker Street, it must have been. Perhaps I can come in? You've led us a fair old dance, young woman."

He held up one hand in an impish little gesture to stop her speaking, turning back into the gloom of the corridor, "One moment."

A quick tread of boots on the carpet, returning, holding a tray. "I believe you ordered these sandwiches, Alex. It is you Alex, isn't it? Lurking behind the arras. And why not?" Turning again to Justine, the smile luminous, "Bottled beer, I fear. Not ideal for the ladies I am aware. Apparently it is all they can do within the law. There you are – how the law dogs us all."

He was playing the gallant old Colonel, playful with the little woman, even a trifle flirtatious. Incredibly, Alex watched Justine thaw, settling herself deeper in her chair, shaking her head at the proffered sandwich, pulling back not quite enough as Archer leaned over to pat her knee.

"Chap downstairs was happy for me to bring them ... saved his legs, you see."

He looked at Alex, the voice changing, "I didn't take to him. Chap like that should be serving his country. Left-handed, I dare say. Still, he telephoned the Unit, we should thank him for that. We're not idiots, Alex. Names are circulated – you knew that. After all, John keeps the list. Did you think Mrs Perry's name would be left off?"

The smile switched on like a lamp, its beam swivelling to Justine, white teeth, hints of gold, "John is a colleague of Alex, my dear. They work together. So don't blame John if hiding was your intent – he was only doing his job, his patriotic duty."

He perched himself on the edge of a chair, committee-style, leaning forward, suddenly serious, bringing the meeting to order.

"Now. Mrs Perry. Justine. May I use your name? We have thought so much about you I feel I know you well. I assume you have explained all to Alex? Lined up a story – that's what you've done?"

Justine remained silent, looking at her shoes. Alex realised she was thinking of Cabot's list, wondering how he could have forgotten that.

"So it's hardly worthwhile quizzing you now. We'll sort all that out tomorrow. Just one thing, though. I want you to promise me you won't run away again."

The smile was back, Colonel Archer hiding inside a caricature of Santa Claus, "At least, not tonight, dear lady. You can do that for me, can't you?"

The sandwiches had rested untouched. He took one, waving it vaguely round the room, "Cheese. That's a comfort. This is a comfortable enough place. You won't run away, will you, because it would be irritating. I'm leaving somebody downstairs, but do us all a favour and stay put. Get some sleep. You look as if you could do with it."

He was standing now, his jutting chest an inch too close to Alex, "That goes for you as well. Eight ack emma. Be there both. I've got news for you, Vere. About our good friend Captain Kessler. But it will keep, it will keep. No, don't get up, my dear. Enjoy your supper."

And he was gone.

Eleven

It was still pitch-black when they left the hotel, long before whatever might have been offered as breakfast. Last night she had kissed him like a little child and fallen asleep, her arms wrapped tight around him, mumbling something about Hansel and Gretel. Late in the night, she woke to find him standing at the curtain, looking out onto the Square and called him back like a patient wife.

The frozen streets were deserted, the air ahead hollow, footsteps a dull echo. Alex carried their only torch, his arm pulled tight round her waist, feeling her warmth, the flakes of snow tumbling through the narrow beam of light strangely consoling.

The familiar Sergeant was standing at the top of the steps, rifle shouldered, a shaded light directly above turning his face to a sculpted mask. A cigarette butt arced down onto the pavement as they fumbled their way across the road, the mask leaning back to call through the black of an open door. Two uniforms jostled out, the little group standing in barrier line on the steps, rifles awkwardly unslung, trying their best.

"It's you Captain Vere, isn't it? I do know you, sir, but I'll have to see your identity all the same. Yours too Miss. Orders today."

Justine mounted the steps, standing level with him, "So if I don't show it, you won't let me by?"

"Now I didn't say that, did I, Miss?" taking her card, stifling a grin. "Mrs Perry, you're expected, Miss. Orders were to escort you … if you don't know the way, that is."

"She knows the way." Alex took her arm barging through the blackout curtain into the hallway.

The place had suffered a sea-change: two uniformed soldiers at the foot of the staircase stopped talking, straightening up. A desk had been dragged out onto the landing at the top of the stairs, accommodating a WAAF officer peering at the keys of a huge typewriter, clicking out letters one by one in the gloom. The Torridon Major stood behind her, looking down at them through the bannister rails.

"Captain Vere – how nice to see a familiar face." The same laconic drawl raised a trifle over the sound of the typewriter. "And Mrs Perry. Odysseus and Penelope all in one go – what a treat. Let them pass, Corporal. Come on up. I gather your Colonel's going to be a little late. We had to tee up transport for him. What a godforsaken hour this is. Can I get you something hot to drink? Or something stronger?"

The curious proprietorial tone jarred. Alex could only wonder who on earth *we* were. Perhaps a coup had taken place overnight, some particularly flagrant misdemeanour finally dethroning Archer. As they reached the top of the stairs, the Major wriggled round the desk to shake their hands.

"I must say I'm extremely pleased to see you Mrs Perry. And pleased you've come to no harm. We were worried."

Down the corridor, Cabot's door, invariably flung wide, was shut tight, a soldier slouched on a wooden chair outside, his rifle propped against the wall. Of Cabot himself there was no sign.

"It looks a little like an invasion, sir. I'm impressed somebody thinks we are so much in need of protection, armed protection at that."

The Major saw Alex glance at Archer's security lock and allowed himself a smile. The door to *Records* was wide open.

"Not my doing. I'm only here on the off chance. I heard you would be coming. No, don't ask … I hear things. Look, why don't we find a quiet place somewhere? I'd so much like a few words with Mrs Perry."

As he started shepherding them through the open door to Archer's room, Justine stood her ground, resisting.

"I thought it was arranged for Colonel Archer to debrief me." Hearing another woman's voice, the WAAF stopped typing, releasing a beat of silence into the cramped space. "I don't want to say everything twice. To tell the truth, I don't want to say anything once."

"There's just one thing ... this seems as good time as any. Colonel Archer can't be much longer."

He closed the door as they followed him inside, pausing with his back against it, listening to the murmur of voices in the corridor.

Justine crossed to the window, opening the curtain a crack, peering into the street below, "I've never seen where you work, Alex. So this is where you spend your days."

The Major gave Alex no time to reply. "I gather you've been in Dundee, Mrs Perry?"

"Yes, since you ask." She turned to face him. "There was somebody I wanted to see. Can I ask precisely how you gathered that?"

"Ah, the *how* question. I'm always a little foxed by that. Actually, in this case I can honestly say I don't know how. Information comes my way. Usually in a file – will that do?"

"I suppose it will have to. It's not pleasant knowing you are being spied on. But the answer is yes, I went to Dundee."

"To interview your fellow passenger from Saint Aunix?"

"I'd hardly say interview. Somebody had tried to kill me. I comforted myself with the thought that it was a mistake. Possibly I wasn't the target. Look ... I'm sure you know all this. She had been in the car that was blown up. I thought that perhaps ..."

"Very reasonable. And?"

"I didn't get far. She wasn't very forthcoming. She went on a bit about the people killed ..." He raised one hand as if to slow her pace, the palm turned towards her, a curiously timid gesture, the expression on his face hard to read – something not far from pain.

113

"No … sorry. I was thinking of something else. Do go on. These people?"

"Somebody close to her, I think. But she didn't say …" Justine looked at him, the smile too bold, "Her lover maybe. You know how these things go? We women in far off places …" He did not return the smile. "No … what I mean is she didn't look as if …" Annoyed the sentence could not be finished - that he had somehow bested her - she stumbled on "… I don't think she … no … Anyway she knew nothing about that operation. Nothing. She'd just got herself mixed up in something. Which leaves me, I'm afraid."

"No names?"

"None that I remember. I would have known if it was anybody in Claude's circuit. I know them all."

"You know them all? You shouldn't really know them all, should you? Not with cut-outs."

"God, is this you interrogating me after all? Why is somebody always trying to trip me up? Listen, Major … I'm sorry … I didn't get your name … cut-outs might seem alright in your world - I dare say they do, and I understand the logic. But you can't operate cut-outs in a tiny village. Just think about it - the whole idea's ridiculous." She turned to Alex, her look desperate.

"Justine's right, sir. In a tiny place like that, knowing other people's business is a way of life. You can't expect secrets to hold …"

"Just a minute, Captain Vere. One at a time." The little gold-cased pad had reappeared, the Major peeling back pages, finding somewhere to write, keeping them waiting, an earnest expression on his face, finally snapping it closed, looking up.

"Interesting."

"You have to understand, Mrs Beyrou didn't want to talk at all. When I was taken to her studio she was working. It was like being ushered into the sacred presence, if you know what I mean. She was mixing something up in a bottle. She asked what I wanted but didn't stop what she was doing. She scarcely looked at me. I don't think she meant to be rude ... no, *rude* isn't the right word ... She didn't seem to care – she could barely bother to look at me. When I ..."

There was muffled rumpus outside, the sudden clatter of urgent boots on the stairs, the Sergeant's bleat, *No you can't sir ... Please sir*, Archer's voice bellowing, *Hands off me, damn you*.

The door burst open, Archer looking in at them, crimson with fury, moustaches flaring.

"What the hell are you lot doing in my room?"

He hung onto the back of a chair, his breath coming in gasps. "Who let you in?" Rounding on the Major, "Do you know that bloody fool down there asked for my pass? A pass for god's sake! Why the hell would I have a pass? Is this tomfoolery your idea, Major? No, don't bother getting up, if you're comfortable sitting there. Was posting a sentry your idea? Was it?"

The major took his time standing, not bothering to supress a smile at *tomfoolery*, raising an eyebrow to Alex as Archer's expression hardened.

"That damn fool went to lay hands on me? Is he under your orders, Major? Because ..."

But they were never to learn the Major's fate. The Sergeant himself appeared at the open door, red-faced, torn between seizing his quarry and crossing the threshold.

Archer cast about for a suitable projectile, falling on Justine's handbag, stubby hands jerking it off the desk, hurling it across the room. The bag flopped limply against the Sergeant's chest, clung crab-like for a second, and fell to earth. Justine burst out laughing.

The Sergeant, at a loss, stooped down to pick it up.

"Leave it! Leave it where it is, god damn you. Step further in here and I'll have you court-martialed. Do you understand? I'll not have it ... I'll not have it. Insubordination. Never seen anything like it."

Realising he was still holding the chair he sank onto it, chest heaving, eyes raking the room, coming to rest on Justine, unforgivable laughter still on her face. It was enough to find his second wind, lumbering upright, grabbing a metal ashtray, beating it into the desk, punctuating his words: "Let's ... have ... some ... order." The Sergeant moved warily back into the corridor.

"That's better. Now ... who stationed you there? No, don't answer - I'm not interested. I don't want to know. Why the hell are you up here? Chasing after me like some damned shop girl. Why aren't you at your post?"

"Orders, sir. Orders not to let ..."

"Don't you ask permission to speak any more? Get downstairs, Sergeant. Somebody asked you to stand guard. Bloody well go and do it. I'm in charge here. I give the orders."

He suddenly noticed the line of pockmarks across the desktop, rubbing ineffectually at them with his fist, finally tossing the deformed ashtray into the wastepaper basket.

The Sergeant stayed swaying in the corridor outside, his face brick-red, head swivelling helplessly from Alex to the Major.

Justine went to collect her bag but the Major beat her to it, scooping it up, letting their hands touch, tapping her wrist, murmuring, "A moment, Mrs Perry, I'll deal with this." He went across to the door.

"It's alright, Sergeant. A misunderstanding. Get back to your post. We're expecting a visitor."

"Permission to speak, sir?" The Major nodded wearily. "A man under guard down there, sir," head rigid, eyes flicking dangerously close to Archer's, "arrived with the Colonel's party, sir ... Corporal Wade's looking after him ... with the other gent."

"Very well, I'll come down."

Archer pushed past, shouldering him aside, "The hell you will, Major. Misunderstanding my backside. Sergeant, escort them up here. Take them to Mr Cabot's room – they'll tell you where it is. Those are my orders. And if you ask any of them for a pass don't expect to keep those stripes. D'you follow me?"

With the Sergeant gone, silence fell on the room. Archer stationed himself in the doorway, his back to them, blocking the way. They could hear his breath wheezing. He did not turn round.

Eventually, the cheerful sound of men's voices floated up the stairwell. Alex made out Cabot's laugh. They were speaking German - apparently exchanging fragments of poetry, vying with each other, capping quotations.

As they passed the door, Archer joined them, calling over his shoulder, "You'll have to tell your tale to the Major, Mrs Perry. I assume that's what he's here for. It may give the two of you something more to laugh over. Other business takes priority over SIS for me. I will eventually be favoured with a report, no doubt. You too, Vere – only don't be too long about it, I shall want to see you. Ah, here you are at last, John - all safe and sound?"

Wedged against the doorframe he managed an awkward salute, "Hauptmann Kessler ... the room on your right. Mr Cabot will show you the way."

A tall man in the uniform of a German Officer shuffled past, Cabot alongside, glancing nervously into the room.

Archer followed them, slamming the door behind him.

Twelve

It was left to the Major to break the silence.

"Not SIS, in fact. Never mind – it's a detail, it's the same war for all. You seem to lead a lively sort of life here, Captain Vere. Is it always like this? Perhaps you have your quieter days?"

"The Colonel was taken by surprise, sir. Armed men about the place ... you know. And we are in his room ..."

"So we are. And you're right. Point taken. But the guard has absolutely nothing to do with me. Perhaps you could explain that to Colonel Archer ... at a suitable moment, of course. I believe the men are from Abbott Court. Part of the prisoner transfer routine. I'm afraid your Colonel jumped to the wrong conclusion."

"He does tend to, sir."

"But it seems he got his man. I'm intrigued."

"Hauptmann Kessler was at Abbott Court. Colonel Archer hopes there's a chance we can turn him."

The Major was checking his watch. "Not much time. My car will be here in half an hour. This debriefing, Mrs Perry - it looks as if Colonel Archer has other fish to fry. Perhaps we can find a convenient time. You as well, Captain."

He had installed himself in Archer's chair, drawing it up to the desk, pushing things about, looking for something to write on, looking up at Justine, the smile disarming.

"There is one thing you could help me with. No, nothing to do with that trip back from Northolt," holding out his cigarette case, "frankly, I can't see why you shouldn't pop off and catch a tube if you feel like it. It's not as if you were a prisoner." He swivelled round to Alex.

"Just a quick précis of the thereafter, as it were ... that would be helpful ... and we do have a few moments. When you were arrested - no chance of running for it, I suppose?"

"I wouldn't have got ten yards, Major. I was in the middle of the road, a sitting target in the headlights. There was an SS Officer in the car. He knew I was with somebody, but ..."

The raised hand again, palm forward, his signature gesture, "Just a second ... how could he know that?"

"Well, he had Mrs Perry's code name – Marie. Perhaps they got it out of Simone. I think they knocked her about looking for her L tablet, but she got to it first. I'm afraid she's dead. There's absolutely no doubt about it."

"No need to be so emphatic. I'm not arguing. I'm trying to keep up."

"The man who arrested me had a copy of Simone's orders, sir. Or rather, not a copy – he had the paper itself, the stuff she was supposed to leave behind at Tempsford. I have no idea how he came by it."

"I can check. See what's missing. And you say she's dead? But you're not dead - you're here. As Colonel Archer is fond of saying, captured agents never come back. You are unique. You can see why we want to know how that came about?"

"It would be quicker to let Mrs Perry ..."

The Major sighed, ostentatiously folding the notepad closed, turning to Justine.

"Mrs Perry? I know you would have preferred to wait for Colonel Archer ..."

She was already speaking, "It may not be what you want to hear, Major. You want to know about the Columbine circuit?"

"That would be a start. Fire away. You don't mind if I jot down some notes?"

"There's barely a hundred people in Saint Aunix. All related to each other, more than they like to admit. It's best not to notice too much who looks like who. Good Catholics, though. Apart from siring children, all else they do is organise funerals. The idea an agent could *blend in*, as you say, is nonsense ..."

"Not my words. It's horses for courses. In small rural communities ..."

" ... Every single person knows you. Knows why you're there. Particularly kids. Children like oddities, don't they? If you want to talk about sides, some of the locals are with us. Most don't care. The choice between us and the Master Race is not that obvious. So *how do you survive*, Major? Any ideas? No need to look embarrassed. Isn't it obvious? If you're a woman you need protection. And I don't mean sturdy peasants singing the *Internationale*. The right people have to look the other way – and to get them to do that is an endless expense." She looked across at Alex, "Of money, of course. But mostly favours. You do understand what I mean, Major? Favours is how we stay alive. You do understand, don't you? You can witter on as long as you like about blending in with the natives, it's favours that count."

She had talked herself to a standstill, hands resting calmly in her lap – SOE regulation pose – daring him to speak.

He sat, head bowed, the only sound the minute scratch of his pen, finally looking up.

"*Witter* – long time since I heard that word. Scottish isn't it? I had a nanny used it. Listen, Mrs Perry, I see what you're saying. I suggest ..."

"I know, I know. You suggest I write a letter. You suggest I come across to Baker Street and give a talk. Explain how ... despite everything ... I end up still alive all these weeks later. Oh, I can explain that alright. Christ almighty, don't you think I've done enough?"

She went over to the window, pulling at the thick curtains, letting a little grey light seep into the room, waving a hand behind her back for a cigarette.

"Do have a seat, Mrs Perry. I can see you're exercised about this. Nobody is implying anything. We can stop if you like."

"I'll tell you a story, Major. About *blending*. My first operation, the briefing was at Castle Kennedy. Some chap gave a pep talk before the drop. *Your initial rendezvous*, he said. Smashing bit of French, nice accent. Your initial rendezvous is the bar in the square, that's what he said. I can tell you, by the way, that the bar's called *Le Sport*. Just go in, he said, order a coffee and wait, somebody will meet you. Sounds easy, doesn't it? Just a few snags. Biggest snag - that bar exists exclusively for the rugby club. The only woman in there is a tart called Nathalie or some such name, on a Saturday night. And you don't *order a coffee*, Major, for the simple reason there's been no bloody coffee anywhere in the South West for months. Alright - I admit I was met eventually, so you could say that part went to plan. And he got me out of *Le Sport* smartish. You could hear them laughing all down the street. I might as well have been wearing a placard saying *English Agent*."

"I do understand your point. Can we get back to Captain Vere. You were going to explain how he got out."

"The situation Alex was in looked worse than it was. For one thing, there is no official SS presence in that area. The local Vichy police are in charge and they're jealous of that. I happen to know an officer in the Gendarmerie - a man called Pascal Renault. He hates Germans treading on his toes. I have leverage with Renault."

"Blackmail?"

Justine looked at him, pondering her reply, glancing at Alex.

"Something like that. You can't keep captured agents in the local cop shop. They get sent on. Renault signed a chit for the prisoner to be transferred up the line. It was a bit unusual, him turning up to do the necessary at the crack of dawn, but there was only an old guy on duty and he did as he was told."

"No, I'm completely lost. How do you know all this?"

"I was there. Consider Renault as my captive, Major – it's not quite right, but it will do. I don't propose to elaborate. The paperwork said Alex was to be plucked from his dungeon and sent off under escort to Limoges. It was obvious to the old guy what was going on - he seemed to treat it as a bit of a joke. Everything was deniable. The place is awash with forged transfer papers. That SS officer had no business haring about chasing parachutes, he should have contacted his superiors. The whole arrest was irregular. I think he had a little free-lance torture in mind. He's a nasty piece of work, apparently. He had to go along with the daring rescue nonsense, because if he didn't he was in deep trouble. There's no story, really. Captain Vere just walked out. We sent him on his way to the safe house ... I know it seems a miracle, but ..."

"It does, rather ..."

Alex broke in, "What's that supposed to mean? I want to add something about Columbine. That prisoner Archer's got confirms what Justine's saying. He claims the Gestapo own the whole of the Columbine circuit. All the WT traffic is through captured sets."

"A slight exaggeration, Captain Vere. I can see they would like us to believe that, but obviously they don't have the whole of the circuit. Mrs Perry is here, isn't she? Unless you're going to raise that business with the car exploding?"

"Obviously that was intended to kill Justine. The thing went off too late."

"Intended by whom? I'm just asking. You need reasons to organise something elaborate like that."

Justine was glaring at him. "I haven't the faintest idea, Major. How do you imagine I feel?"

"Can I ask about this report you were seen with the local Gestapo. Now, there may be a perfectly ..."

"Not this so-called message from Claude Barte? When that was sent, Claude had already been arrested. Whoever sent it, it wasn't him. That Friday night I wasn't even there."

"Please don't shout at me – it gets us nowhere. Just to have something to write down, exactly where were you?"

"I was in Toulouse. Look, if you think I'm in a position to go chatting to the Gestapo, you must be mad. For one thing I can't speak German ...."

As Alex looked up, she grabbed his arm, "Ask Captain Vere - he knows I was brought up in France. Schools didn't teach German. That message stinks of dirty work. German dirty work. Or, more likely, English dirty work."

"I'm afraid I'm losing your thread, Mrs Perry."

"Really? Isn't it fairly obvious? If every member of a drop is picked up on arrival, how do you imagine that trick is played? Somebody is telling them, Major. Somebody at this end ... at your end. I can't believe you've not thought of that."

The Major had long since stopped writing, leaning back in Archer's chair, his expression thoughtful, calculating.

"I'll want to go through all this again. But let's see what we've got to be going on with. By way of concrete evidence, that is. A bit cold-blooded you'll say, but there you are – that's my job. First, we've got this WT operator Simone. Captain Vere claims she was captured and committed suicide. He was a witness to her death. Unfortunately, there are problems with this. First, there are things that Captain Vere can't remember at all. I'm not arbitrating – just playing devil's advocate. By his own account, his memory is unreliable. Now, taken along with the fact we've been receiving messages from Simone since the day she arrived ... No, Captain Vere, before you say anything - all the necessary security checks are present. And no capture codes."

"She's dead, sir. My memory on that score is perfectly clear. She swallowed her tablet. She'd been sick ... what more can I say?"

"As you say, Captain Vere, I think we've reached a stalemate on this point. Let me come to the message concerning Mrs Perry. From the local maquis chef, Claude Barte. Mrs Perry is certain this must be bogus because she is confident Barte has been arrested. Let me put it crudely: the message concerns Mrs Perry and the evidence that it might be bogus has Mrs Perry as its source. You see the problem?"

"Look, I've had enough of this." Justine went to the window, pulling the curtains aside, rubbing at the grubby panes, seeking air.

"If you're going to claim I'm in any way responsible. I'm resigning my commission. You'll have to look elsewhere." She went across to the door. "I'm leaving."

His voice was so quiet she turned to catch his words, "No, you can't do that, can you, Mrs Perry? Do please sit down. It would embarrass the chaps in the corridor. They've orders no one's to leave. Frankly, we've had enough theatre today. Sit down, Mrs Perry. You had something to say about that explosion."

Alex got up and led her to the chair, taking her arm. She was trembling.

"What about it? Am I supposed to be sorry I didn't die?"

His smile, when it finally came, was friendly, "I can see you interpret it as a lucky escape. Your driver was too quick, you arrived too soon. I think the truth's simpler than that. I think the bomb was placed exactly as intended. The targets were the occupants of that car. It had absolutely nothing to do with you."

Thirteen

Justine left with the Major. Getting into the car she had turned to look back, her face caught in sunlight filtering between the looming buildings. She looked frightened. Alex was consumed with the thought that her leaving was somehow irrevocable, that she was being taken from him, that things would never be the same again. As the car rumbled away he managed a half-hearted wave, conscious of the Sergeant behind rattling a rifle into place.

He walked inside, past the loafing soldiers, settling in his own room, waiting in silence for Archer's summons.

It was half an hour before Cabot tapped on his door. Alone, looking excited.

"Archer wants some time on his own with the prisoner."

"Why on earth? He can barely speak German."

"Kessler's English is alright. Anyway, who am I to ask? I've been banished. All a bit fishy if you ask me, secret communion with the prisoner. That's what we're to call him, by the way: *the prisoner*, except when addressing him. So we don't have to accord him a rank. Written orders to follow. I must say, only Archer would think of that. He's sent me to explain things to you. Has your Mrs P gone? I'd have liked to meet her."

"She volunteered to go back with the Major. In the sense it was that or being hauled off in chains. It's depressing. Punished for delivering a few home truths. He didn't appreciate it. She got the choice to share his car back or wait under guard for an escort. I'm to report to him tomorrow. Apparently nobody thinks I'll run away.

What's afoot with this chap Kessler? And all these soldiers hanging about?"

"Archer's furious. He told them it would be alright for him to secure Kessler's parole and for one of us to escort him back and forth. You wonder sometimes which war he thinks he's fighting. The proposal was not well received. We either put up with the extra security or deal with Kessler at Abbott Court."

"But what's deal with him mean? Why's he here? What are we supposed to do with him?"

"That's what I'm sent to explain. Incidentally, Kessler's a student. Literature. Half way through a degree when he was called up. I tried to talk to him about Gotthold Lessing. You know, *Nathan The Wise*, religious tolerance and so forth, but he would have none of it. Said I was trying to trap him. It's peculiar – a couple of years ago I knew dozens of Germans. He's the first I've spoken to since they were all defined as the enemy. He seems quite a reasonable chap - not very well educated, but quite reasonable. There we were, chatting about Schiller, me wondering all the time whether he thought it was his duty to brain me and jump out of the window."

"Quite a reasonable chap - apart from baiting the occasional Jew, you mean?"

"A bit harsh, Alex. Archer pressed him on his anti-Semitism. Kessler is hellish touchy about his background. I was right about his name, by the way. It was comical in a way, both of them pretending and both of them knowing perfectly well."

"You're losing me – what about his name?"

"I told you that name reminded me of something. It's Jewish. Well, Yiddish, actually. It means coppersmith. Our Hauptmann Kessler is Jewish - that's why he kept shying away from the topic, trying to bamboozle us with legal niceties. He claims to be amazed at the French hostility to Jews - says it's irrational."

"Whereas German hostility is, I suppose? But if he's Jewish ... he's military ...?"

"You surely don't suppose he's the only one? Trouble is, Germans will never understand what's going on in France."

"You mean all these arrests?"

"Arrests? More like a purge. You know they've been rounding people up in Paris? The Marais - the Jewish quarter. French police shoving perfectly ordinary citizens into holding camps. Children even. They don't want their land – they just want rid of them. Even the Germans are surprised."

"You think that explains Kessler's obsession with rooting out the Jews of France – is that what you're saying? Make sure you're on the right side before it gets too hot?"

"Yes. But he can't see this is something the French want to do themselves. It's shameful enough - the last thing they want is Germans doing their dirty work."

"But he can't be Jewish, John – it's impossible. He's a serving officer in the Wehrmacht, for god's sake."

"This is Germany – how can you be German and not have Jewish ancestors? How the hell could you avoid it? Why do you think they invented insane rules about needing two Jewish grannies? One's enough in France, by the way – did you know?"

"He'll deny it. He'll know you're just guessing."

"No – I've seen the paperwork. Archer has his French Military Security file. Kessler comes from Breslau. His father had a business repairing violins in the Jewish Quarter. They all died when the shop caught fire. Certainly deliberate - the place had been boarded up. Not Kessler though, he'd left home by then. The French think he bought forged papers - got himself new parents - after the fire. The odd missing baptismal certificate didn't matter too much. At university he became a good enough little Nazi to die for the Reich when he was called up. But it's not going to last. They're on to him. He must know he's not going to survive. No need to look that surprised - I doubt things will be all that different ... when ..."

"When they get here you mean? The ones without degrees in literature. Has it crossed your mind we may not live to find out, given our current occupation?"

"No, I'm being serious. People in my College are forever going on about the curse of all these cosmopolitan intellectuals. Did I ever pipe up and say, you mean the Jews don't you? I even catch myself nodding. I'm as guilty as Kessler: perhaps we all are."

"Come off it, John. You're not guilty of anything."

"I think a lot about the invasion. Wondering how I'll bear up. It's different for you, I suppose. Field agent and all that. The truth is, I don't know how I'll face up to it. I suppose I won't know until … we're all cowards when it comes to it."

He had taken his spectacles off, wiping them on his handkerchief, weak rabbit eyes blinking. Alex was consumed by a kind of affectionate pity, lost for what to say. It was hardly a consolation to state the obvious – that this man with his gentle scholar's face was the sort you might torture to his grave before he would betray a friend. Surely he knew every martyr died believing himself weak?

And recollecting his cell in Saint Aunix he saw Cabot look away, embarrassed, fixing his glasses in place, casting about for a cigarette.

"No need to look so tragic, Alex. Sufficient unto the day. I'm to tell you what the old man has in mind for Kessler. You remember Operation Briefcase? No, don't laugh, Archer thinks there's life in it yet."

"But we've been through all that. Even if there is life in it, SIS will veto the idea. And I can't see how a captured German helps."

"Ah, but you're missing a trick. The idea is that Kessler carries the briefcase. There's no question of dropping anything - he'll be jumping with it. We put him through the standard Ringway course then drop him as part of a scheduled run. Archer suggests Metz, which seems reasonable. He takes the local train, gets off on the French side of the border. Leaves the briefcase on the train. It's clever – the perfect plant."

"So clever he'll report the whole scheme to the local Gestapo. What then? Are we supposed to tick him off and make him have another go? For heaven's sake! He'll chuck the thing in the river and re-join his unit. What's to stop him? Really John, it's as barmy as the man-eating sharks. Let me tell you something. Before you got here, Archer had one of his temper tantrums – really spectacular. I thought he'd expire with rage. In front of the Major. Once that story gets around, god knows what'll happen to us. We're already a bit of a joke – they'll probably close us down."

"He seemed calm enough just now, talking to Kessler. Your trouble is you don't give him credit for low cunning. It's his speciality. He's desperate to keep the Intelligence chaps out of our hair. If he has to seem mad to achieve that, so be it – that's his philosophy. I thought fake madness was your subject. Can't you see what he's up to?"

"The people I was studying are seriously damaged … mentally ill."

"And it doesn't strike you Archer likes putting on a show? Honestly, Alex, he's not nice and he's not very clever, but he's exceeding crafty – don't underestimate him. You know what he just told me? He said he'd been planning this drop for months. *Months*. Puffed his little chest out. He claims he planned the whole thing right from the start, including the phoney squabbles with SIS. He was perfectly happy for everything to be turned down because he was waiting for the right man to turn up. He's sure Kessler's his man."

"You realise that applies to us as well."

"I don't follow."

"He must have recruited us because we were right as well. What brought him to Netley looking for me? It's a long trip. Why me? I suppose it's because we're a couple of wounded ducks."

"You mean because I'm as blind as a bat and you're …"

"… not quite right in my cracked head. You may as well say it - no point being delicate. When I get a bad day, I can barely think straight."

"No, I didn't mean that. You were Archer's way into Abbott Court. Psychology and all that mumbo jumbo – a free pass ..."

Cabot pushed his chair back, struggling to stand, plump face suddenly pink. Archer had flung the door open without knocking. He stood looking into the room.

"Ah, both of you ... good ... why the startled looks? Just to tell you I've agreed that the prisoner's to be kept at Abbott Court. Not ideal, but we can't have this rigmarole every day. One good thing – we'll be rid of this damned WAAF woman kicking up that infernal row and hogging the lavatory. She's to go. All this affects you most, John, because you'll be spending most time with him. You've briefed Alex, I take it? Now ... I've talked with SIS and they agree we can do some initial planning. They were quite tickled I may say. It's to be *Operation Alathea* – what d'you think John?"

"Goddess of truth, sir. Couldn't be better."

"You still in that hotel Alex? I'll drop you on the way. My driver's waiting."

Cabot glanced across, rapidly cancelling a puzzled look. They both knew Archer had made repeated requests for the allocation of a staff car suited to his status, all ignored. His response to this indignity had been to paste something cut from a War Office letterhead onto the windscreen of his own modest Austin 8.

He faced Cabot down, turning into the corridor, "Give me five minutes. Things to do. I'll leave you two to finish whatever you were up to." He left the door open.

"D'you think he heard?" Alex found himself whispering, feeling foolish. "Not that it matters. Alright, I'll sit quiet and keep the mumbo jumbo to myself. Convince me it could work."

Cabot went to close the door, changed his mind and pulled it wide. "Start with the obvious objection. As you say, once Kessler's out of our hands he can simply ditch the whole thing. But here's the clever bit. By the time he jumps, that won't be an option. By then, Hauptmann Kessler will have a different identity altogether. A non-

Jewish identity. We'll have him kitted out with all the right paperwork." He glanced across to the door, raising his voice.

"The Colonel suggests somebody exempted war service - a businessman, high level clerical maybe, somebody expected to be touting a briefcase. It won't be hard to persuade Kessler that his present identity is a death sentence. Once he's convinced of that, we hold it over him indefinitely."

"We provide him with the identity that keeps him alive, and the quid pro quo is he's managed by SOE. Yes, I can see it's clever. So we've turned him, whether he's committed or not."

"Oh, he's certainly not, but that doesn't alter much. It's simpler in some ways, there are always layers below layers with double agents. Better to have somebody by the short hairs. Of course, he can refuse to go, but he knows we will turn him over to the French in London. They can probably justify shooting him for the spying. They've got the proof. He's dropping with a WT set, by the way. Instructions to report back once the briefcase is planted. If there's no corroboration it has actually been picked up things will unravel for him fast. He'll be at the mercy of the local circuit."

"What if he simply reports in to his unit and confesses all? Explains the whole plot - how he was picked up and spirited here, his new identity, everything."

"An officer who's gone AWOL turns up with false papers? The only way he can get out of that is to come clean about who he really is. Passing himself off as an officer. I imagine he'd be shot that night."

"Let me think … he joins the circuit at Metz. His French is alright, so that could work. He can come from Alsace - how about that? We've invented a few Alsatians, remember? I start to think it's not impossible."

They heard Archer's door slam. He stalked past. "Get a move on Alex. Trot, trot."

It was actually the Major's car. Archer installed himself, waiting for the driver to come round to close the door, leaning over towards Alex, eyes glistening, broken veins blotching his cheeks.

"I get the use of a car for Abbott Court if the prisoner's involved. That's where I'm going. You can get out there. Gives us time to talk a bit. It's not a long walk back."

As punishments went, it was not particularly severe. Alex was struck by the pettiness of the gesture: he was to be driven miles out of his way as Archer's response to some vaguely articulated grievance with Justine. She had laughed at him and for that Alex must walk back to the hotel. It would be getting dark soon. Alex remembered Justine had taken the torch with her.

Archer tapped the glass and they pulled away. He held out his cigarette case, running his other hand approvingly over the leather of the seat, "Superior sort of chap, Cabot. Always knows one better, don't you think?"

"He's very intelligent, sir. In fact he's the brightest person I've ever met."

"Brain's aren't everything, Vere."

He was looking through the side window, perhaps hoping to be noticed. He had kept his cap on, "In fact sometimes I think they're a hindrance. You know what Napoleon said? Spare me Generals with imagination. Knew a thing or two, that man. D'you know what I think?" Alex, starting to shake his head, thought better of it.

Archer was still staring through the window. "What I think is that German is playing us for fools. Those names he gave you, for example, including mine, the whole recital. He could have got all that information easily enough. Loose talk, that's the culprit."

"If you think it could have been Mrs Perry, I'm sure you're wrong … is that what you're thinking, sir?"

"You're emotionally involved there, Vere. Doesn't do. But it doesn't matter what I think, does it? I intend to get the truth out of this German. We can do that, can't we? It's your pigeon."

"Truth's a funny thing, sir. If we start using Cardiazol on him, it's a sort of one-way road. Subjects usually end up so scared, they tell the truth alright, but it turns out to be false more often than not."

"Try to make sense, will you, I'm tired."

"I'm sorry sir. What I mean is extracting the truth is not like pulling teeth. It's the same with memories. Get somebody scared enough and they'll actually believe what they're saying – whether it's true or not. That's the trouble with drugs … he'll say anything, and he'll believe it."

"Scared? Why scared?"

"Nobody knows. It's just the effect the stuff has. The books say it induces feelings of dread. There are cases where subjects fainted at the prospect of the injection. If we're going to be talking him into this Operation Briefcase, it will be better to forget drugs."

It was barely daylight outside, the weary fag end of another grey day, London drawing itself in to meet the night, trying its best not to flinch.

The driver pulled over to let him out at the green metal gate in Abbott Court. Abandoned, he stood for a second on the pavement, orienting himself, then turned and walked slowly back towards the city.

He had seen the other car pull up as Archer was making his perfunctory goodbyes. It had been behind them for most of the way. A decrepit Morris, headlamps painted over with black paint, creeping to a halt at the corner, reluctant to stop. The man must have waited until Archer's car masked the view then slipped out of the passenger seat.

They were not the same footsteps. After yesterday's lapse perhaps his allocated walker had given up. Then again, given that Justine was safely tucked up somewhere there seemed no point in following him at all.

Approaching a bookshop, Alex slowed to get a better look, peering down at a collection of yellowing pamphlets. Almost too soon, a reflected form loomed up huge behind him in the glass, feet pounding past. He watched the man hurry on down the street wondering why, of a sudden, his heart was lurching. Days of benign surveillance must have tipped him into paranoia. For reasons beyond his power to fathom he now merited a professional. A surge of inexplicable fear invaded him, screaming alarm. This walker was not seeing him benevolently to his door - he was playing an altogether different game.

Well ahead now, walking fast, putting distance between them. You would say he was hurrying home to the wife, perhaps a little late for supper: a tall chap, long raincoat buckled tight at the waist, a vaguely continental look, trilby hat. At the corner of Clifford Street the man stopped to admire a tailor's dummy, tweed suiting long since unobtainable, letting Alex leapfrog past. The hat had been someone's mistake. The trilby didn't quite work. Plainly, this particular professional had never owned one in his life.

Half way along Saville Row he was in front again, chugging past Alex, metal toe-taps clicking on the pavement. A good ten yards ahead, perhaps more, lolloping contentedly by two burnt-out shop fronts without a second look, turning into New Burlington Street. So he knew where they were both going - his confidence on the point was infuriating. When Alex reached the corner, the street was empty, the distant stream of evening traffic flowing right and left along Regent Street. He would be waiting there, Alex was sure of it – insolently waiting at the junction to fall in behind.

Perhaps it was a response to Archer's infantile spite. Certainly the response featured in no Training Manual yet written, but Alex found himself running. Running as he had not done since he was at school, legs drawing on some memory of their own, lifting him onto his toes, broken glass crunching beneath his feet, carving a suicidal path across Regent Street, threading between cars in a blaze of horns, hands arresting the polished bonnet of a car. By some miracle he was on the other side, weaving light-footed round startled pedestrians.

An awkward flying glance over his shoulder glimpsed a vague form rifling its way down the pavement opposite, head erect, checking to pick a time to cross. He was moving faster than Alex, the trilby hat fallen back giving him a vaguely Mexican look, the brim haloing a face red with sweat.

As they approached Hamleys, the revolving doors were disgorging a woman into the street. She stopped halfway round, tugging the chrome rail, crouching to settle a parcel under her arm. Alex threw himself at the other side of the door scooting it into her back, tipping her out in a confusion of parcels at the feet of the trilby hat.

Walk, don't run. How often had he parroted that injunction at Torridon? Easy to say, a damn sight harder to do. But he was safe enough here, safe enough to walk.

A hot oily smell hung about the place, last week's bomb leaving only half a shop. It was a miracle it was open at all. The girl behind the counter wore a tin hat. Somebody had written, *We never cl* in white paint round the brim, eventually running out of space.

Alex picked up a toy fire engine and stood looking at the ticket. He could see the man now, standing outside, nervously peering up the street, breathing hard. Alex handed the girl a ten shilling note.

"Can you wrap this? It's for my little boy."

As she turned to close the drawer of the cash register he found himself locking eyes with someone along the other counter: someone who inexplicably looked away. God, there were two of them! How incredibly stupid not to realise. This ferrety bloke in the other queue had been waiting. That was why the trilby had risked going ahead, why he was content now to wait beyond the revolving doors. They were not following him at all. They were hunting him down.

Alex went on smiling at the girl as she looked for scissors under the counter, the little man with scruffy ginger hair jostling his way out of the other queue, nothing in his hands. He had stationed himself at the only other door, brazenly watching Alex collect his change.

At least he knew what he was up against. If he left by that door he would only have this new man to contend with. Alex walked briskly out, turning into the jumble of streets behind the shop. *Walk, don't run.* Quiet footsteps, echoing his own, keeping their distance.

They were in a narrow alley squeezed between the backs of buildings. A section of wall hung out across the footpath, casually remodelled by the bomb that had demolished half the shop, red security tape flapping loose across the path. Duckboards over a broken drain formed a narrow walkway between charred baulks of timber. Alex stopped to light a cigarette hearing the following steps falter.

He would take him as he walked past, he had nowhere else to go.

Along the street a daring splash of yellow light briefly framed two women in the doorway of a pub. The sound of a piano surged out.

As the man reached the boards Alex turned to give him room, realising in that second his mistake. He had a fleeting glimpse of bloodshot eyes. Surprisingly clean white hands stretched out towards him. He seemed insanely friendly, this ferrety stranger leaning forward to pinch your cheeks. Even intimate, you might say. And for that fatal second Alex let the thought cross his mind. It was a private enough place, after all. As the man let his hands drop an inch, Alex heard the sigh as if from someone else, realising too late it came from his own throat - the noise a girl might make. Too late. The face close now.

"We're only doing our job, laddie ..."

A surprisingly cultured voice. Funny how SOE always settled on that sort, whatever bit of grubby obscenity they had in hand. You could imagine this one giving lectures on something, *Pissaro and the Glasgow Boys* perhaps – there was something Scottish in the voice. Certainly happier in some College, this one. Happier, that is, than killing Alex in a dark alley behind a toy shop.

Something seemed to be pushing hard against his heart, the smell of stale tobacco everywhere as he caught his breath, knowing he had no breath to catch. Giddy now with the image in the Training Manual, his own manual, the one with the corner torn. A remembered voice, impenetrable Highland accent: *Seven seconds ... maximum ... often found it less, gentlemen. Carotid Choke. Fast and painful, if you do it right. And you will do it right, won't you?* Torridon flooding his mind like a consolation: Justine linking arms with a smiling policeman, the two pads of flesh in Alex's neck like radiating stars, a fearful darkness closing in. Sounds far off now: footsteps near his head. Lying down. Better lying down. Mother's voice: *time you were asleep young man*. Steps scampering away like mice. *Dame souris trotte*. Curious that it should be like this. *Do it right, he will be rendered unconscious in three to seven seconds. Unconscious or, if you prefer, dead*. And then the joke. The Scots like their joke: *You will usually prefer dead*.

Fourteen

They held the post-mortem that night in the hotel room: Justine grim-faced, staring out of the window, Alex sprawled on the bed.

"I shouldn't be in this trade, you know, it didn't even strike me. It was the classic move – one driving, the other waiting. And me thinking I was safe dodging inside. If it hadn't been for the girl in that shop I would be dead. The big toy shop on Regent Street. When I saw the other one waiting there I could have kicked myself. I picked up some toy or other, just to buy time, I must have left it on the counter. This girl came running after me just as he decided to move in. A little ferret of a man, you'd have thought he wasn't capable of much. I underestimated him – a big mistake: he had hands like steel and was as quick as a snake. He was going to kill me."

She was sitting in a cane chair, very upright, as if discomfort might somehow ward off the worst. When she spoke it was so quietly he could barely hear.

"Paying you back for giving them the slip. They hate being made to look stupid, you should know that. They were out to scare you."

"No. More than that. I know the difference. He was going to kill me - the bastard almost apologised for doing it. SOE-trained, that's for sure. You remember the carotid choke? I walked slap into it. He knew his stuff alright. I'm losing interest in an outfit full of thugs. I wanted to be a soldier – a soldier of sorts – not mixed up in a kind of gang warfare. What's the point? "

Justine turned and smiled at him. A smile so lovingly knowing that, for a moment her condescension seemed unbearable, almost he hated her for it. Why did he always end up thinking he knew less than her, the schoolboy late for his lesson? The sad smile remained: she had nothing to say.

"This girl came running out of the shop. That's what saved me. I'd more or less passed out. I felt his hands relax, the relief was incredible. Then he let go. Next thing I know he's running hell for leather down the alley. She was wearing this stupid tin hat, you see. I suppose it was a sort of joke. There'd been a raid on the shop, mess everywhere. It was getting dark he must have thought she was ARP. He only had the silhouette to go by as she came round the corner - thank god he didn't wait around to check. There I was, sitting in a pile of soot looking up at her, trying to speak and all I could do was croak. She didn't look much like a Warden with all those curls. The tin hat suited her. Reminded me of poor Simone. You could see she was wondering what the hell was going on, a bit scared. Shoved the packet in my hand and scooted."

Justine, still silent, waiting until she was sure he had finished. "How did they know you'd be anywhere near Abbott Court?"

"Archer had the use of a staff car. They followed it."

"But how did they know you'd be in it?"

"I suppose anybody could have known. Mind you, it was Archer insisted I came with him. Took me miles out of my way."

"So you know who's responsible, don't you?"

She came and sat next to him, struggling to loosen his collar stud, fingers gently exploring the bruise. He felt her hands trembling. She had drawn the blackout apart at the window and a pale trapezoid of light fell across the carpet.

A continuous low roar had started up over the river, distant clouds blossoming dull red like flowers, oddly disconnected from the hollow crump of bombs.

"It must be the docks again. That's two nights running."

She was staring out into the dark, her voice dead, looking past his reflection into nothing.

"Alex?" Turning aside as he sat up, "I have to tell you about this afternoon. Can you bear it?"

"Bear it? Why *bear it*? What did he say? If you told him you've had enough I can't see what he can do about it. You gave him a bad time, you know. I suppose he wanted his own back. Why the hell did you say you couldn't speak German? He'll have read your record."

"I wanted to jolt the bastard. Wipe the smile off. Make him deny something. I really hate all these tricks. Men sometimes think they're so clever. You do it sometimes – it drives me mad."

"You realise he's probably jealous? There he is sitting in an office, filling out his forms, while you're …"

"… Getting myself killed. Oh, yes, I can see it's not a fair trade. Actually, he didn't shout at all. He was quite nice. Look Alex, there's no easy way I can say this - they're sending me back."

"You mean here? Why not? Where else would you go? Is he bothered about the cost?"

"No, not here. Back to France. I'm to be dropped in two days."

"That's insane! What d'you mean you're to be dropped? He can't make you do that. It would be suicide. You know that."

"If you'd only listen for once. I thought he was taking me to Baker Street. But it wasn't there. It was to some pokey little office down a side-street. I was left cooling my heels for about half an hour. Stuck in a room with paper pasted over the windows. Then he stalked back in with this big bundle of message decrypts. Chucked them down on the table in front of me. They were all from Simone."

"They couldn't be."

"He took me through them. Apart from the very first, they were all clean. No errors, no capture codes, nothing flagged at all."

"Apart from the first - you said it yourself."

"That doesn't mean much. The first message was incomplete, that's all. She forgot to send the header. There were only seconds before the allocated time ended on that frequency. She'd stopped after about ten groups. It wasn't that checks were missing, the whole message was cut off. She must have panicked. It's her first mission, Alex. Everybody agrees she's green. I've seen her picture – she looks about seventeen. Reality on the ground is never like the training, we've all had to learn that lesson ..."

"She's dead, I tell you."

"... And her French isn't wonderful. They assumed she had aborted the transmission to wait for the next scheduled time. That's correct procedure."

"*Assumed* isn't exactly convincing, is it?"

"There's more. He showed me the latest exchanges. That's after the meeting you lot had the other day. A whole series of questions. Your chum Cabot wrote them. I can't remember them all: What car does Edith drive? How many windows in the Section F store? How tall are you? When's your mother's birthday? That sort of thing. Twenty or more. All the replies were perfect, even down to her asking if one was a trick question, because there are no windows in the store. There was one she said she couldn't answer, but that somehow made it more convincing, because it was a stupid question, something anybody might forget."

"What do you want me to say? I am certain somebody is working her set. She's dead. I was there. I saw her."

"And the Major is certain that's impossible. Alex, it does look impossible - unless they own someone who can provide all that personal detail. Some of the questions are things only Simone could know." She looked away, embarrassed, "That's why I have to go back."

"Don't be ridiculous - that's not a reason. It's insane. Remember Aste? You saw me being picked up, for god's sake. They were waiting for us. Kessler confirms it."

"Confirms what? Who's Kessler?"

"The German prisoner I told you about. He's talking."

She leaned forward, suddenly alight, "There you are. Ask him about Simone. Why don't you ask him?"

Alex sat rubbing his bruised hand.

"Alex, my dear. You did ask him, didn't you? What did he say?"

"He knew she was arrested the night she landed. With her WT set. He might be lying when he says he was actually there, but ...."

She took his hand, pulling at it, "That's not the point. Does he say she's dead? Does he?"

She heard his breath, a tiny release of exasperation into the silence. "No. But that's no warrant for a suicidal operation. I'm going to see Archer. I'll stop it. I can do that, at least."

"Oh, my dear, you really can't see, can you? If you keep on saying no like this, you'll have me crying. Do I have to dot the i's, cross the t's for you?"

"Perhaps you do. Stop pretending you know best, that you always know that little bit more than me. I'm fed up of it. You know how I feel. If you go back there ... if I lose you ..."

"Poor Alex, my poor little Guffin, don't start talking about love. Don't you understand what comes first? What has to come before you can lose something?"

"I'll tell you right now I don't trust any of them. Not Archer, not even John Cabot altogether. Not now he's best buddy with some SS creep, all because he can recite Schiller. Above all, I don't trust your sainted Major."

"Oh Alex, my dear, don't you see it's the other way round? It's *you* that nobody trusts. There, I've said it. He's completely convinced you spilled everything when they captured you at Aste. That they did something to you. Either then, or sometime after. He thinks that's why the circuit has been rounded up. Oh, he's prepared to accept you can't remember, but that doesn't alter much, does it? Saying you can't remember: it isn't much of a defence is it?"

"*Defence?*"

"I have to go back because I'm the only person now standing between you and him."

"What gives him ... he has no right ..."

"But he has. If they arrest you and all you can say is you can't remember, it's not going to wash. And it is all you can say, isn't it?"

"Arrest me! Who's talking about arrest? Don't be ridiculous ..." He looked at her standing silent at the window, the distance suddenly a chasm between them, "... no, you're serious aren't you?"

"I told you they were sending me back. That isn't quite true. I asked to go. I persuaded him I can settle the matter."

"So nobody's making you? Nobody's blackmailing you? You're doing it to save my skin. Or rather to save my skin again. Do you think I'm going to let you do that?"

"Don't Alex, please don't. There's nothing you can do about it, is there? In your position I'd resent it as well. They always talk about being stuck in a web – it sounds fanciful, but that's exactly how I feel. There's something rotten about this whole enterprise. You feel it and so do I. But do you think I'm going to let them shoot you?"

"Christ, I begin to wish that girl had arrived a few minutes later. That would have solved everything."

"Don't be melodramatic. It'll be alright. It's a perfectly practical plan. I can find out about Columbine. Discover who's still free, who's talking. I'm probably the only person who can. I know the place, I have the contacts, you know that. Don't worry, there's no question of dropping anywhere within miles of Saint Aunix. They're teeing up a drop somewhere East of Toulouse. I'm to make my way only when it's safe."

"God: two days."

"From Castle Kennedy. I leave tomorrow first thing. King's Cross."

He lay alongside Mrs Perry that night thinking, not for the first time, of husbands and wives, filled with a superstitious certainty that to touch her would be for her to die. She conceded with the familiar knowing smile, muttering she was dog tired anyway and he should have brought his sword if he was going to play Tristan, then fell asleep, her quiet breathing a gentle accompaniment to footfalls in the corridor, whispered voices beyond the door, closing doors, the distant drone of lifts: all the restless secret life of hotels.

Hours later, as he stood at the window staring blindly across the Square, he saw her reach out, paddling naked arms restlessly across the blank of the sheets, searching for his hand.

She would be gone in an hour or two, perhaps this was the last night they would spend together. How easily they had accepted that thought at Torridon. Drunk with the quixotic nobility of their enterprise it had seemed almost heroic. You would lay down your life for that: give yourself away without a second thought. They must have been mad.

What had she said? You have to possess something before you can lose it. But that was a symmetry that worked for things, not for souls. Not for love. It was his turn to discover it didn't work like that. He would lose whether she thought herself his or not. In some ways, she didn't come into it at all.

"What time is it, Tristan?" He had not heard her get up, standing now behind him, pressing the warmth of her breasts against his back.

"*Grise dans le noir,*" no more than a whisper, "a little Verlaine to get you into bed. I can tell you're having mournful thoughts just by the shape of your shoulders. You are, aren't you?"

"You should be asleep. You'll get cold like that. It's quiet now. The raid's over. Mournful doesn't do my thoughts justice. Suddenly everything seems dreadfully fragile. Like walking on ice. What will I do without you?"

"Is that what you plan? It's faith you lack, little mouse. Remember when you were captured? How the man in the white hat came riding in, just before scalping time? Well, this is going to be easier."

She put her arms round his shoulders, pulling him closer. "Come to bed with me. I'll tell you a story, if you're good."

What do you do when the person you love walks away? When the person you love, remembering she's English, straightens her gloves to shake your hand, not even skin to touch, a competent brittle smile, suited to outdoors. Justine gone. Striding along rows of swinging doors, peering up at paper labels, hers not properly stuck, climbing in, the slam of her door echoing along the empty platform.

They were dreadfully early, King's Cross, a cast iron cathedral, smelling of sulphur. What do you do? Alex held on to the latticed steel of the gate, the cold searing his hand, the man at the barrier prodding his arm, *Go in mate, if you like, there's plenty of time*. Too much bother to tell him he was wrong, this chap with his friendly Porter's cap. There was no time at all. Suddenly Alex felt tired beyond belief, felt he could not keep up, the world would have to go on ahead without him. He shuffled out into the first of the weary traffic.

When he reached the TPSU it was to discover his appointment with the Major had been cancelled: a polite note in his box, the signature illegible, suggesting Wednesday.

Cabot looked as if he had been there all night. He was peeling papers out of last year's box files.

"Here - I've found one. Colonel Steffle. Born Cologne. We did three letters denouncing him, remember? You did that one from a fellow student, how he drank too much and – oh the shame of it – criticised our beloved Führer. Surely you remember him? Alex? What's up old boy?"

"Nothing. I just saw Justine onto a train. Feeling a bit *distrait*, that's all. Life's a bugger, isn't it? What about your Colonel Steffle? Yes I remember. Happy days."

"I've a whole stack of his stuff here, Birth Certificate, Medical Records, Identity Card, Army Registration, Travel Pass, the lot. Some of it's first-rate. I was just starting to add a brother. We didn't think of it at the time, but he could easily have had a brother. What do you think of Stefan? Nice name. I'd just given birth to him when I heard you on the stairs. Shall we get him baptised? What d'you think? How about June 1912. Pick a date."

"This is to be wrapped round Captain Kessler, I assume. That would make him about thirty – push it on a bit, don't make him too old. He can't be military, you realise? Archer doesn't want that."

"Absolutely. No, he was a sickly child our Stefan. He's got a medical card as long as your arm. Serious stuff. Hospitals. I was thinking of St. Elisabeth Krankenhaus, but we need to find a Sanatorium for him. Somewhere residential because I'm striking him down with TB. Can you chase a place? Not too far from Cologne. He's a Tax Inspector in the *Gastarbeitnehmer* Guest Worker racket. Enough of those are French to explain all the border crossings. He'll be as popular as the plague with that job. Left strictly alone. Exempted military service on account of the TB - I've done a Certificate about that. And a letter from his brother on the subject. Quite stiff actually, hinting he's not pulling his weight. Full of harsh words about the Nazi project. I can't see Kessler complaining. I'll get a copy of the biography typed for him to memorise. I doubt he'll ever need it, but you never know. From this day forth he's Stefan Steffle. All those sibilants - what on earth was his mother thinking of?"

They worked all day, passing drafts across the desk. By the time the inventory was finished, it was hard not to believe in the consumptive brother of this delinquent officer. It would take no more than a few days for these fictions to take on life. In a week, perhaps less, a pile of dog-eared papers would return from the forgers of Portland Place bound in a thick rubber band.

Alex stared through the window, watching black plumes of chattering starlings in the winter sky. They always seemed to wait for evening. Another day gone. Justine would be there now. Jumping down from the train, letting someone catch her, remembering it's as well to look lively. What it was to be a women in a crowd of lecherous buggers. Squeezing a spot in some ancient jeep, sharing a cigarette, capping the worst of the dirty jokes. Fending off, she called it.

Fifteen

As Alex left for his Wednesday meeting he found Archer pacing the deserted hallway, waiting for the staff car. He barred the way, clutching him by the arm.

"I'm told you've an appointment at Baker Street. I'm off to see our Hauptmann Kessler. I'll drop you off."

"Happy to walk, sir, it's no distance."

"Ah, but you'd best not walk. Rumour has it you can't walk far without villains falling on you. What's the world coming to? In Hamleys of all places. Can that be right? What took you there? No, don't say. You'd best come with me. Fear not, you'll be in good time," the flash of a complacent smile, "best not be late for a roasting. I assume that's what's on offer?"

"I was followed all the way from Abbott Court. I must say it's a mystery how they knew I'd be there."

Archer showed no sign of taking the bait, shrugging incomprehension, striding out to meet the driver.

"Trot on my boy, we've things to do."

"But you heard about the attack, sir?"

He affected not to hear, settling himself into the car, tossing his cap onto the leather shelf behind his head, tapping the glass as they pulled away.

"We'll call at Broadway Buildings first, Corporal."

They jolted to a halt, a bull neck craning round, "Beg pardon, sir, orders were to …"

"Switch the bloody engine off. Come round here."

Archer leaned over to Alex patting his knee, "It's a full time job taming these people. You'd think they had better things to do."

He wound the window down as the driver appeared.

"What's your name, Corporal?"

"Boxer, sir."

"Ah, quite so. The pugilist or canine variety?

"Couldn't say, sir."

"And is there a Mrs Boxer?"

"Sir ..."

"And little Boxers no doubt?"

"Blocking the road here, sir. Permission to move off."

"Forgotten how to salute?"

"Beg pardon, sir. You having removed your cap, sir, I thought ..."

"Given to thinking? Always a risk in the ranks, Corporal. You expect me to stand up in here?"

"Sir?"

"Orders in this car come from me, Corporal Boxer. Is that understood? Now move off, you're blocking the road here. Broadway Buildings. I believe they call themselves the Fire Extinguisher Company."

He leaned over to Alex, huge head close enough to smell something vaguely astringent on his skin, "You think anybody's taken in by that sort of thing?"

His little theatre over, the car jerked forward, Archer smiling malevolently, clicking his cigarette case open and shut, humming to himself.

"You heard the good news, I suppose?"

"What in particular, sir?"

"We don't have to put this chap Kessler through the jump course. He had ambitions to join a parachute regiment. Went through the full training at Wittstock. Got his parachute badge. So no need for Ringway. Avoids involving them."

"He still won't be familiar with our equipment ..."

"God, Vere, you find a cloud in every silver lining. Don't you realise, man, he's trained. A parachute's a parachute."

"I think the German release system is different. We went into this at Ringway. We could check."

Archer sat silently for a moment winding his window up and down a few inches, assessing the mechanism, "Hot in here. Can't see the point of heating a car, one luxury we could do without."

He peered earnestly out as they weaved through the nightmare landscape, piles of sooty brick pushed to the margins of the road, everywhere the acrid smell of burnt cloth.

"That right? ... about the release?"

"Their chutes are a bit different. Larger, I think. Not so manoeuvrable. I can work up a note on it if you like."

"Could you? Good man. Do that, will you? But I can't see it need hold us up."

"We could put it to Kessler himself, sir?"

"No. It's for us to take the decisions. Avoid complexities, that's my rule. Look, we're here," rapping ferociously on the glass with the metal ferule of his stick, "If this idiot can bring himself to stop. Off you go. Write me that note when you get back, will you?"

The Major was sitting at his desk, door wide open, sorting through piles of yellow signals traffic. He stared blankly at the figure in the doorway, recognition slow to come.

"Ah, yes, you're right. We've a meeting," waving him to a chair, holding his place with the tip of a pencil. "Sorry – slipped my mind. Still, you've picked a good time." When he finally looked up, the smile was genuine," Pull the door to, there's a good chap."

"There's very little I can add to my report, sir. If you've read it ..."

"I suppose you know we'd been thinking harsh things about you, Captain Vere. I imagine Mrs Perry told you?"

Alex started to speak, changing his mind, feeling like a tongue-tied schoolboy called in for a wigging. The Major pushed the pile of papers to one side, taking a slender file from a drawer.

"Do sit down, my dear chap. No need to look like that. It's my job to ask questions. That report ... it was a bit vague, you know. I can see that's not your fault. Jumping to conclusions – we all do it. Always a hazard in this game."

"What conclusions, sir? If I'm to be accused of anything ..."

"Nobody's accusing. It's good news for once. Mrs Perry has been on. We've got some first thoughts on your Columbine circuit. It doesn't look as dark as we thought."

Alex stared back, heart racing, lost for what to say, watching the Major idly tapping the pink folder with the end of his pencil. "You heard me, Captain? She's been in touch. Smart work, I must say. Look ... I know some of the background, personal stuff. Can't help knowing. You'll be relieved."

"Relieved doesn't cut it, sir. Thank god. No problems with the drop?"

"Problems? No, nothing at all. And not entirely god's handiwork. A clockwork operation. They do happen, you know."

"You're saying you've heard from her already?"

"Right on cue, o-six-thirty. And no fumbles, either."

"Did she ...?"

"Wait, I'll tell you what she says in a minute. It bears on these," shoving the bundle of papers across the desk, "the people in Signals put them together. Have a gander. They're all from this Simone woman. They go back weeks. In reverse order - the first's at the bottom."

"I really don't think I need to, sir. Mrs Perry told me she was convinced. I don't think my reading them would advance matters."

"Fair enough. The problem is we've a report signed off by you, saying she perished resisting arrest. Swallowed her L-pill, wasn't that it? It looks like you're going to have to wind that back."

"I can't account for it, sir. Simone is dead. How can I be wrong about that?"

"Look, it's not easy to put this. I just wondered whether you could have got confused ...we know you've not been well."

He opened the manila folder, handing Alex a single sheet torn from a message pad, "See what you make of this." A crisp sheet of yellow paper: strings of characters divided off into groups of five with slanted pencil strokes.

"Mrs Perry's, this morning. Wait a minute, I'll read you the decode: it's mercifully short. *Safe home. Claude asking cash urgent urgent. Simone safe and in good spirits. Expect reply 1325 apu. Arthur.*" Alex was staring blankly at the paper. "You see, *safe and in good spirits*. Rather settles it, doesn't it?"

Alex sat on in stunned silence, measuring Justine's words, the space around him dissolving. In some other world someone tapped the door, a face peering round, blue uniform, hands hanging onto the handle, "Sorry chief, didn't know you were occupied, I'll come back. Free later?" A subliminal nod towards Alex before the door closed.

"Can I ask, sir ..."

"Error checks? Capture codes? That's what you're going to say, isn't it? Nothing. A hundred percent clear. By the way, Perry's Morse is surprisingly good."

"She did a special course at Torridon. When the idea was being floated that couriers and WT might double up. Didn't come to much."

"I remember now. It was on her record." He leaned back, shaking a cigarette from a packet, pushing it across to Alex, grinning, "Incidentally, along with the fact she speaks German fluently. I can see she likes to tease. You might mention that when next you see her. It's still a poem code, by the way. Nothing out of the ordinary."

"I know the poem, sir. Why *Arthur*?"

"Not my suggestion. The name's not currently assigned. After that business at Aste, Marie got dropped. Too strong a supposition that whoever arrested you got wind of it. More of *Captain Vere's Consequences*, I'm afraid."

"They got nothing from me, sir."

"Nobody's denying it."

"And *apu*?"

"Yes, you're right, it's not in the book. Irritating. Another teasing eccentricity. You would know. Signals suggested *As Per Usual*: seems right in the context, if less than elegant. Leaning across to retrieve the paper, frowning as Alex held on.

"If you've finished with it, Captain Vere … it has to go back. She seems in good spirits herself. There's a certain esprit about *urgent urgent,* isn't there? This chap Barte is always complaining about money." Alex felt him pull on the slip of paper.

"Sorry sir, all a bit overwhelming. Do you think I could see the decode?"

"Couldn't resist my little bit of theatre, reading it out. Here it is."

Someone had scrawled a line of text across the top of the page, *Noire dans le gris du soir Dame souris trotte,* a faint pencil line through the first repeated letter *e*. He saw Alex frown.

"Apparently she agreed that poem at Castle Kennedy before take-off. The book's in the Code Room."

But Alex was not listening. He had known what he would see before he took the slip of paper. Had known what he would not see. A kind of dumb horror consumed him. The room was stifling hot. How could anyone work in such a place? Ticking off the pencilled words, desperate, his heart booming in his ears. The Major was right: it was short. Short enough for there to be no doubt: no doubt at all.

It wasn't there.

Staring sightlessly at the scrap of paper, Alex was watching Justine against the pillows in Russell Square. Justine lighting two cigarettes, the match flaring yellow across her body. Justine's dark voice, as quiet as death. *The word's WILL, Alex. Just right for a Guffin because that's what you need.* Him pushing her down at that, kissing her quiet, paddling the words into her flesh. *No, I'll think of Shakespeare. He's a Will.*

Staring sightlessly at the scrap of paper, Justine's sombre voice, hours later, drawing him out from sleep, his heart galloping. *You do understand, don't you, Alex? Forget error checks. Forget SOE. Forget SIS. Forget all that. If the word will isn't there, they'll have me, my love. And we're the only people in the world who know this.*

Staring sightlessly at the scrap of paper, little noises in the room filtering into his consciousness: the Major, rummaging in a drawer, pulling something out, suddenly impatient, "You seem very taken with that. Anything we haven't spotted?"

"Mrs Perry and I were very close, sir, I just ..."

"Why the past tense?" Alex felt the paper pulled free from between his grip. Shrewd eyes searching his own, benign. "My dear chap, she'll be home before you know it."

"To be honest, sir, I'm not feeling particularly well. I'm not really over that crack on the head."

"We've asked her for a full report on Columbine. She'll need time to get around, of course." Scraping his chair back, the hint of a dismissal, "That Simone business - we can sort it out later. I'll get your Colonel in on it. Mend some fences – he's rather a character." Standing now, lost for the words to speed Alex on his way, "Don't imagine we're not concerned about this memory thing. Is there nothing ...? Can you try ... rack your brains, as they say."

"It's not a case of trying, sir. But there are avenues, options. Things I've avoided so far. A doctor I knew in Netley Hospital has a clinic in London. I've been considering going back."

"... Good chap. See what you can do. You'll see someone outside waiting. Ask him to come in, would you?"

In the event, neither avenues nor options were called for. Perhaps it had been thinking of Dr Hoffmann: more likely the terrifying certainty of Justine's loss diminished everything else. The persistent torment of inaccessible memory that had dogged his life for months quietly ended. Ceased without notice, a short walk from Broadway.

He recalled passing a worn wooden bench as it came to him, close to the gates of Paddington Street Gardens. Recalled noticing a carved rebate in the wood where a brass plaque must once have been. It was then his memory returned, thinking of memorials for dead husbands. Thinking with a certain nostalgic sadness how *Lovers Remember All* went well in Latin.

More than an hour he sat, a solitary hunched figure in the drizzle, watching a Mallard duck diving for weed.

No way would they take him to the big house. Forget it, the driver said. Braking hard where a narrow track branched off on the other side of the road, leaning over Alex, sweat smelling of garlic, pushing him out, Justine's rucksack bouncing on the hard clay next to his face.

He was lying on a trodden clay path. A stone hut, barely visible among lines of neglected vines, the ground draped thick with un-pruned cords. Lingering diesel fumes gave way to something permanent: the bitter scent of pine, a Torridon smell.

He sat at the roadside, feet dangling in a dry ditch, searching through Justine's pack: Model B tucked neatly down the side, combat knife in its leather sheath, powder compact, cigarette case. And a book - cheap blue fabric, ink-stained, the cover decorated with petal doodles - Le Nouveau Testament. Justine Perry, Ecole Sainte Marie. *Round blue ink.*

The hut at the end of the path was shuttered. Let them come to you – that was the rule. You die for that mistake. He would wait. He took one of her cigarettes, leaning back against the wet grass to smoke, the exhilaration of escape fading. Time had somehow expanded, bringing a sense he had been here always. Although exactly why escaped him.

Voices were moving fast through the woods high above him, stones rattling onto the track. Men talking. Closer, it seemed only one man, an endless monologue, incomprehensible Basque echoing through the trees. Once, it stopped, replaced by some kind of drawn out whistle, as if to call a dog.

He appeared from nowhere. Leaning against a tree, very thin, deep lines etched black across his face. Breaking so abruptly from the trees Alex could do no more than roll into the ditch, Justine's rucksack open on the ground.

"If you want a password, wherever you are, I've forgotten it." The language a kind of French, words buried in ferocious Basque.

Alex stood, holding his pistol, "Stay where you are - I have you covered," blushing at the words.

The man turned to spit into the undergrowth. "So you're going to shoot me, are you? Better get off this road to do it. People coming," gazing past Alex, across to the hut, "you haven't been inside then. Very wise ... the place is full of snakes ... not so lively this time of year ..." Ignoring the pistol, walking past Alex, pushing through a tangle of brambles kicking at the door, Alex tagging breathless behind, scared he would fall and the pistol fire.

"What do you mean: people coming?"

A rank abandoned smell bowled out past them. It was dark inside, the floor piled with hurdles white with frost.

"What people coming?"

The man was picking up hurdles, stacking them, making room, holding one out to Alex straddling the outstretched pistol, a vicious grin cracking his face.

"Some bastard fascist informer. Action Française. They bring them here. Your bad luck it's today." Standing at the door, looking across the banked curtain of pine, head cocked, listening.

"We'll bury him over there,"

"What do you mean bury? Is he dead?"

The man threw a broken hurdle out of the door. As Alex turned, he felt the pistol eased from his hand, the man weighing it in his own, lodging it on a shelf over the door, changing his mind, wedging it in his belt.

"Dead? How would I know?"

They had cleared enough space to sit before they heard the first rough pinking noise of some machine painfully dragging itself up the track on the wrong fuel. A Citroen van, ribbed sides splattered with plaster, breasted the hill, barely slowing, someone pushing a large sack out of the back, jumping out alongside, thumping the side of the van.

Alex helped with the sack. Three men trailing a smear of something liquid to the crest of a bank. Soft underfoot, deep in pine needles. Ripping down the hessian, a sudden hot stench of faeces, head lolling out, the colour of ripe cheese, one unblinking eye suspended loose on milky threads of flesh. It seemed to be watching them.

No more than a boy, sixteen at most, nestling on his bed of needles. Fair hair, clotted threads, caked blood fashioning lips to a pout. Alex felt his gorge rise. If he was alive – could this thing be alive? The crotch of its trousers an open mass of raw flesh and burnt cloth.

"You know, there's life in him. That's a wonder." Probing with his boot, turning to Alex. "Here. You wanted something to shoot … he's best dead if we're to tip him out here." Pushing the pistol into his hand. "Head's best."

Scraping sacking together with his foot, "Not that they'll find him. Nobody comes up here."

Sixteen

Walking through streets heaped with the blackened remnants of other people's lives Alex had been content to lose his way, content for a while to be going nowhere.

When he reached the TPSU, Cabot was crawling across a large-scale map of France spread out on the floor of his room.

"Well timed - I've just about finished. Thought I'd look at Metz: I wasn't sure where it was exactly." He leaned back on his heels, looking up. "I was starting to think you'd been clapped in irons. Was the gentle Major not so gentle after all?"

He scooted a bundle of papers towards Alex with his foot. "There you have it: Stefan's life from his mum's pregnancy bus pass to his inglorious present. You were right about his age, by the way. Our first go would have had his mother producing him at the age of fifteen. We've shifted his date of birth. Nothing else drastic. Push that chair out of the way – it's easier on the floor."

"They made me shoot somebody." Alex realised his voice was not working properly. "Kill him, you understand? That's if he wasn't dead already. They made me. If I hadn't, I think I would have joined him down the bank. I'd forgotten all about it. Had it knocked out of me."

Cabot looked puzzled. "You're not making sense, old boy. Don't stare like that - it's unnerving. What's up?"

"You don't have a drink, do you? I've been wandering about for hours ... should have remembered you can't cut across that park anymore. The streets on the other side have all gone, just dozens of little rabbit tracks through rubble. They don't seem to go anywhere.

Just holes where the houses used to be, full of water, most of them. Where do you think the people are? Where've they all gone?"

Cabot had started rummaging inside a steel cupboard, pushing files aside. "That's the hell of a gloomy question, Alex. There's some whisky in here – my secret cache. I'll join you. Who shot who? You're being mysterious – it makes me nervous. And do stop pacing about. You're dripping on my map."

"John, you knew how my memory had gone? That there was something I'd forgotten?"

Cabot swung round, suddenly inquisitive, "My word ... you don't mean? Am I to know? You look alright. Wet, but not crushed. What's to tell?"

"I'm not sure it's a story you want to hear."

"Tell me all the same. And drink this - departmental contraband. Don't worry, we'll not see the old man again tonight. He's off to Boodles. The draw is fish pie, apparently – lucky devil. We're safe."

"No, John, we're not. Don't you ever start thinking we're safe."

"*Calme-toi, vieux pote.* Remember what Mother said - start at the beginning. I'll believe you whatever it is."

"Archer was so damned sure I had things tortured out of me. What I want to know is where did all those whispers come from? How do you think I felt about it? Why does everybody always believe the worst?"

"Not me, old lad, you know that."

"I suppose I do." Alex waited until their eyes met, Cabot painfully looking away. "All the same, the thought crossed your mind, didn't it? No need to shake your head - I know it did, because it crossed mine. I've never said this to a soul, but the truth is, when I was arrested, I knew I wasn't going to hold out long. The training just fell away, it seemed ridiculous. I'm not made of the hero kind of stuff. Why the hell didn't the people at Torridon discover that about me? It doesn't say much for psychology."

"Don't be so damned hard on yourself, Alex. You can't crucify yourself just because you imagine things. Most of us never get the chance to find out and thank god for that. I happen to think they got you about right, old man. Now … you were going to tell me. What was it you'd forgotten? Nothing so very vital, I'll bet."

"Well it wasn't war, John. Whatever else it was, it wasn't war."

"I still don't know what you're talking about."

As Alex described the body in the sack, Cabot seemed curiously unmoved, his expression no more than distaste. He got up, pulling the blackout across, pausing for a moment to look down into the street, resting with his back against the cloth. With the curtains drawn, the stuffy little room seemed to close in on them. "I thought revenge killings had stopped. If this boy really was an informer, there'd be reprisals."

"You really think those people care about reprisals? So far as they're concerned, if you aren't fighting fascists you deserve everything you get. Anyway I only had their say-so he was an informer. He was just a boy. There were knife marks on him. Cuts. And he'd been shot to wound, not to kill."

"It's alright, Alex, *we know there's a war on*. I quote our leader. Of course, what Archer really means is we're not going to see any of it. The real stuff is somewhere else."

Alex reached down for the bundle of papers on the floor, snapping the rubber band against them. "This is our war, isn't it?"

They sat on, neither speaking, hearing a solitary car creep past in first gear, feeling its way round the square.

"Did I tell you they make you kill a sheep at Torridon?" Alex felt a sudden urge to shock. "So that you know what fresh blood is like on your hands." Cabot's impassive face was barely visible across the darkened room. "I managed it as well. I remember thinking it would be the real enemy next. The poor dumb brute wouldn't have died for nothing. But it wasn't the real enemy was it? Just some schoolboy who'd found himself the wrong friends." Cabot said nothing. "They kept shouting his father supported the chap who banned the Communist Party."

"Daladier."

"Like father like son, they said. That made him a collaborator. I don't think they knew what they were on about. They were laughing at me ... laughing at all of us, I suppose. The stupid bloody bourgeoisie ushering in their revolution."

Cabot walked into the light from the desk, "I'm not sure I want to hear about the politics of France, Alex. Not right now. Not after that story."

"Politics didn't come into it. They kept going on about how the rich bastards would get what was coming to them, how it was better in Russia. Why are we fighting their cause, John? Tell me - I've forgotten."

"Our enemy's enemy, isn't that it?" He shrugged, "I've always thought there was a flaw in that."

"I mean why's Justine fighting their battle? She doesn't want a revolution. I would have packed all this in, you know, if it wasn't for her. Joined a fighting unit, done something useful. I'd do it now if she wasn't ... if they hadn't ... Justine's worth more than this madness. Don't you realise, every single person we work for is crooked."

"You mean Archer? Cunning, maybe – I'm not sure about *crooked*."

"I wanted to go to war, John. That's what I thought at Torridon. Fight the good fight ... like all those chaps getting killed right now. I've ended up in a kind of bureau of madness. Justine is the one island of sanity in all this."

Cabot reared back, tutting in mock indignation, "Not very friendly, old boy."

"And you, of course ... I meant you." Alex forced a smile, "You're sane. God be praised nobody's pressing you to go a-fighting. You're the only straight person in this damnable outfit."

"Nice of you, old man." Cabot slumped into the chair behind his desk, pulling his glasses off, shuffling papers to find a space for them. "Now look what you've gone and done? I'm embarrassed." He looked up, his face pink, "You're a nice chap, Alex. What made the good Lord wish that buffoon Archer on the likes of us? As for your French thugs, I'd put them right out of your mind ... sorry ... unfortunate turn of phrase there. Honestly though, right now revolution's the last thing France wants."

"I'm ashamed to be part of it all the same. You know Justine's gone back?"

Cabot stared at him. "No I didn't know. How's that? What about, *Once captured never returned*? I thought that rule was infrangible?"

"It was me that was captured – she wasn't. They decided she was best placed to find out about Columbine. Who's *they*, John. Why don't we ever get told who *they* are?"

Cabot started folding up his map, stacking it alongside bundles of paper, yawning, "Never drink whisky after midnight. Look, I have to go home. I'm done for. You know what I'd do in your place, Alex? Tell Archer what you've told me – the whole story. That'll put an end to his endless digs about you blabbing secrets. Anybody can see why you wouldn't want to remember something like that. I'd be the same. Worse actually, because I can't stand blood - you'd not get me killing sheep. That's what I'd do. Bamboozle him with how this psychology stuff works. No, don't smile ..."

"Poor old Cabot. You think I've been suffering from psychological repression, don't you? Like some character in a Buñuel film. No such luck my dear chap. I was hit over the head. Probably a fracture. Don't look so crest-fallen. I hadn't finished my story. You remember they were supposed to get me to a safe house?"

Cabot nodded wearily. "Yes, I think so ..."

"They refused to take me. I was left tied up in the hut while they stood outside arguing the toss whether to cut my throat or not."

"Why on earth?"

"The one who'd brought the sack knew I was connected in some way with *The Englishwoman*. He meant Justine. He said he knew she was a traitor. Then they started arguing. The last thing I remember was this big chap coming back into the hut. He had a rock in his hand."

Cabot winced, screwing his eyes up.

"Next thing, I'm lying on my back in a boggy field peering into the blue eyes of a Lysander pilot and wondering who I am. I was slipping in and out of consciousness. He got me on board somehow, bless him. That's how I ended up in Netley hospital with a cracked skull. It's called anterograde amnesia - common enough. Look, don't go yet. Stay with me for a bit, will you, John?"

"Of course. You don't look too good, you know. A bit green about the gills."

Alex stared sightlessly through him, seeing only dawn bringing steel-grey light to the hotel room, the morning Justine confirmed their pact. Ever since, the certainty she was lost had tormented him like an untended wound.

"I have to go back, John. You don't understand. She wouldn't be there if it wasn't for me."

"Go back to France? You know that's impossible."

"I have to. I'll have to tell SIS she's been captured."

Cabot leaned forward, "*Captured?* Who said anything about captured? Are you sure you're alright, Alex?"

As Alex began to explain their secret pact, Cabot got up to close the door, shutting out the faint light from the corridor. The room was very still. "You can't tell them that, Alex. You know what they think about private codes. They'll say she forgot about it."

"No, you don't understand. It was something between the two of us. We ..."

"Let me finish. Agents come up with private codes all the time."

"Do they?"

"It's common knowledge. Chaps hoping to get a message to the little woman back home, that sort of thing. Of course, once the mission's started they forget all about it. And Baker Street gets pestered by demented women convinced poor Jack's been captured.

What evidence have you got she's captured? Hard evidence? Did she send a standard capture code?"

"No, no, nothing like that. That was the reason we agreed on something private. Hell, what can I say? The last thing I expected was you not believing me. I'm lost. She couldn't have forgotten. And don't look at me like that … I don't need your blasted sympathy."

Cabot stood polishing his spectacles, blinking vacantly into the darkened room, lips silently shaping something useful to say.

"The trouble is it involves leaving something out … there's no difference between her sending your code and forgetting to send it." He checked, looking hard at Alex, "You see what I mean?"

"Of course. D'you think we didn't realise that? You're forgetting her message. You're forgetting what she said. She said she'd seen Simone. That can't be true. That's why I'm sure."

"God almightly, Alex! What do you want me to say? You want to use the best evidence we have that Simone is alive as proof that she's dead. Don't you see the mess that will get you into? Me as well, if I start backing you up. We'll get ourselves arrested. Archer's capable."

"Justine went back on my account. She knew she was going to be betrayed and went all the same. For nothing. Have you any idea how that makes me feel? What can I do? I'll go mad if I don't do something. God man, I love her …"

The telephone on the desk burst into life, Cabot turning aside, embarrassed. He let it ring, guiltily dropping the whisky bottle into the wastepaper basket, lifting the receiver, tracing damp lines with his fingertip where his glass had been.

A familiar tinny voice rattled into the quiet room, Cabot looked at Alex, steadying his voice. "No, he's not actually. Not now … I don't know … yes, tomorrow … yes, I'll tell him … righty-ho, let me get a pencil … go ahead …"

An impatient click cut across him as he finished scribbling.

"That was Signals at Baker Street. The Major left orders you were to be told when Mrs Perry acknowledged today's message. She did. Half an hour ago. He particularly wanted you to know."

"They gave you her message?"

"It's short. *Await silk delivery. Will confirm with Barte.* That's it, apart from headers. *Silk?* What's that about?" Not exactly loquacious, is she?"

Alex walked home in the rain, a single word drumming in his head. To fall into bed in a kind of feverish stupor, the night filled with restless dreams of Justine below his window, staring up, her expression indecipherable, an eternity of darkness behind him. He woke drenched in sweat, still hearing the echo of her voice.

He would not sleep again that night: heaving himself up in the bed for a better sight of nothing, praying she would sell his name cheap. Praying for the consolation of betrayal, the dark city beyond the window filled with intermittent sounds of war. It seemed unbearably alien. She had taken some indefinable part of him with her.

The next morning he picked a way to the TPSU through empty streets still dark, smelling of half-burnt gas.

The charwoman in Archer's room looked startled as he passed the door, hastily dropping a cigar back into its box, scuttling out.

He finished the report on German parachute design, one ear cocked for the thump of boots on the wooden stairs.

It was well past ten before Archer appeared, peering loftily through the open doorway, moustaches at the ready, immaculate in thornproof tweed, a tiny rosebud decorating his lapel. He carried a raincoat over his arm.

"Come along to my room, will you Vere. When you've a moment. Your chap Kessler's kicking up. What are you sitting there for? Chop chop. Things to do."

Alex followed him along the corridor. Handed the raincoat, he went to hang it on a hook, only to have it snatched away, Archer wielding a wooden coat hanger like a sabre,

"Know what this is? Never use one? We'd best go to *Records*. Something I want to say."

He had a curious mincing gait, lifting each foot a little too high as if he might slip. He closed the door behind him, his voice adopting its confidential register, a kind of stentorian whisper.

"Kessler says he wants more time. The man knows perfectly well we don't have more time: the moon's in two days. He thinks if he stalls, that's another month gone. I'm not having it," Bewildered watery eyes gazed round the tiny space, "Now … what are you here for?"

"You asked me to come, sir." Archer looked doubtful. "Although actually there was something I wanted to raise with you …"

"I remember now. I went through the briefcase. You two did a decent job. There you are – praise when it's due. A decent job, given the notice. You'll have more time with the next, of course."

Alex winced as his arm was grabbed. "You were going to write something about parachutes. Where is it?"

"Done sir. I just need to tidy it up. But if Kessler completed the parachute course at Wittstock, he'll know about British designs. The Luftwaffe actually copied them: they thought ours were better. We used to sell them to the Germans before the war. Funny to think they're using our kit. But if he says he doesn't know, he's lying."

"He hasn't raised the matter. It was you started that particular hare."

"It was worth checking he could jump with our gear. And he can. The papers were ready yesterday, sir. There's just the border pass. It has to have a date stamp. If there's a delay …."

"There'll be no delay. He's going whether he likes it or not. Thinks he can play games. Look, it's hot in here. Why did you bring me in here?"

He pushed his way out, prancing along to his room, calling over his shoulder, "I'm going to Abbott Court when my car gets back. To tell him he'll go when I say. Now … what did you want? Can't it wait? I've a lot on at the moment."

Of course, the request to go back to France was dismissed. But in a minor key, merely a hint of impatience. Hurrying down the stairs, Archer had listened to the story of the body in the sack, struggling into his overcoat, barely suppressing a smile, perhaps remembering some similar distant exploit of his own.

"These things happen." He held up a massive hand, hairs sprouting from stubby sausage fingers, "Changes nothing. Gratifying you've coughed it all up at last. We'd been wondering when you'd get round to that. Can't change the fact you were seen. Seen and docketed. Reason enough to keep you here."

He walked out onto the steps, shouting over his shoulder, "And you're wrong about that WT woman. She's alive and kicking. Alive and in good spirits."

"If you accept Mrs Perry's message at face value."

Archer skidded to a halt, turning back inside, breath hanging in clouds of mist, blurring his face. "You'd try the patience of Job, Vere. The answer's no. No today, and it'll be no tomorrow. Understood?"

"Have I your permission to ask the people at Broadway? They might take a different line … interpret the case differently …"

"No, you bloody well don't have my permission. Not that that will stop you. Come here."

Alex felt a finger stabbing his chest, orchestrating the words, "You go skulking round behind my back – *prod* - consorting with that SIS lot – *prod* - and you get no more favours from me."

The final prod met vacant air as Alex stepped back.

"Forget it Vere, you'll get nothing out of them except grief. They'd veto their own granny. You're needed here. Understood? And I want that bloody parachute report on my desk. Ah, there's my car."

Seventeen

Alex approached SIS about going back, any pleasure in this defiance of Archer blunted by the discovery that they already knew about his recovered memory. It was infuriating: some subterranean current seemed to flow through this shabby building, information materialising by a kind of osmosis.

The Major had heard about the body in the sack, even adding his own colourless recital of the event. How he had come by all this? Surely not Cabot? But if not Cabot there was only Archer, and informing his enemy, even to secure a petty advantage, breached every principle the old fool held dear.

The fact remained, the well had been poisoned long before Alex could drink at it, the futility of his request so plain he barely listened, mulishly staring at the wood-block pattern of the lino.

"Your Colonel didn't like it, you know that? You asking to see me."

"He knew I was making the request, sir."

The Major's smile was genuine. "You make a decent spy, Vere. Lying with the truth. Didn't someone tell me you were studying that? The psychology of lying. No, *lying's* a bit strong. How about *evading*?"

"I'm not sure I understand."

"I think you do. Did Colonel," scrabbling for a piece of paper on his desk, "did Colonel what's-his-name ...?"

"Archer, sir."

"Yes. Did Colonel Archer refuse you permission to return – yes or no?"

"Yes ..." regretting the peevish tone, Alex felt like a schoolboy caught out in a lie, adding - because the smile had not yet been completely withdrawn - "but he said he knew I'd ask."

The Major began pushing his pen across the desk in an unconscious gesture, releasing it to let the tilt of the surface roll it back to his hand. He must have done it a thousand times before.

"D'you know what day it is?"

"Friday."

"No, not that. It's Christmas Day, can you believe it?"

"I'm afraid it passed me by. Too many things on."

"What makes you think I've the authority?" Alex recognised it - a sheet of TPSU letterhead under the Major's thumb, familiar purple scrawl filling the page. "What makes you think it's for me to say yes?"

"It was something the Colonel said a while ago ..." Too late to call the words back, Alex cursed himself.

"And what would that *something* be?" the Major's face suddenly bleak, "there's a damn sight too much loose talk about. And your setup's the worst."

"I meant he knew his refusal would not stop me asking. It seemed to me he was inviting ... or at least not expressly forbidding. Perhaps I was reading too much into it."

The Major turned the sheet over. Florid purple ink filled both sides. He stared vacantly at it, perhaps wondering how it came to be in his hand, the same calculating expression Alex had seen that day they had raided Archer's office.

Noises from elsewhere in the warren beyond the door filtered into the room: feet hurrying past in the corridor, muffled telephones, the hurried irregular clack of typewriters. Far away, the mechanical chatter of a teleprinter surged out as a door opened. All about them a steady hum of life, the murmur of bees. It seemed improbable, but this was what it came to - the prosecution of war. War on Christmas Day.

The Major folded the letter, sliding it back into its envelope. "He had rather decided views about your arrest in France – your Colonel."

Alex glanced at the envelope. "Yes sir."

He looked up, "Not altogether dispelled. But if it will relieve your mind, I can tell you we do want you to go back. God knows why that would be a relief to anybody. There's more risk than usual at the moment, as you're well aware. I've told Colonel Archer you fly down as part of his *Operation Alathea*, that business with the briefcase. You can keep his prisoner company down to Metz. After that we'll take you West, drop you near Saint Aunix."

"Saint Aunix. We're sure that's secure, sir? I'm thinking of Kessler's story."

"Not dropping blind, of course not. They're laying on a reception committee. You're a land Surveyor – a local *arpenteur-géomètre* checking last year's crop records. Name, Georges Harcourt. Not much going on this time of the year, I doubt you'll have much talking to do. You won't be there long enough." He tapped Archer's envelope.

"Your Colonel did agree, by the way. Can't say he was overjoyed, but he agreed ... eventually." He looked up, the smile suddenly friendly, "That's that then. Surprised?"

Alex was no longer listening. For days his every waking moment had been spent with Justine, watching her life trickle away alongside his own, his head filled with a mindless chatter of prayer. Godless prayers that she might live, knowing well enough it was better she should die. Knowing the best he could hope was to die with her. Staring at the Major, overwhelmed by a sense of hypocritical betrayal he wanted to scream, *She's captured, damn you. Don't you realise? She's a dead woman. Damn you all.*

"I fear you're not with me, Captain. I asked does the decision surprise you?"

For a second Alex could not place the voice against the blare of his thoughts, the Major leaning across the desk towards him, face lined with fatigue, glancing from his watch to the door – the rituals of dismissal.

Perhaps, after all, now was the time to confide? Explain his certainty Justine was captured. Explain how the Major's acquiescence in his return sealed his own fate. He felt words spilling towards his lips. "Sorry sir, I was thinking of something else. No, not surprised really. Obviously two would be better for a job like that. It's what I was briefed to do first time round ... when I was captured. We need to get to the bottom of Hauptmann Kessler's story about Columbine ... and Mrs Perry is alone."

"She's hardly alone, is she? She has her WT with her. I'm afraid this Simone is not going to forgive you, the way you insist on killing her off. You're still doing it."

He had returned to his pen: rolling it, catching it, rolling it, catching it, the hint of a smile. "But you're right. You'll have your work cut out. We need the full story - not Mrs Perry's enigmatic signals - understood? We'll get you back in a couple of days. You report direct to me."

Archer now spent his days at Abbott Court. He had taken over Kessler's interrogation, obsessively determined to sift the truth from the story of circuit penetration. The day after the decision to send Alex back, he burst into Cabot's room demanding to know which cabinet in *Records* was allocated to Captain Vere. Finding nothing more sinister than three French newspapers he had ripped them into small pieces, leaving a heap of torn shreds on the floor. An angry monologue in what might have been Hungarian ended abruptly as Cabot came to investigate.

The following morning Alex arrived to meet Archer descending the steps to his waiting car. He was cut dead. Thereafter, orders came through Cabot, although confirmation of his dismissal made further orders irrelevant. This was delivered by dispatch rider from Abbott Court on TPSU notepaper: a transfer to Baker Street *pending operational duties*. A scrawled addendum in Archer's purple hand pointing out that access to the TPSU was strictly restricted to staff assigned duties in the building. The word *strictly* had been so heavily underlined it had punctured the paper.

Cabot helped Alex clear his desk then left for the British Library, saying he wanted to look at something – anything - that wasn't forged.

Alex had made no effort to put any kind of personal stamp on his allotted room. Divested of weeks of accumulated clutter it had returned to its aboriginal state. Even the original smell was creeping back: something dry and papery, like musty biscuits.

Since he had nowhere to go and time on his hands, he pulled a chair to the window and sat looking down into Bedford Square, forehead pressed against the glass. A grey staff car had drawn up, the Major emerging to help a young woman out of the passenger door. They stood for a moment talking then parted, exchanging a double kiss in the French manner.

She stood on the pavement looking tentatively into the stairwell directly below where he sat. Dressed in a long black raincoat, the belt fashionably tied round her waist in a knot. Realising she was overlooked, her face tipped up, large eyes meeting his own. She made no pretence of looking away, raising a gloved hand, almost a wave, as if to keep him at his station.

It was not long before light footsteps brought her to his door.

"Captain Vere? You are Captain Vere, aren't you? Can you spare me a few minutes? I was told I might find you."

He had forgotten about perfume. Justine rarely wore it. A dark musky scent had come into the room with this woman. She seemed to be in mourning: even her hat with its tiny silver pin was black. As she shook his hand, he was conscious only of something cold, feather-light, barely touching his skin. An aura of gaunt vulnerability surrounded her.

"I'm Lucile Beyrou. Possibly Mrs Perry mentioned me to you? She came to Dundee to see me. I wondered whether she was here … I gather she's not."

Alex came across the room half barring the way, the gesture bringing a faint smile.

"How on earth did you find this place? I'm sorry Mrs Beyrou, but I have to ask. It's not exactly public. How did you find …?"

"Oh, I asked around. TPSU. Nobody knows what the letters mean."

"But asked around who? I'm not sure you should be here."

"I'm sorry. I'm being dreadfully rude. I know someone who told me where to come. He said I shouldn't tell, but you must have seen him. I saw you watching."

"You mean the Major?"

"Is that what you call him? He's my brother." Her eyes were unsettling, somehow belying her voice, challenging him to contradict her.

"I remember we got you out of France last November. He never mentioned you were related … no reason he should, of course. Somebody said you're an artist. You'll have to forgive me …"

"It's quite alright, you can say it: you've never heard of me." Smiling, she suddenly seemed years younger, almost pretty. "To tell you the truth, I've never heard of me either. I'm incognito for the duration. Silly, I know, but there you are. But I don't need to tell you about secrets, do I? The point is, I've been lucky enough to find you."

"Luckier than you realise. This is my last day." He stepped back, pulling a chair out from the desk.

She shook her head. "No, I won't stay. It was just a message."

"I knew Mrs Perry had met you. You appreciate there's very little I can say about that."

"Oh, I'm not here for secrets. I wanted to tell her I knew I wasn't very helpful when she came to Dundee. I'm sorry about that. She caught me at a bad time. I've come to make amends. Too late. Funny, isn't it? Amends are always too late. Perhaps you can give her a message?"

"I'm not sure I can."

"She came to ask me what I knew about that explosion." Seeing his expression change, she checked, "It's alright, I know you can't talk about it. I can't, either. Different reason. I meant to tell her that I feel responsible. I'll carry that to my grave. You see, one of the men who was killed … one of the men they sent out to bring me back was my brother. "

"Your brother? But you said …"

"I had two brothers. Stuart was the pilot they sent to get me out. They'd sent him in case persuasion was necessary, I suppose. Anyway, I'm the reason he ended up in that damned car."

She pulled a cardboard box from her bag, placing it in his hand. "That's where we've been. To a sort of ceremony. It's Stuart's medal. You can look, if you like."

The box was tiny, the lid embossed with a Fleur de Lys in lurid yellow. Alex prised it open. Something like a freshly minted copper penny lay inside on a bed of cotton wool.

"The ceremony was in a church off Leicester Square. I'd never noticed the place before – jammed between shops. It's been bombed but they're putting it to rights. Catholic. I suppose that's natural, being French."

Watching Alex struggle with the lid, she retrieved the box.

"Ian said it was best I keep it: it's not much is it?" Seeing him frown, she tried again, a tiny smile, "My brother … your Major. He doesn't believe it was an accident, you see - he's certain somebody intended to kill Stuart." Her voice breaking, there was something shocking in her passivity, outstaring him, dark eyes welling tears. "I don't understand … war ought to be about more than things like this."

Alex looked away, embarrassed. "If it was his job to rescue you, I don't think you were responsible for anything. You should put your mind at rest on that score."

"When Mrs Perry came to Dundee I couldn't understand her interest. I told her what I knew but she must have thought I was demented. It sounded so melodramatic. The truth sometimes sounds bigger than you intend, don't you think? I mean when it comes to other people … sorry … I'm not making much sense."

"No, I understand perfectly." He sounded so vehement she leaned back. "You see, I know Justine Perry. I know her very well."

"I didn't recognise her, you know. Not at first. Then I did. She was standing in my studio looking at me and I suddenly remembered her on that aeroplane. That same look. It made me ashamed. I'd never been in an aeroplane before. I was terror-stricken. She was so perfectly calm in the middle of that hell. I remember thinking I'd never seen anything so brave."

"Oh, there are braver things than that."

Eighteen

Three days later, Alex walked from the station to the gates of Tempsford Airfield. He was directed to yet another stately home, operational briefings being now conducted at Hazell's Hall, a damp Palladian country seat, an inconvenient distance from the airfield.

He was never to discover who believed carved panelling, draughty bedrooms and alabaster cornices were adequate consolation for the certainty of death. Hazells's Hall, being truly ancient, was inevitably less impressive than the fake Scottish pile at Torridon, but raw timber and new concrete walls served the same brutal purpose in both. It exuded a desperate air of make-do, a ramshackle conversion completed with almost vindictive incompetence, reeking of unsound drains. Dusty shrubs lined a driveway scored with lorry tracks. In the entrance, chequered marble was littered with the final stubbed cigarettes of numberless departing men.

It was a pity. Memories of Tempsford had been charged with a magical sense of high endeavour, one recollection above all: the sight of Justine stepping from her jeep, bringing a dissolution of dread. That single frosty moonlit night, filled with indefinable exultation, had determined the course of his life.

He spent the best part of a day pacing aimless corridors waiting for his briefing, the truth gradually dawning that he was so incidental to any operation, he had been overlooked. When finally called, the affair was scandalously perfunctory. Half expecting the Torridon Major, he found a flustered Captain from Signals hurriedly sent down from Donnington sitting alone in an empty room. He was spreading the contents of his briefcase across a dusty table like a salesman.

"Sorry, old man," hardly daring to look up, "got drafted into this ... not my usual game." He consulted a slip of paper like a prompt card, "Captain Vere, is it?"

"Actually I've been Georges Harcourt, since I reported. If you look at the log. Still ..."

"Right-ho ... sorry. You've to hand over your paperwork. There's a bundle of printed silks to be collected with your kit. You know about them - ready-made code keys? You've been told?"

"I was told I'd be carrying them. Nobody seemed all that interested. It's a change from when I was here last."

Relieved of the burden of explaining, the Captain relaxed, "Point is, you don't need to know. It's the WT needs to know."

He picked up a tiny paper package. "Here. To give you an idea of the size," pulling from his pocket a square of silk folded to a thumbnail of nothing like an amateur conjuror.

"Neat, eh?" Laying it down unfolded – line after line of black print, letters, numbers, an exquisite calligraphic pattern. "No more of your poem codes. That means no more undecipherables our end ... or at least fewer of them. You've no idea the errors those poems threw up. All that transposition – I can't see how you put up with it."

Alex was about to say they hardly had a choice when he realised the Captain was lost in thought, head bowed, spreading the silk across his hand. "Here, I'll show you. You take your line, cut it off and there's your key. Use it, burn it. Secure as a one-time pad." He pocketed it before Alex could speak.

"One thing, though. Mind you tell him to cut it carefully. It has to be scissors, you understand – otherwise the silk unthreads and you're in queer street. They're working on it."

Alex was thinking of an end to *Dame souris*, trying not to think of how you were supposed to conceal scissors. Perhaps that would be easier for a woman. "It's not a him, actually. The WT. It's a woman."

"Right … right you are. No, I didn't know that," eyes nervously raking the empty room as if he half expected her to appear. "Well, she'll tell you all you need to know."

Shaking out a cigarette and lighting it, he held the packet out to Alex, suddenly remembering something, diving back into the briefcase, blushing scarlet. "And this. I'm to give you this. They said you'd be *au fait*. There's a new one. It's blue. You're to keep it apart – but you'll know that. A quick-acting sedative. Poison at that dose. They said you'll know where to keep it. God, the world you chaps live in."

The tiny tin was flat as a button, the colour of lead. Alex squeezed it into his palm. "Yes, that's alright. *Au fait's* the word."

The Captain was already snapping the catch of his briefcase closed, pausing to look at tatty posters pinned to the walls, scraping his chair back, launching himself unsteadily upright.

"If the safe house is no go, keep away from the church … Wait a sec, I need to check," retrieving the slip of card from his pocket, "*The hotel in Saint Aunix – ask for Jules.* That's what it says. That's your last resort."

"You mean *Le Sport*? You're not going to tell me to order a coffee?"

"Coffee?" He peered at the card, puzzled, shut out of a private joke. "No, nothing about coffee. Oh, I'd forgotten how you fellows go on … sorry. No it just says make for the hotel, not the church. You're to ask to speak to Jules. Wait to be contacted. He ought to identify himself with a passphrase … it's in French, not my strong suit – here, you read it."

"*Ô bruit doux de la pluie.* It's alright – it's somebody's idea of a joke."

"It says exercise extreme caution - I don't imagine you'll have to. *Last Resort* - sounds a bit dramatic. I'll be off then. Your stuff's at the barn. The driver will take you."

"The barn?"

"Farm buildings. Gibraltar Farm they call it. Fake, of course, but damned convincing. I've seen the aerial shots."

"I hope the plane's not fake."

"It's where you're kitted out ... oh, right ..., sorry," pausing a beat too late, concocting a smile as he caught up, "you'll have to forgive me ... I've not done one of these before ... I suppose it shows. Bread and butter to you chaps, seen it all a dozen times I dare say. Look, is there more you need to know?"

Discovering he was staring at a poster about venereal disease, he scooped up his briefcase, scattering papers across the floor.

"What do I do now? What's usual?"

Alex collected the debris and stood up. "Shake hands, I suppose. Wish me luck. That's usual."

Take-off twenty-three hundred - earlier than last time. Everything was filled with last time. No frost, though, just a chill settling clammy on your face. Alex stood in the hangar mouth looking at the phosphorescent blur of a full moon above the trees, risking a final cigarette, remembering Justine hugging him on this spot, stuffing her rucksack with cash, grinning like an excited schoolgirl.

It had started to rain, grey clouds bowling up from the West. As the first engine of the Hudson coughed painfully to life, faint streamers of yellow light came glinting across lying water on the grass.

Suddenly aware of someone behind him he turned, his heart jolting. But that was last time. This WAAF, awkwardly saluting, was not Justine.

"I'm your transport, sir. Jeep's over there. Anything I can help with? You're not to smoke here, sir. Although ...."

"No, you're right," tossing it onto the grass, watching the red end refuse to die.

"Just me in the jeep?"

"There's a bit of a hitch with the others. I'm to drive you across. Get you aboard the bus," an embarrassed pause, "that's what he said – the CO."

"Things wouldn't be normal without a hitch. How many others?"

Dumping his pack into the jeep, her glance back across the apron was oddly precise, the pause a fraction too long.

"Couldn't say, sir."

Alex followed her eyes, his hand wet on the handle of the door. A huddle of uniformed men was silhouetted in the mouth of the hangar. The Major – it could only be him – was stepping round puddles, sparing his shoes, pausing to stoop over something bundled on the ground.

Standing a little apart, huge in a calf-length greatcoat, another shadow loomed across the asphalt: barrel-chested, florid cheeks shaded white with protruding fuzz. Archer turned away as their eyes met.

"Wait a sec, will you? That's my Colonel."

"Orders were to …" but her voice was already blown away.

The Major shook his hand. "Came down to see you off, Vere." He was unaccountably lost for more to say, patting his pocket, searching vainly for cigarettes he could not smoke.

"We've had confirmation of your reception committee, by the way. But you'll get the gen on board," looking across to the jeep, "that your transport? Don't keep her waiting."

"If I'm to go down with Hauptmann Kessler, perhaps I'd better wait."

"No, you push on. We'll see to the prisoner. Best get you on board. Get you settled. Flight will explain things."

"You're not flying, sir?"

"Me? God, no! But I wanted to be in on this." His voice rose to pull the sulking Archer in. "Something to remember, wouldn't you say, Colonel?"

But Archer was not to be drawn. Ignoring the Major, he cast a full cigarette into the darkness, watching it arc down to the grass.

"Step aside Vere, would you?" Alex felt himself steered into the darkness, his elbow gripped, fingers squeezed hard against the bone, intending to hurt.

Away from shelter, rain fell in angled lines across the shaded lights at the hangar's rim.

"Got your own way, then?" closer now, bringing the smell of whisky, chiselled English accent, always slightly phoney, hot in his ear.

"What the hell makes you think you have special rights? Just asking. For my information, you understand." As Alex pulled away the grip tightened above his elbow, fingers wriggling hard against the bone. "Stand still, man. D'you imagine I didn't know your game?"

For a fatal second Alex stiffened, thinking of Justine. How the hell could he know that? Archer sensing something, rearing back, mad ox eyes searching his face.

"You and that man Cabot, sneering all the time." He was speaking in a ferocious stage whisper, flecks of spittle on his breath. "Think I don't know?"

Alex wrenched his arm free. Hearing Archer grunt, the WAAF stepped back into the dark. "I understood you agreed this mission, sir. And with respect, I'm no longer attached to the TPSU. Your orders ..."

"Respect! You don't know what respect is. Creeping about behind my back. I specifically ordered you ... you're a bloody menace, Vere. If it was my decision I'd have had you locked up, you understand? But ... it's not ... it's not ..." Teetering absurdly on tiptoes, scouring the field beyond the jeep, Archer's words petered out.

As Alex turned away, a new grievance swept over him. "Don't walk off like that when I'm talking. Stay where you are. I'll just say this. Raise a finger against my operation and by god ... by god ..."

Exceeding crafty. Thinking of Cabot's phrase, Alex understood why this manic display left him unmoved. There was something absurd about passion bellowed out to no purpose. It was all he could do not to laugh in the old fool's face - the man really was ridiculous. Or was there, after all, a purpose? Alex had an uncomfortable feeling this display served some end, although god alone knew what or why.

For some time he had been dimly conscious of the group of men at the hangar piling gear into the back of a jeep on a kind of improvised litter. They had scrambled on board, the driver gunning the engine.

Archer stood watching their lights bounce over the field, tracing a pattern in the wet grass with his toe, fumbling for his cigarette case, accepting the lighter Alex held out.

"About going behind your back, sir ... " Archer blinked, puzzled to find Alex still there. "About SIS, sir ..."

"You'll have to excuse me, Vere. I really can't stand about chewing the fat with you all night. That young woman's waiting. You do realise you're holding things up?"

He installed himself in the back seat of the jeep, tapping the shoulder of the WAAF to move off, Alex scrambling onto the wet leather alongside, fumbling to close the door.

Glancing across, he saw she was smiling.

At the waiting Hudson, two mechanics were abandoning efforts to push something at head height through the open door. Not an improvised litter, after all: a standard army stretcher tied with bands in three places down its length. Hopelessly too wide for the door.

Keep back a minute if you would, sir, the Sergeant from Abbott Court moved across, barring his way. Beyond, a tall figure in RAF uniform staring at something on the ground: the MO from Abbott Court, it seemed, was a Wing Commander.

The Major called across, irritated, "Bear with us a moment, Vere. Weren't you to be boarded first?"

"Can I help, sir? A medical case?"

"Not really," the ambiguity of his reply shutting Alex out.

Archer pushed past, staring defiantly at the Major, an unhealthy flush on his skin, jutting face oddly demonic. He seemed unfamiliar with embarrassment. This must have been the reason for the pantomime at the hangar - he had taken it on himself to hold Alex back while the stretcher was boarded. He had not considered the door.

Two sweating bearers finally yanked the stretcher out, cabin lights falling on a red blanket as it snagged back. Hauptmann Kessler, a waxy sheen on his face, lay peaceful in death, strangely impressive in uniform. An oval badge had been pinned to his lapel: a swooping eagle clutching a swastika, glinting yellow in the cabin lights. This German parachutist dressed for war was surely no tubercular clerk. His right arm had been braced under the top-most band, a briefcase chained to his wrist, the tiny handcuff an effeminate affair in mottled tortoiseshell.

They had him unstrapped at last, running the blanket underneath, shipping him easily into the waiting arms of the crew.

Alex turned to find the MO at his side.

"Bad do." He turned away to cough, glancing at Archer, receiving a savage glare in return. As the MO dropped his voice, Archer leaned closer.

"And if you're going to ask, my advice is don't. About responsibility I mean. If you're going to ask who's to blame."

The Sergeant was steering Alex to the foot of the steps, the MO tugging at his sleeve. Shaking the Sergeant off, Alex turned to look back at a brief pinprick of light near the hanger, conscious of an inexplicable sense of menace. Nothing but distant shapeless forms against a blur of rain.

"He bullied us into it … your Colonel." Rain on the MO's face fell like tears.

"Mind you, written orders, full medical authority. I've kept them … I've kept them alright! Kept saying he wanted the truth. All available means to be used."

"You're talking about Kessler?"

Alex saw the Sergeant stride across to Archer, watched him salute, erect in the pelting rain. "I helped plan this operation with Mr Cabot. The two of us did it all. Cabot's not here, but I can tell you there's something dreadfully wrong. Kessler can't drop like that. The paperwork for one thing ... everything's wrong"

A man framed in the doorway of the plane was unhooking the emergency light, looking down at them.

"Look, you know about those drugs," the MO's voice an ingratiating whine, "that's what I couldn't get through to your Colonel. You know you can't just keep on upping the dose. You stop when there's nothing left to wring out of them. Stands to reason. The dose yesterday. I told him it was mad. The poor bugger's heart gave out. Nothing we could do about it."

He pulled out a cigarette case watching helplessly as rain beat down onto it. "How old was he? Seemed young. D'you know how old he was?"

"And did you get the truth?" Alex knew his voice carried. Archer stood huddled in his greatcoat, cupping his hands round a flickering match, face yellow in the flame. He turned away, striding into the darkness, rain bouncing off his shoulders.

"I asked did our sainted Colonel get his truth? Did he?" It seemed worthwhile screaming.

The MO stared. "What do you think?"

"What do I think?" Howling like a madman at the distant greatcoat, already no more than a shadowy blur. "It's bloody obvious what I think. The operation must be aborted."

Alex cast round for the Major, the field strangely empty.

"We need to know what's going on. Cabot as well. We're responsible ... responsible, do you understand?"

He did not hear the Sergeant. He came up fast, footfall hidden in a sudden bellow of engines. Arms stronger than his own wrapped around him, binding his chest, lifting him by the armpits like a child. Hands grasping his wrists from above, jerking him brutally over four metal steps, onto the soaking sill of the open door, rutted grass running under his flailing legs, glinting in the cabin lights.

Nineteen

Darkness retreated to a green light, smooth and velvety, engines beating to some kind of harmonic of their own, felt more than heard, too slow to be safe.

"Channel coming up. About ten minutes." The voice was so close in his ear he thought at first it was his own.

"Flak there most nights. Skip usually flies under it. Captain Vere - you alright?"

Rolling on his side, Alex stared into a child's face flushed with exertion.

"Somebody pushed me."

No, two faces, looking down: schoolboys, dressed unaccountably in khaki flying suits.

"Nothing to do with us, old boy. Blame Number Two. It was him saying get a move on or you'd miss your Toulouse rendezvous. All hell broke loose. Mind you, he has a point, we need the dark to get back."

The other schoolboy was nodding, straightening Alex up, his arms surprisingly strong, "Bit of a panic back there. Had to get you in."

This one had an earnest, spotty face, pocked with acne, unruly hair stuffed under a cap. There was the dark smudge of a moustache on his lip. He could not have been shaving long.

"Somebody pushed me."

"Right you are, squire. Heard you first time. Saw it myself. Wanted to get you aboard, pronto. Army type. Stepped up on the double. Orders, I suppose ... weird, all the same."

"Whose orders? You can't be ordered ..."

"No point shouting. You'll end up hoarse. Take it up with teacher when you get back. Here, have something to drink," A metal bottle, strangely heavy, stopper hanging loose, warm liquid slopping over his hand. "Only water. Careful where you sit. Some nights the floor in here ... you wouldn't want to know."

Their metal prison was painted grey, punctured by tiny squares of sky, bright with stars. A ribbed metal floor sloped to a metal door swinging idly onto a metal oasis pinpricked with yellow lights, the backs of two men, leather helmets a little awry. A vast moon stared in through windows glazed like a greenhouse.

A distant sound, oddly festive, corks popping, the cabin suddenly tilting through a sea of bouncing air. *Pop ... pop... pop ... crump.* The last closer, its breath trailing smears of oily red past the greenhouse. *Crump ... Crump.* Space itself lifting like a kite, heeling over tiny quartered fields, engines straining, silver flashes of open water to port.

"Shouldn't be flak here," the voice close again in his ear, "buggers keep moving ... only light stuff. See if you can get some kip. It's alright, skip's got the orders about the passenger. Metz in about an hour."

Passenger Kessler lay quiet in the crook of the cabin wall, a red blanket for his catafalque, parachute backpack propping him forward. The handkerchief draped over his face had fallen away.

He was kitted out for rescue at sea, a distress flag stuffed into his boot, a circlet of flares clipped round one leg. He looked as if he was waiting for something.

Alex thought of the German's last days with Archer. Old soldier Archer running rampant in Abbott Court, believing there was more to know, certain he was being cheated. Old soldier Archer, employing men to lie, searching for truth. What had he wished on this poor devil? Surely Kessler had expected to die, but not like that.

Not lost in the endless fictions of sodium amytal, not swearing each lie truer than the last.

They must have used cardiazol at the end, persuading themselves that ill-defined urgency justified anything. After that, there would have been nothing but demented ramblings for Archer to pick over. The chap must have died of fear. Alex felt unaccountably complicit, ashamed.

At Torridon, Justine once had asked him to pray for her soul, taking him unawares, suddenly angry as he turned away mumbling he didn't know how she could believe all that stuff. At least Catholics had it worked out, she said, none of the woolly graveyard claptrap his lot went in for. She would not let go, talking him into silence: *What if there were souls, Alex? What if there were? Have you thought?* And of course he'd thought, shouting there were some things god had no right forgiving, didn't she know that yet? That was when she had started to weep, her silent tears breaking his heart.

With Justine dead, prayer seemed too small a gesture, somehow demeaning. He had none of the words anyway. Surely there were special words? Would holy angels really bear your soul to paradise for the sake of a word or two? It seemed improbable.

Cabot was wrong. Justine would never in a thousand years have forgotten their pact. He would wager his life on it. That second message, with its reckless brazen *will*, was certain confirmation. She had wagered her life on it, and lost.

It was staring into space, this Jewish Catholic corpse. Too late for Hauptmann Kessler to deliver his soul from the pains of hell. Perhaps in those final drugged hours he had forgiven himself. Kessler's impassive waxy face across the cabin gave nothing away.

Archer must have planned all this from the start. Archer and his pretend enemy, the cynical Major, snaring Cabot and Alex into a futile game of make-believe. Archer must always have intended Kessler's death, believing it served some warped view of a greater good. The creation of Herr Steffle was no more than a convenient cover for murder. The two of them taken for fools. Impossible to believe John knew - it would take a consummate actor to fake that kind of obsessive dedication.

He should have felt angry at the thought of their eager, ingenuous, pointless work, at their infantile gullibility, at their betrayal. It was too late - the most he could summon was a kind of anaemic pity for the dead Kessler, for Justine's life thrown away, for himself, hurtling to the same end.

A pity he would never understand who had brought him to this.

Approaching Metz, he watched them shuffle Kessler to the jump hole, limp legs dangling in a slipstream of mist, an awkward ventriloquist's dummy propped against their knees, head lolling back, dead eyes watching the drop light.

When they came to it, the affair was not unlike a burial at sea, Flight even managing a sort of tottering salute, shamefaced, but not wholly ironic. Below them through the hatch, the city spread black like a stain against the lighter black of forests to the West. Tiny farms, careless of the blackout, pinpricks of gold.

Shouted commands now between the leather helmets beyond the flailing metal door, the Hudson impossibly low, sweeping over rail tracks, silver with frost, twisting along the glint of water. Far ahead, desultory fingers of tracer started up, raking the Eastern sky.

"On my go," he sounded like somebody's son, this pimply child, straining against his safety strop, shouting to make himself heard. A few months back this voice had been calling for a sneaked single in house cricket. Cracking now, touched with fear.

"Christ we're low, bloody water everywhere … hold steady … steady … green … GO."

He was gone. Hauptmann Kessler sent to his rest, flailing chute a narrow cylinder of furled silk, tip flapping like a flag. To be discovered tomorrow, or next week, by some rambler. Snuffled over by hedgehogs, but nothing worse.

Kessler, the first move in a chess game still in need of an opponent, briefcase stuffed with pointless artifice. Waiting in the mud.

The jump light off, Alex scrambled onto Kessler's blanket, thinking it somehow his proper place, the plane pulling up, sprawling him hard against the bulwark, thunder pulsing his chest, pain in his ears breaking only to hurt again. Puffs of icy cloud swirled free as they closed the jump hole.

The next green would be his. Long before the lights of Toulouse those waiting on the ground would hear the engines delivering Alex to his death. It seemed inconsequential.

In the cockpit, leather heads leaned together, calmer now, sharing a quiet joke, gigantic towers of cloud parting briefly onto patterns of stars.

Due West, engines settling to their beat. Lumbering through a comforting cocoon of piled grey. They had lost the moon.

The cockpit door pushed back, Skip weaving an unsteady path to where Alex sat, shaking hands, accepting a cigarette, pulling hard on it. Tall, this one, almost gangly. You could hear his mother explaining how he had not quite grown into himself. Too young, this child pilot with his old man's smile. Three hours, he said, perhaps a little more - there was a head wind. He seemed proud knowing a thing like that.

Three hours, and Alex would be perched like Kessler, legs dangling, Flight clipping his line to the rail. Three hours, and his turn to watch the red light with dead eyes.

The thought had lived with him ever since Archer's petty deception outside the hanger. When you collect your rig the thought is always there: was she paying attention, the WAAF who packed this one? If you ask for another, the girls never mind. They know about accidents.

He had collected his rig at the Barn, neatly tagged *Vere/Harcourt*, a padded helmet perched on top. The WAAF standing guard had offered Georges Harcourt an ironic salute. How could he ask her whether the trailing cords had been cut?

Flight was propped against the bulwark opposite, legs stretched out, venturing a timid grin. He was no Iago, this one: murder was far from his mind. He would dutifully clip the line, check it was secure, give that reassuring double tug, the shoulder tap, the squeak of *on my go*. Before the fall.

Remembering those few seconds on the hotel balcony in Russell Square, Alex felt only an immense weariness. If oblivion was what they had arranged, so be it. It was too late anyway: with Justine gone, the whole damned thing was too late.

He woke to the sound of engines relaxing. Flight was up, stretching the stiffness out of his back, mouthing *descent* to Alex, flapping a hand to keep him in his place. A sudden rush of clean air filled the cabin. Different air, smelling of land, Skip looping a hand high in the air high above his head, the jump light pulsing red.

It was happening too fast, this business of joggling him to the hole, this business of falling to his death. One cheerful boy clipping his line, the other tugging for good measure.

Low now: lower than Metz, engines drumming back from a sense of trees, nothing but trees, hydraulics wheezing tiny nudges … down … down. A distant wavering triangle of lights reared up dead ahead, three flaming points swaying against a vast purple sky, Flight's grip tightening on his arm, head angled back to catch the jump light.

Upturned faces below were already scanning for the billow of silk. Those were German faces craning up, not French.

Thoughts of Justine ravelled themselves to a scream of hopeless rage, releasing the startled hands at his back. He wrenched himself away, tumbling desperately into the consuming black, his last sight a glimpse of startled eyes. The jump light was red.

The chute deployed into a fierce up-draught, the triangle of flames jerking behind the crest of a wooded hill. Trees everywhere.

At Ringway there had been a session on trees.

I won't waste your time, Captain Vere, trees boil down to this. Avoid them. If you can't avoid them, come in face to wind, minimise speed over the ground. The theory is the canopy breaks the thinner branches, let's you down nice and gentle and Bob's your uncle. That's the theory. More likely you knock yourself out. Or to be really cheerful, you strangle yourself. The Manual says entangled more than eight feet up: wait for help. If no help comes, pray. Less than eight feet up, I'd give it a go. Better than getting shot. Shoulder straps first, then legs, Face in crossed arms. Drop. I'd pray anyway.

It was on him before he could think: a huge cedar, rearing dead ahead. Face to wind ... face to wind ... where the hell was the bloody wind? Too late. Tight cones like lemons banging his face, the silk above wrenching him round: holding, slipping, tearing, holding again, everywhere the cold resinous smell of Christmas. Mother hanging glass baubles, singing to herself. He wriggled to free his chest strap, feeling the blow as his arm released a springing branch.

Eight feet? Didn't they know it would be dark? Somewhere below his dangling legs was the painful earth. Leg straps gone he leaned back into the sweet air, a sudden surge of liberty bringing thoughts of angels. The grunt as the breath thumped out of him seemed to come from someone else. He lay on his back in a bed of needles. He had forgotten to pray.

The dull rumble of the Hudson refused to wane, a huge shadow coming round, horribly close, shaking the trees, pounding the air. Straight and low, screaming into the night, pulling up steep.

Alex risked the torch. At Aste-sur-Torre they had overshot by miles, much closer this time. You could smell the target fires in the air. Half a mile, or less. The go-around had given him a line due West, bless them for that. Somewhere ahead they were waiting, scanning for a chute. Puzzled by the second run, but waiting all the same. He hitched the pack onto his back. At least no swooping car this time to take him unawares.

The route was through an abandoned coppice of sweet chestnut, dense tufts of fresh growth covering lines of stumps. The going was easy: meandering woodcutters' tracks with only hanging ropes of spider web to contend with. He made for a faint cloud of blue smoke where the trees thinned against a lighter sky.

At the crest of a rise, the track dipped sharply down to a metalled road. It was closer than he thought. Two fires still smouldered on the wet grass. There was a smell of petrol everywhere.

The drop site was on the other side of the road, hedged round on three sides by trees, a moon throwing the empty field into shade. A last few burning embers were blowing red in the wind.

Where were they? They would know he was here, would sense something in the silence. No reception committee would seriously expect him to walk out. *Never show yourself first*: that was the rule. A faint scent of tobacco blew on the wind. Far away, someone coughed.

A narrow beam of white light broke out of the woods, jerking across the grass to the centre of the field. A tall figure, torchlight catching the hem of a long raincoat. It swung round to signal the woods behind, receiving an answering flash. They were biding their time. Whoever it was had stopped no more than thirty yards from where he stood.

There was a whistle from the distant wood, like someone calling a dog. As if in response, a shaft of torchlight, glinting wet green, raked the leaves over his head. Alex held his station. Flashes now, pulsing Long-Short-Long-Short-Long. The All-clear.

Where were they?

The torch flared again, held low against the waist, tilted up to throw a face into vivid relief. Justine – small against the expanse of dark, unbearably vulnerable, stark white face scanning the trees where he stood.

As he dared to move, the torch swung back to the woods behind, her voice calling clear in the night, a voice he would die knowing, "*Es ist hoffnungslos ...Ich habe Ihnen gesagt, dass er nicht kommen würde.*"

German uniforms burst from the trees, lights bouncing across the grass. "*Ta guele, bordel!*" Her torch spinning into the night, the blow felling her. She pulled herself up on one arm, grunting with pain as he kicked again.

Paralysed with the horror of it, Alex had not seen the trap. A third man running from nowhere across the grass, pausing to ready his rifle. Boots were clicking fast on the metalled road below where he stood, the slam, slam, of car doors echoing. An engine coughed into life, then another. In a second he would be surrounded. Across the field, Justine was vomiting as they hauled her to her feet, the white blotch of her face turned full into the moon.

Run!

Her cry collapsed into stifled silence as another blow fell.

Twenty

Some sixth sense kept him upright, barrelling between trees, leaping stumps, careless of bramble tearing at his legs. His only advantage was the sinuous road to the village. If he ran like hell he would get there first.

He stumbled out onto a clay track, houses closing in on either side. Rows of cabbages, tiny garden plots. To his left, a cobbled lane running hard against the side of a church into the square beyond. A stone colonnade in silent shade.

He climbed some steps into the dark of a shop doorway, bent double, an ugly cough racking his lungs. The square was deserted, the only light a single gas lamp hissing yellow green. On the other side, the battered menu board of *Le Sport* swung drunkenly from an iron hook.

At Torridon in the session on the Last Resort some wag had called out, *What's the first then?* forcing a wintry smile from the solemn man tasked to explain to them what you do when there is nothing to be done. Most of them had skipped the session, Alex sharing their superstitious dread of last things.

Strange to think Justine had once been in that dingy hotel, standing at the bar, fending off. *You don't order a coffee, Major.*

Alex drew further into the shade, her voice vivid like a pain.

The church clock struck the half hour, the sound too loud for the empty square. Twenty yards of exposed pavement and he would be there.

No following cars: they should have come by now. It was almost an irritation to realise he had not merited a chase. He stepped down onto glistening cobbles and padded softly across the square.

The bar was shuttered, dusty curtains clumsily drawn across a glass door, the room beyond dark. A metal gate at the side of the building led onto a tiny terrace set out with rickety tables, each with its metal ashtray, the back door a little ajar showed a line of feeble yellow light marking the hem of the blackout.

Alex unhitched his rucksack, pushing through the curtain into a panelled vestibule smelling of pastis and stale smoke.

The night porter had wedged his chair against the wall to get comfortable, feet cocked up on the counter. He was reading a newspaper.

"We're full." The accent was Basque, black suspicious eyes sizing him up. "Don't you know what time it is? You shouldn't be wandering about. Forget the curfew, did we?"

"Do you think I could have a word with Jules?"

He swung his feet down, sprawling forward over the counter for a better look. "I thought it might be something like that. D'you expect me to fetch somebody at this time of night? You're not from round here, are you?"

"Does that make a difference?"

"It might."

He went back to the newspaper, folding it over at the race results.

"Look, I can pay in advance. Not a deposit – the lot."

"Oh, it's a room you're after. I thought you wanted to see Jules. I told you, we're full. Who sent you? Not Claude Barte?"

"Claude who?"

"Haven't seen our Claude for a while. What's he up to?"

"I told you, I don't know him. Look, I can pay. I don't think you're full. I just want a room."

The man spun the register round. "It's five thousand for the night." He pulled his sleeve back, peering at his watch, an exaggerated gesture, enjoying his moment, "What's left of it. Another thousand and you can fill the book in tomorrow. That's a convenience, isn't it? Mind you, it's tomorrow now. I'll need your

Carte in the morning. They'll likely come asking. If I don't have your papers that's going to be your look out. In advance, you say?"

"Here's the money. Nobody will be asking for me."

"Number 22. Top of the stairs, this end of the corridor. Second door. It's open. If you get visitors you'll hear them on the stairs."

A narrow wooden staircase opened onto a shadowy long corridor, doors along one side. The electric bulb had been removed, the only light coming from shafts of faint moonlight through two tiny windows.

The window in his room was open to rid the place of the smell of pipe tobacco and some kind of leathery hair pomade, reminders of the last occupant.

Alex locked the door, pocketing the key. He threw his rucksack on the bed, stretching out alongside it, staring vacantly up at a faint splash of sickly light on the ceiling from the street lamp outside.

The room was cold, but he was sweating from the run, his throat raw from coughing. He had not eaten since Tempsford. He was desperately thirsty. There would be food in the pack - Belgian chocolate, far too sweet, but better than nothing. And water, you'd be mad to drink from the tap. With luck, a quarter bottle of cognac, the story at Hazell's Hall was you got that on French drops.

He pulled at the straps of the rucksack, the packet of silks falling onto the bed. His mission. The waxed package rolled onto its side. He could barely remember what he was supposed to do with it. He began fumbling in the dark for the other things. The water flask was not there. No chocolate, either.

His heart unaccountably pounding, he got up and closed the curtains, turning on the tiny bedside lamp. The Model B was there, stubby suppressor screwed in. The ammunition clip had shaken down to the bottom of the pack. It was empty.

He remembered the Signals officer at Hazell's Hall pushing a wallet with his papers into the side pouch of the pack. A brown leather thing, cracked with use. The one here was red. It seemed brand new.

He pulled it out, tearing it open. His *Carte d'Identie* – where the hell was it? He must have that *Carte* to survive. What would he do when that avaricious creep downstairs asked for his papers? Georges Harcourt, travelling travelling *Géomètre* with a Dutch accent, asking to see Jules, was never going to be very convincing. Without papers the pretence was ridiculous.

There was no *Carte*. No pass for the Gers border. No train tickets. All the little bits of circumstantial colour – cinema ticket stubs, ration cards, the picture of his little boy – all gone. He had watched that clumsy fool of an officer from Donnington pack them. Watched him carefully check them off against his list. Innocently watched the officer whose phoney incompetence had duped him like a child.

The wallet wasn't empty. A thick wad of papers was stuffed into a side pocket. He flattened one out. It was a chart. A stretch of coast past Le Havre, the tongue of the Seine snaking inland, hatched zones labelled *mined* in red ink. A small square marked *Artillery* had been crossed out, reinstated in a new location. It was headed: INFORMATION SHEET – NOT TO BE TAKEN INTO THE AIR.

There was a sheet of teleprinter paper, torn along a perforated edge, still crisp:

ETA 0245 STOP CONTACT ARTHUR AND SIMONE ST AUNIX EARLIEST STOP CONFIRM ARRIVAL 4.2 MHZ 1830 DAILY UNTIL ACK STOP ARCHER STOP END.

The signal confirming his drop – his own copy. The one he had handed over for destruction at the fake barn at Gibraltar Farm. He remembered the Donnington Captain taking it from him, stuffing it into his own briefcase, tutting impatiently as it snagged against something. The blundering Captain who wanted him dead. As a betrayal it seemed inexplicably vindictive.

And to think he had felt sorry for him - how the bastard must have laughed at that. Laughed all the way home to his masters, whoever they were. Remembering Justine clubbed to her knees, that seemed the only question that mattered.

There was a greasy passport in the wallet. Issued in Paris to Adam Walenski, March, 1935, the photograph, slightly blurred, a clean-shaven man with haunted eyes. At a pinch it could have been Alex. It was empty apart from three Customs stamps for the crossing at Vogelbach dated, January, February and March, 1938. He had never seen it before.

The face staring back at him from the tiny mirror over the sink was flushed, two spots of bright red high on the cheeks. With the curtains drawn the room seemed unnaturally bright, his hands sticky with sweat. He filled the bowl, plunging his head into water smelling of sulphur.

He switched off the light and drew back the curtain, cold air rushing past him into the room. The square below was wrapped in eerie silence, tiny houses on the other side above the colonnade shuttered and dark. A huge moon hung over the church steeple against a black sky.

Wait and you will be contacted. His instructions.

Pressed to say wait how long, the man in Torridon had turned away.

Alex undressed and lay on the narrow bed, pulling damp blankets round his shivering shoulders, an irresistible tide of tiredness sweeping him into a sleep as dark as death.

Always the same dream: the figure below his window looking up, light so bright it hurt his eyes. He sensed someone in the darkness behind him but could not turn to see. Someone waiting to push him through quartered panes of glass, splinters cold on his face like falling snow. Justine below his window, looking up, her mouth shaping a cry. Impotent, his arms pinioned in clinging cloth. Conscious of a huge face, not his own, looming too close, stale tobacco breath, a booming whisper, filled with fear.

"For god's sake, quiet! If someone hears we're lost."

The Parisian accent was subtlety coarser than last time. "You remember me?"

"Yes ... yes, I think so ..." Alex struggling to sit up, the room unaccountably a misty blue. "The Gendarmerie. Last year. You're Colonel Renault. What time is it?"

Framed against the window there was something hallucinatory about the impassive figure stooping over him: stiff cap decked out with gold filigree, long polished boots, crisp purple piping buckling at his knees, a glint of gold epaulettes.

"It is a little before six o'clock."

"Dawn?"

"It is evening. I had to wake you - they would hear you downstairs. You were screaming. A fever, I think."

Filled with a sudden exultant recollection of Aste, Alex strained forward, hopelessly scanning the room.

Renault followed his gaze, shaking his head. "I also remember our last encounter, Mr Englishman. No, she is not here. We are alone," pulling at the bedclothes, "can you stand? There is not much time."

"Am I to be arrested? Is that why you're here? To arrest me?"

"The question is absurd," Renault sounded angry. "Arrest is out of the question. Incredible that you come to this place. I will do what I can to remove you - and do not thank me. I do it reluctantly."

"Justine?"

"She told me you might come here. Why, in god's name? Only a madman walks into the same trap twice. Are you a madman?"

"How did she tell you? I don't understand. She wasn't dropped here. Why is she here?"

"You are wrong. Mrs Perry was dropped at Saint Aunix. And arrested. Like all the agents sent here." His hoarse whisper had a venomous edge: "You know that your network - your ridiculous *Columbine* - is compromised? You know your agents are captured? Yet every moon you send more. Are you all insane?"

A door slammed in the hotel vestibule below. Renault tossed the end of his cigar into the fireplace hurrying to the window.

"No, nothing. The night porter must not see us leave. You were never here, do you understand? This hotel is unsafe. It is used by SS officers. For … recreation. Yet you come here?"

Alex was not listening to him, "Justine. Do you know where she is?"

"You really don't know?" Standing close, tossing his cap onto the table. "She is in a prison block attached to the wireless station. German technicians operate your sets. How could you not know that? The Major in charge, I know him a little. His name is Gliess – he cannot believe his luck. His little army of phantom English agents."

"Not Justine – she's nothing to do with that."

"Are you sure? I have been there. Gliess has a chart in his room - the complete SOE command structure. The English agents have been purchased. If they cooperate they will be treated as prisoners of war." He stopped to light another cigar, walking to stand at the door, listening. "And they believe this."

"Justine wouldn't talk."

Renault sat down in the chair next to the bed. "You will think me insulting, Captain Vere, but I ask myself how you came to be selected for active service. When I arrive, for example, you were asleep. Is it not a symptom of hysteria? When the animal can no longer cope, it sleeps."

He raised a hand, as Alex was about to speak. "No, you must listen to me. Reports come to my desk. I received one two days ago. *Captain Alex Vere, under the command of Colonel Archer of the TPSU.* How do you think it was obtained? Of course she talked. Would you want her to resist? Prisoners in the care of Major Gliess are not treated well. He looks the other way. Now get dressed. You have very little time."

Alex stumbled about the room gathering scattered things, all the time hearing Renault's quiet voice.

"The day before yesterday I was ordered to the wireless station. The accidental death of a prisoner." He smiled. "*Accidental.* That is what I was told. Germans are not without a sense of humour. Accidents are a matter for the French police. I was ordered to bring with me a doctor. One not too interested in the condition of the body."

"Why are you telling me this? To shock me?"

"Shock you?" Renault looked puzzled. "No. I am talking about Justine." It was the first time he had used her name. Pronounced in the French manner, she seemed almost another person, softer.

"You're lying. She's alive. I've seen her."

"You misunderstand me. I took the opportunity to bargain with Major Gliess ... to plead for her. I gave him reasons to keep her alive. You can imagine them if you wish. Humiliating, I agree. Reckless ... but we are all a little reckless at the moment. The Major found my request amusing. He said he had a better idea, pointing to priorities between brother officers, explaining that a German Major had precedence over a French Colonel. *Precedence* was the word he used. Obviously he was baiting me."

"I don't know what you're talking about." Alex was cramming the packages of silk into his rucksack, fumbling with the buckles. "Where are you going to take me? I'm sorry, I don't understand what you're talking about. *Precedence?*"

"Ah, perhaps because you think I am trying to shock you. I will explain. Major Gliess gives his prisoners little freedoms, secured against their parole. He is the psychologist, you see. He knows the English will not violate a promise if others would risk execution. I suppose that is admirable."

"What freedoms? *Little freedoms.*"

"Nothing much. He brings them to the bar here"

Alex stared at him. "Justine?"

"She is not to be shot. I secured that much."

"But's she's a prisoner of war ... you said ..."

"I will tell you something. Something you also may not find shocking. Shortly after we signed our armistice, I met with my opposite number in the Abwehr. He explained what was owing to an occupying power. Making particular mention of women. *Our women*, is how he put it. He told me his men must have their fun. Warned against a hysterical reaction."

Renault released a haze of blue smoke into the cold air. He seemed to have stopped, sitting quietly, tiny noises from downstairs floating up the staircase outside the room. "The last woman to come the way of Major Gliess killed herself. Do you remember?" Alex looked at him. "He looked on that as an injustice. Justine does not have that option."

"She won't …" Alex checked himself, "…no."

"So you understand Gliess sees her capture as a particular prize. That is what he said. His French is not good. He said *prize*."

He stood up, looking for his cap, turning at last to look at Alex. "He has started to bring her here in the evening. Commandeered a room for the purpose. I imagine this will continue until she leaves. That is what he meant when he said he had other ideas. It is a way of tormenting me. And now I torment you." He shrugged. "My regrets."

"What do you mean, u*ntil she leaves*?"

"All the prisoners are to be shot. I have been given orders to make the arrangements. The executions are set for next week. There is paperwork to be completed. The promise they would be spared must be legally annulled, you understand … it was a contract. This is France … there are formalities. As I said, Germans are not without a sense of humour."

"Justine?"

"She is to be sent to a camp. A place called Ravensbrook in the North of Germany. We arrange shipments every day now from Mont de Marsan. Two thousand at a time, mostly Jews. They are called *shipments*. There are even detailed manifests." Something seemed to be breaking in his voice, "It is a little like the movement of cattle."

"When will she go?"

"When Major Gliess can no longer think of an excuse to keep her here."

"At least she will be alive."

Renault looked at him, anger evaporating into a kind of exasperated pity. "They are freight waggons, Captain Vere. The French State is now obliged to remove Jewish citizens ... former citizens ... but the rail company will only provide cattle trucks for the purpose. They say the risk is too great in a war zone. A journey of two thousand kilometres." Hearing his voice thicken, Alex looked away. "There is only room to stand. No water. No sanitation. She may survive. I am told it is the young who are alive at the destination. They need the young - Ravensbrook is a work camp. For women."

"For pity's sake - this is France! Not some vassal state. You've got your damned armistice. You've kept your army. And you stand there looking sorry for yourself. You let this happen. You are as responsible as Gliess."

"You think I don't know that? Why do you think I am helping you? And no – it has nothing to do with Justine. It is because I can. Do you understand? It is something in my power to do. Have you any idea what is happening in France? We are removing one hundred thousand. That is virtually all we do: count Jews."

"And if you refuse?"

"What – like some quixotic Englishman? You think that is an option? Listen. My service - the Gendarmerie has no wish to refuse. Quite the reverse. Since the summer fifteen thousand Jews have been arrested in Paris. Not by Germans, you understand. By us. By my service. No, perhaps *arrested* is not the word. I should say *rounded up*. That's what we do now. We round up women and children. In Paris the first lot were herded into the velodrome on the Boulevard de Grenelle. You know the place? Thousands and thousands, you understand, crammed in and left. No food, no water. Nothing."

"They must have been released eventually."

"They were not released. They were sent to special camps. There is one not far from here. They are to go to Poland, I believe." He was staring at Alex, "They will not be coming back. There is nothing I can do. That is why I do this."

"Look ..." Alex was feverishly pulling at the buckles of his kit, "Whatever you think of me ... I don't care ... I can use a knife. You say Gliess comes here. What protection?"

Renault pulled the kit bag from his hands, threading the buckles closed.

"He has his driver. But Major Gliess needs no protection."

He was fumbling in an inside pocket of his tunic, pulling out a sheet of typed paper. "I am unsure whether this is strictly legal ... it is a matter under consideration. By a German tribunal, you understand. The proposed tariff of reprisals." He opened it out, rattling through phrases at random, "... *intentional death of an ordinary soldier ... five persons at the discretion of the Commune ... Jews to be preferred ... children and pregnant women excluded ... junior officer ... thirty, no exclusions ...* Shall I go on?"

Standing very close, his voice a desperate whisper, "If there is even an attempt on the life of Major Gliess, Saint Aunix will be burnt to the ground. You understand? Every inhabitant will be shot where they stand. Or burnt alive."

He tossed the half-smoked cigar into the fireplace, "Put your absurd knife away, Captain Vere."

"You say he will be here? Here tonight?"

"Possibly. After you have gone. He is always very late."

"And she will be with him? You will see her?"

"The bar is a public place until the curfew. I can buy a drink for whoever I like."

"Can you give her something?"

"A message? Impossible. Gliess knows my interest. We may exchange a greeting ..."

"No, not a message."

Alex was pulling at the webbing at the bottom of the rucksack, feeling for its secret cache, fingers closing round the tiny metal tin.

"This. Find some way to give it her. It would be a kindness."

Renault took it, experimentally palming it from hand to hand, abandoning the gesture, pushing it into his pocket, shaking his head.

"Perhaps she no longer looks for kindness."

"Do it if you can. For her."

Renault checked the window again, turning to survey the room. "We must deal with you. I will wait here. Go downstairs. Walk through the vestibule. There is a road directly across the square. Three doors down, a cake shop." He looked at his watch, "You still have time. They will be closing. Say you want directions to the church. Say, *perhaps there is a back way?* Exactly those words. They will show you."

"What if they don't?"

"There is only one kind of stranger that makes that request. Behind the shop, a little lane, at the bottom a wooden shed. Pass the night there. The police patrol will stay away. I will keep this passport. It may be possible to arrange for some papers ... possibly not ... the name is unfortunate. Early tomorrow morning, I will ..."

The sound of wheels on the cobbles outside sent him hurrying to the curtain, a car skidding noisily against the pavement under the window. Doors clicked open.

Renault stood, careless of the light, muttering a stream of slow curses.

In the square below, a German officer was emerging from a polished staff car, finishing some fragment of conversation, adjusting his cap, calling out to someone, laughing.

Alex did not see her at first. She stood alone on the far side of the car, gloved hands resting on an open door, her face bearing the faint uncomprehending smile of someone not quite following a joke.

The man walked round, taking her arm as she seemed to stumble, dark eyes huge in the white of her face.

Renault closed the curtains, turning back into the room, switching off the light.

"If they find you here, we are both dead," picking up the rucksack, turning it over and over in his hands. "You bring your damned luck with you. He was not expected until ten. Here, help me pull this bed away. Lie against the wall, I'll push it back. I must go downstairs. I will leave the door open ..."

Twenty-One

A smell of cooking drifted through the open door: something frying, not altogether agreeable. Down the stairs there seemed too many people jammed into the vestibule, all talking, Renault making an entrance, greeting people from the car, managing stilted German phrases, the reply querulous, too loud for the space, demanding drinks like a thwarted child at a party. They moved through to the bar, swing doors flapping, Alex desperate to catch her voice.

He pressed his head against the dusty lino, hearing a slow creak of leather boots on the narrow staircase, torchlight flaring wild across the ceiling in the corridor. Someone pushed the door hard against the wall with the tip of a boot, torchlight raking the bed, lingering a moment on the wall above his head. The man moved away, breathing heavily, tapping pointlessly at a door at the end of the corridor, pushing it open - the guard for Gliess getting something to sit on. He was humming to himself.

Alex tried to draw into his skin. A buckle on the rucksack Renault had bundled behind him was biting into his leg.

At Torridon they had acted out situations like this, analysed their essential instability, the paramount necessity to kill before being killed. An alert guard always sensed a presence, however hidden you believed yourself, however still. No one knew how or why: perhaps some unconscious awareness of sound, more likely the scent of fear. Alex readied his hand to snatch his knife, remembering his kit was strapped tight. He would not stand a chance.

The man had stopped humming, the sudden silence broken by the scrape of a match, coarse cigarette smoke drifting down the corridor, hideous Russian stuff - curious how soldiers always ended up preferring that brand. He seemed a restless chap, this sentry, idly scraping his boots on the floorboards, endlessly clearing his throat. How long before he decided to take another look at the room with the open door? How long before he wondered about the recent smell of expensive cigars?

The double doors from the bar flapped open, disgorging a babble of voices into the vestibule, Renault complaining about something, his voice a little too loud, pausing to let the German labour over some elaborate parting formula in French. A burst of false laughter capped a dirty joke.

Gliess was coming upstairs. Alex was sure it was him: the intuition confirmed by the sentry heaving himself to attention, the floor shuddering. The peevish voice stopped in the stairwell, struggling on in mangled French as if speaking and walking together were too great an effort - determined to make his point, to get it right. He sounded drunk, fighting to catch his breath, wheezing like Archer the day he came to Netley. A burst of officious German sent the guard thudding downstairs.

And another voice. Alex once believed himself happy to die thinking of that voice. She was here. So close he could have reached out and touched her shadow darkening the doorway. Speaking French, mumbled words that stopped his heart: *No, not here, Monsieur, the end of the corridor*, Gliess grunting an inarticulate reply.

He could see her shoes - black leather, a little masculine. She had perched on the edge of the bed putting them on, the morning she had left for King's Cross, a lifetime ago. *Sensible*, she'd said, as if answering a question.

They moved off, walking like furtive lovers. The faint rustle of cloth, Justine's dark voice again, *Not here, Monsieur*, Gliess laughing, opening the door.

Braced against his wall, Alex cursed the tense silence that had fallen over the hotel. The cramp fluttering where the bag pressed against his leg would sooner or later betray him.

In the room at the end of the corridor conversation had started up, voices clear through the flimsy walls: Justine talking about the dreadful wallpaper, switching to German to say she would pour him a drink. French again, protesting he would tear her dress. Gliess, an oily teasing tone, voice thicker, no more than a rumble.

A shoe fell to the floor, Justine squeaking in mock alarm, telling him not to paw, Gliess louder, importunate, Alex flooding his head with words. *Dame souris trotte, Dame souris trotte* again and again and again - a pagan prayer. Sweet Jesus, anything not to hear.

They were quiet at last. No words, only the barely audible adjustment of bodies. He knew those tiny adhesive whispered moans, had lived them all, believed they were his own. Straining against the silence, waiting in dumb horror for some end, he knew each step of this sexual liturgy.

Gliess was calling out, untranslatable words rising above the rhythmical creak of the metal bed. Perhaps not words at all, thrusting, grunting, wresting a climax from pain. And threading through the hellish mix, burning his brain, Justine's voice - Justine liberated as Alex had never known.

The pain in his leg had become so much part of his impotent fury that for a second it seemed the muffled call had been his own.

A wooden chair clattered to the tiles downstairs, heavy feet stumbling up the staircase, thudding past, Justine's voice surging out of an open door, French, then German, her throat raw: *Fetch someone. Quick! What are you gawping at, man? Can't you see he's ill? Fetch someone. A doctor. I don't know. Only hurry!*

The swinging doors in the vestibule below clacked open onto bedlam: Renault ordering a press of voices back to the bar, taking the stairs two at a time, meeting the sentry running back, both speaking at once: *A doctor at this time of night ... What emergency? ... Are you mad?* Shouting at a press of strangers on the stairs. *Get those people back! And shut up, for Christ's sake!*

Another voice. The night porter, half inside his room, whispering obsequious German. *I know where he lives, Herr Colonel Sir. The doctor. It's a fair way.* Renault barking: *No ... telephone the Casserne ... Damn it, it's too late. Go with him. I'll deal with it. Get a move on.*

Voices in the square outside: shouts echoing clear in the frosty air, conjuring an engine to life. A skid of wheels, fast on greasy cobbles.

Then they were gone.

Alex sensed he was not alone. Someone was breathing, a shadow stretching across his patch of floor, Renault's polished boots silhouetted against a faint light.

"Captain Vere," the voice low, almost conversational. "Nobody is here. Get up. I have to lock this door. Damnation! The fool of a porter's taken the key."

"No, I've got it," Alex struggled to his knees, fumbling desperately for his pocket. "No. Try another room - all the keys will be the same."

Barely standing, he watched Renault pull the curtains back, the sudden flare of orange light hurting his eyes. God, he was going to faint. Why was he talking about keys? Things were running away from him: his life lost, and all he could do was talk about keys.

"What do you mean, *Nobody here*? Has Gliess gone? Justine? Where is she?"

"Too many questions. Can you manage? Here, hold on to me."

The bedroom door at the end of the corridor was open wide. A wall of heat struck them as they went inside, logs still burning in a stone fireplace. The shade from the bedside lamp had been taken down, throwing sharp unnatural shadows high on the walls. The place smelled vaguely unclean - the sweaty fetid scent of sex.

Justine's frock lay draped like a body along a brocade sofa, her other things scattered on the floor. Gliess had folded his clothes over a chair, his dress cap perched on top.

He lay face down, naked apart from stockings held by elastic suspenders. Slumped across Justine's body like some blasphemous *Pietà*, his buttocks, gelatinous blue mounds, rearing up. Patches of flaky skin showed through matted hair, his head nuzzling against her breasts. He was obviously dead.

"Get the bastard off me, will you?" Her look as Alex gripped Gliess by hairy shoulders was frigid, not yet recognition. As he rolled the body off, she pulled free, stifling a hysterical laugh, "God almighty! It only needed that."

Gliess lolled back onto the sheets, a grotesque priapic doll, penis stubbornly erect.

She struggled to the side of the bed fumbling with a gloved hand to find her blouse.

Alex leaned down to help.

"It's alright, I can manage," wincing as he took her wrist. "My hands hurt. Best not that one, the bastards did something. I've not dared look. I'm such a coward," dark eyes wide with pain. "Oh Alex, my dear, you look worse than me. Leave me be – I want to get straight."

"He's dead." They had forgotten Renault standing immobile in the doorway. His voice was flat. It was not even a question.

"When that sentry came in, what did he see?"

Justine avoided his eyes. "What do you mean, *what did he see*? What do you think? You gave me the bloody pills." She raised a gloved hand in mute appeal to Alex, "I knew who they came from - it was knowing that kept me alive."

"You don't understand. Did he touch him?" Something urgent in Renault's voice made her look at him, seeing him for the first time.

"Did the sentry touch him? Of course not. He didn't come in. Stood where you are. He was only interested in me. He couldn't take his eyes off me. You'd think he'd never seen a woman before. He stood in the doorway ogling like an idiot."

"But he could see he was dead?" He stepped into the room, moving towards her.

She paused, weighing the question, "No. Why would he think that? I'm sure he thought Gliess had just passed out. He seemed very young. Fainted with passion, he must have thought. It was very hot in here."

Renault picked a glass up from the table. "The pills, tell me what you did."

"Only one pill. The new one. I put it in his brandy. He didn't drink it all. Too keen to get at me. They said it acted fast – that's a joke." She stood unsteadily in front of the wardrobe mirror, straightening her dress. "Why do you want to know all this? I feel sick. I want to be sick. Hell! My coat. I just remembered - what's happened to my coat?"

"Your coat is in the bar downstairs. Listen to me, for god's sake. I have to think. When he drank the brandy – what then?"

"Nothing. Absolutely nothing. These trick things never work. But he was drunk anyway."

Renault kneeled at the side of the bed, gingerly straightening out the body, pushing the head back, examining the neck. "No mark … so far as I can see."

He stared up at Justine, some obscure embarrassment flushing his face, "The state he was in … I have seen it before. At Fresnes prison. Men when they are hanged." He waited for their eyes to meet.

"When he started to come off, my hands were round his neck. He asked me to ... begged me ... only so far, you know. He wanted pain … any pain. He was screaming, *Harder, harder.* You must have heard. The whole place must have heard. Pathetic bugger."

Raising her head to Alex, wide blue eyes embracing him, the first hint of a wounded smile. "Carotid choke."

"He didn't resist?" Renault let the head fall back onto the bed, "*Why?*"

"Oh, he resisted … he resisted like hell … but you can't resist that … you're always too late to resist. The way he looked when he realised - God, I'll always remember that. I made it ten seconds. I counted a bit fast I suppose. But he was dead long before ten." She extended a hand towards Alex, "I killed him."

Renault had pushed a pillow under the scrawny neck, letting the head sink into it, gesturing for Alex to join him.

"He's older than I thought. I have a question. Perhaps you know. Can people die like that? Die of … how you say? *Congress?* Is it possible?"

Alex was raking his memory, dredging for the one undergraduate lecture nobody forgot. "Possible, yes. I believe it's a question of blood pressure. If it's high … if there is a history. I'm not a doctor … a doctor would know."

"This one they have gone for – I know him. He is a friend."

He stood up, turning to Justine, reaching out to touch her arm, his voice desperate.

"Tell me again. Our lives depend on it. More than our lives. Tell me the truth. When the sentry looked at Gliess, what would he have concluded?"

"I'm telling you the truth. Why should I lie? What do you conclude when you see your officer's backside like that? If you're asking did he think I'd killed him, I'm sure not. There was a bit of a smirk on his face. He drew the obvious conclusion – a climax of passion. It will be the talk of the barracks in a day or two. I told you he was young. Probably surprised to discover old men fuck at all."

Renault's eyes widened, "Direct as ever, Madame."

He opened the door and went out into the corridor listening to the buzz of muffled sound below, finally turning back inside.

"Captain Vere, the rendezvous for your return? When is it?"

"*Return?* There isn't one! We're not intended to." Justine blurted out a reply before Alex could speak. "Pascal … it's too late for all that. You know it is. It's over. We're not going to get out. Can't you leave us here? Don't get involved."

Alex sat fiddling with the buckle of his kitbag, warding off rising claustrophobia. Justine slumped down onto the sofa, her arms trembling violently, grinding her nails into the pink brocade, staring at him. She did not know who he was.

This dreadful place would be his last sight of freedom. There wasn't room for four crammed into this stifling little space. No, not four – one was already dead.

"Leave her," Renault was pulling him aside. "It's a reaction. It will pass. She is wrong - that guard will tell no one about this. Tell me - the rendezvous?"

"I don't know how long she meant to be here. Weeks I think. But it was all nonsense. She was betrayed – they were bound to arrest her."

"The pickup would be Castelnaudary," Justine's voice was trembling, "I was to be dropped there. Except I wasn't. How do you imagine we get to Castelnaudary, Pascal? How do we manage that?"

The two men looked away, Renault standing, his back hard against the closed door.

"She doesn't understand." He was speaking to Alex, his voice low, almost a whisper, "You believe someone betrayed you? Whoever it was still waits for news of your arrest. You see the consequence?"

"Frankly, no, I don't."

"It will be impossible to annul your return. That was to be where?"

"Here, of course - the field at Saint Aunix. In two days. No, that's not right. Sorry ... I've lost a day. Tomorrow. It was scheduled for tomorrow. Eleven hundred hours."

"I suggest you keep the rendezvous. Both of you. You will have to risk the patrols ... but ..."

Justine started to laugh, "Do you believe all this Alex? Alex, my love, can this be right?"

"Quiet!" Renault pushed the curtain aside, staring into the empty square. "No ... nothing. We are still safe." He looked at his watch.

"There are people in the vestibule. When I go downstairs I will take them with me into the bar. When you hear the doors close, make your way out into the square ..." he paused, staring at Justine's gloved hand, the expression impossible to decipher. "Do you think you can walk to the house at Aste? A long way, but not impossible. The house there is still safe. The owner has been happy to accommodate fugitives ... even Jews." He was still staring at her gloved hand.

She struggled up, swaying slightly, resting it on his arm. "Worse things happen, Pascal." She was quieter now. "I can manage. I know the house. But there are Germans billeted there."

"Only one. And he is not there - nobody is there. It is empty. One thing, Captain Vere. Those papers you are carrying- they are a death warrant. Give them to me."

Justine supressed a choking kind of laugh, looking desperately at Alex, "What's he mean, a death warrant? God, my coat. It's in the bar."

Renault released her hand, "It will not be there tomorrow, Madame," turning to Alex, "wait at the house. I will bring a car. If I am late, wait." He shrugged, "If I am later than that, you will have to make your own way ..."

"And him?" Alex looked at the bed. Justine did not turn round.

"There is somebody in the bar. A girl. When you have gone I will talk to her. I think her name is Nathalie. She comes here on Saturdays. The German boys like her because she is willing to be friendly. They are happy enough to pay what she asks. It's little enough. We arrested her once for a moral offence. Her father complained. About Germans, you understand, not about her selling herself."

"You're going to mix her up in this?"

"When the doctor arrives, she will be detained. Not an arrest – after all it is hardly an offence. The sentry has no reason to involve himself further."

Alex stood looking down at the corpse, no longer tumescent. "I recall that word - the term is *coital death*."

"That is what the doctor will certify. I will contact Feldkommandant Kloss about the event. It will be very late. It is better to wake people up for this sort of thing - they rarely make sensible decisions. I can offer to intercede with the doctor to obtain a less specific certificate, for the sake of good relations. If Kloss can suggest a more appropriate place to die I will offer the services of the local Gendarmerie to transport the body. Kloss will tell the sentry how little he saw."

Twenty-Two

For the last mile Alex carried her, heavy in his arms like an injured child, finally persuading her onto his back, one gloved hand pressed against his neck. As she drifted into unconsciousness he would stop, bending forward, gently shaking her awake.

They found the house by the last of the setting moon - a blue shadow across lawns ragged with frosty thistles, dead leaves piled against double doors braced shut with an iron bar. The place looked abandoned.

Alex made for a pantiled building set apart from the house, pushing at an open door, the smell of turpentine rushing out. The light switch worked, a single bulb festooned with dangling spider webs. Frames and paintings were stacked three-deep against whitewashed walls.

An ancient easel with a wooden crank filled the centre of the room. Facing it, the polished reflector of an acetylene lamp gave the scene a curious arrested air.

The portrait looked complete - an old man standing unnecessarily erect, jaw jutting forward, dark suit suggesting someone just back from church. A mean face, heavily lined. The German lodger, surely, although no uniform. Perhaps imagining his warring days over, posterity in mind. Something disquieting about the vacant stare reminded Alex of Archer. It was hard to believe the sitter would be all that pleased.

She had seemed conscious when they arrived, able to stand. Now she slept in the chair where he had placed her, erect and silent, a bruised face in repose someone he had never known.

She stirred at the scent of woodsmoke as he lit a few sticks in the fireplace. That had been half an hour ago. He sat watching. Her mouth a little open, a desperate beat to her breath, clinging to a kind of sleep.

There was a cardboard box of baking soda on a shelf over the sink, perched among empty paint tins. Alex stirred some into a glass of water and began easing off the glove. It was too big for her hand, white cotton, embroidered with flowers at the wrist. He had never seen her wear such a thing. As he pulled at it, a lump of bandage came away, caked black.

The nail on the little finger was gone, pink flesh, horribly exposed, met the frayed remains of the cuticle, vivid lines running blue across her hand.

She gave a tiny instinctive flinch as he began sponging, water in the glass darkening red. Reaching open flesh he realised he was weeping, tears blurring his view, turning aside to meet huge dark eyes close to his own, staring wide.

"Hello Guffin," coughing, snatching the wounded hand away, pawing empty air. "Hell, that stings. I'm done for. Did I pass out? How did we get in?"

"The door was open. Do you remember keeling over in the wood? I thought you'd tripped."

"Bloody shoes. No, all I remember is dogs. I thought they were following us with dogs. I remember you carrying me piggyback … made me feel like a little girl." She turned to him, her face charged, "Can it be safe here? I don't think I can manage any more … I'm sorry."

"Renault said it was safe. It's quiet enough. Nobody's here, the big house is locked up."

Justine looked at the portrait. "She lived here, you know? D'you think she painted it?"

"Who?"

"Your artist woman. She lived here. She was picked up from here the morning of that bomb. I was supposed to die that day, Alex."

She slumped back, "You know who she is, don't you?"

"The Major's sister – she came to see me. She told me they sent her other brother out to get her. He was killed in the explosion."

"It seems so long ago. That bomb was meant for me, I'm sure of it Alex." She seemed very close, searching his face, "Were there really dogs?"

"Strays. The woods are full of them. Try and get a bit of rest. There's some bandage in my kit."

She was looking down at her hand as if she barely owned it.

"You know, this is the first time I've seen it. It's started hurting again," stretching out her other hand, holding it against his cheek, "not your fault, my love … it had to be cleaned."

She watched as he began winding bandage round her hand, crisp white against smudged bruises. "I knew you'd go crying on me. I didn't want you to look."

"It all seems so senseless."

She reached out, resting her other hand on his head, ruffling his hair. "You followed me here. It's that I can't believe. Standing in that field, I was in such a panic. They worked out your drop had gone wrong. One of them came up with the idea of using me as bait. He had a rifle."

She pulled the glove off her lap. "Throw it on the fire, will you?"

She flinched as Alex tightened the bandage, "They knew I'd try to warn you, right enough. All he needed was a clear line of fire. When they heard you running away they hadn't a clue where you were going, why you were bothering to run. They were so sure you'd be picked up soon enough. Why on earth did you go to that hotel? You should have been told it's not safe."

"That was where I was told to go. The man who briefed me said to treat it as the Last Resort. He was lying."

"Most nights it's full of Germans. It's a sort of brothel, I suppose. That's what Gliess said. Showing off he was one of the lads. When he went into the bar Pascal as good as told me you were upstairs. Lots of hand shaking - that's how I ended up with your little tin. In case I didn't cotton on, he started quoting bits of poetry – mice trotting about. Gliess knew something was up, but he couldn't work out what. He put it down to gallantry. I think that's what they hate about the French: that gallantry comes natural."

"He doesn't think much of me, your friend Renault. He thinks it's my fault you came back here."

Alex nestled the bandaged hand into his own, stroking it. "No, Justine, let me say it. You're keeping something back, aren't you? Renault as well. It's about London, isn't it? You know who's behind all this."

"Oh, love, no. He knows nothing at all. He's angry he doesn't. He thinks London is wilfully stupid. That's why he started helping – until the rumours started about him. He knows his time's up. Getting us away might be the last thing he does. He told me once why he's playing this double game. You know what he said?"

"Yes, I think I know. He told me about the Jews."

She nodded. "It's this Vichy setup. It's really changed since the Germans moved South. He said it made him complicit, ashamed. The way people have accepted things. Not just looking the other way, actually helping. The truth is most of them aren't even particularly unhappy. You know the motto's *Work, Family, Fatherland* now? Poor Pascal, he just can't stomach the idea of a fatherland. He wants his Marianne back."

"Or his Justine?"

"No, Guffin, not that – he was ashamed of that as well. Don't think ill of him. He's making amends. But he doesn't know anything about London. Perhaps there's nothing to know – has that thought never struck you?"

"Why didn't you tell me you were going to be dropped here?"

"I'm sorry Alex, I'm too feeble to talk much. Look, is there anything to drink? I'm horribly thirsty. And something to eat? Can you look?"

Alex fetched a glass of water from the sink. He walked round the studio, opening cupboards, calling out over his shoulder: "There's a box here with biscuits. Very fancy. German. And brandy. Lots of brandy. Artists seem to live on the stuff."

He turned towards her, holding out the bottle, to discover she was speaking, almost to herself, a numb quiet voice he barely recognised.

"I was betrayed – that's all it comes to. You remember that day I was taken away? No, listen to me, Alex. That day, the Major told me the drop zone would be near Castelnaudary. Even showed me the spot on a map. Explained about the local reception committee, names, pass phrase, all the usual stuff. My orders were I was on no account to come scouting round Columbine until there was intelligence that it was safe to move."

"What was the pass phrase?"

"Why d'you want to know that?" The sweetness of her sudden smile stopped his heart, "You still don't think I'm lying, do you? It was *Fête Galante* if you must know. Oh Alex, have we come to that?"

"It's him I want to know about, not you. I don't trust him. That was one of the Verlaine pass phrases. The Major once told me he didn't know anything about them. So how did you end up here."

"The flight down was a lot longer than I expected. And I couldn't get a word out of the crew: they said they were under orders to keep mum. As soon as they got the hole open I knew something was wrong. It was nothing like the approach to Castelnaudry. We were miles lower than we should have been. And the landing markers seemed familiar somehow … the pattern. I had this weird feeling I'd seen it all before."

"You mean the Aste pattern?"

"Three times I'd been on that approach. We were right over Aste-sur-Torre. I realised just before they shoved me out. There were no buildings, for one thing, just trees. By the time I hit the ground I knew exactly where I was."

"You're saying this was some kind of cock-up? I can't believe that – not complete with landing markers ..."

"They were waiting on top of that little hill, above the road. They hadn't even bothered to cover their uniforms. There was nowhere to run, not with a harness pulling me. Gliess himself was in the car keeping out of the cold. He knew every last detail of the operation. Exactly like the time we dropped together."

"You mean the local circuit …?"

"No, no, of course not. They couldn't change a flight plan. London orders all that."

She held out her glass, shaking her head as he went to add water, gulping it down.

"Go easy with that stuff. We need to be ready."

"Not *we*, Alex - *you*. I'm not going to get out of this, am I? You realise I'm all in. I can't walk – are you proposing to carry me? It's miles."

"You won't have to walk anywhere."

"You really believe in Pascal and his car? I thought it was me that believed in miracles. He's probably been arrested by now. No, you'll have to leave me here. You'll make it alright walking on the road."

She reached out, pressing her finger against his lips. "Be kind. No quibbling. This is where my six weeks end."

"He'll come. You didn't see the look on his face. Your Renault will get you out of here if it's the last thing he does. Me too, but it's you he's thinking about."

"He's not my Renault, Alex. And it's nothing to do with me … except it was me killed Gliess. With us out of the way, what he ought to do is get rid of the body. He should forget fancy stuff with the doctor, get the local maquis to deal with the driver then dump the two of them somewhere in the mountains. They do things like that if you pay them enough. A long way from Saint Aunix, anyway. Don't go thinking Pascal's doing anything for my sake. It's reprisals he's thinking about. You don't know what those bastards will do. But if you want me to say I shouldn't have …"

She seemed unaware she had stopped speaking. Her head had slipped forward, eyes fluttering. He rested a hand on her shoulder, feeling it yield like a dead thing. She seemed already asleep.

"Justine. If we're going to get away you must try to keep awake. Look, I need to know what happened after they arrested you. If only one of us makes it back ..."

She started up, "That's right. Sensible. Pour me another glass of that stuff, will you. A shame Pascal took the pills off me. Benzedrine's what I need."

"Wait a minute ..." He dragged a chair across to the open door, helping her onto it.

Dawn had broken, feeble sunlight slanting across the lawns, turning the track to the house red.

He kneeled down at her side. "You can breathe better here. And we'll have a couple of minutes to scram if it comes to it."

Justine downed the brandy. "They didn't take me to the Gendarmerie, if that's what you're thinking. No Pascal. He didn't find out I'd been arrested until later. They took me to some kind of barracks the other side of the village. It was dark, but the place was obviously a wireless station, masts everywhere. I was marched in behind this man Gliess. No ... sorry, I'll have to stop ..."

"You're doing fine," cradling her bandaged hand in his own, "tell me about this man Gliess?"

"It's alright, Alex, it's stopped hurting. Gliess was horribly polite - I think he believes that's what the English expect. He said he wouldn't bother interrogating me, he doubted I could add to what he already knew. His English is very good, but now he's got this wireless game going he fancies himself in French. He's a cocky bastard ... God, I've just realised he's dead."

"Renault said there were English agents there ... prisoners."

"Wait a minute. He gave me this lecture about how easy it was to cheat the stupid English WT people. Then he came on friendly, apologising that the English saw fit to employ women. I've seen friendly like that before, believe me. He said I was to operate under German orders, *like the others*."

"How many others?"

"I'm not sure. Five or six, I think. I never saw them. I heard them talking the next morning … English. They sounded alright … quite cheerful."

"Six? Renault said there were more."

"He asked for my parole so I could be treated like the others."

"He couldn't ask for your parole, could he? Not really."

"You mean given I'm not a fighting man? That didn't seem to worry him. He pulled this letter out of a drawer in a fancy desk. He's kitted the place out with bits of furniture, even carpets. Stuff looted from old grannies, I suppose. Antiques. Pictures on the walls. It's a concrete air raid shelter, for god's sake! He treated this letter like it was the Magna Carta. Covered in signatures and red stamps. Told me it had been initialled by Adolf Hitler himself. He read bits out. Very florid German. In return for compliance, a guarantee of treatment as a POW. He called it a pact. Went on and on about how it was honourable, given we were under French jurisdiction and France was not at war."

"I know about that letter. It has saved nobody. Hitler issued a secret order that all irregular forces are to be shot. It makes Gliess's thing worthless. The prisoners are to be executed."

"I guessed something like that. Later … after they'd got things out of me … he changed. Everything changed. They started dismantling everything. I knew we weren't going to last long."

"You know Renault went and pleaded for you to be spared."

"Oh, yes. Gliess thought it was so funny. *Like an earnest schoolboy* he said. I felt like killing him then."

She looked at Alex, her expression defiant, daring him to pity her, "Do you really think it needed any pleading to spare me? You surely know what *spared* means? No … no, I'm sorry. What am I shouting for?"

Holding her, Alex felt her breath coming short as if she were drowning. She peeled his arm away, leaning forward, drawing in air.

"You don't have a cigarette? I'll be alright."

Alex lit two cigarettes in his mouth, handing her one.

"I was to be taken to the wireless room to call London and ask for instructions. He said they'd got my set working. They're not supposed to be able to do that, Alex. There's a key. They had everything - times, frequencies, everything."

"The Major showed me your message. The one with *will* missing, with our word missing."

"I realised what it would do to you. We never thought of that, did we? I almost funked it. Then I knew I had to. It was one thing we had between us – do you understand? It was a sort of goodbye, Alex."

She raised his head from her lap, cradling it, letting it fall.

"I do love you, Guffin, despite your jealous looks. I suppose I always will now. And I was so sure you couldn't come following." He felt her squeeze his arm, "Then you did just that! *Why?*"

"Isn't it obvious?"

"The Major? There was something strange. He ordered me not to use standard capture codes - I was to send completely straight. He explained Baker Street have got a machine now that can tell whether it's your fist that's sending. When I got to Castle Kennedy, he'd changed his mind. This wire arrives. Urgent. If I was sending under duress I was to use any non-standard abbreviation. That first message I abbreviated *as per usual* and sent it as *apu*. The Jerry operator jumped on me about it. I told him it would look suspicious if I spelled it out."

"The Major said it wasn't important, you were always doing irritating things like that."

"You know that's not true. I've never sent anything at all before. That's why I did that course at Torridon."

"All he went on about was you confirming Simone was alive. Beat me over the head with how I'd got that all wrong."

"Gliess added that bit. He was keen to get one more WT operator on his books – even a dead one."

"But why would the Major lie?

"You said it yourself. Given he wanted you out of the way, he was hardly going to tell you the truth."

"You weren't there, Justine. He was incredibly convincing. I know a bit about lying. I can't believe he was lying."

"Isn't that what you lot are paid for? No point being a bad liar, is there? But our code – the word *will* missing – he didn't know about that, did he? You didn't tell him?"

"No. I was scared he would veto the mission. I still don't see him lying. Nobody is that good."

"*Lying* is too kind a word. After the message with *apu* had gone off, I was bundled into a little cubbyhole next to the wireless room. I guessed they were waiting for the acknowledgement from London. You know that comes back in seconds and they were taking the hell of a time about it. After about a quarter of an hour, I was hauled back in. There were three of them – German WT operators - looking at this bit of paper. A horrible tense silence in the room. Then Gliess himself comes rushing in. In a dressing gown. Face like thunder, really angry, asking to look at it. He shoved it in front of me. It was *en clair*, from London, on the same frequency. Asking for confirmation *apu* signified *as per usual*. And would Arthur please avoid non-standard abbreviations."

"God almighty!"

"After that, Gliess had me back in his office. He'd got dressed. He was so deadly calm it was terrifying. The man's not normal ... I think he's really insane." She stopped, suddenly solemn.

"I'll tell you something: the world's better off without people like him. Some people do deserve punishment ... I really believe that. He was pacing about, cursing god and the devil, saying he couldn't believe a woman would try to trick him. Then he started pawing me, pulling at my dress. Was I real woman? A German woman would never do such a thing ... and so on. As they were taking me away he called after me. Said he wasn't responsible if others were less tolerant. I knew what he meant. I could see it in his face. I was so frightened, Alex. It's my problem. I know I look solid ... but all the time I'm scared stiff inside. It's been eating me away ever since I joined up."

"I'm the coward – I know what you're going to say and I want to stop you. I don't want to know."

"It's best I tell you. It's not so terrible. That way you won't go imagining. They took me to a cell downstairs. The place was just like they said it would be at Torridon – horribly dirty and cold, concrete floor. It smelled like a sewer. There was a bucket, but the floor round it was slimy with shit. A grubby little light bulb in the ceiling. No window. A sort of mattress – really filthy - on a wooden bench. I remember standing there, knowing I couldn't sleep on that thing."

Thinking of his hopeless hours in that cell in Aste, Alex felt her hand move on his head.

"You remember what it's like, don't you? I don't know how long I stood like that. I began to think I was paralysed. Then I heard them coming. Two men chatting along the corridor. I thought they were bringing something to eat. They left the door open so there was light. One of them was carrying a metal cup. They weren't in uniform. They'd brought this weird smell in with them – methylated spirits, I think. This big fat bloke suddenly got his arm round me and shoved my hand down on the mattress. The other one had a pair of pliers. They were in the cup. I remember they were dripping ... and this meths smell was everywhere."

As Alex raised his head she pressed him down, his face buried in her lap.

"He did it so quick, Alex. As if it was nothing. Gripped the end of my nail and snapped it back. I couldn't believe it had happened. I was watching blood bubbling out of my finger and it didn't even hurt. No pain at all, just this hot feeling down my back. Then something bigger than pain. I didn't think you could hurt that much and stay alive. I was jumping up and down, trying to get out of myself. Howling. They just stood there watching me skidding about in all that slime, waving my hand, praying the bloody thing would drop off. Then the bloke with the pliers put them back in the cup and they walked out." He could feel her breath coming fast. "I'll have to stop ... I'm not sure I can explain the rest."

"It's alright, Justine, it's alright. Stop. There's no need ..."

"No, I've started. You haven't heard the important part. After they locked the door I remember I fainted. Gliess must have come down later and had the cell opened. I was lying on my side across this bench thing looking up, seeing him standing there with a handkerchief over his face, like I was something in a dog kennel. I was taken back to his room. Stood up in front of his desk. He apologised for the injury – that's how he put it, *the injury*. Then he said the business with the transmission was a shooting offence."

As Alex lifted his head she raised her bandaged hand, arresting him. "I know what you're going to say. *Make silence your only goal*. All that Torridon stuff. That book wasn't written for me, I know that now. Stuck there with Gliess in his horrible little fake *salon* it didn't make sense. I felt sick. Then I really did throw up, all over his carpet. I think I fainted." She managed a tiny smile, "Nothing in the book about that."

"It's the book that's wrong."

"When I came round, some poor Corporal with a bucket was wiping up sick. They'd put a sheet over a chair and propped me up in it. Gliess was mauling me about, slapping me, not hard, more like I was a naughty little girl. On my backside. There was this excited look on his face ... aroused ... you know. He kept saying I must do what he wanted. A horrible sing-song Daddy voice. I didn't understand what he was on about at first, whispering in my ear. I was going to obey or a nail would be removed from my hands. One every ten minutes. He made it sound like some kind of medical operation. Something he could watch. The ten minute interval was because I might die of shock. Then these same men came in again, and that awful antiseptic smell."

"Barbaric stupidity. There's no need ... Christ - there's drugs ... you can get information. They know that."

"Of course there's no need. That's what he wanted."

"Hurting, you mean?"

"It's more complicated than that. He wanted to deal with the aftermath. I knew what was at the end of that road."

"Your L tablet, Justine. Didn't you ...?"

"You know why. I left it at Castle Kennedy. It's funny – even when I was praying they'd do me in, I knew I couldn't have done it myself. But I left it behind, all the same. To be on the safe side. It's a mortal sin, Alex, don't you know that? No ... you don't know, do you? Eternal death. Better be punished here than face that. It's alright, my love, you don't have to understand. I don't understand myself – that's why I left it behind."

She had stopped. A small bird began an echoing wintry song somewhere near the door. He strained to listen for the sound of a car. Renault was dreadfully late. For the first time in many months Alex felt at peace. He would not be leaving her here. It was enough to sit together looking across to the dark line of the woods.

"I wonder what makes us so sure we'd never betray a friend?" She was weeping. "Because it's the easiest thing in the world. I suppose that was my punishment. *The punishment of Judas* – you see? One kiss too many ... you never understand that until it's your turn to do the kissing. You're not going to make me explain, are you? It's too hard to say ... about us. Once I'd started, even Gliess seemed surprised. I couldn't stop. I told him everything I knew."

"It's not betrayal if he already knew it ... you can't call that betrayal."

"That's your friend Cabot talking. Saying clever things doesn't alter anything, Alex. I told him everything. I let him kill me inside because I was terrified of being hurt again."

Remembering *her name is Justine Perry*, Alex felt her breath close on his cheek, tears running unheeded down her face. He drew her close against him. "Stop now. Please stop. Please don't go on."

"The worst is I gave them us. My poor little Guffin. I gave them you. Gave them our pathetic little code ... the word *will* ... everything. Colonel Archer, Captain Vere, Mr Cabot, and so on. When I said your name I thought of that hotel. You talking about love. And now every time I kiss you … I was starting to believe in the future … stupid … but I really did believe. It was like killing us, both of us. Killing everybody I'd ever known. Killing the children I'll never have. God knows how long I went on for. I was desperate not to forget something, leave somebody out. I think Gliess stopped me - told them to take me to the ablution block and put me in a hot bath. I was to be put in a room in the Officers' Block. A room with a bed."

They sat for a long time huddled together, staring through the open door, a violet sky hanging low over the line of the woods. A light rain had started up, pattering on the leaves, nothing very much. Somewhere far away, dogs were barking. Alex looked at his watch thinking it a mercy that hopes faded so gently. Renault was not coming: certainty slipping away like a retreating tide.

"I know why you were sent here, Justine. Why we both ended up here. If you were captured, they had all the proof they needed the Columbine circuit really was dead. That's all they wanted to know. You're a justified sacrifice – I once heard Archer use that term."

"*They*? Who's they?"

"Does it matter? Perhaps that's what always happens when you start calling people agents. Proxy people. Once they have you, you're not really a person anymore. That code the Major gave you was always going to be one-way. That message told him all he needed to know. You're a sacrifice worth paying. I can just hear somebody saying it at one of those interminable meetings. Somebody coming up with *brave young woman* or some such pious claptrap. They'll look solemn for a second and then get on with their war. God, I despise the lot of them! As for me - getting me back here was the surest way of never seeing me again short of murdering me. And they'd tried that already. Killed in action. I might have got a medal."

"But you're not dead, are you Alex? You've not called in. They don't know your call sign. They won't risk faking it, not with Gliess dead. Renault is right - the RAF will run the pickup, they will have had the order ages ago and there's been absolutely no reason to cancel it." She tried to look at his watch, "You'd better be going soon."

"D'you know what my orders were? *Make contact with Simone.* Cynical bastards."

"What time is it, my love?"

He put his arm round her, pulling her close,

"He's a bit late. Nothing serious. The French are always late."

Twenty-Three

They let themselves be herded through sheeting rain to a broad arch of corrugated steel, animated clumps of men in blue sheltering in the mouth of the hanger around trestle tables, trading jokes like schoolboys.

At the desk in the far corner Alex faced a pair of dead eyes: civilian clothes, steel-rimmed glasses.

"Mrs Perry here needs somewhere to rest, can you fix that? She's not too good."

The spectacles turned to Justine, perhaps hoping for some response – they didn't get many women here. Something in the expression that met his own made him look away.

"They put fighters up over the coast." Alex remembered a stream of obscenities as the pilot corkscrewed blindly into cloud, streamers of rain whipping the cockpit. "Ours, thank god. I don't think they knew who the hell we were."

"Christ! You were on that Lysander? Landed crab fashion. Still you were lucky to have the rain ... nothing but bloody rain here."

Alex found he could no longer speak, his jaw frozen. There was something wrong with his left arm, rattling against the wooden ledge of the counter.

"*Lucky,*" he got the word out, "yes, I suppose so."

A hideous stink of burnt rubber had blown into the hangar. Justine at his side retching, murmuring, "God, I'm going to be sick."

"We were to be met."

The man strained forward to catch the words, "Met? What name?"

Alex glanced at the soaked trousers wrapped round his legs, knowing this interrogation would draw him back into a hopeless world of paper. He felt unbearably vulnerable.

"Archer, I would think." If anyone was to meet them, it would surely be Archer. You couldn't see Cabot finding his way past the gate.

"Yes, Colonel Archer. It'll be him."

"Unit?"

"You can hardly miss him, he stands out, rather. He'll have come down this morning."

"That narrows it down nicely, squire – do you have any idea how many …? No, you don't, do you?"

He threw a weary grimace to draw Justine in, "You alright Miss? Sit down over there, take the weight off. A unit really would help, sir."

Alex looked past him to a varnished wooden door incongruously bolted into the metalwork, "Perhaps if you asked …"

"Archer, you say? We don't go by names. Mostly it's numbers. But we've logged the flight in. I don't suppose …?" A slow shake of the head, "No, I suppose you don't. What name?"

"I just told you – Archer."

"No, your name. And you're together?"

"This is Mrs Perry. I'm Alex Vere … Captain Vere. My unit's TPSU. I'm attached to that. No, that's not quite right." An exasperated release of breath, as the man let his pencil fall. "I mean, I'm not currently with the TPSU. Okay, forget all that. I'm part of Colonel Archer's outfit, that should do."

"Archer … Archer …" pulling a thick sheaf of stapled papers from a drawer, running a pencil slowly down a column on the first page.

"We don't have an Archer … No, sorry, I'm a liar … correction, what about this one? *Lt Colonel Neville Archer, MC.* That him?" He frowned at the paper as Alex nodded. "It says *Second Directorate.* What's that when it's at home?"

"I'm sorry. I can't help you."

"No contact details. Nothing. There wouldn't be." He dismissed the pile of paper. "You're with him? That's the two of you?"

"I'm being transferred. Look, is all this necessary? If you'll just find him ..."

"Right-ho, old boy. Homing in on that task. Difficulty is, he's not logged in. Meaning he's not here. He can't be. We do know who's here, you understand?"

Something indefinable in the taut expression facing him made him relent, "Okey-dokey, I'll see whether the Winco is free," waving an arm into the blue haze of empty air. "Park yourselves over there, I'll go looking."

They sat together on a battered sofa pushed against the wall, leatherette arms punctured with cigarette burns like black wounds. Justine lay slumped, her body flaccid, eyes closed. Since the landing something seemed to have snapped inside her: something had gone. She seemed barely alive.

There was a Christmas copy of *The Beano* on the seat. Alex had seen a man in uniform abandon it, hurrying off to join the voices echoing down the distant metal corridors. He picked it up. A picture of kids dancing round a huge flaming plum pudding, a girl in a brown dress, the edges snipped to make her look vaguely elfin.

The rain had stopped. A tiny plane screamed past the mouth of the hangar, teetering against the wind. On the far side of the field a little bleak sunlight sparkled through wet leaves. The plane gone, the place was eerily quiet: apparently no war today.

A door behind the desk pushed open, a man in uniform leaning out. He seemed disappointed they were still there.

"Sorry to keep you," coming round, hand outstretched, "Captain Vere, is it? The Wing Commander's apologies. He doesn't know your Colonel. TPSU was new to us. Bedford Square – that right? He says there's a story about that, but you'll know, of course. Yes, we can lay on some transport. There's a car going in about an hour."

He glanced down at Justine asleep, cradling the grubby bandage in her other hand, his voice suddenly softer, "She won't mind sharing with RAF types, will she?"

After he'd gone, Alex walked to the mouth of the hanger, feeble sunlight throwing long shadows across the grass. A row of red fire buckets hung under a *No Smoking* sign. He lit a cigarette.

Justine's head had fallen onto the pock-marked arm of the sofa. She was breathing quietly, drawing in the tainted air that had defined her life for more months than he could remember. Marking her out for death in a cause neither of them would ever be permitted to know. He walked to stand over her, keeping guard, wondering whether she was dreaming of liberation.

Liberation, when it arrived, was predictably banal. A gleaming Citroen hearse progressing majestically up the drive to the safe house, like god's last joke. Pascal Renault, newly shaved, easing himself out of the driver's seat, surveying the house, pausing to light a cigar. He helped her onto the polished leather, answering the question on her desperate face with a single laconic, "As you see."

He stayed with them at the field, waiting on the narrow path, thin rain dripping through bare trees, scanning the sky.

It took them unawares: the cough of an engine high above, feathered props fluttering suddenly too close, a humming suck of air, wings dropping to the grass.

Renault watched Alex clambering awkwardly aboard. He peeled off his gloves to take Justine's hand, leaning close to catch her words against the roar of the engine. She let him slip her arms into his overcoat, rising tiptoe to brush a kiss against his face.

The Lysander was already moving as he strode back to the car.

It was late afternoon when the promised transport reached the TPSU.

Milky white water smelling of Dettol was puddling down the steps onto the pavement, four neat holes in the brickwork all that remained of the plaque at the foot of the stairwell.

A man at the top of the stairs stopped whistling, clumping down to meet them, khaki puttees over huge spit-polished ammunition boots.

"Can I come up?" Alex had never seen him before.

"I'm not sure as you can. There's nobody here. You're not the van, are you? I'm waiting for a van."

"Removal van, you mean? What's all that about? Is Mr Cabot in?"

"Nobody in, mate. His room was done yesterday. The amount of stuff ... books ... like a bloody library. Anyway, he's not here."

"Colonel Archer then. I won't take long."

"Take as long as you like – he's not here either. Like I keep telling you, nobody's here. They've all gone. And don't ask where. I haven't the foggiest."

Alex peered up into the stairwell, nodding for Justine to stay where she was.

"I'm Captain Vere. I work here."

"Sir ..." The voice suddenly resentful, "Sorry, sir ... didn't appreciate ... you not being in uniform. Well, you'll know then ..."

"Alright, Corporal. Look, there's your van. I'll just have a quick look round."

Alex shouldered past him, up the stairs.

Cabot's room smelled of damp and old tobacco. The familiar battered desk had been left sizing up the narrow doorframe, its drawers, stripped of linings, stacked in towers on the floor.

Everything else had gone.

There was something obsessive about the depredation: even scraps of newspaper had been torn from their pins. Cinders were scattered over the floor where the fireplace had been raked out.

At the end of the corridor the door to *Records* had been taken off, square patterns in the dust all that was left of the line of cabinets. There was pile of spent matches on the floor.

Odd to think he had been standing in this cramped little space - when was it? - not so many days past, a tide of Archer's fury sweeping over him. Archer, the old soldier playing spies, not knowing his adversary had written the rules of the game.

Perhaps old soldier's games always ended like that, with nothing much to show for the effort. Certainly there was nothing to show here: everything gone. Not that *everything* had ever amounted to much.

How easily they had been duped, even Cabot, for all his intelligence. Tricking out this dusty corridor said all you needed to know. How many agents had ended up in a stinking cell in Auch at the will of old soldier Archer? Would they have thought it worthwhile? How could anyone in their right mind have been deceived by all this ham-fisted nonsense?

The Corporal, banging along the bare floor, seemed startled by the sudden flush of anger as Alex turned to face him.

"Beg pardon, sir, they say as how they have to dismantle the desk … if you don't mind. And I ought to get your names, sir. The lady downstairs. If you would …"

"Do you know where this stuff is going?"

The guileless face turned towards him had seen off better than Alex. "I can't say as I do, sir." He gave a little deprecatory shrug. "Orders were to secure the place once cleared. Lock up, you know."

"Where are you to take the key?"

He grinned. "No key, sir. I'm to slam the front door."

Alex returned the smile, starting off down the staircase, calling back: "The name's Captain Vere, Corporal. You'd better write it down. For when you report back."

"That's alright, sir. I'll remember."

"Report back where, exactly?"

"Couldn't really say, sir, I'm to go with the van." He tossed Alex a final bone, "Not far, though, I wouldn't think, not at this time of day. I reckon they'll be settled before the blackout."

It took all night to reach Oxford, the last train from Paddington moving in spasmodic jerks, finally coming to rest in open country.

Justine had slipped into a deep sleep, passengers leaning over her crumpled body to watch the undersides of clouds flaring dull red in the distant sky.

They were shunted into Oxford station at first light on Sunday morning. The Refreshment Room was closed.

Not so The Queen's College: huge oak gates pushed in, offering a cold glimpse of immemorial grass, less trim than usual, a grudging concession to a war that had otherwise passed it by.

A board leaned against a trestle outside the empty Porter's Lodge, the time of Morning Eucharist scrawled in chalk.

Justine stood in the stone tunnel letting a biting wind catch her hair. "I think I'll go. I suppose I'm allowed? Would you mind?"

"Go where? We only have to find his staircase."

"You can go looking, he's your friend. I'm going to the service. Ages since I went to church."

"You'll be awfully early."

"I'll wait." She squeezed his arm, "It's alright Alex, I'm not running away. If you can't find your chum, come and sit next to me. We'll listen to the sermon together. It'll do you good."

He found Cabot bent over a tea chest just inside his room, fishing books out, mumbling titles, adding them to towers ranged behind him across the floor. His door was flung back.

Hearing the timid tap, he looked up, darting a glance beyond Alex into the darkened hallway, the smile a little awkward.

"Alex! My dear chap! Like the proverbial bad penny. I was just thinking about you. I knew you'd end up here. Late, of course, but then, you're always late."

"You don't know the half of it. I've been searching for a familiar face ever since we got back. What on earth's going on? I was beginning to think I was a character in one of those modern plays – you know, that I'd invented everybody and now they'd started to slip my mind and disappear. I'm so pleased you're here. Well, aren't you going to ask me in? It's alright, I can jump over."

Cabot, stepped back into the room. He seemed embarrassed, "Of course. In you come. My humble abode. And no, you didn't invent me - perish the thought. Find yourself a chair, old man. I'm unpacking ... hateful task ... almost finished."

Alex made his way to the window, looking down onto the grass.

"You knew I'd be coming? How's that? I mean, how could you know?"

Cabot was dipping low into the tea chest, his voice muffled, "Oh, I got wind you might be on your way."

"But got wind how?"

He stood up, easing his back, his face flushed from stooping,

"How did I hear, you mean? Oh, the usual tom-toms. Drums along the river, you know?" The smile, always a little uncertain, had evaporated, "Forgive me Alex, I can't tell you - you know how it is?" He glanced again at the open door, "Mrs Perry? She with you?"

"Justine? No secret about that. She's in the Chapel as a matter of fact. Morning Service."

"My word ..." inexplicably relieved, Cabot pushed the door to, turning a long silent scrutiny onto Alex.

His rooms were larger than Alex expected: heavy figured panelling picked out in black and gold. Paintings hung against the wood, uncomfortable modern things he felt he should recognise. Junior Fellows seemed to do themselves surprisingly well.

The place was furnished in bachelor style: overstuffed armchairs on either side of an unlit fire, Persian rugs showing just enough of wide polished floorboards.

The desk faced a window, deep stone mullions framing diamonds of thick glass. The surface was empty apart from a pile of unopened letters and a tall bottle, uncorked. Three glasses were set out on a silver tray.

Cabot stayed with his back to the door, warily seeing the place through his visitor's eyes, gauging an opening gambit.

"About Kessler ..." immediately changing tack, walking to the desk, "rude of me, I should have asked. I've opened a bottle. Something to drink the New Year in. To think, it's 1943 tomorrow. Anyway a homecoming for me ... and you, of course. Hock. Would you like some? Or fake coffee? I'll have to make it, but I don't mind. Sorry it's so cold in here – my devout scout's idea. Apparently the Almighty has set his canon against fires on Sunday. The things you learn in Oxford. Do sit down, old man, you're looming rather."

He poured the drinks, taking his own back to the window, staring into the quadrangle, a beam of dusty sunlight catching his face, softening it. He held up a hand as if he had somehow conjured the deep diapason of the organ from the distant chapel.

"He must be rehearsing. It's Buxtehude, I think. Majestic stuff. I rather envy Mrs Perry."

"I'm sorry. I didn't think. Do go if you want to. I can come as well."

"Not me, old boy. I've a superstitious horror of sacred places, always have had. I think it's the idea of being secretly watched."

He seemed to make his mind up to something, turning to face Alex. "Yes, Kessler. Funny how all that business turned out."

"Because he ended up dead, you mean? Not all that funny for him."

"You know what I mean."

"Actually, I don't, not really. It's why I'm here. I've news you'll find hard to credit. We have to talk. I feel complicit in that Kessler affair. I don't know how much you know, but we've been taken for fools. *Operation Alathea* was changed at the last minute. God knows who by, but whoever it was decided we didn't deserve to know. And now Archer is nowhere to be found - vanished. Shut up shop. I'm not going to drop it, you know. I'll go over his head if I need to. We don't owe him anything."

The sunlight framing Cabot against the window had converted him to a black silhouette, patiently sipping wine, the rim of his glass twinkling yellow, waiting for Alex to finish. A clock outside in the quadrangle began to beat slow asynchronous chimes, the order not quite right.

"The plan wasn't changed, Alex." He was tracing patterns on the misted window with his fingertip, his voice barely audible, "At least, not in essence. I thought you knew. The idea was that his parachute would fail. Surely you realised? Kessler did."

"The thought crossed my mind. Archer's insane enough to think of something like that. But that would be murder."

"You're sounding a trifle gothic this morning. We're soldiers aren't we? Well, you certainly are. And I suppose I am, in a manner of speaking. Soldiers kill people in times of war – it's what they're for. Anyway, the failing parachute is academic. The problem went away."

"That's a bit cold blooded. I thought you liked Kessler. You're suddenly sounding very well informed. You're not suggesting his dying was intentional?"

"Drug overdose wasn't it? Not my ticket, old man, more your province. I suppose accidents happen. All I'm saying is, given it was deemed Kessler had to arrive dead, somebody brought his death about. Let's be grateful for small mercies. If that's cold blooded, so be it."

Holding his glass by its foot, idly gazing through the window, he seemed to have finished, letting an embarrassed silence fall into the room. It came to Alex how much he resented this violation of his private world. Apparently the camaraderie of the TPSU, always a little asymmetric, did not travel as far as Oxford.

He came across to where Alex sat, standing over him, an irritated edge to his voice.

"I'll tell you what he was carrying, if you like. Is that what you came to hear? Incidentally, why *did* you come? It's early for a social call."

"What d'you mean, *Tell me?* You can hardly make a mystery of what we were up to. I know perfectly well what he was carrying: all that fake junk about German resistance. You know, it came to me on the train today. What we are up to. You only have to get away a bit, see it in perspective, none of it would fool a child."

Cabot had slipped into the other armchair, the smile friendly at last.

"You're a nice chap Alex. You know, I didn't realise until this minute, just how nice. Scout's honour - I really did think you knew. And now I'm going to feel bad, because apparently not so. Kessler didn't take our Steffle stuff. That was all smoke for prying eyes. Honestly, I thought you knew. The operation involved something altogether different."

"*Different?* How different? And how come John Cabot knew? How come you, and not me? How do you imagine that makes me feel?"

"Left out?" A yelp of a laugh was instantly cancelled, Cabot taking his spectacles off, polishing them, a tiny apologetic gesture.

"Sorry, old man - that was a low blow. This place makes one waspish. It was unworthy. I take it back. *Betrayed*, I suppose. Then again, that's an ugly word. Let's settle for *let down*. But we're all let down one way or another in this business, aren't we? Look at Archer - not a clue, poor devil. All his blind rages wasted on the desert air."

"You were right first time - *left out* will do perfectly well. Frankly, I got used to it. I looked for you at the TPSU."

Cabot said nothing.

"You know I was in France. You wouldn't believe these past few days. The situation there is unbelievable. And before you say anything, I was with Kessler – his body - on the flight down to Metz. D'you know what's going on?"

"Rather a generalisation, old chap. Can you be a bit more specific?"

"Sorry - I'm fagged out. Bear with me. I mean who changed the plan? Is that specific enough?"

"*Changed* – that's a loaded word, Alex. What our lawyer friends call leading. I'm not talking about changing things – you are."

He was back at the window, looking down into the quadrangle.

"When they recruited me I had orders to divulge nothing to a living soul." He whirled round, "The same for you - correct?"

Alex returned his stare, "I suppose so. You make it sound dramatic, in my case ..."

"I do as I'm told, Alex. Didn't you notice that trait? Until a few minutes ago I thought we had both been playing the same game, neither of us letting on. All your world-weary stuff about being left out of the scheme of things - I thought it was for my benefit. You were so damned good at it, as well. I was quite jealous. You and your lost memory! Priceless. Alright, I was wrong ..."

"*They* recruited us. Who's *they*? You mean Archer? I was recruited by Archer."

"So you were, Alex ... in a manner of speaking ... so you were. And you never thought to ask who recruited Archer?"

"No I didn't. Is that such a lapse? Archer's bad enough. Look, are you going to explain? Or would you be breaking another sacred oath?"

"And now you're getting angry. Please don't. The whole operation's probably dead anyway, thanks to you. Or thanks to the famous Mrs Perry at her prayers. Alright, I'll explain, if you insist."

Twenty-Four

Cabot went out into the hallway, looking into the panelled gloom of the corridor. He turned to come back in, pulling the outer oak closed, his expression a kind of defiant embarrassment, the reluctant host saddled with the wrong sort of guest. Finding his way barred by an open tea chest he plucked a book out, turning it over and over in his hands, sensing the tension in the room.

"You won't believe me, Alex. I'm at a loss as to where to start. For heaven's sake, why the long face? We're still friends, aren't we? Let's not fall out over this. About this war we're all fighting – as good a place to start as any. Haven't you noticed it's pretty well lost, Alex?"

Cabot had always been a little inclined to talk down, to fall into an air of proprietorial superiority. Alex wondered whether he had always been beaten over the head with his own name like this. He could not remember.

"No, I haven't noticed, John," watching Cabot widen his eyes at the name, "high strategy's a bit out of our league isn't it? If you learn one thing in Bedford Square it's that this war isn't really our affair. We'll have to wait to see who wins, if they bother to tell us. Meanwhile, we do what we're ordered."

"There, you put your finger on it. We're ordered to tell lies. You can't be selective about lies: *Lie to one, lie to all*, as the saying goes. You know, people will look back and say that was the defining spirit of our age, our *Zeitgeist* - a time to tell lies."

He perched himself warily on the edge of a hard chair by the desk, keeping his distance. "Take that cover story for Kessler, his sickly childhood and so on. Tell the truth - you knew it was nonsense right off. I remember you had dozens of reasons it couldn't work. What changed your mind?"

"Actually, you did."

"Are you sure? Perhaps you didn't want to face the truth. Didn't inventing Herr Steffle take your mind off what was really going to happen to Hauptmann Kessler? Did that never cross your mind? Or is that me playing the psychologist?"

He checked, frowning slightly, lips silently rehearsing a phrase, the words, when they finally arrived, spilling out in a rush, "Truth is, Alex, we planned for Kessler to be carrying maps."

"Who's *we*? This isn't about me at all, is it? You've been playing some kind of double game. Deceiving me - is that it?"

He knew the question was idle. That morning, walking alongside Justine through echoing Oxford streets, a prayer had been beating in his head: *Let it not be Cabot. Not the only one I trusted. Let it not be him.*

In truth, he was here only for confirmation.

Cabot's mild face regarded him, the gentle perfect scholar, ingenuous smile a little awry.

"Deceiving you? Well, you could put it that way. Mind you, deceiving Alex Vere wasn't exactly the alpha and omega of the business. Why the resentful tone? You said it yourself – we're under orders. I'll be perfectly frank with you. The plan was that maps would be planted on Kessler's body. Maps. Nothing else."

"What maps? No, wait a minute, how could you know it was going to be a body? That he would arrive dead?"

"How you do harp on about that. It's tiresome - you're beginning to sound like Miss Marple. All I was told was that the matter would be arranged. And it was. As for the maps ..." His face dissolved into a curious tentative smile, the proud schoolboy up for his prize, "The landing site for an eventual invasion of Northern France. Disposition of forces. The best I've seen Portland Place come up with. An incredible job."

He opened his hands, a weary little *nothing to declare* gesture, "So now you know."

Alex felt a surge of embarrassed relief, blushing for the shame of it. It was difficult not to return the smile.

"Come on, John - don't tell me Archer's sold you his version of the Haversack Ruse? Archer's at least one war too late for that game."

"Colonel Meinertzhagen and his devilishly cunning deception. Interesting chap. I've met him. I wonder whether he really did it. Perhaps it doesn't matter, it's such a good story."

"Well nobody's going to fall for it twice, that's obvious. Honestly John – you let Archer get to you. Too many hours in the museum, that's your problem ..."

Seeing Cabot's face, his conciliatory laugh turned a little false. "I'm sorry ... I shouldn't mock. I thought you were serious for a minute. It's not the quality of the printing Jerry will be thinking about when they find Kessler. The idea's typical Archer - barking mad. Only an idiot would be taken in. No, no ... sorry, I don't mean ..."

Cabot sat on, calmly contemplating the cold grate, perhaps wondering whether to put a match to it. When he looked up, the expression was a kind of bleak exasperation, honed through numberless hours with struggling undergraduates. He glanced down at the place on his sleeve where his watch might have been visible.

"Not *completely* mad, Alex. But you do put it awfully well. As you say, only an idiot ..." reaching out to gather the empty glasses. "You know, I think this stuff is rather good. Would you like some more?"

Alex stared dumbly at the convoluted pattern of the rug at his feet, feeling strangely outmanoeuvred. "But you do see it's completely barmy? A German officer kitted out for a landing at sea in the middle of a field."

Footsteps clattered along the corridor outside, loitering at the door, drawn to the sound of voices. Cabot raised one hand, waiting until someone shuffled noisily away, a heavy distant door echoing shut.

"Speaking of idiots, Alex, old man, that was your definition of Colonel Archer, if I recall."

"The man's a fool."

"No, *idiot* does perfectly well. Our flamboyant Colonel provides an endless source of merriment for spies from Whitechapel to Mayfair. All those watching eyes."

He settled back into the armchair opposite Alex, patience finally exhausted.

"For heaven's sake, Alex! You're not usually so slow. For months the German High Command has been asking why we're still hanging on. We do read their signals traffic, you know," tapping Alex on the knee, harder than necessary, beating the words into him, "you understand? You understand?"

Alex wriggled back, "Understand what, for heaven's sake?"

"Their Intelligence people have concluded we really are irredeemably stupid. You understand the consequence of that?"

His puffy face was tight with satisfaction, a slight sheen on his skin: the tutor giving the struggling pupil one final chance to leap the humiliating gap. Alex felt sick.

"You could have explained without all that rigmarole. And I'm not slow – just bloody tired. I've been on a train all night. Yes, I see what you're getting at. Whatever arrives in the briefcase defines itself as false – is that it? Not deception - cover."

"Hole in one, old man! I knew you'd get there. Here, I'll top you up."

"And this was really Archer's idea? It sounds too clever-clever for him."

"Nothing to do with Archer," Cabot sounded irritated, "and it is clever. It's given us the perfect channel."

"*Us* again?"

"Sorry, you know I can't say who. I've already said too much. You can't expect me to be entirely frank."

"You never have been, have you? All that stuff about the short-sighted German scholar. What else isn't true? Look at this place. Is this how Junior Fellows live?"

"Well I *am* short-sighted." Cabot allowed himself a faint self-deprecating smile, "And I do claim to be a German scholar, you know. Quite a sound one, as a matter of fact. Did you never think to check?"

He was close now, the flowery scent of hock on his breath, his tone curiously intense. "We've another drop next moon. Same idea. French maps again. And it's going to work. They'll think they know what we want them to believe …"

"And flag it as disinformation?"

"Of course! The most cack-handed transparent disinformation you can imagine. Irredemably stupid. If we claim we're landing for certain at a place, the only sensible conclusion is *anywhere but there*. We've had the army types on it. It could be worth a Division if Jerry swallows the bait. That's ten thousand men in the wrong place. Gold, Alex, pure gold."

You could almost smell the triumph on his skin.

Alex got up, feeling like a cheated lover. From now on, humiliation was always going to have the cold foxy smell of this room about it. He looked round, wondering whether he'd brought anything with him.

"I think I'll be off. See whether Justine's service has finished."

"But you can't go - you've barely arrived. Stay for lunch. Oxford's safe enough, you know. I heard the other day that the Führer intends to settle here. He says he won't bomb us if we won't bomb Heidleburg – he gets the better of that deal, I must say."

"I suppose I shouldn't ask who told you. I shouldn't have come – I can see that. I thought you could help with something. One more thing I was wrong about."

Cabot followed him across to the window, peering down into the quadrangle, looking at his watch.

"Bear up, Alex. It doesn't suit you - all this hurt pride. What do you want me to say? That I'm sorry we misled you? Well, I'm damned if I will. It wasn't in my power to disabuse you, you know that perfectly well. Do stay. Can't have you standing outside in the rain nursing your grievances. The Service hasn't even started. You're perfectly safe here. Mrs P knows where you are."

When he grinned like that he was the old Cabot again. Alex remembered watching him on all fours like a plump baby crawling across his giant map.

Feeling Cabot's arm on his shoulder he flinched away. "I'll stand in the rain if I feel like it. And why harp on about being safe? Why shouldn't I be safe? You surely don't think I'm going to give your game away?" Intending to sound angry, Alex realised he sounded merely infantile.

"Look, I'd better go, I wouldn't want to be in your way. You'll have your next drop to think about. Another prisoner, is it? How are you going to arrange for that one to be dead?"

Cabot stared at him, rabbit eyes blinking behind huge lenses. "It's unfortunate, you taking it this way. I didn't appreciate you were so touchy. What can I say? The other briefcases won't involve personnel if that's what's pricking your conscience."

"Nothing to do with *my* conscience. How am I supposed to take it? Months and months we've been working on one insane project after another, all the time you going behind my back, knowing I was wasting my time."

"And now you really are angry. But it's not true you were wasting your time. The TPSU will get the credit, after all. In as much as you were - how shall I put this? - a necessary decoy, not wasted at all."

"I'm meant to be consoled by that? A bloody *decoy*!"

"A little humiliating I grant - not a role I'd like myself - but not wasted effort. That French setup in Duke Street is riddled with German spies. You've been watched ever since Archer netted you."

"But you're not working for Archer, are you? Who *are* you working for? Can't you say? That's surely not a state secret."

"Isn't it?"

"Oh, it's not so hard to guess. Isn't it obvious? The Major ..."

The laugh, when it came, was an infuriated bark. "I know damn-all about your Major. Apart from the fact he's an infernal nuisance and has some weird personal agenda of his own. You know he's chased me down here? Keeps leaving his card at the lodge like some Victorian suitor. Thank god for the porter - I am resolved to be not at home. I suppose he's found out I organised that damned explosion that went wrong."

He was standing too close, small broken veins under his eyes a purple smudge. He looked desperately tired.

"Look, I'm employed to deceive people. Apparently I'm good at it, that's why I was picked. Rather wounding, as a matter of fact – it makes me feel cheap. Go if you want to. Please yourself. What did you come for, anyway? What do you want?"

"That explosion. It was meant for Justine, wasn't it?"

Cabot stepped back. "Not you as well? People endlessly going on about one little pop in a field. For god's sake, *yes*. The answer's yes. Does that satisfy you? What's more, the local people had good reasons for doing it."

"Good, but completely false. She would have died for nothing at all."

"The fog of war, Alex. Why go on about it? As I said, she's a lucky woman."

"You know the Major's brother was killed in that car?"

Cabot stared at him, "No … no, I didn't know … His brother, you say? No, I didn't know that. How could I? Now that is unfortunate."

Alex followed as he retreated to his armchair, standing over him.

"*Unfortunate* - is that all you can say? It's bad enough you're responsible - you have to humiliate the poor devil into the bargain."

"That's nonsense."

"Is it? How d'you think you'll feel when you discover somebody's pulling *your* strings? It's always somebody like you, isn't it? Always some bastard who knows better. You know what I came here for, don't you?"

Cabot gave a momentary flinch of distaste as a fleck of spittle caught his cheek. "My dear chap, of course I know. You wanted to play catch-the-spy. You had your doubts about the good Major and now I've dispelled them, all at once he's a poor devil. So you turn to me. I'm right aren't I? Do you really think this is a job for a psychologist? Not exactly your *metier* is it?"

"There's no need to sneer. You don't know bloody everything. Real people have died on account of your pathetic cack-handed meddling in the Columbine circuit. And for nothing. You could have killed Justine. For no reason at all. I'm not surprised the Major's looking for you. How long do you think you can avoid him? I know what I'd do in his shoes."

"Oh, I think I'll survive." Cabot leaned back, hands steepled, "You were going to explain what I don't know? Do tell. Is it a long story? Are you cold? Shall I light the fire? I can make an exception."

Alex ignored him, "Do you know how many missions we've deployed in the South West?"

"Missions? Are we to talk about missions? No, I don't know that. Twenty perhaps."

"While you've been going behind my back playing with briefcases, every mission has failed. Agents dropped to reception committees have been arrested on the spot. Those dropped blind have been picked up in a matter of hours. The last was Justine. She dropped right into a trap. The same trap was intended for me."

"Yet you say she is here in the Chapel. And you are here with her. You do both seem to lead charmed lives. But yes, of course I know some agents are sending under duress. It's unavoidable. You're not saying I'm responsible?"

"Of course you're not responsible. You have no idea what's been going on. And it's not *some* agents - the Gestapo are working all our sets in Saint Aunix. They have a WT station doing nothing else. Now let me tell you something else you don't know. We've been dropping supplies straight into German hands for months. The resistance groups we've been supplying don't exist. They're fakes. It's been a catastrophe."

"Alex, my dear chap, captured agents have been turned for years."

"I'm not talking about that. Somebody's been helping them on their way. When Justine Perry was arrested she transmitted a capture code. One she was expressly ordered to use if she was sending under duress. You know what London did? Queried the code over an insecure channel, *en clair*. Whoever did that was signing her death warrant. What name would you use for whoever did that?"

"What do you mean, *expressly ordered*?"

"She got the order by wire just before take-off. From the Major."

"You know, Alex, I find that rather hard to believe. Are you sure the Major sent it? Are you really sure?"

Cabot left the question lying in the silence between them, the faint smile on his earnest face striking Alex like a blow. For a moment the room appeared smaller than it should be, tumbled piles of books leering at him. Suddenly, it seemed there was not enough air in this cold place for both of them.

Twenty-Five

It was an age before Cabot spoke, leaning his head back against the leather of the armchair, head cocked to one side, the familiar moue almost an apology.

"Why do you think I was against Mrs Perry going back to France, Alex?"

His name again, mutating into an assurance that he was wrong about something. Had always been wrong - fatally wrong.

"Justine? Were you against her going? Perhaps you were, I don't remember. What's it to do with you, anyway?"

Annoyed at the slight quaver in his voice, Alex felt something in his chest scudding too fast, something drumming in his neck. "All I know is she was betrayed."

"You do keep using that word. Let me tell you why I was opposed. She could have done immense damage to a vital operation."

There was a slight hoarseness about his voice, as if words could not do justice to the immensity of his thoughts, as if speech somehow demeaned them.

"Aren't you getting things out of proportion? Alright, it's a clever idea, but Justine didn't even know about Kessler. How could she possibly damage your precious plan?"

Cabot batted the objection away, suddenly impatient, "You remember that day you came back with Kessler's story about captured WT operators? I was so relieved. I thought the two of us finally had something we could talk about. That was the day I realised you weren't just pretending you knew nothing. You really did know nothing. The two of you blundering about in the forest like bloody Hansel and Gretel. Look at your face - you still don't know what I'm talking about, do you?"

Alex turned to stare through the window, Cabot's voice behind him coldly addressing some invisible audience of its own. "There we were, about to launch the biggest disinformation project ever undertaken – really huge - and by some stupid mischance two agents risking the whole thing."

"This is mad, John," rounding on him, "it's the TPSU you're on about. You work there. It couldn't launch a teapot."

Only the tone of Cabot's dry recital changed, his voice more reflective. "The first WT operator we dropped into France lasted quite a long time - a couple of months, I think. His codename was Patrick."

"How could you possibly know that? That's field stuff. What the hell did it have to do with you?"

Cabot paused, irritated, "I'm afraid I wasn't entirely frank about what I was up to before Archer's TPSU business. I spent most of last year designing protocols for the code room at Baker Street. I'm attached to another unit now." His expression was dismissive, "No reason you should know more." Alex barely recognised him.

"One day, Patrick came on out of hours with news his courier had been arrested. Nothing after that for several days. The next message, both capture codes – the bluff and the second."

"He'd been arrested ... of course ..."

Cabot shook his head, "For god's sake Alex, will you pay attention for once in your life. Do you want to discover what perfidy is? Shall I tell you about perfidious Albion, Alex? I really wonder if you deserve to know, Alex."

"I do know who I am, if that's your concern – there's really no need to remind me. And yes, I know what capture means. You forget I've experienced it. In all probability this chap Patrick was tortured to get that second code."

A curious expression, not quite pain, fleetingly crossed Cabot's face. "You really are infuriating you know. Why won't you sit down?

Do you think you're intimidating me pacing about like that? You're missing the most obvious point. Capture codes are completely worthless? *Completely*. There is literally nothing anyone can do with them."

"You don't think it's important to know an agent's been captured?"

Another weary shake of the head, "No, not really. Not from the agent himself, anyway … not a sensible source. Capture codes as such are pointless. And that includes the one I arranged for Mrs Perry to send, by the way. I sent her that wire - it had nothing at all to do with our obtrusive Major scuttling along the corridor outside. It was one last effort to make them believe we thought her safe. Futile, of course, given what she knew. Alas."

"I'm getting tired of *we*, you know. This unit you work for? Are you going to say?"

Cabot bowed his head, a kind of mock apology, "Can't, old boy, and that's that. The substance of Patrick's message was a request for the coordinates of a drop. I suggested we reply, saying his Morse was garbled, asking for a re-send. Mrs Perry would recognise the tactic. Two days later we went ahead with the requested drop. Exactly as if he was safe and sound tucked up in bed."

"Dropping what?"

"God almighty! Ever the irrelevant question. What on earth does that matter? Small arms, I think, ammunition, explosives. All in perfect order. Over the next month, three more messages, obviously sent to dictation. We bounced the capture codes. Went ahead with the drops. It served as a trial run."

"Trial for what?"

Cabot blinked at the question, the first slight hint of a smile, "I'm coming to that, old man. Patience. The fourth time he came on, he included the letters CAPT in plain English mixed in with the cipher. I admit that was unexpected. It was his last transmission. I'm afraid it has to be assumed he perished. Of course, he was a dead man from the moment he was arrested. But we had turned his capture into something really significant."

"Can you imagine how he must have felt, thinking he was betraying the circuit?"

"You're being sentimental, Alex. By then, we had intercepted a message to Berlin from a Major Gliess, the lucky communications officer. Excitable chap. Crowing that he was working a fake agent trusted completely by the fools in London. In other words, his very own golden goose. He had his proofs - arms drops, food drops, explosives, medical supplies and so forth. Of course, they were not going to buy that. After all, perfidious Englanders play games - I'm sure Berlin has read about *haversacks*. But this time Berlin already had proof enough. You know who, of course?"

"You mean that poor fool Archer?"

"Exactly. Archer and his pathetic briefcases. Transparent Colonel Archer, busy fighting a war in which the Hun is even more stupid than he was last time. Beyond belief, the English had put this lunatic in charge - they couldn't believe their luck."

He reached out for his glass, sipping, a long theatrical pause. "All we had to do was give Archer his head. Soon enough Gliess was boasting he had information about drop sites, circuits, safe houses, contacts, cut-outs, everything. We have all the signals traffic. He believed he was pulling the strings for a whole circuit. In fact, you know its name, Alex. Patrick dead, Gliess could barely wait for the next arrest."

"If you're going to say what I think you're going to say, perhaps you shouldn't."

"Oh, for god's sake, man. He believed he'd got himself a completely reliable source. Can't you see what that was worth? Gliess was a godsend."

"Not any more. He's dead."

Cabot looked up, surprised. "Yes … I heard. A heart attack apparently. Visiting an ack-ack battery near Auch. In the middle of the night. I wouldn't have thought that was his sort of thing. Odd you knowing that."

"Even odder, you knowing. Friends in high places?"

"You're a rum character Alex. Maybe you really do know something. Why don't you sit down? Finish your wine. I'll tell you about the first story we planted through Patrick. A planned raid on the harbour at Toulon."

"You never considered Patrick's part in this? What he thought? Poor devil."

"On the contrary. He must have denied everything, thrown sand, anything to convince them something was wrong. They would take all that as confirmation, of course. Gliess swallowed the Toulon raid story, by the way. They still have a sizeable force waiting for it. He's never once smelled a rat. We've been feeding him for months. He's swallowed every single story. It's a miracle."

"But it wasn't just Patrick, was it?"

"You want me to talk about that WT Simone, don't you? Yes, she was *enrolled* - I suppose that's the word. We cleared her arrival with Columbine."

"You might as well have cleared it with German Intelligence. In fact, that's precisely what you were doing."

Cabot shook his head, "Arrested WT operators are well-treated ..."

"You really believe that? Have you any idea ..."

"... accorded POW status if they cooperate. Frankly, it's more use having Gliess think they're working for him than ..."

"Than have them think they're working for us. Than have them carry out their mission? Is that what you mean? God almighty! I don't believe I'm hearing this."

"Even if you're right, Alex – and you're not - Simone was bound to be captured. It's part of the deal. I've never understood it – how you people blind yourself to the truth. Feelings of invulnerability – or is that me playing psychologist? No, it's just a matter of time. Six weeks – isn't that what they say? You know perfectly well that's an overestimate. The German Direction Finding is now so good, operators are refusing to transmit. You can't blame them, but what use is that? The truth is we thought she'd be a useful addition to the Gliess setup because her Morse was so error prone. Nobody expected her to take her own life."

"Now I know why they were waiting for Justine. And me. If it hadn't been for a cock-up at the drop zone …"

"But you came back to us, Alex. And Mrs Perry." He looked up, eyebrows raised, "Obviously she has somebody protecting her. We'd give a lot to know *who*? Any help in that direction?"

Alex stared him down, feeling the blood rise in his face, "How could she possibly be protected? Who would risk that?"

"Well, some other time then," the familiar grin had returned, "you're a dreadful liar, Alex – it's endearing. I really can't fathom why you're in this trade. You see now why it was quite impossible for her to go back. She only had to let slip we knew agents were acting under duress and Gliess would realise he was being fooled. And she did know, Alex."

He got up, emptying the fag end of the bottle into his glass, settling back into his chair. "She knew - because Alex Vere told her. I ordered Archer to veto her drop. I'm afraid telling him I had the authority precipitated another bout of wrath. He cursed me in purple for five minutes. Told me to go to hell. You have to admire him, don't you? I smiled sweetly, explained I was already well on the way there and would shortly be leaving his employ. But it was all too late. Your damned Major decided to send her back before we could do much about it apart from change the drop zone."

"I suppose you know she was tortured?" Alex found himself shouting: "Tortured, John. Do you want to know about that? You couldn't wait for more arrests could you? You've been hurrying things along. It's not much of a step from waiting for an arrest, to ensuring one takes place. I'm right, aren't I? At least fifteen times right. And one of those was intended to be me."

Cabot looked at him. "I didn't know you when that drop was planned. That's the truth. You have to believe me."

"Oh, I believe you, alright. What are friends for, after all? And what was to happen to me? Am I allowed to know?"

"It was thought Captain Vere would break under interrogation ... look, do you really want to hear this? If you must know, we thought you would talk yourself into a hole. Something about your interest in the Ganser Effect. It's in your Torridon Report."

"And John Cabot saw my Torridon Report, did he? Go on, finish your sordid little story."

"You believed you were carrying forged currency. I think the idea was if you were captured ... and yes, Alex, it's *if* ... they would be holding a senior intelligence officer completely convinced of a plot to flood the French market with forged Reichmarks. Then you had to embarrass us all, turning up alive and kicking. Obviously, once you'd met Kessler you couldn't be allowed back. Fortunately, Archer was only too willing to believe you'd talked."

"I asked what was to *become* of me? Or isn't that consideration part of the equation?"

"I didn't make you expendable, Alex. You made yourself. You were expendable as soon as you signed on. I'll ask you a question. Do you really believe dropping rifles to disaffected farmers is going to win this war?"

"Bugger your sophistry. Dropping agents to certain capture. There's a name for that."

"Not certain capture, Alex - not certain. Take you, for instance. And not murder, if that's what you're implying. Perhaps a kind of suicide, I admit. But volunteering for your business is already a kind of suicide, isn't it? Part of your equipment is the means to commit suicide – is that not so? Operational life measured in weeks. I've never understood how you people can do that."

Alex came to sit in the chair opposite Cabot, waiting for their eyes to meet. "Would you like to know how Patrick died, John? No, don't ask how I know. I'm going to tell you and you're going to listen. Then you will have to hope I can bring myself to walk out of here without wringing your superior neck."

Cabot drew his legs in, feeling in a pocket for his case, half rising to light a cigarette.

Alex put a hand on his shoulder, "No, stay there. I want you where I can see you. Patrick was taken to a house in Saint Aunix. I know the place. It used to be a butchers shop. He was hoisted up onto a meat hook in the cellar. Did you know there's a way of piercing the wrists?" Cabot looked away. "No? Surprisingly, it takes the weight."

"Look, Alex, I know what you're trying to do. Really, you're wasting your time. I don't live in your world - don't you understand yet? You're embarrassing yourself."

"You're going to hear anyway. Perhaps I can live with being embarrassed. For god's sake! Do you think that matters?" He leaned across, their faces inches apart, whispering, "They beat him with a length of electric cable. Nothing very sophisticated. What came to hand, you might say. Other things as well. Worse than anything you could even begin to imagine. It's not your world, is it? Cigarette burns - heard about those? There's a mincing machine in that shop. Frankly, you don't deserve knowing – he's worth better than that."

Cabot had taken his spectacles off, mechanically polishing them, weary red eyes blinking in cigarette smoke. He seemed to be curled into himself, waiting. Alex broke away, leaning back.

"And do you know why they did all this? I'll tell you. They wanted the code he used to assert that his messages were secure. They didn't get it. Oh, not because he held out. People don't hold out – virtually never. *You will succumb* is the first thing you learn in this business. It's our motto. No, they didn't get it, because there wasn't one. There was nothing to give. After a few hours they took him down. They managed to put some clothes on him. Not shoes - you need complete feet for shoes. Then he was shot. In the yard at the back of the Gendarmerie. Executed. You're not allowed to beat people to death in France - it's an orderly place. There's due process."

Alex stopped, aware his voice was shaking, the pain behind his eyes beyond bearing, squeezing them closed. Tears ran hot across his cheek.

Cabot went on looking at the end of his cigarette like a man forced to hear a tiresome story he'd heard before. "Tell me this, Alex. What if my Gliess bluff helped get us into Africa? All things considered, that's a miracle. Don't you think that was worth the life of a soldier?"

"Oh, no – you're not getting away with that. That's *your* cheap little comfort, not mine. And if you're talking about Patrick, you have your answer. He didn't volunteer to be deceived. It's as simple as that."

"That's an absurd thing to say. You always were slightly absurd, Alex." He looked at his watch, frowning in disbelief, "I think I'll forego lunch and get away myself. It was interesting meeting up again. There's an earlier train. At least I'll miss the customary New Year hoards of drunken Scotsmen. It's only a walk to the station."

As he struggled up Alex prodded him in the chest, feeling plump flesh yield to his finger, registering the indignity with an expression of pained distaste. Watching him fall back, bouncing slightly, it seemed to Alex his whole life had been contingent on the indulgence of people like this – people who knew better, people one crucial step ahead. The noble cause for which he would have given his life no more than a grotesque charade designed to deliver him hog-tied to his enemy - reality itself predicated on lies.

Cabot sat on, lips nervously forming silent words, oblivious of that part of his web of betrayal that was truly unforgiveable. Justine, her future snuffed out, casually consigned to hell. The justified sacrifice. Alex felt nails bite deep into his bunched fists, an emotion he had never known before consuming him. Torridon had schooled him in the precision of violence - where the blow must fall for maximum harm. Had schooled him how to sidestep the inevitable spurt of blood that would blind his adversary, the nose crushed to a broken mass of flesh and mucus. It seemed he almost felt the pain of that initial blow jarring his wrist as Cabot's upturned face registered sudden alarm. And in that instant, Alex realised a single blow could never be contained, would spawn a hellish frenzy of others, until all that remained of that gentle scholar's face pressed back against the chair would be a single filmy eye hanging loose.

"You really don't know what you've done, do you? You don't have the faintest idea. Don't you know what you did to her? You and your kind. Our masters, that's what you think, isn't it? God damn you ... God damn you to hell." Clotted with impotent rage, Alex heard his voice lost in the dead book-lined space. "You snivelling cunt. That's the word. You want to know how I feel knowing I've been mixed up with a cunt like you? Ashamed for the whole bloody human race. No, don't turn away. Let me say this - you made a mistake telling me that story. I could beat the life out of you right now ... god knows why I don't ... for Justine's sake ... Justine."

As Alex stepped back, Cabot eased himself warily out of the chair, slipping past to pull at the door of a panelled wardrobe, reaching inside for a raincoat. When finally he turned to speak, his voice was steady. "Odd word that ..." balancing a coat hanger in his hands. "*Cunt*. As a term of abuse, I mean. You get it in Catullus ... about a mule, I think. I always found Catullus slightly obvious - you know ... gross. As for your threat - it is a threat, isn't it, Alex? Mixed in with that extraordinary little scatological outburst. Why do you think I told you?"

"I've been wondering. I suppose treachery needs a knowing victim. Dante worked that out, if I recall, and by god there's a circle in hell for friends like you. You couldn't resist telling, could you?"

"Resist? Oh, I think I could do that alright. Not everybody is worth boasting to, Alex, not even you," glancing at his watch again, a flash of starched cuff. "In a little over two hours I shall be explaining how Captain Vere has come into possession of a significant state secret. *Unauthorised* knowledge of one of our most secret operations. Why don't you think of it as an infection? You're infected with knowledge. Knowledge you really shouldn't have. What do you imagine the remedy will be?"

"You mean somebody strangling me in a dark alley?"

Cabot looked pained. "I'm a back room man, you know that." He folded the raincoat over his arm. "But I suppose you do need to take care, old man. Now ... where's my briefcase? You're an incredibly lucky chap, you know – enough to get one believing in angels. I really must go. Pull the door to, if you would. We don't shake hands in this College – did you know that? As well, really – avoids any last minute unpleasantness."

Outside in the quadrangle it was raining, lines of black running down buttressed stone walls. The Chapel was dark, hazy blue light from tall stained glass windows reminding Alex vaguely of the interrogation room at Abbot Court.

The place seemed empty, a single candle in a stand on the chancel steps struggling restlessly to stay alight. The organ was still playing. Alex walked a little way along the central aisle and stood leaning against one of the wooden stalls to listen. Bach: one of the trio sonatas, counterpoint like a relentless argument that would never reach a resolution.

He was about to leave when a figure in a stall near the altar rail struggled to its feet, sensible shoes clicking towards him on the wide stone flags. She was smiling.

"Hello Guffin. There ... you've caught me about my secret rites. Would you believe it? There wasn't a single soul for the Service. Well, I suppose two souls if you count me and the vicar or Dean or whatever he's called. He seemed nice. Very old. I was his congregation. Really shocking hearing it all in English, though. Had me blushing when he came to the *Dearly beloved* bit. I didn't go up, of course ... What's the matter? You look bad."

Alex frowned, "Go up where?"

"It's a Mass. I didn't take it ... couldn't really ... of course I couldn't."

She took his arm, drawing him in close, her face tipping up to his.

"Don't you bother your heathen head about all this now. How did it go with Cabot? Did you get what you wanted?" He felt her lips brush his cheek, "You've been drinking."

"Oh, it went well enough."

The music ended abruptly in mid-course, echoing briefly in the stifled space. Justine pulled him aside into a stall, sliding along to make room.

"Here's as good as anywhere now that racket's ended. There's something I want to tell you. You remember how I was miles early for the service? I was sitting quietly up there when I heard somebody come in. In a stall behind me. He wouldn't have known I was there. Over there. D'you know who?"

Alex shook his head, finding the musty-sweet silence of the place vaguely menacing. He glanced vacantly at Justine at his side, her face turned to his.

"It was the Major. What on earth was he doing here?"

"Same as me, I think. Looking for Cabot. There was somebody in the corridor outside the room. I guessed it was him. He must have heard our voices – anyway he went away."

"He saw me when I turned round. I sort of waved and he walked along the side there until he was quite close. It was then I saw. He looked terrible."

"You mean ill?"

"No, not ill." She checked, suddenly embarrassed, "I almost feel I shouldn't say. Completely distraught. Rubbing at his face like mad. I know that look, you can't fool a woman about secret tears. He came up, fake smile and all. Went to shake hands, then saw this bandage thing. The way he looked at me. I don't think I'll ever forget it. He just turned tail and walked out. Didn't say a word. Why would he do a thing like that? I can't understand."

"I think he'd just realised his whole life this past year has been a kind of fiction. I know how he feels - your life suddenly defined as a humiliating show put on for other people. A pathetic bloody pantomime."

"What other people?" She squeezed his arm. "No, you don't need to talk about it if you don't want. I knew as soon as I saw you. It's that Cabot chap, isn't it? He's not right, is he?"

Twenty-Six

They spent the weeks after Oxford like fugitives, in a flat Alex barely remembered as his own, venturing out after dark to eat at a tiny restaurant, the cellar of some long-abandoned town house, neither willing to assign any concrete form to Cabot's nebulous threat. Uneasily marking time.

At the end of the first week in January Justine returned from Baker Street clutching a bunch of tulips.

"It was a woman. A nice old biddy dragooned in to wish me well. Said all the right things. She said these were in Amsterdam a few days ago. I'd rather not have known that."

Alex filled a vase with water and watched her strip off some of the waxy leaves. "Don't tulips mean eternal love? I think I read that somewhere."

She took the vase from him, avoiding his eyes. Starting to force the stems down into the water, she suddenly stopped, letting the flowers fall, "I think I'll do this later." As she turned to walk away he realised she was weeping.

Orders for Alex arrived on Wednesday morning the following week. It had been snowing heavily and the embossed envelope shoved under the door was already limp with damp. He took it into the bedroom to read: marked *secret* in superfluous red ink, headed, *War Cabinet Office - London Controlling Section*. Three lines of laconic prose informing him that a car would collect him the following day at eleven hundred hours.

That night she kissed him on the lips, which was rare, pulling him close, protesting when he tried to speak, murmuring, *Time's up for us, Guffin*, a crushed teasing tone he did not like, tears wet against his face. Later, when she thought him asleep, *One kiss too many*, clinging to him like a child.

The summons was to an address in Whitehall, an anonymous stone portico shored up with sandbags. There was barely room for two in the tiny room, blue with smoke, a man in civilian blue, almost a uniform, standing far too close, craggy face walnut brown like a piece of carved wood.

"No need to sir me. You don't know me, after all. That correct?" Alex had the wit to nod, conscious of sharp blue eyes sizing him up. "Your Colonel said it might be otherwise." He waved a bundle of limp paper, florid purple ink bleeding through to the other side. "*Psychologist*? Lying your speciality, right?" His expression was a kind of controlled distaste.

To his surprise Alex found himself pushed down into a hard chair in front of the desk. "Look, don't misunderstand me. I'm not saying your setup's a waste of time."

"You mean the TPSU, sir? With respect I don't think Mr Cabot would agree with you."

"Cabot? He's out of it now. Anyway, what d'you know about that?" He leaned down, his face suddenly very close, "No ... what I mean is you chaps get things out of proportion. Just that."

He broke away, walking across to the window, rubbing at the grimy glass, peering through it. Apparently finding nothing to see, he turned back to Alex.

"D'you want to know how wars are won? I'll tell you. High explosive - the rest's just decoration."

He sat down at the desk, pushing papers aside to clear a space, staring at Alex. When it seemed nothing could break the silence he suddenly barked: "Stalingrad – heard about it?"

"Not very much, sir. Apart from that the Russians seem to be holding out."

"*Holding out*. Is that what you heard? No, you're wrong. Stalingrad's certainly lost. It's a matter of days."

"Lost? You mean ..."

"I mean Corporal Hitler has got his way - the Germans have lost. The master strategist has watched the whole of his sixth army wiped out. Do you have the faintest idea how many men? Hundreds of thousands. More even than that. We'll never know how many. You can ask me why I'm not smiling if you like."

"I'd rather not do that, sir."

"No, perhaps not ... perhaps not. But it means you've won your war, young man. Or rather somebody has lost it for you."

He scraped up a sheaf of papers from the desk, rifling through them, searching for a name. "Now ... your orders, Vere. You're to go back to Torridon. You know the place?"

"Of course, sir. I spent a few weeks there. You mean training? Colonel Archer said ..."

"No, not training. You're doing the training this time. That's what we want you to do. Tell the buggers about lying. That's what you know about, right? Tell them all you know."

"But if I did that, sir, perhaps there'd be fewer of us." It was too late to call the words back, but they produced no more than a weary smile.

"Spotted that, did you? Pick up a travel warrant on the way out. The desk at the end of the corridor."

Alex walked home, spoiling his shoes on pavements lined with low walls of snow. Content to be lost again. Hoarding the minutes he could still believe Justine might be there to greet him.

She had left her ring on the breakfast table. No note: nothing to decipher.

The man at the desk in Boodles directed him to a private clinic in St John's Wood. Archer had been taken ill making a speech at a dinner to celebrate Allied victories against Rommel. Needing to read something out, he had failed to lay hands on his spectacles. Apparently he had fainted. Perhaps Alex could tell them how the old Colonel was doing. You couldn't deny he was an awkward customer, but then, the club had lots like that and not all of them were MC.

It was a cottage hospital, set back from the road. They had given Archer a private room. Less on account of his status, more that he had begun calling the others in his tiny ward to order in the middle of the night.

He seemed quiet enough now, sitting erect against pillows, beady magpie eyes feverishly popping from object to object in the room. He had not been shaved for several days, untidy grey stubble competing with the white fluff of his moustaches.

He looked up as Alex closed the door. A large illustrated book lay open across his legs.

"Says here there were tigers in Hungary. Didn't know that." He seemed suddenly angry. "But who's to say different? Who the hell are you?"

"I'm Captain Vere, sir, do you remember? I heard you'd been unwell."

"Well you heard wrong there. And I remember you perfectly well - just couldn't put a face to the name," glancing at the door, leaning forward, suddenly conspiratorial, "do you know the people here? I can't seem to get out."

"You mean a nurse? I'm sure ..."

"Sure, are you? That's more than I am. Don't bloody well patronise me."

He grimaced, shifting awkwardly on the sheets, "Look here, can you fetch somebody?" craning his neck, looking eagerly beyond Alex at shapes flickering white against the beaded glass.

"I wondered whether I could ask you something, sir? Only if you feel up to it ... it won't take a minute."

"Why shouldn't I feel up to it? I feel fine. Ask about what?"

"I worked at the TPSU ..."

A faint wrinkle of distress creased Archer's forehead, the look defiant, "And?"

"With Mr Cabot. John Cabot. We worked under your command."

"I remember Cabot. Slippery chap. Wouldn't trust him as far as I could throw him. Wouldn't trust him with my spoons. Always sloping off to the museum. Even when it was shut. Thought I didn't know. Can't stand that sneering type. What about him?"

"It's not him. I wanted to ask you about a Captain Kessler. A German prisoner. Do you remember him?"

Archer looked offended. "Didn't take too many prisoners in my day. Nowhere to put them. What is it you want to know?"

His face suddenly brightened, "Weren't you with that woman? Set yourself up in that place in Russell Square?" He closed his eyes, nestling back into the pillows, a slight smirk, "Can't say I blame you. Nice little thing ..." A single alligator eye blinked open, "Gone missing again - that your problem?" tugging at his arm, the familiar sadistic smile a little lop-sided. "*Perry*, that's the name. Knew it would come to me. Left you in the lurch, has she? Gone to ground? I remember your friend Cabot had something to say about that, insolent beggar."

"I've been assigned new duties, sir. I think it was your suggestion."

"*Me*? What's it to do with me? Taking her with you?"

"Mrs Perry is not involved. She has resigned her commission."

"Looked like you wanted her, all the same. You want to marry her? Got that in mind? You can't find her ... that your problem?"

Alex had forgotten Archer's need to hurt. "I'm not sure where Mrs Perry is."

"Ah, but I found her, you see. I knew where to look. Something else you forgot."

"I can come back if you prefer, sir. If you're tired ..."

"*If you prefer* – too bloody polite for your own good. You'd be tired cooped up in here."

Archer wriggled restlessly under the book on his lap, handing it to Alex, "Here - put it where I can get it, there's a good chap."

The weight off his legs, he seemed more alert. "Kessler – what about him?"

"You interrogated him at Abbott Court. There doesn't seem to be any record."

"Writing things down, you mean? Why would I do that? I'm not a clerk. I don't write things down."

"No, no, of course not. I wondered what he said about our Columbine circuit. About it being played back to us under Jerry control. Do you recall that?"

Watching the huge bewhiskered head slowly oscillate, Alex realised he had, long since, lost his audience. It seemed futile to press on. Fatigue, or something far worse, had consumed what was left of Archer.

"He's dead, you know. Damned unfortunate business," the expression was comically wary. "That what you're here about?"

"Did he ever mention someone called Gliess? A Major Gliess."

"Name rings a bell. Who is he? Look here, can't you fetch somebody?"

"You mean a nurse. Sorry … I'll call one … are you alright?"

"I need my pot if you must know."

Alex stood with the MO in the corridor, the two of them side by side at a window, staring out over a patch of turned earth that might once have been intended as flowerbeds.

"You'll need to go easy on him. He's very ill, you realise?"

"No, as a matter of fact I didn't. I didn't even know he was here until I asked at his club. He doesn't seem too bad. A bit confused. But he can always put that act on - the old devil."

The MO did not return the smile, "It's not an act. He's had a stroke. A bad one. Lost his temper once too often, I suppose - old chaps and their blood pressure. A curse for me, I've orders to keep an eye on him. Have they got you on the same game?"

"Me? No. I found out he was here, that's all. There was something I wanted to check. But surely the people here can keep an eye on him?"

The MO shrugged, "Not that sort of an eye. I'm here to stop him blabbing. You get a bit garrulous in his state. Walls have ears, to coin a cliché. Got myself saddled with the job. I think they imagined I wouldn't stick out too much, being an MO."

Alex wondering who *they* might be, the MO seemed to sense the question coming and steered away. "As if I didn't have better things to do," leaning forward, beating his forehead against the glass, a comic display, "what's the old boy supposed to know that's so important? Any idea?"

"I'm afraid not. I worked for him for a while. His unit's closed now. There were only the three of us and I've been posted away. With Archer gone, it would have left Cabot on his own."

The MO stepped back, conjuring a curious solemn expression onto his face, "Yes, dreadful business, that."

"Oh, I wouldn't say that. He's happy enough. Oxford's his world really."

The MO seemed suddenly embarrassed, "Hell. There's me talking out of turn again. You don't know then?" His face flushed with irritation, as if Alex had somehow tricked him, "How can you not know?"

"Know what"

"That chap Cabot. I should have kept my trap shut … I was sure you'd know … About the accident? I'm afraid he's dead. I can't understand you not knowing." He sounded aggrieved, "Mind you, I know nothing about it."

"*Dead*? I was with him just the other day. He was perfectly well. We're talking about the same person?"

"Worked for Archer. German specialist. Some sort of don at Oxford."

"Yes, that's him. But ..."

"Mixed up with London Controlling Section, the wallahs who ran your show."

Alex felt his colour rise. "Colonel Archer was my CO," turning aside, mumbling, "I don't know anything about a London Control thing."

"Well, that's me shot then." The MO grabbed his arm, giggling, "It's alright, I'm not always like this. I do know about denial. We're all in the same damned boat ... utterly ridiculous."

Alex stood looking across the wasteland to the distant traffic, a surge of guilty relief giving way almost instantly to something else. Sudden death was commonplace enough these days: somehow, death didn't suit Cabot.

"*Accident*? Was it a raid? I thought Oxford was pretty safe. When was this?"

"New Year's Eve. At the train station. But it wasn't a raid." The MO struggled on, Alex staring through the window, silent, immobile. "There's a through train before the London one ... it belts right through the station. This Cabot chap was trying to get to the other end of the platform. That's where first class on the London train ends up. The place was jam-packed. People said he seemed to be looking for somebody ... kept turning round ... he lost his footing. Ended up on the track."

"You mean somebody pushed him? Is that what you're saying?"

"What an extraordinary notion." He glanced nervously at Alex, instantly looking away, "Why would you say that? No, the police said it was an accident, pure and simple. He fell. You knew him, of course?"

Alex reached for his cigarette case, opening it out for the MO.

"Well if the police ruled on it, that's settled. Mind you, Cabot was not without enemies. You may number me among them." The MO looked puzzled. Alex squeezed his arm. "It's alright, I've an alibi. I've been a bit out of circulation, that's why I hadn't heard this tale. How did you hear it, by the way?"

"That Major chap told me – the one at Tempsford the night you nearly missed your flight. I bumped into him in Baker Street. Gave me the whole story. The two of them were waiting for the same train." He broke away, "Look, if I've said more than I should, I'm sorry. I know nothing about it. I'm going in search of tea. If you want time with Archer you'd better catch him. He tires quickly. Don't leave him on his own when you're finished. Get them to come for me."

"It's really bad?"

"It's not just the stroke. His heart's in terrible shape. In fact, the drugs are the only thing keeping it going. If they go on with them, he'll have another stroke. Not much they can do. If you ask me, he's unlikely to see the week out. Don't quote me – I'm not treating him."

"I didn't appreciate that. I'm sorry." To his surprise, Alex found he meant it. There was something reassuring about Archer's bovine stupidity. "He seemed lucid. I had been hoping to get some information from him. I won't press."

"Ask away. Mind you, I won't guarantee you'll get the truth. Lying's second nature. He's as crafty as a cage of monkeys. Drives the nurses barmy. But at least while you're quizzing him we'll all get a bit of peace. Just go easy. By the way, he breaks into a foreign lingo when he's really steamed up. That's the sign you're best to stop. Possibly Hungarian. Nobody here has a clue. Not Polish, anyway."

"He's Hungarian. I know a few words, I'll see if I can make it out. I suppose it's the stroke … you know, drawing on what resources he's got left."

"What is it you want to know? Can I ask? Or is it a secret?"

"Actually I don't want to know anything. I want to be sure he doesn't know something."

"Best of luck with that."

When Alex went back into the room, the book was restored to Archer's lap. He was mechanically turning pages, devoting a brief inspection to each. It was hard to believe he saw what he was looking at. He turned in the bed as the door opened, leaning on one elbow.

"Wondered whether you'd come back, Vere. I remember you perfectly well. You're the chap who spilled the beans - had things squeezed out of you. You've a cheek coming here pestering me. No, damn it … don't flounce off like a girl. Come here. Fetch that chair. That name - what was it again?"

"Gliess, sir. Major Gliess."

"What about him?"

"Nothing specific. I just wondered whether you knew anything about him."

"Fishing, that it? Well, you're not going to hook me."

"But you do know of him?"

"I can do better than that," beady eyes suddenly cunning, "it won't be what you want, but it's all you're going to get."

He stretched painfully across to a tiny table by the bed, tugging at a knob, the effort eventually defeating him, "It's in here. Can't reach. Get it, will you. My wallet."

Alex swung open the little door. A flat leather wallet lay alongside a metal urine bottle.

Archer took his time peeling papers out one by one, opening each, pressing them flat, folding them back. Finally, a familiar yellow sheet from a decrypt pad.

"Got this from your chap Gliess," flapping the paper, teasing him, "shan't tell you how, so don't ask."

"May I?"

Alex caught the paper as it dropped to the bedspread. Someone had written in ink under the message header, *Arrived en clair - English language as original*. It was dated the day after Justine's capture.

FOR THE KIND ATTENTION OF COLONEL ARCHER STOP TPSU STOP GRATEFUL THANKS FOR YOUR MANY GIFTS STOP REGRETS OUR GAME IS OVER STOP PERHAPS WE SHARE A CIGAR IN PARIS IN BETTER DAYS STOP HERMANN GLIESS STOP HEIL HITLER STOP END

"I won't ask *how*, sir. But it would be helpful to know *where*? Can I know that?"

"You mean where did I see it? Where d'you think? Baker Street, of course, can't you see who it's addressed to? Impertinent bastard."

"This word *game*?"

"Nothing to do with me. I don't play games."

"But what do you make of it, sir?"

"Make of it? Boasting he'd got our men, I suppose. Ask your friend the Major. Not that you can. Somebody in Boodles said he'd gone to America. Here give it me," clutching the wallet to his chest, eyes suddenly vulnerable, darting round the room. "Bad do, that man dying."

"You mean Kessler, sir?"

"Pour me some of that water, will you." As Alex handed him the glass he found his wrist wrapped in a dry hand, the grip transferring a subterranean tremor to his own.

"Come closer," hot sickly breath smelling of chocolate, "that's why they put me here. Out of the way, you know. Because I killed him."

"You mean Captain Kessler?"

"You know what?" His glittering filmy eyes seemed to know more than their owner, "You know what? I'd do it again." The lopsided smile still sadistic, still triumphant, "Can't let them get away with that ... won't do."

Alex stood up, "I've a message from your club, sir. To pass on."

"The Boodle Boys?"

"For a speedy recovery. For a speedy return."

Archer looked thoughtful. "They said that? Must think I'm here for good. *Return*, eh?"

"It must have been around the New Year?"

"Fishing again, Vere?"

"No sir, not really, I just wondered ..."

"Operation Torch. Heard of it?"

"Of course, sir. The North African campaign."

"A little dinner. That's all. Here, read this," opening his wallet, tugging at a folded slip of paper, "read it out if you like. Remind me. I can't see so well."

It was a letter, very short, apparently unsigned: *Dear Colonel Arthur, General Eisenhower has asked me to convey his thanks for the invaluable contribution of TSPU to recent operations.*

Alex read it out, correcting the errors. Archer had closed his eyes. He seemed content.

The MO had slipped back into the room. Alex looked up, feeling like the fretful spouse at a deathbed. "It was something he wanted to hear. He just fell asleep."

The MO leaned over, taking Archer's wrist. Each inhalation of breath came separated by a pause so extended it seemed certainly his last.

Alex prised the wallet from his grip, pushing the letter back inside. Bending down to the little cupboard he found huge sightless eyes close to his own, fetid breath unnaturally hot.

Jó hogy itt vagy, Fanni.

The MO looked at him, eyebrows raised.

"Like I said. When he gets worked up. Make anything of it?"

"Just some girl called Fanny. He thinks she's holding his hand."

"Some people get all the luck."

"Is he alright?"

"He's not dead, if that's what you mean. Just tired. It takes you like that. Did you get what you wanted? Come again tomorrow, if you like. He'll perk up again."

A little thin sunshine was waiting for him outside, casting long shadows, the afternoon drawing in that imperceptible fraction later, a tiny presage of Spring. Alex decided to walk. Aimlessly at first, then with resolution as his destination seemed more certain, the Russell Hotel sprawling greedily across one end of the square, layered nine storeys high like some vast wedding confection. A terracotta palace,

Venetian colonnades glowing pink, row on row of silent windows watching as he crossed the square, fluttering pigeons rising at his feet to fall again like restless waves.

Also by Alan Kennedy published by Lasserrade Press

Lucy [ISBN 978-0-9564696-7-0]

Lucy Beyrou is a painter. She has everything: fame, money and reputation. She also has Oscar. At least, he has always been there. One fine day, she will do something about that. It was, as she says, hardly a love affair, more a kind of marriage. Perhaps, even war-torn France is safe enough on the Oscar front. But Lucy is deceiving herself. Set before and after the second world war, in London, Edinburgh, Saint-Valery-sur-Somme, Dundee and a remote village in war-time France, two painters struggle to come to terms with the casual brutality of war. A love story.

www.lasserradepress.com

www.ingramcontent.com/pod-product-compliance
Lightning Source LLC
Chambersburg PA
CBHW031114030726
47496CB00002BA/537